The Desert of Souls

The Desert of Souls

HOWARD ANDREW JONES

Thomas Dunne Books 𝔐 New York
St. Martin's Press

This is a work of fiction. All of the characters, organizations, and events portrayed in this novel are either products of the author's imagination or are used fictitiously.

THOMAS DUNNE BOOKS.
An imprint of St. Martin's Press.

THE DESERT OF SOULS. Copyright © 2011 by Howard Andrew Jones. All rights reserved. Printed in the United States of America. For information, address St. Martin's Press, 175 Fifth Avenue, New York, N.Y. 10010.

www.thomasdunnebooks.com
www.stmartins.com

Library of Congress Cataloging-in-Publication Data

Jones, Howard A.
    The desert of souls / Howard Andrew Jones. — 1st ed.
        p. cm.
    ISBN 978-0-312-64674-5
    1. Iran—History—640-1500—Fiction.   I. Title.
    PS3610.O62535D47 2011
    813'.6—dc22

                                  2010039301

First Edition: February 2011

10   9   8   7   6   5   4   3   2   1

To two great ladies:

For my mother, Shirley Jones, who first guided me to The Shire and Riverworld, helped kindle my imagination, and always believed in my storytelling.

For my best friend and muse, Shannon, who brought unflagging energy and a razor-sharp intellect to help breathe these characters and their world to life.

3460

Acknowledgments

This book would not have been possible without aid from a talented team of readers and advisers, among them Ahmed Khan, Eric Knight, Bob Mecoy, and Scott Oden. Wise sages John C. Hocking and John O'Neill rode in with support and sharp swords for cutting Gordian plot knots. Editor Pete Wolverton leapt into the fray with his own fine sword, urging me on through dark valleys while steadfastly guarding my back. I thank you all.

The Desert
of Souls

1

The parrot lay on the floor of his cage, one claw thrust stiffly toward the tiny wooden swing suspended above him. The black olive clenched in his beak was the definitive sign that Pago was a corpse, for while he had fooled us all by playing dead in the past, he had never failed to consume an olive. To be sure, I nudged the cage. It shook, the swing wobbled, and the bird slid minutely but did not move a single feather of his own accord.

"He is dead," Jaffar said simply behind me; simply, but with the weight of the universe hung upon the final word.

I turned to my master, who sat with his back to me upon the stone bench of his courtyard. The second-story balcony, from which the cage hung, draped Jaffar in shadow. Beyond him, sunlight played in the rippling water that danced from a fountain. Flowers blossomed upon the courtyard plants and wild birds warbled gaily. Another parrot, in a cage upon the far wall, even called out that it was time for a treat, as he was wont to do. But my master paid no heed to any of this.

I stepped into the sunlight so that I might face him. Upon another bench, nearby, the poet Hamil sat with stylus and paper. There was no love in the look he bestowed me, and he returned to his scribblings with the air of a showman.

"Master," I said, "I am sorry. I, too, was fond of Pago."

"Who could not be?" Jaffar asked wearily. He was but a few years younger than my twenty-five, but due to time indoors looked younger still, no matter his full beard. His face was wan, from a winter illness that had also shed some of his plumpness.

"He was the brightest bird here," Jaffar continued in that same miserable tone.

"Brighter than many in your employ," Hamil said without looking up.

"Too true," Jaffar agreed.

"Is there some way that I can help, Master?" I was the captain of Jaffar's guard and sometimes his confidant; the matter of bird death, however, was outside the field of my knowledge, and I did not understand why he had summoned me. It is true that I had found Pago entertaining, for in addition to playing dead, he could mimic the master and his chief eunuch, and even sometimes answered the call to prayer by bowing thrice. He did this only when it pleased him to do so, which, as my nephew Mahmoud once noted, was far too much like many men he knew. Also Pago had once perched upon the poet's chest when Hamil had passed out from consuming the fruit of the grape, and pinched his long thin nose heartily. That had pleased me so that I brought Pago the choicest of olives whenever I knew I would pass by his cage.

"Do you suspect he has been killed?" Jaffar asked.

I blinked. "It had not occurred to me."

"The master lay ill for weeks," Hamil said with the patient air of one explaining to a simpleton. "Might it be that someone, in failing to poison him, poisoned one of his most cherished companions?"

"It may be," I replied, wishing that someone had, instead, poisoned the poet, "but the hakim did not believe the master to have been poisoned."

"The hakim has declined to examine Pago," Jaffar said, "saying that he is no expert on birds."

"I shall look at him," I said. "But, Excellency, if I may be so bold, Pago was your father's before he became yours. He lived a fine, long span of years. It may be that his fate was writ."

The master did not answer. I stepped back to the cage containing the rigid parrot, uncertain about what I was expected to see, but fully deter-

2

mined to ape the manner of someone looking with full concentration upon a weighty matter. It occurred to me then that the olive might be poisoned, and so I opened the cage. Pago, dead, was no easier to part from an olive than when he'd been alive, and that tiny beak resisted my attempts to pry it open. I resorted to sawing the olive back and forth until I'd worked it free. I stepped into the sunlight, the fruit between thumb and forefinger. There was nothing obviously wrong with the olive save the shredding it had endured at my hand. "I see no sign of poison, Master."

Jaffar sighed. "I did not think there would be."

"He is but a captain, Master, not an expert of poisons, or birds. Perhaps a specialist should be called." Hamil seemed determined to make much of this occurrence.

"Perhaps," I said. "Why don't you go fetch one?"

"I," the poet said, brandishing his stylus, "am composing a memoriam for Pago."

It was all a bit much, what with the self-important poet and my morbid master, and the parrot's last meal held tightly between my thumb and forefinger, and I chuckled.

The poet's head snapped up. Jaffar fixed me with his own eyes, his brow knitted. The very air was charged then with tension; Jaffar was a kind master, it was true, but he was one of the three most important men in Baghdad and only a fool would mock him to his face.

"He laughs!" said Hamil, and mixed in with his incredulity was a note of pleasure. A stunned smile spread across almost the whole of his narrow face.

"I laugh," I said, "because an excellent idea has come to me." I do not know who inspired such a fine lie, but it gave them pause, and at that moment I would have thanked hell-bound Iblis himself if he were responsible.

"What sort of an idea?" the poet prodded, with all the manner of a cat playing with prey.

"I am not sure," I said, bowing slightly to my master and thinking rapidly, "that it is appropriate to discuss at this time."

"No, please, Asim," Jaffar said. By all that was holy, I had gained his interest, and I had no idea whatsoever what I might say. "What is your idea?"

"A diversion," I managed, thinking as I spoke.

The master raised his hand dismissively. "No poem or pageantry would wash this sorrow from my soul."

"Of course," I said, a desperate inkling taking shape, "no ordinary diversion would help. Only a truly unique experience would gladden your wounded heart."

"I await astonishment," the poet said quietly, setting down his stylus, "and will be astonished if it arrives."

"When last the caliph visited, did he not regale you with a fine tale?" I asked.

Jaffar bowed his head in assent. "Yes."

"He and his comrades dressed in common attire so that they would not be recognized, and walked the streets." The caliph had said he would have invited Jaffar, had he not lain ill, and, recognizing the disappointment upon my master's face, told him he hoped Jaffar would join him on some similar venture in the future. The master had mentioned the incident regretfully a number of times since.

Jaffar shook his head. "Yes, but the caliph hunts this week. I cannot venture forth with him."

"I had not forgotten, Master. It is my idea that you venture forth with comrades of your own, so that you might have an adventure to share with the caliph upon his return."

Jaffar did not brighten, exactly; his head rose and he ceased movement altogether. The little poet watched him for reaction, probably wondering whether he should mock or praise me, though he would certainly prefer the former. At the upturning of the master's lips, Hamil quickly said, "I think you have something there, Asim. If you go on this mad enterprise, Master, I hope that you will allow me to accompany you, so that I may record all that transpires."

Jaffar was nodding. "Yes—it would be good to leave the palace. We might go down to the market and see what has come from downriver. In disguise, I would be bothered only by beggars."

He referred indirectly to the courtiers who would always swarm about him wherever it was that he set his feet.

"Indeed, Master. But Hamil should remain so that he may finish his composition in silence."

"Hah! Who then will tell the story to the caliph?"

"I will do the telling," Jaffar said.

"But surely"—the poet halted in midsentence—"You need men of wit to accompany you. Who does Asim plan? A trio of guardsmen, I suppose?"

He knew me too well. That is exactly what I had planned. A brief foray out; my master well protected. I smiled only.

"You might as well go in accompaniment of dung merchants," the poet said. "Nay, you need me. Allow me to suggest other companions, as well."

"Nay, Master," I said. "Take the scholar Dabir. He is crafty, and does not lack for wit."

Jaffar nodded and climbed to his feet. "That is a fine thought. Go and gather him. Tell him that we shall meet at the west servants' entrance. Just after midday prayers. Oh—tell him not to wear anything extravagant. You, too, should disguise yourself. Something common."

I bowed. "I hear and obey."

The poet was still politely protesting as I left the courtyard and made my way through the palace halls. The master's palace was nearly the size of the caliph's, and no place for an aimless search. While I was friendly with Dabir, I did not know him so well that I was familiar with his rounds, and thus I asked directions from one of the slaves.

The little man bowed. "At this hour he is most likely tutoring the mistress, Sabirah, off the main courtyard."

Of course. It was only my miraculous escape from potential dismissal or death that had left me unthinking. The slave's expression was blank, but there was a hint of derision in his tone, as if all the palace surely knew Dabir's daytime assignment. I left him and made my way through the hall.

That a male tutor should be used for the master's niece had set many tongues to wagging. The situation had begun after our return from the dig in Kalhu, where my actions and those of Dabir had not only brought us higher in the eyes of Jaffar, but, through him, garnered a word of praise from the caliph himself. The master had brought me closer into his confidence, and augmented Dabir's position, entrusting him with the teaching of his beloved niece.

Sabirah's father, Musa, had declared that as God had seen fit to bless his daughter with so excellent a mind, God must have meant for it to be used. Musa had been appointed governor of Syria, but had left his eldest child in Jaffar's care with instructions that she receive the best education available in Baghdad.

I neared the twin doors to the room where she was being taught and caught the warm tones of a young woman's laughter from within. She sounded no brighter than any other girl. I rapped on one door and then walked straight in, as was my right as guard captain.

Two crones looked up from a backgammon table. They apparently did not mind their charge giggling at a man, but fixed me with a glare that would shrivel a ready groom. Dabir and Sabirah sat at a nearby table, each holding a book.

I did not look first at Dabir, but to Sabirah. Though I sometimes saw her without a veil, she had been told to wear thick ones while under Dabir's tutelage. In that day, amongst the wealthy folk, it was not uncommon to show hair, but this too was concealed. She was a slip of a thing, with a slim nose. For myself, I preferred a woman of more ample curve, but I admit that her eyes were large and clear, her voice sweet.

"Good morning, Captain," she said.

"Good morning, Mistress. Forgive this interruption."

"The mistress is taking lessons," one of the crones told me curtly.

"Are they lessons in courtesy?" I asked her, then looked back to Jaffar's niece.

6

Sabirah's eyes crinkled as though she smiled.

"I come at your uncle's behest to fetch Dabir," I told her.

"He's not in trouble, is he?"

"Oh, no."

"Why do you need him?"

She had me there. Apparently my well of inspiration had run dry for the morning, and I stood statue-still for a moment too long trying to think of an explanation that did not reveal my purpose.

"It must be something very important," Sabirah prompted.

"Yes," I agreed, though it was not important in the way that she supposed. Doubtless behind her eyes lurked the fancies of a maid; that Dabir was needed to consult about some important affairs of state involving marriages and horses, most like. In truth, I felt suddenly awkward, for I understood then that if I had maintained my composure around the stupid poet, the girl, the scholar, and the crones would have gone the morning uninterrupted.

"Take him if you must, then," Sabirah said. "Though I would gladly have read more."

"Read on," Dabir said, "while I gather my things. First in the original, then translate."

The girl began to recite curiously worded Greek.

Dabir stood, searching me with a look. His eyes were a clear blue, more vibrant than that of the blue jubbah he wore, a gift from Jaffar. In those days the hair below his turban was dark and thick. There was no gray yet in the well-trimmed beard, shaped spadelike below his lips, nor in the mustache perched above. Elsewise his beard was thin, only following the shape of his jaw. He searched, I think, for some reassurance that all was truly well, and I nodded once.

"Some lucky Thracian has my noble shield," Sabirah continued. "I had to drop it in a wood. But I got clean away, praise God. I'll get another, just as good."

Dabir chuckled as he stuffed his own papers and a stack of books into his satchel. "Quite right. You see?"

"It mocks the Spartans," Sabirah said.

"Yes. What do you think? Is pragmatism more important than glory?" Sabirah stared into space as Dabir closed his satchel.

"It must depend upon the circumstance. Practicality might excuse evil practice."

Dabir nodded. "Well said. Keep reading; we will meet again in the morning."

"You won't be traveling, will you, Captain?" Sabirah asked me.

"Not very far," I said. I judged by her look that my reply brought no satisfaction, but she wished us good day and said nothing further.

Dabir and I walked at each other's side then, down the hall.

"What has happened?" he asked.

I told him that Pago had died and that the master craved a diversion. "Hamil had suggested he go; I thought of you."

"I see," he said, not sounding especially pleased.

I bade him stop in the shadow of a column, and lowered my voice. "It is folly, but I hope to make the best of it. The master desires clever conversation. You can provide that, but you also have a head upon your shoulders. I expect you to help me keep watch upon him."

"Where does he intend to go?" Dabir asked.

"He mentioned the market."

"We should shape his steps, then, to safe places."

"They must also hold his interest," I said.

"Of course. Do you suppose we should take him to a seller of birds?"

"I would prefer to keep his mind from the parrot."

I conveyed the rest of the master's instructions. Dabir listened without question and then we parted, he for his preparations, me for mine.

All too soon came the call to prayers, and then I hastened to the west servants' entrance. There I found Dabir already attending the master. The scholar had donned a dusty brown robe. Jaffar smiled and nodded to me. Boulos, the plump old eunuch, stood behind him, making final adjustments to the master's turban, which seemed especially bedraggled. On any other day the master would have pitched the dirty cloth through a window. His own jubbah was threadbare and stained; I am not sure from where it had come, but it was considerably worse than my own travel garments. It did not quite work, in truth, for his beard was so well trimmed, his nails so clean that he seemed less a poor man than a child playing dress up. The master was well known for his handsome face and fine figure—though of course poets exaggerated—and he carried himself with confidence that belied his clothing.

"How do I look?" he asked me.

"Your garments are suitably ragged," I replied.

"I was thinking," Boulos said, "that a smudge of dirt upon one cheek might complete the look."

"Do you think?" Jaffar asked. He turned to me.

I wished to say that he would then resemble a clown, but Boulos, no matter that he was slave and eunuch, had more power within the palace than I, and only an idiot antagonized him.

"It would be a fine touch," Dabir said, "but the girls will look with less favor upon His Excellency then."

"I seek adventure, not wives," Jaffar said.

"Oh, you should always be prepared," Boulos said cheerily. "Who knows when God shall send some tidbit to cross your path?" He and Jaffar laughed; I groaned inwardly.

Boulos bent to buckle on Jaffar's sword belt.

"Is it sharp?" my master asked.

"It was seen to. I found you an older sheath, though."

"Thank you, Boulos," Jaffar said, and again I groaned internally, for a proper warrior would see to his own weapon; it had not even occurred to Jaffar to be embarrassed to ask. He turned eagerly to us. "I'm quite pleased with all this. Are you two ready?"

"We await only your word, Master." I bowed.

"This was a fine idea, Asim," Jaffar said. Boulos hustled forward; the two guards waiting to either side of the door pretended not to notice us, although they reached for the door pulls.

The master held up a hand and the sentries stepped back. "I'm sure you know," he said as he turned to us, "that you are not to call me by title, or, indeed, by any honorific whatsoever, once we leave the palace."

"Of course, Master," I said.

"Of course, *Andar*," Jaffar corrected with a smile. "I am to have an adventure, so why not name myself after one of the greatest adventurers?"

"An excellent idea," Boulos said. "Captain, see him safely home."

"Of course."

"What time shall we expect your return, Master?" Boulos asked.

"There is no telling," Jaffar replied. "We may be gone through the night." He turned to the door, thought better of it, and faced Boulos again with raised finger, as though he were ticking off a point from an invisible list. "Do not let word spread of our adventure."

"Of course not, Master."

"Dabir, Asim, let us be off."

Once more the sentries reached for the doors, eyes focused blankly above our own, lest they be in on a secret they should not know. Outside was bright and fragrant, for even here at one of the side entrances were a row of bushes in bloom. It was but a short walk to the gate in the outer wall, likewise guarded by sentries. One opened the gate for us while the other advanced to push back the crowd of folk who tend to gather about all palace entrances. Dabir and the master and I stepped around them; the assorted beggars and job applicants and onlookers watched us curiously; one even pulled at Dabir's robe, pleading for alms, and then we were past.

I think the master was more bewildered than amazed by the cacophony of the streets. Baghdad teemed with people and their attendant smells, and we were in the thick of both. It is not that the master had never been out of his mansion, it is just that he never ventured forth without a buffer of servants and guardians.

When Jaffar asked where we should go, Dabir suggested first the nearby market in south Al-Rusafa, the wealthiest quarter of the city, where we spent the greater part of the next hour. Merchants could not know the master's true identity, but even a fool could tell at a glance that he was a nobleman in disguise because of his fine manner. They bade him look at the best of their baubles and silks and perfumes and nearly everything else under the sun. Jaffar paid them little heed, but he examined much, listening with interest to the outrageous lies regarding the rarity of certain cloths, or the unmatched skill of a bootmaker's leatherwork. He was especially taken by the elaborate tale of one jeweler's perilous trip to Baghdad from India. I found it tiresome and stepped away. Dabir joined me.

"Is *your* sword sharp?" he asked quietly.

I did not take his meaning at first, then saw his sly smile and chuckled.

"We must give thought as to our next course," Dabir said, "for he will grow bored."

"There is a place across the river where men often race pigeons," I said.

"That involves birds, though," Dabir wisely pointed out, and I nodded agreement.

"Do you suppose he would like to see some wrestling?" I asked.

At that moment Jaffar returned, passing each of us a small gold ring.

"Thank you . . . Andar," I said. Dabir echoed me. I slipped the thing over my smallest finger and admired the effect.

"It is my pleasure." Jaffar ignored the beckoning calls of other merchants and turned his head this way and that, searching the distance. Because the market was crowded, there was not much to be seen but the turbans and backs of shopping folk.

"The jeweler spoke to me of a woman who deals in magical things. She is down one of these side streets."

Dabir and I traded a quick look while the master was looking the other way.

"Is it not said that upright men should turn their face from magics?" I asked.

"Andar," Dabir said, "our last encounter with magic was . . . somewhat . . ."

"There will be no Greeks involved this time," Jaffar said airily. "Besides, *that* wasn't really magic."

Dabir and I exchanged a glance. The master had never fully believed our accounting of the events with the Greeks, having been drugged at the time. "*This,*" he continued, "is simple marketplace magic, in our own city. There can be no real harm. Let us seek her. The jeweler said she is very good."

"She is probably the man's aunt," I said, "who will share our monies with him."

"Asim, must you always grumble so?" the master asked. "I thought we were going to have fun today. Let us see this magic woman, then find some food."

I would have preferred that we find the food first, for I had neglected a proper meal while preparing for this venture, but Dabir and I followed the master down a winding side street, stepping past running urchins and around a series of foul-smelling brown puddles. After a time it was clear that Jaffar had become lost, so we gave alms to a graybeard who then provided directions, and in the next quarter hour we sat on the rugs within a small, dark front room. From elsewhere in the house came the enticing sound of sizzling meat and a most pleasing scent of lamb.

None was offered us, though, by the stripling who had answered the door and told us to sit, and nothing was offered us by the bent woman who emerged from behind the curtained doorway and bade us welcome to her home. Her voice was like that of an old songbird, for it was clear, but tired, and a little thin. She fished for information about us, as fortune-tellers do, whether we were young men looking for wives or taking a break from important business, all the time watching us with dark eyes. In the shadowy room there was no seeing through her veil, and her gaze revealed no emotion or sign of her thoughts. I took in the room, ordered neatly with strange things, both rare and humble. High shelves stood out from the dark walls. I could see few of the contents perched on those directly to my right, so close were we to the wall itself, though I thought I saw a small bird's claw hanging off one ledge. On the shelf to my left was a hodgepodge of wooden balls adorned with strange symbols, chips of colored stone, a clay goblet decorated with what looked to be emeralds, and the mummified head of a ferret. The peculiarity of these items lent an ominous mien even to the more mundane trappings—that kettle hung from a rafter, for instance, might hold more than emptiness. And what had those dark wooden spoons on the wall been stirring?

My sword lay ready to hand and so too did my knife. As my fingers brushed over its hilt I felt the magic woman's eyes upon us. Just then she asked us for coin and Jaffar revealed his station by bidding me pay an initial fee. The woman passed the coins without comment to one of two similarly dressed youths, identical in feature and hair save that one was a few inches taller. He disappeared briefly then returned with small pastries, which he sat before us. He retreated again. The older boy sat quietly upon a stool in the shadows.

"You seek magic," the woman said, sitting. "Why?"

"Because I am curious," Jaffar answered.

"You are bored." The woman glanced over at me as I munched on a treat. It was fresh, and seasoned with honey. It can never be said that I dislike sweets. "Do you seek magic only because you are bored?" she asked Jaffar.

"My friend has witnessed true magic," Dabir said. "Dark magic. He has no interest in that."

The master's mouth turned down at this.

The woman turned to Dabir, appraising. "What sort of magic does he desire?"

Jaffar spoke up. "A merchant outside told us you are gifted with an understanding of future events. I would hear them."

"Would you?" She cocked one of her thick gray eyebrows. She leaned closer, her voice dropping. "Do you know for what you ask? It is a dangerous thing to know one's fate. The knowledge has driven some mad. Some spend the whole of their lives twisting and turning and scheming to avoid what they have been told, until they realize they are wrapped within the coils of the serpent they thought to escape."

"We are not afraid," Jaffar said.

Perhaps he was not; I covertly made the sign warding against evil, hiding it behind my thigh.

She paused a moment more, staring into his eyes. "You have paid the price," she spoke without sentiment, "and I will honor your coin with my service."

She motioned to the boy, who brought forth short red candles, which she lit. They gave off but little smoke. She then presented us with parchment, one small square each, of a peculiar wrinkled texture.

"What manner of paper is this?" Dabir asked.

"It is fashioned from the skin of Egyptian cats," she said, whereupon my master fell to examining his own paper more closely. In truth it did not look to me to be animal skin, but I said nothing.

Then came the presentation of an especially old-looking stone inkwell, in which black ink rested, and a pen with a marvelously colorful feather. This she handed to my master.

"Breathe deep of the candle fumes, then write your name upon this parchment and set it within the bowl." At this word, the youth placed a small brown bowl before each of us. I looked at Dabir, wondering if he too were concerned by Jaffar revealing his name to this woman, but he kept silent; Jaffar hesitated not at all.

My master leaned close to breathe in of the candle—which smelled faintly of cloves—put the parchment across his knee, and boldly wrote out his name. He then folded the paper and set it within the bowl. Next was my turn, and then Dabir's, who had watched us closely at work.

In light of later events, I wish that I had paid closer heed to how the woman brought the bowls to her, but I saw only that she reached forth and set them near. She closed her eyes and began droning indistinct syllables. I thought them words of magic, and made again the sign casting off evil. It may be that she spoke some prayer. Whatever it was, she sat thus, with eyes closed, and back straight, mumbling for some minutes. The fumes spun about us and the flames of the candles flickered and the air felt heavy. The atmosphere was cavernous, as though we were somewhere quiet and secret, deep beneath the earth, rather than a mere few feet from the entrance to a Baghdad alley.

When the woman's eyes opened, it was with such suddenness that my master flinched. Trancelike she reached for each bowl, held the parchment over the nearest candle, and dropped it back within. Three times she did this. Dabir started to say something, but held his tongue. The master and I were silent, though he glanced over at me, eyes alight with excitement.

Each of the papers flared and went out, leaving black ashes that glowed red at their tips; these the magic worker stirred clockwise three times with her fingers and observed in turn, her eyes blinking seldom. Finally she set the last of them down, and straightened.

"I have read the fates. Be warned—you may not wish to hear."

"Speak!" Jaffar demanded, breathless.

"You." Her gaze fastened upon Dabir. "You shall be known far and wide as a slayer of monsters and protector of the caliphate. Fame will go before and after you; heroes shall listen to tell of your exploits with envious ears."

Dabir's brow furrowed and he looked as though he might have asked for further detail, but the woman's eyes fell upon me. I found that I could not help but meet them, and it was not at all like staring into the eyes of a courtesan; it was more like studying the immensity of the night sky above the desert.

"Your bravery will not be unknown, but in later days it will grow when you will take up the difficult weapons of pen and parchment; the fruits of these labors shall carry your name down the ages."

Her veil rippled when she turned to face Jaffar. "High have you risen and higher still shall you rise, until you lose your head when you dare to love a woman beyond your station. Your master will weep, but he shall not spare you."

The master blinked, then stared with rapt fascination and horror. His mouth opened, moved up and down, yet no sound came forth.

"You stand at a juncture," the woman said to all of us. "If you delay, if you do not rise and take immediately to the street, none of this shall come to pass, and your lives shall be forgotten in the greater misery that shall follow."

"Ah—" the master began, but the woman's head fell forward, her shoulders slumped, and her breathing grew shallow. The stripling hurried to her side, and she reached feebly for him. He helped her rise.

"My grandmother must rest," he said in a high piping voice. "No more than a few moments. If you wish to ask her further about her sight, you may wait."

She leaned heavily upon him as he guided her through the curtains. My master meanwhile was still silently working his mouth, as though continued exercise might see sound evolve there.

"I suppose," he said eventually, "that we should depart." Saying this, he rose, staring hard at Dabir. He stared hard at him again as I opened the door. I did not think him happy. Who would be, after such news?

Sunlight flew at us in a blinding rectangle, and the noise of people haggling just down the street, and the laughter of children, even the snort of a horse, reached us with all the scents of the bustling city. I preceded both men, surveying the street as my eyes adjusted.

The master was quiet as we walked, and his tread was slow.

"I would not trouble myself overmuch about any of this," Dabir said, by the sound of his voice smiling as he spoke. I thought it false cheer.

"I do not know what to think," Jaffar said. "Did you not hear the truth in her words? There was magic there."

I dropped back to his side. "There may have been, Ma—yes." I had forgotten what I was supposed to call him.

"But I think, perhaps, that she confused the bowls. Consider." Jaffar raised a finger. "Dabir is no slayer of monsters, he is a scholar! Surely she must have meant you, Asim. *You* are the warrior. I think that God plans great things for you."

"I hope so, Master."

"And me—I have often thought that I might take pen in hand. I have

16

been inspired to create many stories, but never set them down. You have heard me tell of some of them, I think?"

"Yes," I agreed, though I had always thought he went on a bit long before reaching his point.

Now Jaffar looked long at Dabir, even as we stepped in to the main street.

"She must have confused her fortunes," the master said with surety. "There is no other explanation. Dabir, do not think me harsh, but I think you should leave my service. For your own safety."

"Master—" Dabir began.

"Andar," Jaffar corrected. "My niece is fair, I know. She is young and well spoken, and it was unwise for me to present her with a tutor instead of a suitor." He smiled. "You see," he confided to me, "I do have a way with words." He looked back at Dabir. "Clearly the woman confused the bowls."

I brushed past a kneeling man begging with upthrust and dirty arms, fearful no longer for myself, but for my friend, whose livelihood was jeopardized because I had suggested he join us.

"Master—Andar—she was just an old woman in a rude hut. If she were truly a mistress of magic, would she not reside in a palace walled with rubies and emeralds? Surely we can look upon it all as a jest. A lark."

I saw from Jaffar's expression that he was not convinced.

Again he raised that index finger of his. "I think—"

I was never to learn what he thought, for at that very moment a bleeding man stumbled into our path, clutched vainly at Jaffar's robe, then pitched into the dust before us.

2

Before I could draw breath, four bold rogues rounded the corner and stopped short at the heels of the wounded man. Three wore fine clothes shabbily treated, as if they liked the look of them but did not know their proper care. More to the point, swords were in their hands.

I slung free my sword; I knew a surge of pleasure as the weapon came clear and sat in my fist, curved and gleaming. It was a blade my father had won from a Turk. In practiced hands, its shape allowed faster unsheathing than the straight blades borne by most folk of the caliphate.

"Back, dogs!" I said.

The first of the ruffians, broad-shouldered and large-bellied, gave way. "That man is a thief," he said, pointing at the fellow lying before us.

I pressed forward a half step. "Then the magistrate will decide his fate."

"He has something that belongs to us." This from the second man, tall and rangy, with a dirty turban. The third, big-boned and surly, was like enough in mien to be his brother.

The fourth of them watched quietly. He was smaller than his companions and dressed simply, but I did not discount him. They were oxen, he was a snake. Angered oxen are dangerous, true, but are mostly bluster and would sooner stand about eating grass or chasing females. A snake kills for its living.

Dabir stepped to my side and drew his own sword. There is, of course, a vast gulf separating the competent from the skilled, but the ruffians could not see that gulf as Dabir took a confident stance; he held his blade well.

Jaffar, behind us, had knelt and was speaking softly to the injured man, but I could not hear, for the fat rogue spoke again.

"He has stolen our property," he said petulantly. "Give aid to honest citizens and step aside."

"That may be," Dabir said. "Let us sheath weapons and consult reasonably."

This puzzled the fat one, who glanced to his right, where the snake waited.

"Kill them," the little man hissed.

The fat man bellowed, as is the manner of bulls, and charged Dabir. The tall one leapt at me with an overhand swing. I sidestepped and his blade whished past even as my own sliced through his abdomen. I was certain of the strike and did not watch the impact or subsequent fall, for my eyes were already upon the one with the surly grimace. He, too, charged, and his strike at my head was more skilled than his comrade's. Almost I threw up my right shoulder, but I remembered I did not wear armor, and dropped to one knee. I felt the wind of the sword's passage over my head.

There are those who say combat is a whirlwind that leaves no time for thought. I find that the world seems slowed at such moments, also that my thinking is clear and steady, and that my soul sings with life.

Dabir and the fat man traded wary blows to my left while the snake watched.

I sprang to my feet. The big-boned one caught my blow with a desperate swing. There was power there, but no finesse, and I locked blades and forced his down and offside. He was wide open, and his eyes were wide as my sword tip sliced across the front of his throat. Blood sprayed. He clutched his ruined neck with his hands as he fell.

The snake cursed, backed away, and darted off. The fat man sprinted after him, puffing heavily. Both disappeared around a house and I started to follow before recalling my first duty was to safeguard Jaffar.

My master had turned the man over onto his back. Dabir sheathed his unbloodied blade and knelt now at the dying man's side, seeking for his wound. A simple look at his blood-soaked clothing told me there was no bandage wide enough to save him—surely there was more blood without than within. His face was pale as winter sky.

Yet Dabir exposed a wound in the man's trunk and was wiping the blood and gore clear with the fellow's clothing so that he might see the extent of the injury. Jaffar, a kind man, cradled the fellow's head and pressed a water sac to his lips.

The fellow drank once, then shook his head, agitated. "The door," he muttered. "You must tell . . . the caliph . . ."

"The caliph?" Jaffar asked. "What?"

"The door—the door pulls. Do not let them put them on . . ."

The master looked up at me, then back down at the man, whose eyes relaxed and looked upon the angels and the glory of God.

While Jaffar considered the dead man soberly, Dabir investigated his satchel.

I do not mean to suggest that I am now, or that I was then, a connoisseur of doors or their ornamentation, but like most folk who have made their home in cities, I have seen many doors, and as an intimate of the powerful, I have passed through or by my share of doorways gilt with decorative patterns and precious things. I remember few details about them, but I still vividly recall the splendid door pull Dabir discovered in the dead man's belongings, gleaming all the brighter for its rude container. The pull itself was a solid ring of gold, held in the mouth of an exquisitely rendered roaring lion. It was set into a gold plaque bearing three rubies, beneath which was peculiar writing—geometric shapes and lines like chicken scratches. Dabir had once told me that folk in olden days were still perfecting their letters and had not yet designed beautiful script.

Upon finding this pull within the dead man's satchel Jaffar immediately declared that he wished Dabir to translate the writing, also that he hoped to place it upon one of his own doors. He wondered aloud if a craftsman might be found to fashion its twin. He seemed to have momentarily forgotten that he had dismissed the scholar. Dabir puzzled over the thing only briefly before lowering it back into the satchel.

"All this," he said, rising and taking in the three bodies with a sweep of his hand, "is part of a greater mystery. He sought for you, Andar."

"Do you think so?"

"He was one of those who waited outside the palace when we left this morning," Dabir answered. "I must examine all these bodies before they are shrouded. We may yet learn more from them."

Jaffar agreed.

A crowd had gathered swiftly after the spill of blood, and I spread enough coins around that no one troubled too much over the renting of a cart, horse, and the rug we threw over the bodies. The master meant us to return immediately.

We reached the palace in late afternoon and grimacing slaves conveyed the bodies to the same workroom where Dabir usually tutored Sabirah.

After the corpses had been deposited upon the old rugs, Dabir put down the satchel and suggested I set to work, saying that he would return soon with books.

"What will I look for?" I asked.

"Study them, Asim! You do not lack wit. See what you can learn. I shall be back soon."

He departed, and I was left alone with the three dead men and a smattering of flies, busy about the blood. I hoped we would be through the task soon, for the flies were certain not to diminish in number.

I stood at the booted feet, staring down at the bodies. Dabir had instructed that they lie faceup. I scratched my beard and wondered when the slaves would bring the food. I'd had naught but tiny pastries since morn.

I had seen enough death that bodies did not trouble me overmuch. In truth, apart from the corpses and the flies, it was rather a comforting room, paneled with dark teak and decorated with old Persian wall

21

hangings. One I especially liked showed Rostam's taming of the horse Rakhsh, his lariat depicted with such skill it looked somehow like it had just been flung. A crowd of elders looked on the youth in horror, and one fat fellow was actually chewing his beard in consternation down in the corner of the tapestry. His expression made me chuckle.

I then bethought of the dead men and held off laughing, stepping over to the bank of scalloped windows. Here, too, was a goodly sight, for Dabir's study looked out on another of the master's gardens, one floor below. I breathed in the scent of water from the fountain, and took in a faint scent of rose as well.

Still there came no food, so I looked over the other tapestry, considered the scrollwork on the large chests against the wall, glanced at the red and blue glazed game pieces the crones had left to see who was winning, then returned at last to the corpses.

The door opened, but instead of a slave with food I faced the poet, who slid through and closed the portal behind him. His mocking smile disappeared quickly as he considered the grisly display. He tugged on his wispy beard.

"Are you through with your poem?" I asked.

"Almost." He joined me by the bodies. "The master said many curious things had transpired, and that he was going to write of them. What are these?"

"Dead men."

"What wit! Did you slay them?"

I only grunted and looked down at the slain men once more. I expected the poet to grow bored and leave me be.

"Why do you stare so? Do you admire your handiwork?"

"Dabir set me to examining the bodies."

"For what?"

"For information."

"You seem somewhat far away to learn much information."

"You seem somewhat sober for a drunkard."

"Huh. I would see this gold the master spoke of."

"It is there, in the satchel."

Hamil stepped around me while I considered what might be learned from the dead. Two were murderers and thieves, one was a victim. I could tell that the victim had once taken greater care with his person than the other two had likely ever known, but his clothing was travel-worn, his face and hair dirty with road dust.

"This is quite a treasure," the poet said from my right.

"Yes." I glanced over, saw him slide the pull back in the satchel.

"And Dabir can read the language on the gold?"

"I believe he went to find some books about them."

Hamil came and stood at my elbow. He was a short, slight fellow, and the height of his turban was barely level with my eyes.

"Have you seen to their money yet?"

"No," I answered.

"Let's count it, then. Those money bags look full."

I couldn't see how that would help anything, but it was a better suggestion than I had developed, and had been offered without malice. "Very well," I said, and in a short time we had cut free the coin purses, dumped their contents in a pile, and sorted them. I kept watch on the poet to see that he palmed no coins, but he seemed motivated more by curiosity than avarice.

There was more in those purses than I would have guessed, but the poet and I separated the money into piles in a short time. We were uncertain what to do then, but fortunately for us, the servants arrived at last with food, so we washed, moved the platters away from the bodies, and set to eating. It was one of the few amicable moments Hamil and I had ever shared, united as we were both by the mystery of the events and our own consternation, for we could not imagine that anything useful might be learned from the dead men's possessions.

We were to be rudely surprised.

As I was wiping my hands on a napkin, Dabir entered, burdened with books and scrolls. I hurried to assist him as the poet rose with a greeting.

I caught one of the scrolls as it rolled about on top of Dabir's stack. "What did you find?" he asked me.

"More coins than you might think."

Dabir set the books and papers on a table and walked to the piles of money, which he eyed critically.

"We counted them for you," the poet told him.

"You mixed the coin purses together?" Dabir sounded horrified.

"Yes," Hamil answered.

Dabir put his hand to his face.

"What?" I asked.

"Are you trying to ruin me, Asim?"

"What is it?" I was solicitous; I was all too aware that I had put the man's career in jeopardy by suggesting his name to Jaffar earlier today.

"Which coins came from which man? Do you have any idea?"

The poet and I traded glances. "Well," I ventured, "the man who had the door pull had few coins upon him at all. The others had a month's wages."

"Your pardon—what could the coins tell us?" Hamil asked.

"All manner of things," Dabir said quietly, "to those who would look."

"I looked," I said, "but I did not see anything."

"Exactly! Those Greek coins, there—from whom did they come?"

"The ones who attacked us," I answered.

"Are you sure? Are you absolutely sure? It might be important!"

"I'm sure," I answered, although now that he mentioned it, I couldn't be, completely.

"He is right," the poet said.

"Why do you think these Greek coins were in the possession of these men?" Dabir asked.

"They're Greeks?" the poet offered helpfully.

"No, a Greek paid them," Dabir said. He stepped to one of the bodies. "Look here, at these men, and their finery. These are not their normal clothes, judging by their treatment. Do they otherwise seem the sort of men to wear such excellent garments?"

"Do you think them stolen?" the poet asked.

"No—see how well they fit. These are but recently purchased. Someone paid them well to do something."

"Somebody Greek," I said.

"Probably." So saying, Dabir bent over the men who'd attacked us and tore open their jubbahs to reveal old, stained undergarments, as though to confirm his earlier suspicion. He studied their footgear momentarily, then spent a much longer time going over the victim, inspecting boots, belt, sleeve, even his beard. The poet hovered nearby, watching all.

"What do you see?" Hamil asked.

"These two are no more than we supposed. I would we could trace them back to the neighborhood from which they were hired, but I lack the necessary information. This man, though . . ."

Dabir undid the fellow's sword belt and opened his robe. Beneath it was a thin white garment. "His sudre. He was Magian. Note also the belt he wears here. I glimpsed it while I was seeing to his wound."

"A wool belt? It holds nothing up."

"It is a symbol of faith. Those who revere the fire tie and untie it while praying. It is woven," Dabir continued, "from seventy-two threads, to honor one of their holy texts."

"Was it a Magian door pull?" I asked.

"It does not seem to be." Dabir climbed to his feet. "Hamil, would you call for the slaves? These men must be shrouded. This other—the Magians have different rites."

"The fire worshippers leave their dead exposed to the elements," the poet said. "As like we can throw him into the alley."

"They do not worship the fire," Dabir said. He sounded faintly annoyed. "Do you worship the rug upon which you kneel?"

Hamil stared at Dabir in answer.

"Send word for a Magian priest. They will want the body. It may be that they will recognize this man."

The poet bowed his head and left without complaint. I did not yet understand that Dabir could inspire people who might normally be contentious into aiding him because they desired involvement in the unraveling of his mystery.

Dabir carefully rubbed his hands with a cake of soap and rinsed them in the bowl of water the slaves had brought, then considered the food. The sherbet had melted; Dabir selected a wrinkled fig.

"Dabir," I said, "if you translate the scratches on the door pull, Jaffar will be so pleased he is likely to forget the magic woman's words."

"He will not forget. He knows I can translate this, which he desires. If it pleases him, he will pass me on to some other house, likely the caliph's."

I smiled. "Then you will wax higher."

His look was dark and long, and I could not escape the feeling he thought me stupid at that moment. His tone, when finally he spoke, was not welcoming. "The caliph's household is large; he is surrounded already by courtiers who do not wish for rivals. And I am not especially interested in sparring with them for a place. Besides, I am pleased with my work here. Was pleased."

I spread my hands. "Allow me to speak with Jaffar, on your behalf. I think I can persuade—"

"You have done enough, I think, today." Dabir sat down heavily with one of the books and began to read. He made no other sign to me, nor did he speak.

Almost I spoke against his rudeness, but I held my tongue as I departed, though I did not leave off slamming the door behind me. Somehow it did not satisfy.

It occurred to me that the old woman had, indeed, confused the bowls and that Jaffar likely did Dabir a favor that he did not appreciate; moreover, that if it had not been for me, Dabir would not have learned he was destined to die for love of Sabirah. Now he might yet change his fate, if such a thing could be done, and he had me to thank.

I spent the rest of the afternoon rounding through my duties; inspecting the arms of the men, the organization of the barracks, and the overall security of the palace. All the men under my command there were dependable, for Jaffar had given me authority to hire and fire as needed, but that did not mean they were not tempted sometimes to cut corners. I set three to work polishing helmets that had been neglected.

For most of that afternoon and early evening I thought only of my duties, but my mind turned occasionally to Dabir and the bodies and the pull. Would he be able to translate the thing, and what would it say? Were the men I'd slain after it solely because it was gold, or had they, too, valued the words? Would I be renowned as a slayer of monsters? What monsters, and from whence would they come?

What use asking questions for which I had no answers? I put them from my mind.

I was leaning over a shatranj board across from my nephew Mahmoud—my chief lieutenant—just after evening prayers, when there came a knock upon the door. Mahmoud bade the knocker to enter, and Boulos himself stuck in his head and asked for me. The chief eunuch explained why as we walked.

"Mistress Sabirah desires a word with you," he said.

"What is this about?"

"You do not know?" he asked.

"No."

"Hmm. I was hoping you did." He chewed on that thought a moment as we advanced through the shadowy corridors. Here and there torches flickered in cressets set into pillars, but despite them, evening always lent the palace a cavernous feel. Expensive carpets dulled our passage, but every eight feet or so there was a gap, and our boot heels would echo on the flagstones for two paces before we crossed again to fabric.

"Did you really slay two men in the space of a single breath?" Boulos asked.

I thought for a moment. "Perhaps three breaths."

"Zip, zip, zip!" Boulos brandished an imaginary sword before him, then chuckled. "A Magian priest arrived and spoke with Dabir at length before leaving with the other fellow's body. I would give much to know what they said! You know how closemouthed Dabir is. And he seems in a mood besides."

"He said nothing to me."

Boulos tried prying out more information about our trip, but I was seasoned enough to ask if Jaffar had shared details with him yet, and Boulos was wise enough to admit to me that the master had not.

"The master," I said, "may intend to surprise the caliph with the story and not wish it spread."

"You can tell me, Asim, for I am the very soul of discretion."

"Boulos," I said, "you are known far and wide as a fine relayer of tales, which is to be commended. But in this instance, it is not to be encouraged."

Boulos pouted, but fortunately by this time we had reached the harem. Here the halls were not so lofty, and more narrow as well, though decorated with even finer hangings. Gold filagree showed upon some of the door lintels. The floors were of stained wood.

He conducted me through the central hall and into Sabirah's apartments. She sat beside a screened window, through which fading sunlight shone. A candle flickered upon the sill.

Boulos and I were both permanent fixtures of the house; he the chief slave and me guardian of the family blood, and thus Sabirah did not bother with the veil. Perhaps it was the wan light or her grim countenance, but she seemed older than her eighteen years. One of her serving girls sat in the corner reciting a sura. Sabirah corrected her, then requested she leave off.

"Mistress," Boulos said, "here is Captain Asim, as you requested."

"Thank you, Boulos. You may go."

"You do not wish me to remain?" There was almost a rebuke in the tone of the smiling eunuch's question.

"Ghadya is here," Sabirah said, flicking her fingers toward the serving girl.

Still Boulos hesitated.

Sabirah was unexpectedly sharp-tongued. "Do you linger because you did not hear, because you do not trust the captain, or because you are desperate for new gossip?"

Boulos bowed. "Your pardon, Mistress." He bowed thrice more and backed out, closing the door behind him. Sabirah watched him the while, and so he dared no instructional side looks to me or Ghadya.

Sabirah listened for the creak of Boulos's feet upon the floorboards as he departed, then turned to the serving girl. "Leave us."

"Mistress?"

Sabirah pointed to an archway on her right. The servant girl rose and left, with a backward glance at me. She worried, as did I, as to Sabirah's unseemly behavior.

"Sit, Captain. What? Do you fear my uncle believes me in love with both you *and* Dabir?"

"I worry as to your reputation and my head." I reluctantly settled onto the floor in front of the door.

"My uncle has told me that Dabir is to be sent away and that I am to be married soon. What do you think of that?"

"Eh. Congratulations, Mistress."

She scowled. "I am still in mourning."

Two years prior her marriage had been but a week off when the would-be groom died on the wrong end of a Greek lance. Sabirah had never met the fellow, but had expressed grief with great alacrity. The charade had been taken up by both Musa and Jaffar as an excuse to further the education the girl so craved, but everyone knew another marriage had been delayed too long. My own look at that moment must have conveyed my opinion on the matter, for she stared sharply at me. "What did you do?" she asked in a fierce whisper.

"Me?"

"This is all *your* doing!" Sabirah pointed menacingly at me. "Jaffar tells me that it was you who suggested Dabir accompany you to the market. What happened there? Uncle will not say!"

"I do not think—"

"Tell me, Captain!"

"If your uncle would not say, then it is not—"

"Did he forbid you from telling me?"

"Nay."

"Then I command it."

God had seen fit to heap troubles upon me that day. "Mistress," I said slowly, "it is not that simple, and you well know—"

"I command it, Captain. So help me—" She stood up from her cushion and began to pace in front of the window. "You do not want me for your enemy!"

"Indeed, nor do I wish to anger your uncle."

"Surely it would anger him to hear that you had not obeyed a command from me?"

I said nothing, and her eyes narrowed. She stood over me, glowering, while I considered my options.

"It is true that I suggested Dabir accompany us. The rest was but fate."

Bit by bit, pacing most of the while, she pried the story from me. My battle held little interest for her. Again and again she asked for details about the bowls and the fortune-telling.

"It is clear to me," I concluded, "that the magic woman confused the bowls."

"Is it?"

"Dabir is no monster slayer, and I am no writer."

"So you trust this woman to read your futures?"

"Well, I suppose so."

"So you believe that she is wise enough to foresee the plan of Allah, yet can become confused about the contents of bowls?" Sabirah seemed almost to be quaking with anger.

"It could happen to anyone," I admitted.

"You yourself said she was looking right at you as she pronounced these destinies!"

"Yes, that is true."

"That she seemed to be in a magical trance."

"Yes. That is probably why she was confused."

"Or perhaps," Sabirah countered, "that's why you should believe her the more! Ah! God help me, but men are idiots." She faced the window.

"Dabir is not in love with me, this I know." She turned back to me suddenly. "You will make it right! I do not mean to cease my learning and give over my life to child rearing! You will march yourself straight to Jaffar and put things as they were!"

"How, Mistress?"

"Remind him that it was his fate, not Dabir's. Use the same reasoning that I have just used with you! Is it not reasonable?"

"Can you not tell him your reasoning?"

"He will not listen to me when I speak to him of this."

"He does not want to think it his fate, Mistress."

She sank back onto the cushions. "That is the problem." She curled hair ends about her finger and looked up through her lashes. "You could confess that you are the one who desires me, Captain. Then Jaffar would dismiss you, and not Dabir."

I blinked at her. "I would not lie to the master." What else was I to say? Was everyone crazed today?

"Mostly I jested." She sighed and dropped her hands. "Why did you ask Dabir to accompany you?"

"Because," I said, "I knew that he would be a better man than the poet to help safeguard your uncle. And," I added, "because I enjoy his company more than Hamil's."

"Have you asked Dabir what he thinks? Surely he can find the words to make this right."

"He will not talk to me. He says that I have done enough already." I sighed deeply, feeling the weight of the day's events rest on my shoulders. "I did not mean to anger either of you."

"Perhaps the woman could be arrested and proven a fake?"

"That would not be just, Sabirah. Of all things, your uncle believes in justice."

"So do I." She groaned. "This is so unfair!"

Sabirah could sound like the wisest of counselors one moment and half her age the next. For a moment I'd forgotten that I spoke still to a young woman.

"I will talk to your uncle," I said, choosing my words carefully. "I will remind him of Dabir's faithful service. I could suggest to him that the woman was merely playacting. It might be that she recognized us and played upon our hopes and fears."

"I would not doubt it. It is the way of the souk, to mislead and exaggerate."

"The problem," I said, wondering whether or not I should mention the issue, "is that the fortune-teller predicted something important would take place if we left immediately and lo, she was right."

"So you said. Argue to Uncle that it was coincidence." She must have seen the doubt in my eyes, for she continued. "Clearly you think well of Dabir—if he is your friend, speak for him."

I rose and bowed to her.

"Captain, perhaps such a duty requires reward. I have funds at my disposal . . ."

I bowed once more. "Mistress, Asim el Abbas needs no compensation for right action."

She bowed her head to me.

"Good evening to you, Mistress. I shall speak with the master immediately."

"Good evening, Captain, and thank you. Go with God."

Boulos lurked just down the hall, and fell in step with me as I left. "What was that about, Captain?"

Our shadows were stretched out along the corridor as we left. I listened for the muezzin's call, knowing it would come soon. "The master spoke to her about his trip to the market today."

"Whatever for?"

"To make my life more difficult, I'm afraid. I must see the master."

"This is all quite puzzling," Boulos said in an attempt at a casual tone. "What could have happened in the market that would so upset the mistress?" He awaited an answer.

"I wish that I could say, Boulos. It does not bode well for either Dabir or myself, though."

That seemed to whet his appetite for information even more thoroughly, and his neck craned forward, as though to better gauge me.

"I really must see the master, Boulos. Do you know where he is?"

Information was the chief slave's main source of power, and he nodded, smirking. "He will be in the private mosque, and then means to play backgammon this night." As if I did not already infer his meaning, he winked.

I sighed. The year before, Jaffar and his older brother Musa and some friends had attended a party where there was much wine and many courtesans. One, a sloe-eyed dancing girl, had painted all visible flesh in alternating triangles of black and brown, and a drunken Musa had confessed to my master—and to any within earshot—that he was determined to learn whether the designs had been painted across the whole of her body. Jaffar joked after morning prayers the next day that his brother must have played backgammon with her the whole of the night, and ever since it had become a euphemism within the palace. A rather tired one, by that point.

The master being occupied, I returned for evening prayers with Mahmoud, asking Allah to send an angel to the dreamland, one with wise words to aid my argument when I spoke with Jaffar. Then I finished a shatranj game with Mahmoud before I lay down to sleep. I planned to make my case with Jaffar just after he broke his fast, when he was always in the best of moods.

It was fated to happen otherwise.

3

The Greek entourage arrived early the next morning, three bearded officials and a dozen servants clothed all in gold silk, bearing baskets and boxes. The master's chamberlain guided them to the reception room where they were offered refreshments. I supervised the placement of two dozen guards within and without the room, emphasizing both that they should be wary and that they should hold off from rash acts, and then reported to Jaffar in his chambers. He sipped fruit juice from a mug amongst plump cushions and rich furnishings, surrounded on every hand by brilliant wall hangings.

I had hoped to speak with him alone, but Dabir sat at the master's right hand, conversing in low tones. Jaffar looked bright and animated, in high spirits. Dabir's manner was subdued. There were dark circles under his eyes, the blue of which seemed somehow duller.

"Ah, peace be upon you, Captain," Jaffar said at sight of me.

I bowed low. "And also upon you."

"You slept well?"

"Yes."

"Both Dabir and I were up many hours," Jaffar said. The master looked immaculate and well rested. But he was almost always thus. "Inspiration struck," he continued, "and I worked upon the writing of verses describing that door pull. And Dabir was hard at work deciphering the runes upon it." He smiled at Dabir. "I think my work was less taxing. And," he added, raising his index finger to make his most important point, "my strength is back from the illness."

Jaffar's illness had begun as a simple cough, then lingered long, afflicting him so that it became difficult to both breathe and sleep. He had grown so weak from fatigue that the caliph himself had sent his best hakims to care for his friend. Under their ministrations Jaffar had mended. Usually Jaffar sat in judgment upon weighty matters that shaped the course of the city and the caliphate. The caliph had made him leave off his duties for more than a month while he regained his strength, much to my master's frustration.

"So," Jaffar asked, "what do you think of the Greeks?"

"They have come with many presents," I said.

"They desire the door pull," Dabir said.

Jaffar and I both looked at him.

"How can you be sure?" I asked.

The master answered instead of Dabir, a smile on his lips. "I see! You think that this must be related to the Greek coins you found on the cutthroats."

"Yes, Master. It appears that they went to a great deal of trouble to obtain this door pull, spending far more than its apparent decorative worth."

Jaffar considered this information, then nodded decisively. "Let us see what we can learn from these Greeks. Asim, I want nothing revealed to them. Show a face of stone, and we will see what they say."

"As you wish, Master." I bowed my head.

"I shall be there shortly. See to the security of the situation."

I bowed again, debating telling him that I'd already ensured his safety. Also I still hoped to speak a word in Dabir's favor, yet was unsure how to accomplish that with the scholar in the room.

Jaffar sipped at his juice, then looked up at me. "Is there something else, Captain?"

Dabir eyed me sharply. Did he mean to communicate something particular from that glare, or was he truly that angry with me?

"No, Master." I bowed, then left. I would have to seek him out after the reception with the Greeks.

There was no harm, I decided, in checking over the men again. It would press upon them the importance of the meeting.

Jaffar's reception room was a grand, colonnaded space, long and tiled, with narrow raised pools to left and right of the carpeted walkway leading to the dais. Fish swam in that sparkling clear water, and light from the high-set windows flashed along their scales. The room itself was built so that those who waited at one end could not hear the conversation before the dais, which kept courtiers and supplicants wondering as to events that were not their own affair.

The master entered to recline along a settee upon the dais, somewhat in the manner of the caliph, though he did not wait behind a curtain. Mahmoud and another of my lieutenants stood grim and silent behind him. I stood at Jaffar's left, Dabir on the right. This day both Jaffar and Dabir were in their finery, complete with gold thread wrapped through their turbans.

The chamberlain, well-fed old Abdul-Rafi, presented the master's titles to the Greeks, then preceded them to Jaffar's roost, bowed, and formally announced their names before the dais. Old he might be, but few could match the booming power of Abdul-Rafi's voice. "The Archduke Theocritus, his son Nicephorous, and their translator, Diomedes." Also there were servants carrying boxes.

Diomedes was all smiles as he bowed. His gaze fastened briefly upon me, then flicked to Dabir and back to Jaffar. The Greek's dark, protuberant eyes were striking in a sharp, dangerous way: I had the sense that he weighed all he saw for import.

Theocritus, thickset with distinguished sprinkles of white hair along his temples, spoke. Diomedes cocked his head, listening.

"The archduke thanks you for seeing us at such short notice," Diomedes said, his voice almost a purr, "and wishes to bestow upon you a number of marvelous gifts."

Jaffar brushed his curled and perfumed beard. "Tell the archduke that I am pleased to make his acquaintance. I hope that he finds Baghdad and my home to his liking. I thank him also for his gifts." Diomedes translated this, and both the archduke and his son, a thinner, younger cut of cloth with a sharper nose, bowed their heads. The archduke then chattered at the servants, who brought forward the boxes. Two of my men walked with them.

Diomedes introduced the gifts as they were presented, and Jaffar either pretended interest well, or was sincerely curious. For my part, I found the carpets and gold baubles and sundry fabrics only an irritating delay. Were the Greeks truly after the pull? Surely for the cost of these gifts they could fashion more gold in its shape.

After a tedious quarter hour the baskets and boxes had all been opened and the servants dismissed, escorted out by two of my soldiers.

"The archduke is quite generous," Jaffar said to Diomedes. "Convey my thanks to him."

The large man chattered some more. "The archduke says that your reputation is well known even in Constantinople, and that you are judged a fair and honorable man."

"I thank him."

"The archduke and his son had traveled to Baghdad to consult scholars within the household of the caliph."

"How interesting," the master said. "The caliph mentioned nothing of it to me."

Diomedes bowed his head and relayed this. "It may be," he answered, "that the caliph himself did not know of the matter, or that he simply thought it beneath your interest."

"Oh, I doubt that." Jaffar smiled now. He was enjoying himself. "I would have been very interested to learn of a Greek deputation arriving in Baghdad. You are in an official capacity?"

"Somewhat," Diomedes said, after consultation with his master. "You see, the archduke hopes to present the Empress Irene with a gift soon, a rare item from antiquity. Certain sources reveal that the gift's twin might lie within the treasure vaults of the caliph."

"What manner of item is it?" Jaffar's voice was awash with innocence.

"A door pull, Excellency, all of gold, with several jewels. The archduke brought it with him to Baghdad in the hope that he might compare it to that rumored to be held by the caliph. If indeed they matched, the archduke hoped to purchase the pull from the caliph's estate."

"Very interesting," Jaffar said, rubbing his beard.

Diomedes conveyed this to the archduke, who studied Jaffar for a time before speaking again.

"Lamentably," Diomedes said, then paused, listening further to his master, "the pull was stolen from some of the archduke's servants, who were murdered by the thief."

"That *is* unfortunate," Jaffar replied.

"We set men on his trail, but the pull itself was taken by *other* men."

"Wicked behavior yields wickedness," Jaffar said.

"I suppose so, Excellency." Diomedes bowed.

The archduke said something to Diomedes, who shook his head no, but said nothing.

"I have to ask," Jaffar said, "why you have come to me about this matter."

Diomedes bowed once more. "Our men were closing on the thief when they were confronted by three men near the souk. We think . . . the archduke has reason to believe that they were men from your household."

The master said nothing.

"If you know anything of the matter," Diomedes continued, "the archduke would be grateful for any information about the door pull; if you find that your servants did, indeed, recover it, he hopes that you would facilitate its return. He means to well compensate the pull's discoverers," Diomedes continued quickly. "Obviously they had no part in its theft."

Jaffar nodded, and held up a hand. "I will look into this matter immediately."

While the Greeks bowed and expressed their thanks, Dabir bent to whisper to the master's ear, so quietly that I could not hear.

"A fine question," Jaffar said, nodding, then returned his attention to the Greeks. "Why did the archduke not have an identical door pull constructed based upon the pattern of the first?"

Diomedes consulted softly with his master before facing us once more. "It is said that the pulls are not completely identical; there is an ancient pattern upon them both, slightly different."

Dabir leaned toward Jaffar and spoke into his ear. As he straightened, my master asked: "From whence did these door pulls originate?"

Diomedes held a brief, whispered conversation with the archduke, then bowed. "The archduke's explanation may inspire incredulity, Excellency. He does not know for certain."

"What has he been told?"

"He believes they may be from a ruined city of the ancient Greeks, Excellency."

"Indeed? Most interesting! Which city?"

"Mycenae," Diomedes answered sharply, without consulting Theocritus.

Jaffar exchanged a glance with Dabir, then opened his arms to the Greeks. "Please stay in my palace. Be my guests, while I seek the truth."

The Greeks thanked Jaffar with many bows, and then the master exited with Dabir and me.

"You," he said to Dabir as we walked the dark hall together, "are to go to the caliph's palace. I shall write a note. Bring forth this pull, if it exists, and study it. See what it reveals."

"Master," Dabir said, "is it wise to remove the pull without the caliph's knowledge?"

Jaffar dismissed this worry with a casual hand wave. "The caliph would ask me to look into the matter, were he here." It was true that Jaffar was the caliph's closest friend, but I, too, wondered as to the wisdom of the action.

"The Greeks are keeping something from us, Excellency," Dabir said. "Did you note something odd in their manner? The translator was too freely elaborating what the archduke said . . . adding details, and the Greeks seemed almost deferential to him as he did so."

Jaffar stroked his beard thoughtfully, and I wondered if he had failed to see this and did not wish to admit it.

"I presume," Dabir continued, "that there is some important message hidden in the text on the pulls—which is assuredly not any kind of ancient Greek."

"What did the first pull say?" I asked.

"It introduced the device as the 'opener of ways to the Keeper of Secrets.' Also there were magic symbols."

"What do they mean?"

"I have not yet finished the translation."

"Go with him, Asim," Jaffar instructed. "See that this second pull is recovered. We will keep the Greeks occupied while Dabir studies it."

As Dabir and I walked for the stables I ventured that the master seemed kindly disposed toward him, and he agreed that it seemed so and the conversation died as surely as if I had stabbed it. Before long we were mounted and riding our mares out through the streets.

I have journeyed through many cities in my years, and Baghdad was the loveliest of them all. Admittedly a few portions were filthy and rank smells sometimes assaulted the senses, as will happen whenever you crowd humanity behind walls, but there were fountains and blooming gardens and vast stretches of waterways and canals, spanned by bridges.

In this, early spring, there was not yet the suffocating heat, and the streets and marketplaces thronged with folk on their way hither and yon, sometimes with children in tow, or leading mules laden with baskets and bags. It was a cacophony of sound but a joyous one.

To reach the gilded palace that was Baghdad's heart, we left the quarter of the city where Jaffar lived and crossed the Tigris on one of its three great bridges. The outer wall of the Round City, as Baghdad's center was known, watched over the river from a height of eight spear lengths. This grand wall was interspersed with even taller watchtowers, the mightiest of which was the highest point in the city. The Iron Tower, however, was never visited, for Harun al-Rashid's brother and short-lived predecessor was said to haunt its balcony. Hadi the Brute had planned to replace the standard towers with a series of more fortified structures, each fashioned from thick-walled stone and rising more than a hundred feet, but had perished with the plan barely under way. Allah be praised, he also died before any of his many attempts to poison his brother were successful.

Between the height of the Iron Tower—so called for its locked and rusting door—and the triple walls, was the mosque of Al-Mansur. The glittering golden spires of this, the city's most glorious structure, dazzled all who stared at them from the length and breadth of the city, for it was decreed they be polished always to a high sheen.

Once behind the palace walls, Dabir and I were in a sea of black, for all the government functionaries dressed in dark cloth; not to do so was tantamount to resignation. The road passed through the outer gardens, which were decorated with flowers blooming in verses from the Koran. Barefoot slaves tended yew and cypress belted with jewel-studded metal. Soldiers and couriers passed us along the road, some bound perhaps for palaces across the city, others to the ends of the earth.

It happened that the master, his father, and his brothers all maintained apartments within the palace, and thus I was not unknown there to the staff. We were admitted and then introduced to the chamberlain, who asked first after Jaffar's health and then read his letter, brushing his gray beard all the while.

"This is a peculiar request," he said finally. "It may take some time to lay hands upon such a thing, if it does, indeed, exist."

"Do you know of anyone who has made inquiries into it before now?" Dabir asked.

"I have never heard it mentioned."

"Do you know of any Greeks who sought it?" I asked.

The chamberlain shook his head no.

"It may be that they asked about it by letter," Dabir suggested.

Again the old fellow shook his head. "But I am not familiar with every dispatch that reaches these walls."

Dabir frowned. "If one were to come from an archduke, do you think—"

"Ah, well, then I would surely have been apprised. Any request by a foreign official would be examined carefully."

"The Greeks lied?" I prompted.

"So it would appear," Dabir said.

The chamberlain was intrigued enough by the story to send his top assistant with us to look into the matter.

Poets might say that the treasures of the caliph are beyond counting, but that would be a falsehood, for all the treasures have been counted and cataloged, and it is the duty of a harried triptych of thin, black-garbed clerks to track their outflow and inflow. The caliph or his brother Ibrahim and other assorted relatives were at constant pains to diminish the treasury whereas the vizier was at constant pains to bring currency into the state coffers, so these three were ever busy. It is not just money that flows in and out, but gifts as well, bequeathed by this ambassador or governor or foreign potentate to the caliph, or gifted by the caliph or some member of his household to a distant king or a song girl whose voice was especially pleasing. Thus there is a vast warren of underground cubbyholes and shelves and halls, sealed behind lock, key, and swordsmen of massive girth and fearsome manner. That the tracking lies mostly upon the shoulders—or, in truth, necks—of but three men is a testament to their skill.

Once the chamberlain's assistant described our need to them, one looked up from the paper where he was scribbling figures, called for a boy, and bade him take us to a certain hall and a certain room and look along the left.

Within a half hour of our arrival we had passed treasures and splendors to set a miser fainting in envy and a thief perspiring with greed. The boy filled my mind with wonder, chattering as he went about this or that rumored treasure. Beyond a heavy door were niches where the boy claimed the very staff of Moses could be found, along with the crown of Cyrus, the sword of Iskander, and a book written by the angel Gabriel. We saw none of these, but left in possession of a door pull identical to the first. At least I thought so. Dabir indicated to me that the characters were different, but when the characters are nothing but scratches and geometric symbols I cannot know how a man is supposed to judge the differ-ence. Dabir was eager to return with it so that he might compare it in more detail to the first, and begin work upon the translation, and thus we begged off the invitation of my cousin Rashad—a lieutenant in the caliph's guard staff—to join him for a meal before prayer at the Golden Mosque, and hurried back to Jaffar's halls. I thought surely to be done with the matter, but before long Boulos conveyed that the master wished me, personally, to guard the pull while it was in Dabir's hands.

Thus I spent a dull afternoon as the scholar sat staring alternately at the two pulls and all manner of scrolls and books. We were joined in the late afternoon by the old women, resuming their game, and their charge, Sabirah. Then pupil and teacher both sat hunched over the old pulls, making notes.

Sweets were to be had, and I ate them, but that did nothing to allay the boredom. For a while I looked over Dabir's shoulders and saw for myself that the little markings differed between the pulls, but nothing else. For a time I looked back and forth between the girl and the man, seeking for sign of a touch, or a long look, or other such cues. But their love seemed to be one for symbols and Dabir noticed my scrutiny and condemned it with a hard stare from lowered brows, whereupon I retreated to the room's far side. None of the other hangings were as fine as that one of Rostam, so by and by I looked out through an open window at the garden.

My older brother, Tariq, may God bless him, once showed a strange trick to me. A dog lay on the ground outside our window, and he said he would gain its attention neither by calling its name nor making any other noise, nay, nor movement. The dog had his back to us, so the latter would have been impossible in any case. I was but ten, and very curious, so I watched as my brother stared at the beast. Within a minute, the creature turned and stared at him. I raised an outcry, asking my brother if he had learned magic, and he laughed. "No," he said, "the soul shines through the eyes, and when you stare at a man—or a beast with sufficient wit—he will sense your gaze. Try it yourself."

I never forgot the lesson, which showed that there are senses beyond the ones we catalog. I mention it now because, after I sat there in the shadows by the window for a time, I felt that strange prickling sensation that I myself was under examination. I saw no man, though, or even a dog, but a small black bird upon the rim of the upper pool of the garden's fountain. It might have been a statue, so still did it sit, and I wondered if it were an omen of some kind, and made the sign against the evil eye. At that, it stirred, and looked past me. Its eyes were particularly brilliant, shining less like eyes and more like gemstones. I had never seen its like. I watched the bird for a long moment, but it did not move again.

I tried dismissing the notion that there was anything threatening about a bird that I might slay with a flick of my hand, but as it perched there, quiet as death, I found nothing common in its appearance or reassuring in its behavior. Would not a normal bird have been hopping, or picking at its wing, or flapping to another roost? It just sat there, looking through the window.

I crept from my own perch, quietly and slowly, so as not to startle it, and backed into the room. I found Dabir just where I had left him, tediously poring over the books.

"Dabir," I said softly, "there is a strange bird outside."

You might think he would have rolled his eyes or cursed me for my foolishness, but he answered without looking up. "Is it a small black bird with shining eyes?"

"Bismallah!" I could not hold off a cry of surprise. "It is! How did you know?"

"It was there during our battle yesterday. And it flew overhead when we rode to the palace."

"You joke," I said weakly.

"I do not."

The course was clear to me. "We must slay it."

"Nay; we will not let its masters know we know they watch us. They might send some other guardian we would not see."

"Can I see the bird?" Sabirah asked. "How could it tell anyone what we're doing?"

"That is an excellent question," Dabir admitted. "Some birds may speak, but they rarely say anything of use."

"Who sent the thing?" Sabirah stared toward the window.

"Do not pay it too much attention," Dabir said, motioning her back. His eyes dropped again to his papers. "I think perhaps it comes from the Greeks, but I cannot say. There is much here that is shielded from me."

Sabirah chewed her lip thoughtfully then returned to unroll one of the scrolls.

"What have you learned?" I asked Dabir. I stood over him and the pulls, placed side by side on a brown rug, their gemstones twinkling.

"These are very old, for one thing."

"How old?"

"Older than Noah, may peace be upon him. This is cuneiform script, similar to that we saw in Kalhu, but of an older make."

"What does it say?"

"These"—he pointed here and there to strings of symbols—"call for the blessings of djinn these folk worshipped as gods. But the blessings are strange."

"It's all about magic," Sabirah said from her cushion. "The folk of Ubar wanted these pulls on doors that open to a place called the Desert of Souls, where—"

"Ubar?" I repeated, my mind reeling.

Dabir gave Sabirah a hard look. "Aye, Ubar."

There were none who failed to hear of the splendors of Ubar. The wealth of a dozen kingdoms had been funneled to the ancient world's finest artisans in crafting the fabled city, but it had been destroyed by Allah in a rain of fire and covered over with a sea of sand because its people had turned their face from right thinking.

"Did the Greeks find the pull in Ubar?" I asked.

"No, Asim. I think they tracked this one down, or, likely, stole it. What they intend with both of them I am not sure."

"What good are they?" I asked. "Apart from their gold and gems. Ubar is lost."

"They may plan to find it," Dabir said.

I laughed shortly, for men had sought the riches of Ubar for millennia. Some few returned with stories of nothing but failure; most did not return at all. "No one has ever found Ubar; no one ever shall."

"Do not be so sure, Asim."

The door was opened behind us and the master strode in, followed by Boulos. Jaffar's mouth was a stern line. Boulos's head was bowed, and I had the sense that he was both quite interested to observe and somehow ashamed to be involved.

Upon seeing who entered, Dabir rose and bowed his head.

The master did no more than glance at him, demanding instead of Sabirah, "What do you here, niece?"

"Dabir is instructing me." Her voice was carefully neutral.

"Was it not clear that your studies with him are at an end?"

Sabirah rose, her head bowed only slightly. Her eyes burned. "Perhaps I was too simple to understand your meaning."

Jaffar scowled. "Do not play games with me, girl! I am trying to see to your protection!"

"See to your own!" she said, abandoning dispassion. "May God see fit to open your eyes!"

Jaffar was astonished by her rudeness. She brushed past him, wiping at her eyes. Jaffar ordered Boulos after her, to see her to her quarters. The old watcher women scuttled in his wake.

Jaffar faced Dabir. "What is your excuse, Dabir? You are not a willful child."

"Honored One," I said, "I saw no evidence of desire between the two, save the desire for learning."

The master rounded on me. "I did not ask, Captain! But since you intrude, how is it that you did not put a stop to them? You knew that I meant to dismiss Dabir from my service!"

I bowed. "Forgive me, Excellency. He yet remained within your service. The order had not been given, and I thought—"

"I do not pay *you* to think! I pay *him* to think!"

46

"Forgive Asim, Master," Dabir spoke up. "And forgive the girl. I need help with these texts, and hers is an agile mind. When she came for her afternoon studies, I set her to work."

"Your lie exposes you! What possible use could she be here? She does not know this language!"

Dabir explained quickly. "She has a mind that, upon reading a thing, will not let it go. It is greater for this purpose even than mine. She scans the references, and—"

Jaffar put his hand to his head, rather dramatically, and Dabir fell silent.

When the master spoke at last, it was as a disappointed father pleading for reason. Stern, but disappointed. "Dabir, I need your aid in unraveling this knot. But do not use that need to your own advantage. I can call upon other men, if need be."

"I understand that, Excellency."

"Do you deny that you are in love with Sabirah?"

I thought to immediately hear Dabir counter, but he hesitated. I think this hesitation even surprised Jaffar, and I was reminded that Jaffar might still be trying to convince himself the fortune-teller had confused the readings.

"I have affection for her," Dabir said. "As is only natural for a teacher with a talented pupil."

The master waved this off. He seemed almost relieved. "You deceive yourself, Dabir. It is easy to do, with pretty eyes. But she cannot be for you. Her marriage must be a political one."

That was only reasonable.

"I hope that you will find more tutors for her," Dabir said. "She chirps after knowledge as a newborn sparrow for worms."

"That soon shall be her husband's lookout. It is time to obey Musa's wishes, as I should have done months ago. Her father has been after me since autumn to marry her, and I keep writing him that we should delay. She flashes her eyes at me and says 'Uncle, do not marry me—I wish to continue my studies.'" He shook his head. "Now come, it is almost time for evening prayers. When we return, I wish you to show me what you have discovered."

Dabir locked the gold pulls in a chest and dropped the key in a pouch belted to his waist.

The mosque on the grounds of Jaffar's palace was not quite as large as that upon the grounds of the caliph's palace—my master knew better—but the calligraphy decorating its walls rivaled or perhaps even surpassed the caliph's in grandeur. We made ablutions, then set to our prayers.

When I am troubled, I bow to Mecca and pray to God, and my spirit is eased; it is as though a mighty river sweeps me up and carries me upon its current, my back to the streambed, my face to the stars. Prayer both soothes and comforts. Yet this day my mind was elsewhere. My brother Tariq had warned me that I must always mean the words, but that day I dishonored his memory; that day my spirit was uneasy and I focused less upon the marvels of God than upon the burdens of Dabir, and the legends of lost Ubar.

After prayers Jaffar put off the servants who demanded this or that from him, and put aside the request of one of his wives to join him for a fine meal, and returned with us to the room of study. Along the way he was at his charming best, alert and witty, although it was plain to see Dabir was troubled. I think Jaffar meant to put him at ease.

As it happened, God had veiled the sky with black clouds, so that it seemed night chased eagerly after the evening. The halls were dark.

A particularly loud blast of thunder heralded our arrival at the study room, rattling the palace just as Dabir pushed open the doors. Darkness can clothe the unknown in malignance, thus when the dark man-shapes hunched by the chest whirled at our entry, I thought them dwarf demons sent up from hell.

4

A lightning bolt slashed the sky outside the window and in a split second the dark furred shapes were revealed as monkeys larger than any I had seen, taller even than my knee, with dark glittering eyes and fangs. There was something especially malefic in their all too human reaction to us, as though they were two burglars interrupted in the act of thievery. The chest was open and each clutched one of the gold pulls to its furry bosom. The bird that had watched us sat gripping the opened lid with dark claws.

Then the lightning was gone and the monkeys were scurrying for the window.

"Come, Asim!" Dabir cried.

I was a heartbeat behind him, for I paused to draw my sword. The bird rose up, flapping at my face; I swung and connected and it did not come again, but I did not hear it fall or see where it landed.

The first of the monkeys reached the window and clambered onto the sill, the gold pull still clutched to its chest. Dabir grabbed for it, but was too slow. I was a moment behind him and swung at the second creature even as the first leapt over to the wooden screen outside and climbed swiftly out of sight. I threw myself forward, chopping with my blade. I did not miss. The sword sliced clean through the monkey's leg, which flew free. Yet the monkey did not react. In silence it leapt after the first, climbing more slowly with two limbs and tail while it kept the plaque and its dangling ring-pull tight to its furry body.

Dabir thrust his head through the window. There was room enough for me to join him in time to see the second beast clamber over the roof ledge and disappear.

Dabir's study chamber lay on the second floor. Ornate wooden screens blocked the second and fourth windows. All but one of the others was closed with shutters. It was this open window through which the monkeys had fled. I threw down my sword and climbed out onto the narrow ledge after them. Thunder roared all about me.

Holes suited for the claws of monkeys are not as useful for a warrior in boots, and I struggled for a foothold in the wooden screen. I jammed my toe in a round hole and reached up for the overhanging roof only to hear a loud crack. I thought at first it was the thunder, and then my foot gave way.

I sprang off my left foot, caught the roof ledge with my fingers, and pulled myself up. Dabir urged care; I do not think he heard my response, as I was too busy not falling to answer clearly, and my words do not bear repeating. I slung one leg up, then clawed my way over the edge and stood as another lightning bolt shattered the sky and showed me the length of the roof.

There was no one up there but me. I looked quickly to right and left, dreading that the monkeys might lurk in the shadows, but there was nothing to see but a splendid view of the mosque and the courtyard where Pago had died. The thickening shadows beyond the edges of the flat roof disclosed no sign of our quarry.

Jaffar, I thought, *would not be pleased.*

I had more immediate problems. Simply getting down proved difficult, as the roof overhung the second floor, which meant that I could not quite reach the window ledge even though I dangled out from it. Fortunately Dabir noticed my difficulty and came over to grasp my leg and help pull me in. There followed a brief moment of tangled exertion, and then I was once more upright within the study.

Dabir had lit a lantern in my absence; there was no sign of Jaffar.

"Did you see which way they went?" Dabir asked.

"No. They were gone."

"The master ran out to call for the guards and is moving to arrest the Greeks."

I nodded. "I must follow."

"Hold, Asim." Dabir touched my shoulder and pointed down. For the first time I saw that the lantern light spilled upon a furry, severed limb.

"I struck it from the monkey," I said.

"I have looked at the leg, and I have looked at your blade. Tell me, did you wipe your weapon?"

"Nay." What sort of question was that? I had been in a hurry. "I cast it down and climbed."

"There is no blood upon it."

I stepped to where my sword lay, on a rug by the window, and lifted it.

Lightning scorched the air and I saw the blade's hungry gleam as thunder set the walls to shaking.

"There is no blood upon your weapon or upon yon limb."

"Strange," I said.

"The monkey's leg is dry, Asim. As dry as dust."

I bent with him to examine the thing. There was no blood; the flesh was thin as parchment, and wrinkled. The bone was brown with age. The muscles were lean, shriveled.

It looked as if there had been no blood anywhere within that limb for a very long time. "It had a withered leg," I said, pretending that I did not feel a chill along my spine. I did not believe my own words.

"Nay, you saw how swiftly it moved."

A thought struck me then, and I took up the lantern and set out across the room, searching the floor.

"What are you doing?"

"The bird flew at me," I said. "I hit it—"

I found it cut in twain near the south wall. I walked but slowly toward it, already seeing that it, too, lacked blood that should have stained the floor beneath its little body. Dabir knelt beside the two halves. He announced what I had already seen.

"It was dead when you slew it. Look; it is stuffed with sawdust. And its eyes are black jewels."

I backed off and raised my hand, spreading my fingers in the sign against evil. "What does it mean?"

"It means the pulls have greater power than we know. Our enemies have spared nothing to gain them."

I lifted my blade. "Jaffar may be in danger. Come!"

We ran the length of palace to the guest wing, and my mind thought the while of those jewels that had watched me that afternoon. They must have watched us for many hours, if Dabir were right and the thing had followed us from the fight with the ruffians and to the caliph's palace. How could such a thing be, and who had sent it after us?

Mahmoud and two guards stood at Jaffar's side in a small reception room. The archduke and his son sat on cushions across from them, their eyes downcast in fear.

The master's head snapped up and his eyebrows lifted at sight of us. "Dabir! You speak Greek! Talk to them! Asim, did you find the pulls?"

"The monkeys were gone, Master." I started to add that they were already dead, but it seemed an improper time. And the idle thought dawned that there probably was no proper time to speak of monkeys that had no blood, yet moved with the strength of life.

"What shall I say to them?" Dabir asked, a little breathlessly.

"Ask them why they sent monkeys to steal the gold!"

"Master," Dabir said, "if they sent the monkeys, then they are fools to remain here."

"Do you think they will dare deny it?"

"I think they will."

"Ask them!"

So Dabir muttered at them in Greek. "It is as I thought," he said after several short exchanges, "they deny knowing anything about monkeys."

"They lie!"

"They may. Yet there is something more here. If I might have your leave, I will question them further."

The master waved him on impatiently.

And so Dabir fired questions at them and the Greeks answered with speed, though mostly the old one did the answering. After a time it seemed to me that he denied much, and I saw that the young one stiffened. I smelled fear upon them.

"Master," I asked, "where is the Greek translator?"

"I know not," Jaffar snapped. I think he was most worried that he had borrowed a treasure of the caliph's only to have it stolen.

"Diomedes," Dabir said after a much longer exchange, "is the true master. Not these."

"What?" Jaffar demanded.

"These are but actors."

"Then their punishment shall be swift," Jaffar said in a low voice.

The Greeks were chattering now at Dabir, who held up a hand to them without turning from Jaffar.

"They are iconoclasts, unloved by Empress Irene's court because they do not revere and worship images of the Christian saints and the prophet Jesus. They have been blackmailed into playing their parts."

"How do you know they do not lie?"

"I suspected something amiss when Diomedes spoke for them. I thought at first he was merely too clever for his masters. But Diomedes has fled, and left them to take the blame, and they do not know what they should do."

"They should pray to God, who is merciful," the master said. "I am not disposed to be." His voice was grim, but it sounded more tired than threatening. He put his hand to his head, but it was not so dramatic a motion as it sometimes was. "What is it they want from the door pulls?"

Dabir spoke to them in Greek once more. "They know almost nothing of the pulls."

"What do they know?" Jaffar snarled.

Dabir spoke with them at length. There was much wringing of hands and bowing from them and Jaffar's gaze went back and forth between the worried pair and Dabir.

"Where is Diomedes?" he said finally.

"He is fled with a Magian, a master of dark sorceries. They do not know what either of them desire to do with the pulls."

"We must recover them both," Jaffar said, grimacing.

"Yes," Dabir agreed.

"But how? Mahmoud, take these away; they and their servants are to be kept in the dark until such time as I am better disposed."

The Greeks tried to bow, but Mahmoud and the other guards marched them off. Jaffar ignored them and paced up and down. As the guards were leaving, Boulos slipped inside the room.

"You two must find them," Jaffar said. "You must!" He shook his head. "But I do not know how."

"Master," Dabir said, "I may have the answer."

"Indeed? What is it?"

"Give me leave of three hours. On my return, I may need a boat, or cavalry troop. I do not know which."

"Both will be readied." Jaffar eyed him. "You think Diomedes will flee by land or by water."

"Yes."

"How will you learn?"

"I have only a suspicion, not yet an answer."

"Go, then. May God grant you victory. Captain, guard his steps."

Thus did Dabir and I ride forth from the palace for the second time that day. The differences could not have been more marked. On the first, the sun had been high and its rays had warmed our backs. Now the winds were high and the dark sky growled all about us like an angry beast. Dabir and I rode at a gallop whenever possible. The streets were all but deserted; only a few very devout hurried through the murk, bearing lanterns for nighttime prayer at the mosques.

The muezzin's summons echoed through the city, but we rode on. Long had it been since I ignored the call to prayer, and I thought it a bad night to distance myself from God, when I was riding off to parts unknown for a purpose hidden from me. I would like to have asked Dabir for further details, but we moved too quickly; it was not a time for speech.

After prayers were surely over, we reined in before a long dark building set across the street from a dilapidated bathhouse. Dabir swung down from his saddle and tied his mare under one of the building's porticos.

"Where are we?" I asked as I joined him.

"A Magian temple."

"Are the thieves here?"

"Unlikely. We're after answers, Asim. Come!"

I went with him, though I felt only slightly less confused. I was loathe to leave my mare in such a place; even if there was no one about, skulkers were certain to be watching. Still, I followed him to the cedar doors standing at the height of three stairs.

Dabir pounded upon the wood. It sounded thick; an emblem of fire was carved with great skill on eye-level panels in both doors.

"What kind of answers do you need?" I asked. "Do these Magians know where the thieves are?"

Again he knocked. "That's possible," he told me, "but unlikely. I think the first door pull was stolen from the Magians. I want to know what *they* know of the things."

One of the doors was pushed open just far enough for a youth to lift a lantern near his smooth face and stare out at us.

Dabir addressed him hurriedly. "Quadi Jaffar has sent us here. I must see your dastur."

While I had no idea what a dastur was, the youth must have known the term, for he opened the doors to us, sketched a brief bow, and bade us enter.

We found ourselves in a large chamber held up by decorative arches. The young man said he would fetch the dastur then closed the doors, handed Dabir the lantern, and trotted into the darkness.

"What's a dastur?" I asked.

"A holy man of the Magians. It is a priestly rank." Dabir lifted the lantern and inspected the tapestries hung along the wall. Several depicted a white-robed, gray-bearded man of kindly demeanor. It was not a Muslim place.

"Who is that?" I asked.

"Zarathustra," Dabir told me, "prophet of the Magians."

"I know him not."

"You should; he was very wise."

I grunted. "You have been to a Magian temple before?"

"Nay, but I have read the Gathas, the most sacred text of the Magians."

"The Magians," I reminded him, "are not People of the Book." Even the smallest children knew that God had revealed his word to the Jews and Christians, who had gotten some matters wrong, then finally to the Muslims.

"Wisdom is wisdom," Dabir retorted shortly.

"Welcome to the hall of Zarathustra," a measured, reasonant voice said from behind us. I turned; through the door the youth had just departed emerged an old man dressed all in white—robe, turban, and belt. He and Dabir exchanged bows.

"Dastur Esfandiar. Peace be upon you."

"And upon you."

"You know this man?" I asked Dabir.

"I met Dabir earlier," the dastur explained, "when I was called to the home of Magistrate Jaffar."

"This is Captain Asim," Dabir said. "Please accept our apology for this late visit."

Esfandiar nodded once. "Why have you come?"

"The plaque with the door pull I spoke of earlier; it has been stolen. As has its mate." Dabir waited, watching the old man.

Ai-a—why had he said anything of the pull to the old man?

"That is grievous news," the dastur said at last.

"I cannot imagine what someone intends with these pulls," Dabir said. "But I think you might."

The old man sighed. "Come, then." He turned to address the youth. "Gather refreshments for our guests."

"We do not have time for refreshments," I said.

"Oh?"

Dabir clarified. "Your pardon, Dastur. The longer our delay, the greater the distance the thieves can run."

The dastur stiffened. "You would discuss sacred matters standing in an entryway?"

After a moment, Dabir lowered his gaze. "Bring refreshments," the dastur said to his underling, turning once more toward the door.

"Might someone also see to our horses?" I ventured.

The dastur arched an eyebrow at me, then nodded his permission. His assistant disappeared into the night.

"It was once said," the dastur proclaimed as he led us through his archway, "and you will forgive me if I do not recall the source, that a wise warrior cares first for his horse, then for his men, then for himself."

I grunted my appreciation, still rankling over the slow speed of this enterprise. We did not have time for consultation with old men, who were ever wordy. I hoped Dabir knew what he was doing.

Esfandiar diverted right and we turned up a narrow flight of stairs. At their height the priest parted curtains for us and we looked in upon a small rectangular room, hung with a single Persian tapestry of great merit, woven with gold and crimson and vivid azure threads. The carpet and cushions were old and worn, though well cared for. Two candles already flickered in wall sconces; the priest stepped to a scroll upon the floor, rolled it tight, kissed it, and set it in a small chest along the wall, which he then closed.

He bade us sit, and lowered himself upon the carpet across from us. He did not speak until we joined him.

"I thank you again, Dabir, for turning the body of a believer over to us."

"It was the proper thing to do," Dabir replied. "Have you learned his family and name?"

"No. He was not, as I said, known to me."

"He was a dastur," Dabir said evenly. "This I saw. Likewise I recognized from the fabric in his kusti that he was from the north. Likely Mosul."

The old man's eyebrows rose. "You are correct. He was from Mosul. A message has been sent, and his family will be found."

"That is good."

"Did you also know," the dastur said slowly, "that Mosul is where such a relic as you showed me has long been held?"

"I thought so." Dabir stroked the edges of his spadelike beard, but did not elaborate. "One of your priests and a Greek agent have gone to great lengths to obtain the old door pull, and another much like it. They spent great monies to do so, and used dark magic. They set life to dead things to spy and steal for them."

The priest frowned, but said nothing.

"I mention sorcery," Dabir prompted, "and you do not blink."

The scholar was right. I looked back and forth between the two book readers, more than a little impressed once more by Dabir's ability to divine information.

"I know the man who stole this thing," the old fellow finally confessed. "He was a priest, banished from his post three years prior. He . . . lacks balance."

"Was he also from Mosul?" Dabir asked.

"Yes. His name is Firouz. He was clever, even as a boy. Once he was wise, even kind. But hate has twisted him."

"Firouz," Dabir repeated, almost as though he was not learning a fact so much as confirming a suspicion. He hesitated, glancing at me. "What does he hate?"

The priest studied Dabir for a time. "Firouz hates the caliphate, for its practices."

"What practices?" I asked, perhaps a bit too sharply.

"Have you dwelled only in Baghdad, Captain?" Esfandiar's voice was patient but chiding, as though he addressed a child. "The gold that floods the Round City is harvested from the provinces. The vizier is most efficient. If a farmer cannot pay rents due, then vizier Yahya buys his farm. If a merchant cannot pay his taxes, then Yahya confiscates his goods. Ever he reaps, even as the grain stalks groan beneath the scythe."

I frowned at him. "You speak like a rebel."

"I am no such thing," he answered steadily.

Dabir held up a hand to me. "That is not helpful, Asim. Dastur, what does Firouz mean to do with these door pulls?"

"What mean *you* to do with them?" the priest countered.

Dabir stared hard at the old man. "I do not know what they are capable of. You have not told me."

Silence fell then among us, filled only by the steady drum of rain against the roof. The thunder now was distant.

I wondered where the youth was with our refreshments.

When the dastur finally spoke, it was tiredly, as though the weight of ages hung upon his words. "Long years past, before the coming of the prophet, there was a great city in the desert. It is known by many names in this day, and your book calls it Ubar. It was a place of glories, where goods flowed in and out like water, where the streets themselves were lined in gold. In this city was built a doorway that opened into another place. An entry point into the land of djinn."

Stories for children, I thought, and might have said as much except that Dabir gave me a sharp look when I grunted doubtfully.

The dastur continued. "The folk of Ubar traded readily with the djinn that dwelt nearby, the Keeper of Secrets. So long as they paid the proper price, they could ask anything of him."

I realized with a start that the Keeper of Secrets had been mentioned upon the door pulls, or so Dabir had said.

"What was his price?" Dabir asked Esfandiar.

"The Keeper of Secrets," the dastur said with a searching look, "wanted nothing less than the souls of men."

Dabir let out a low whistle. "Thus did the folk of Ubar grow rich with knowledge."

"And invite the wrath of God," I added.

"Aye," Dabir agreed. "So these pulls were set upon the doors that opened this . . . entryway. Firouz must plan to open it himself."

"Ubar," I said, "was destroyed by God." So did all know, for Ubar's end is described in one of the shortest of suras, those first learned by children. "There is nothing left of it. What can this Firouz hang the pulls upon?"

Neither man answered.

"And if God destroyed the city, would not he have destroyed this djinn?"

"Firouz must not think so," Dabir mused. "Djinns are said to be immortal."

"What does this Firouz want to know from a djinn?" I asked.

Dabir shook his head. "Whatever he seeks cannot bode well for us. Neither he nor his ally, this Greek, is a friend to the caliphate."

"We must stop them," I said.

"Yes. Dastur, if Firouz wishes to find the Keeper of Secrets, he must know the location of Ubar. Is that possible?"

The priest licked his lips but did not answer for a long time. "It may be," he said finally.

Dabir and the priest measured one another with their eyes.

"You know where the city lies," Dabir said.

"I may."

"Subhan'Allah!" I cried. "How can that be?"

"You must tell us the way," Dabir told him, ignoring my question.

Esfandiar eyed him soberly. "What then will you do, Dabir?"

"I will stop these men. And you must help me."

"But if you stop them, and these pulls fall once more into your hands, and thence into the hands of the caliph—what then?"

"I shall pray to Allah, for guidance. Now is not the time. You worry about good men tempted to villainy when villains already command the situation. If you know the way to Ubar, you must help so that we may stop them."

The priest's shoulders slumped as he rose. "I will draw no map and write no instructions. Such could fall into other hands." He sighed. "I will come with you, though I feel it shall be my death."

5

Both a boat and a team of horses were ready for us upon our return, for my nephew was efficient, but as Esfandiar thought it most likely the thieves had left via river, Dabir declared we would board the boat. There was a brief delay for the gathering of my own gear—which did not take overlong—and for the gathering of Dabir's. While the scholar was in his apartments and the priest aboard the boat, Jaffar pulled me aside. We stood under a portico next to the dock outside Jaffar's palace, watching the vessel rock on the waves beneath an assault by the rain. The lightning had given out at last, and the night itself was black as pitch. Only the glow of the lanterns, each surrounded by a gold nimbus of light, held back what seemed the very breath of Iblis. Surely he had aided the departure of the thieves, for how might we be expected to find our way after them in such weather?

Dabir had briefed the master, who now looked grimmer than I had ever seen him. He waved Boulos back so that it was only he and I standing together, master and servant, and our voices were pitched low so that they might not be heard over the patter of the rain.

"You heard all that transpired?"

"Yes, Master."

"What do you think?"

"It is hard to know." I took in a deep breath so as to weigh my thoughts. Jaffar watched tensely.

"I have seen many strange things this day," I confessed to him. "A dead bird that flies. A monkey trained to steal—"

"You really think the bird was dead before you killed it?" Jaffar asked. Though Dabir had briefed him in more detail, he remained skeptical.

"Look to the body, master, filled only with sawdust. And look upon the dry limb I sliced off the monkey."

"It was a small leg," he answered, "and you likely splattered all the blood out when you struck it off." He sounded doubtful even as he spoke, hoping, I think, to convince himself more than me.

I did not mean to argue that particular point. "It may be. But you must concede, Excellency, that strange things are under way."

He nodded agreement.

I pressed on. "This tale of Ubar and an angry Magian priest leagued with the Greeks seems no less mad than any of the rest of it. This priest we brought seems an honest man, and Dabir believes what he says."

"You truly think he can help?"

"He knows the way to Ubar, or thinks he does. I suspect there is more to this than the Magian has so far told, but—"

"He has kept things from you?" Jaffar asked sharply.

"Nay. We were in a hurry, and the matter was complicated. I think he will tell more to Dabir as we travel."

Jaffar sighed. "Much hinges upon Dabir. He is in command. If his are the eyes which see, you must be the hand that wards."

"I shall be the sword that cuts, and the arm that shields."

He nodded, looking slightly more pleased. "Be it so." He looked back over his shoulder and stepped closer. "There is something else you may need to be, Asim, though it saddens me to say it."

He did not speak, and in the end I had to prompt him. "What is that, Master?"

"An executioner."

"Of whom?" I asked, though I feared I already knew the answer. Even so, when he said it, I repeated the name in shock.

"Dabir."

"Dabir?"

"God will it not to be so. But I worry, Asim. I know that he, too, lusts for knowledge. And he has reason to be angry with me, does he not?"

"Master, I do not think—"

"Would not you be angry with me, were I to dismiss you?"

"But I have done no wrong."

"So must he be thinking. Much depends upon him, Asim, and sooner or later he will realize that his is the power. Whatever it is that these men seek, be careful of Dabir should it fall to his hands."

"I hear, Master." I hoped my voice betrayed no reluctance, though I inwardly shrank from the thought of such a deed.

He nodded.

"But, Master," I ventured, "I have seen nothing but loyal service from Dabir."

"You are his friend?"

"I suppose that I am," I answered, though he was not the sort of friend of my youth, nor, indeed, one with whom I shared many common interests.

"Remember, Asim, where your loyalties lie."

I bowed. "Master, I did not mean—"

He motioned me to rise, impatiently, and looked once more over his shoulder. "Likely it will not come to it."

"Master, I—"

"Here is Dabir," he said quickly.

And the scholar joined us, one servant bearing a chest behind him. Jaffar unnecessarily reminded us both then as to our duty to recover the gold door pulls, and then told us to go with God. We boarded the rocking ship in the night and quite soon were on our way.

I cannot say much of the journey's first night, for I spent much of it hunched over the boat's side, heaving, and the rest of it lying under the boat's awning wondering when next I might. Between the wondering and the doing I groaned occasionally and for the first time in my life looked back fondly upon the time I was knocked unconscious from a blow to the helm and lay stunned in the dirt of the practice yard.

The worst was over come the gray dawn, and I slept fitfully then. I was awakened not by the sun—for the sky was overcast and the light dull—but by the twang of an oud. I opened my eyes a crack to find the cursed poet sitting beside me, an instrument to hand. His long wisp of a beard quivered as he grinned at me.

I growled at him to go away, but instead he sang, plucking at the strings all the while.

I was kitten-weak and weary. Yet the idiot sang, an insufferable smile upon his long face.

> "With mighty groans he left his bed
> And crossed the planks with staggered tread.
> With shaking hands he gripped the rail
> His eyes were red, his face was pale.
>
> "He retched and moaned and lurched away
> And lived to fight another day
> Or night, for he returned again
> And fought the foe but could not win.
>
> "And now his eyes alight once more
> And color's back, though rather poor.
> I must confess I've never seen
> By morning light a face so green."

Hamil then had the audacity to chuckle at his own composition, and from somewhere close by other voices rose in laughter.

I cursed him roundly.

"Ho, Asim, master of the sword!" Hamil put the instrument to one side. "Has the slayer of mighty foemen been overwhelmed by a stretch of water?"

"Would you like to swim it?" I pushed up to a sitting position. All around me were the sounds of a ship in motion—the rattling of ropes and rigging, the lap of water against the hull. Dabir looked up from the scroll of vellum he considered nearby.

"Leave him be, Hamil," Dabir instructed.

Hamil grinned at Dabir, then at me. "Fear not, Asim. No one thinks the less of you, just because you were the only one upon the length of the vessel that fell sick. Even the ship captain's son, a scrawny nine-year-old, had but kind words—"

"Begone, poet, or I will smash that oud over your head!"

He stepped away, chuckling.

"What," I said to Dabir, "is he doing here?"

"Jaffar sent Hamil to observe so that he might tell the tale and make it easier for Jaffar to write." Dabir had set down the paper to hand me a small green leaf. "Here, chew this."

I did as he bade, though the leaf was bitter, then quaffed deeply from my water sac. I was more thirsty than I had first supposed, and a foul taste from my vomiting lingered in my mouth. I washed the water about with my tongue but the unpleasant flavor did not altogether leave.

"Where are we now?" I stretched my shoulders, then stood, belted on my sword, and checked my turban. It was awry, and dusty, so I brushed it free and rewrapped it as Dabir answered.

"Half a day south of Baghdad. We made good speed."

I eyed the reed-lined riverbank to right and left, and the scrubby grassland spread beyond it. It seemed a bright, empty place. "It strikes me," I said, stepping close, but not so close that my reeking breath might reach him, "that a horseman could overtake us swiftly."

"True," Dabir conceded.

"Thus, if they were on horses, they might be well ahead of us."

"Ah, but will they have a steady change of horses, and a safe road?"

Dabir shook his head. "They are upon the river. They must reach Ubar by sea, from Basra. And Basra is most swiftly reached by the Tigris."

I expected to see a map; instead, Dabir's parchment proved to be awash with mathematics. "What are those numbers for?"

A brief, proud smile brushed Dabir's lips, and his eyes shone a bright blue. "I have been calculating the speed of our ship and the likely speed of those we pursue. Certain variables cannot be known, of course, but . . ." Dabir pointed to one set of figures. "We can assume that Diomedes the Greek and Firouz were not within the palace when they sent the monkeys for the pulls. They would have left shortly thereafter. Either the monkeys brought them the treasure outside the palace and the men fled to the boat, or the monkeys brought the treasure to the boat itself. In either case, the boat can only be a few hours ahead of us."

I nodded. I was not sure why the numbers helped in this deduction, but did not ask.

"Further," Dabir continued, "ours is a new ship. We can assume that theirs is not."

"Of what bearing is that?"

"Ours shall be trimmer, with less growth beneath the water, fewer leaks, finer sails. Likely they hired a vessel. We," he continued, "should gain on them over the course of this day. We might well see their sail before noon."

"We might well see their sail even now," I said. "There are hundreds of boats upon the Tigris. How to know which is theirs?"

Dabir let the paper roll shut and frowned. "That is a problem mathematics will not solve for us. Here is the thing, though. If we make speed, we may overtake them, and await them at the site of the ruins."

"Waiting in hiding like a lion," I added.

"Exactly."

For a scholar he used his words with economy.

I left him and walked forth to familiarize myself with the boat. She was a two master, a broad tub built for river travel. For much of its length the Tigris is but six to thirteen feet deep, which has the depth to kill a man but hardly to welcome the ocean rigs. This vessel had deck space to spare—all the better for Jaffar to hold parties upon—although on this journey she carried little but supplies to see us downriver with as few stops as possible.

The sails were brown triangles that caught the wind as the tanned sailors slung the cloth to meet it. We were aided by the current, which I was told always strengthened in the spring months with rain swelling the banks and floodwaters rushing down from distant mountains.

It required a surprising number of men to tend the sails, a dozen in all. Aside from these there was the stout Captain Ibrahim and his shadow, a gap-toothed youth who stared as I walked past. The captain only nodded, for he was engaged in shouting at a man in the rigging.

Mahmoud and five of my best soldiers idled on the deck, striving not to grin at me. Mahmoud rose and came to attention.

"Did you sleep well, Captain?" A smirk tugged at his lips.

"You are to watch for black birds," I told him.

All pretense of humor vanished from Mahmoud's manner. "Birds? What sort of birds?"

"Black birds."

Mahmoud peered at me as he might a drunkard. "The skies are full of black birds."

"I would hate to interrupt your shatranj game," I growled. "Watch for birds who are watching us. The enemy employs magic." I passed on, leaving him scratching his head.

I had no particular aim, merely the desire to look as if I did, so I strolled on to the front of the vessel, which sailors call the prow. Here sat the priest, neither at prayer nor with a nose in a book; he merely watched the horizon. I could not tell if he scanned for other ships, or if he watched the empty land to right and left, and I did not ask. While I had questions for the old man, now was not the time, thus I passed on.

Back from the prow was an entrance to the ship's hold; I made it seem as though this had been my destination all along, for I felt the eyes of the men upon me and did not mean to provide further opportunity for ridicule. I threw open the hatch and descended the steep ladder steps.

Soon I stood stooped in the dark space, which smelled of wood shavings and rope and tar. About me were crates and wicker baskets, and also the squeak of rats, for the vessel was not so new that they had failed to find their way aboard. Surely there was a cat stalking them as well, somewhere.

I walked hunch-shouldered amongst the crates and paused, wondering what I might say I had been about down here.

It was then that I heard a woman's voice, whispering a name. "Abdul?"

In ordinary circumstances the moment would not have held any sinister aspect, but there in the dark of the hold, with the events of the previous two days playing in my mind, the voice set spurs to my imagination. What woman would lurk down here in the shadows? No one but a witch in league with those we pursued, naturally, so I put hand to hilt and crept forward. My shifting weight set the planks complaining.

"Abdul?" The voice came again.

The space was too close for sword work, so I freed my knife. "Come out, witch," I said.

There was no answer.

There was a narrow space between two of the baskets. Into that I lunged, my left hand outstretched, the right hand with knife lifted. I grasped clothed flesh.

"Unhand me!" came the indignant shout.

I was not so strange to female flesh that I failed to recognize a thigh, which I released, for I also had recognized the voice.

"Sabirah?" I said.

"Captain Asim?"

A faint trickle of light leaked down from narrow gaps between the deck planks above, revealing a feminine silhouette on a narrow, waist-high shelf; a kneeling woman, one arm drawn protectively across her chest, the other raised with an upturned jug, brandished like a cudgel. I caught a whiff of her lavender-scented perfume.

"Come out from there," I growled.

She lowered the jug. "Captain," she pleaded, "do not reveal me—"

"I most certainly will! Why are you here?"

She did not answer me that. I sheathed my knife, stepped forward, grasped her wrist, and pulled her roughly from her alcove. She resisted only a little as I led her out and up the ladder, where she stood in the light, shielding her eyes. I blinked, too, for even a short time in the darkness rendered the overcast sunlight overwhelming. I heard an outcry of surprise, and then all was silence. By the time my eyes adjusted, Mahmoud was before me, shaking his head in disbelief.

He rubbed his beard, staring overlong at the girl in my estimation, before turning back to me. He was sufficiently surprised that he failed to address me by rank. "How did you know, Uncle?"

I did not lie. "I am older and wiser, Lieutenant. Did Dabir go below at any time?"

"Nay, I do not think so."

"Dabir knew nothing," Sabirah said. "I snuck aboard myself!"

"And why would you do that?" I asked.

Sabirah stood straight and stared defiantly up at me. "To help, of course!"

"Who is Abdul?" I demanded.

I saw her jaw set determinedly behind her thin veil. Dabir and the ship captain and the poet all crowded up to us then.

"Who is this?" the captain demanded.

Dabir talked over him. "Sabirah! What are you doing here?"

"I came to help," she repeated weakly.

"Help?" I said. "Now we will have to turn back!"

"Ai-a," the captain was saying, tearing at his beard. "There should be no woman on my ship!"

"This is Quadi Jaffar's niece," Mahmoud explained.

"What were you thinking?" Dabir demanded of her.

The girl turned away and stalked for the awning. Dabir held up a hand when I started to follow. "Let me speak with her."

The poet watched them walk off, shaking his head. "This can bring nothing good."

The ship's captain nodded his agreement. "Truly said."

"Is there someone on your ship named Abdul?" I asked.

"My son is named Abdul," the captain answered. "Why do you ask?"

"That is who Sabirah called out to when she heard me approach."

The captain growled, furious. "The wretch must have aided her!" He strode off, calling his son's name.

We watched Sabirah and Dabir confer at length. Mahmoud and I remained by the mast, with Hamil lingering nearby. I did not welcome his presence, especially as he wandered back and forth seeking a better angle on the scholar and maiden, occasionally obstructing my own view of them.

"We will have to turn back," the poet asserted suddenly. "We can go no further with the vizier's granddaughter."

"We cannot turn back," Mahmoud countered. "Our orders are clear: recover the treasures. Any delay and they'll be lost."

"I'm sure the master did not figure her into his orders," the poet replied. "If there is battle we will be exposing Sabirah to danger."

Mahmoud was unconvinced. "There's no more danger for her going forward than sending her back. We can guard her better than anyone."

"What if there's a fight on board the ship? She'll be in the thick of it!"

"Dabir is in command," I told Hamil curtly. "The decision is his."

He fell silent then, Allah be praised, and it was not too much longer before Dabir rejoined us, Captain Ibrahim at his heels.

Hamil could not hold off asking questions, even though Dabir clearly was readying to brief us.

"How did Sabirah come aboard?" the poet asked. "And why?"

"She claims to have disguised herself as one of the cargo bearers," Dabir said. That must have seemed as unlikely to him as it did to me. "I think she protects some slave or servant she bribed for help smuggling her on board."

"And Captain Ibrahim's son must have been taking her food," Mahmoud said.

"He was." The ship captain's eyes blazed fiercely. "I swear that I did not know. That boy shall rue the day—"

"Go easy on the child," Dabir said. "He was being commanded by a noblewoman. And he is not so young that a pair of flashing eyes do not convince, yes?"

Ibrahim only grunted.

"Why did she come, though?" Hamil asked. "Does she really think she can help?"

"She believes she can."

"How?" the poet demanded.

"You will have to ask her, I think." The annoyance audible in Dabir's tone seemed directed more toward Sabirah, at whom he cast a backward glance, than the poet. "I would not speak to her immediately, though. She is not, currently, talkative."

"So we're taking her back, right?" Hamil asked.

Mahmoud objected stridently. "Then the mission will be lost."

"Mahmoud is right," Dabir said with quiet conviction. My nephew's broad face widened in a proud smile as Dabir continued: "We cannot risk losing the pulls. I anticipate great danger to the caliphate if we do not recover them. Sabirah must remain with us and if we haven't overtaken them by the time we reach Basra, she will return to Baghdad with Captain Ibrahim when we transfer to an ocean vessel."

It was a simple enough plan, and wise, so that no one objected further. Hamil's curiosity, however, had been piqued. "It's certain the caliph will be angry with Jaffar—and he with us—if we do not recover the pulls, but how does that endanger the caliphate?"

Dabir ignored him. "Asim, may we speak privately?" He motioned me to the rail.

"Of course." I nodded at Mahmoud, who stepped away.

Dabir waited for him to retreat, then spoke softly. I felt certain he would confide some important piece of information Sabirah had shared, or further explain his concern for the safety of the caliphate. He said nothing of either. "Tell your men to keep watch for birds such as the one you destroyed."

"I already have," I said.

He looked startled at that, and then nodded. "Good."

I made a mental note to give the instruction to the rest of the men.

He started to turn away.

"Dabir," I said.

"Yes?"

"The girl—this will not look well for you. The master will seek to blame you."

"Jaffar is a reasonable man."

"Not where this matter is concerned."

Dabir frowned. He lowered his voice. "What would you have me do, then, Asim? Which would anger him more? Keeping the girl aboard, or losing any chance to recover the pulls because I turned back with her?"

I nodded. "You are between two bad places."

"Indeed."

"We might send her back on some other boat."

"Then who would guard her? Think, Asim. We can afford neither the delay nor the loss of soldiers to transfer her to a northbound ship— for I'd send her with no less than three of your warriors."

I saw that he was right. We might need every one of my men if it came down to a fight over the pulls. "Suppose," I ventured, "that Sabirah comes to harm on this journey."

"That is the worst possible outcome. We must both strive to ensure that does not happen."

I nodded. "And if we don't recover the pulls?"

He smiled thinly. "There is always Spain, I suppose. That was a jest," he added.

"I know."

"I do not wish you thinking that I would consider—"

"I know a joke when I hear one," I said. "Even a bad one. Tell me, though. How does she think she can help?"

"She expects to decipher any further puzzles we encounter—but also she is angry with Jaffar. She wishes to remain my pupil. So she came."

"Does she not see that she puts her favorite tutor in greater jeopardy?"

"She is a brilliant girl," Dabir said, "more clever than you realize. But she is eighteen. She can speak languages of the past, but she does not see more than a few days into the future. She lives for the moment."

I grunted my acknowledgment.

If Sabirah hoped for a continuation of her lessons, she was sorely disappointed, for Dabir ignored her that evening, and through most of the next day, although he was courteous.

Sabirah did not outwardly take offense at having her wishes thwarted; she merely turned to other tutors. She spoke with whomever she could, and you can be certain that every sailor was eager for a word with the pretty noblewoman. She asked many questions about the waters and the sailing craft and life along the shores. Sabirah shared gentle jests that the sailors found amusing, and they in turn presented her with little treasures— bits of wood that they had carved, or choice fruits. I suppose most of them were in love with her a little bit for her delight in the simple pleasures of seeing a flock of heron erupt from the grass, or in hearing one of the sailors croon a sad love song from the southern marshes. If she was no beauty of the ages, she was pretty in an unassuming way, in no small part because of her charm and grace and quick-wittedness.

I ordered my soldiers to stay clear of her, which they did unhappily. Hamil was under no such orders, though, and spent long hours speaking with passion about the works of the great poets and reciting fine passages from memory. It pleased him to be near a woman, I think, and to be expert in a field, for he carried his small frame with even more pride than usual as he walked off to speak with her.

For my part, I kept close watch though I maintained a distance. In truth I had never assumed a more nerve-wracking duty than watching every movement and gesture around the girl, and I slept poorly when I slept at all.

Sabirah was all smiles and politeness; Dabir, though, seemed more irritable by the hour and took to walking around the prow of the ship when he was not talking with Esfandiar. By the second day, on the heels of afternoon prayers, she asked him a question about the life cycle of a fish. He hesitated, but in the end could not help but answer.

Thereafter tutoring began in earnest once more and Dabir seemed happier for it, even if he remained rather tense and formal. He continued to enlist the aid of the poet and, occasionally, Captain Ibrahim or a sailor. Even the old Magian priest was brought in to the circle to offer instruction. I was skeptical of this at first, for I thought it unwise to allow teachings from a man of another faith. A follower of Zarathustra is apparently taught that truth is best of all that is good, after God, which I found a fine thing. So much of what Esfandiar said made sense that I asked him if Zarathustra was one of the unnamed prophets of the Koran.

As is the way with wise men, his answer was cryptic. "Some have said so. Surely he was a prophet of God."

"Then it must be so," I said.

"I am glad you hear wisdom in Zarathustra's teachings," he said.

So the days passed in conversation. The mornings would dawn fresh and clear and the waters would lap the sides of the boat as we sailed on our course. The heat rose as morning waned into afternoon, and then Dabir would conduct his studies with the girl, breaking only for mealtimes and prayers. These seemed happy studies, for there was much laughter. But then Sabirah was alight with laughter. She was the very queen of the little kingdom that was our boat. She was like the sun, for she warmed all who came near. Even the sailors and my soldiers were more docile in her presence, and cursing and rude behaviors were at a minimum. Mahmoud not only groomed his hair each morning, but saw to it that his garments were kept clean, as well as those of the rest of the men. Dabir enlisted him to tell of great battles, for my nephew had read widely upon the subject, and had sat at the feet of officers who'd seen many campaigns.

We watched always for boats, and we saw them aplenty, as large or larger than ours, heading upriver toward Baghdad or downriver to Basra, laden with goods. I knew that woolen garments, silk, porcelain, and perfumes came from Baghdad. From downriver came goods from India, China, and other stranger lands: nutmeg and cloves, teak, sandalwood, tin, and peculiar curiosities. None, however, obviously carried a pop-eyed Greek, an evil Magian, and a parcel of undead birds and monkeys.

The journey seemed a spring idyll on the river, one that I had to remind my charges was actual duty, not a pleasure cruise, so that they might keep watch. Only Mahmoud truly believed me about the birds, I think, though all claimed to study the skies.

As night fell the next evening Dabir talked to Sabirah of the stars. Already she knew more about them than I, for there were old tales told from ancient days, when the Greeks were brave heroes and not schemers clinging to a dying dream. A few of us gathered around to listen, including Hamil, and he claimed he was put in mind of a story, if anyone wished to hear. Naturally all of those in earshot did, so a number of us sat down on the deck while he spoke to us of Rostam and his seven quests. I thought it was finely told. So, too, did the other listeners; little Abdul begged that another story might be relayed, and Hamil was debating out loud whether or not he should speak again of Rostam, or perhaps a story of love—playing with the audience's desire, in actuality—when Mahmoud clapped me on the back.

"Uncle Asim has a story," he said. "Tell them of what happened in the ruins of Kalhu."

"Nay," I said. "I am no poet." Moreover, I was tired, and in little mood to listen to Hamil's mockery of me should the tale go poorly.

"Jaffar has told it many times," said Hamil. "I could tell it, if you wish."

"Well," Mahmoud said doubtfully, "Uncle Asim and I were both there. With Dabir."

"Why don't you tell it, Asim?" Sabirah asked me, and Mahmoud, too, offered encouragement. I looked over to Dabir and he looked back with a nod. Their gaze was strangely insistent. I did not guess why.

"Very well," I said, and decided to humor them. How best to set the mood, though? "Think not of the river," I told them, "or of the night, but of day, and of the plains far to the north." I cast around for a good place to begin. "It was the spring of last year that a wily Greek came to Jaffar. It seems that the Greeks always bring trouble when they come visiting, doesn't it? Corineus was his name, and he was witty and charming. And he had a lovely daughter."

"How lovely?" the boy asked quickly.

Mahmoud leaned over to him. "She was beautiful, with huge dark eyes and . . ." I think he might have said something else, but he glanced over at Sabirah and his voice trailed off.

I took his hint. "Lydia was almost as lovely as Sabirah, if truth be told. Between her beauty and that Greek's silver tongue, Jaffar somehow was convinced that he should journey to Kalhu. Now there is little enough reason to wander about any of the ruins of old Ashur. They sit naked and gray, abandoned on the plains like old bones, and all their treasures have been looted for a thousand years. Yet this Greek lured Jaffar out there with the promise of fabulous artwork to be seen in the wreckage of a dead king's palace, and since Jaffar went, that meant there also went a team of slaves for digging, servants to raise and lower tents and see to any of His Excellency's whims, herders to care for animals and cooks to prepare them, and, of course, soldiers, which is why Mahmoud and I were there. Jaffar also invited some of his counselors, which is how Dabir became involved.

"It was a week's ride to Kalhu, and no easy task for me in arranging protection for the master and his many attendants, but Jaffar looked on the whole thing as a merry jaunt, never dreaming what the true intent of Corineus and his daughter could be."

"What were they planning?" Abdul asked.

Hamil shushed him. "A good storyteller will take you there in time. You must be patient."

Was that a compliment, from Hamil? If so, it was the first I had ever heard for me from his lips.

I cleared my throat and continued. "I don't want you to imagine shining ruins gilt in splendor. There was almost nothing whole—foundations, yes, walls, an occasional gateway, but mostly there were shattered towers and building stones. Corineus set the slaves to work digging. I posted soldiers—for there were lions about, and there might be thieves, too, and I familiarized myself with the city's extents.

"On the morning of the expedition's third day, I stopped during my patrol rounds to admire a faded and cracked fresco of a bearded archer in a chariot hunting lions. On the whole the people of Ashur had wrought their art with skill; mounts were carved in mid-gallop with lifelike detail, the armed hosts along the walls with startling ferocity. The figures themselves were somewhat stiff, but the detail was extraordinary, for one could see all the ringlets in a man's hair and beard, and all the hairs of a lion's mane; also the muscles in the horses' legs. It was pleasing to contemplate such finely fashioned martial scenes.

"While I examined that ancient chariot, I heard the sound of feet swishing grass blades and turned to find that a scholar from Jaffar's household was standing behind me, with Mahmoud behind him. Both now gazed at the stone. This was Dabir, though I did not know his name."

Dabir interrupted, "Truly? We had met twice before."

I shrugged by way of apology. "I have never had the knack of recalling the names or duties of the countless hakims, scholars, and courtiers who frequent the master's palace, though a few have since become unforgettable." Dabir looked thoughtful at this, but said no more. I continued. "The scholar's eyes held that intensity of purpose you're so used to seeing. A sword hung off his left hip.

"'Behold the artist's trick,' he said to me with an amused smile. 'A thousand years ago he fashioned this piece.'

"I saw no trick and looked back and forth between him and the art, wondering at his words.

"'Now his work pleases us,' the scholar continued, 'two men he never met. Perhaps it will delight other unknown men in a thousand more, when we two are as forgotten as he. The artist defeats the ages.'

"It was strange to think so far into the future to a day when I myself might be dust, but there amongst the battered remains of the ancient city it seemed altogether proper, and I found myself nodding and studying the stone in more detail.

"Mahmoud bowed his head to me in some excitement, and told me that he and the scholar Dabir had found a goat, that it was most disturbing, and that I should come see. I had little interest in goats, and told them so.

"'One was missing from the pens yesterday morning,' Dabir said. 'One of Mahmoud's men found the carcass.'

"I thought Mahmoud foolish for bringing such a concern to me. Some wild dog or daring lion had doubtless snuck into the camp and drug off the hapless beast. 'What of it?' I said, but Dabir shook his head.

"'No animal or thief slew this goat,' he said ominously. 'Someone killed it to use for magic.'

"I did not ask how he came to this incredible conclusion. I thought perhaps he was bored or trying to make himself important, but his expression was grave and I saw I must look further if only to satisfy my curiosity. So I bade them to show me the body.

"We wound our way through the heaped mounds of masonry and the remnants of long, high walls. What remained of Kalhu stretched for many acres and the main body of our encampment was out of sight when my nephew stopped before a rough waist-high block and pointed over it. Beyond was a weathered rectangular pit two spear lengths deep and three spear lengths wide, bordered by stones and accessed from a set of crumbling stairs. At its bottom was a small mound of dirt, a spade, and the carcass of a goat, its head separated from its body." I could tell I had my listeners now. Even Esfandiar had come over, and the gathered crowd waited expectantly for what I might say next. There was nothing to be heard over my pause save the croaking of frogs in the rushes.

"The smell was worse than I had anticipated. I stepped close enough to see that the goat was not eaten, by beast or man, as the scholar had said. Its body was intact except for its stomach, where pale little worms writhed in a long, straight slash.

"'Someone has removed its entrails, to read them,' Dabir informed me, and I made the sign warding off evil." I made the sign then for my listeners. "Then Dabir stepped over to the eyeless head. He explained that someone had carved peculiar figures in the horns, but that was plain to see. They were incised all up and down their length with symbols and letters unknown to me. I stared at it a long time without touching it, though I did wave away flies. Finally I stood. 'Very well, I'm sure you're right,' I said. 'Someone needs to be punished for goat killing. Likely they were trying to work a love potion or something.'

"'This is not the magic of the marketplace,' Dabir insisted. 'This is not about health or love. This was done under cover of night with great care, and those involved do not wish others to learn of it.'

"I did not challenge these assumptions. 'How did you learn of it?' I asked. 'And who are you?'

"'I,' he said, 'am Dabir ibn Khalil. I thought you knew me, Captain Asim.'

"I merely nodded, irritated, and asked if he were a goat herder as well as a scholar.

"'No,' he answered without hesitation, 'I overheard the report one of your soldiers made to Mahmoud when they found this goat's body, and when I expressed interest, he invited me to accompany him.'

"Mahmoud spoke up: 'Latif had been patrolling this quarter when he noticed some wild dogs nosing about this old pit. He chased them off and then saw that they'd been scratching at the loose dirt in this corner. The horns of a goat were poking through the soil, and when he pulled them free and realized the slain goat was probably ours, he came to give me account of it.'

"Dabir pointed to the head. 'It is missing both tongue and eyes. The symbols carved on the horns are Eblaite, I think—an ancient language similar to Akkadian. And look here. Do you see this, in the wall?' He moved to the far side of the pit where a fierce bearded face looked at us from the nearby stone. Time had worn away portions of some of his curling hair, but his scowl was etched deep. Dabir stepped to that visage and touched his left hand to first the lips and then one of the hollow eye sockets. 'There is blood here.'

"'Why would they have smeared it there?' Mahmoud asked him. His eyes were alight with interest.

" 'I am not yet sure.'

"Mahmoud seemed inclined to stand there and stroke his beard, watching Dabir think. The more I contemplated the goat's empty, staring eye sockets, the more they bothered me, so I took the shovel, threw dirt over the goat head, then handed the tool to Mahmoud and bade him to bury the rest. As he set to work I considered Dabir in a new light. He was right to have been drawn to this peculiar matter, and, while I knew nothing of the symbols or his claims of magic, I too suspected some sinister purpose. 'Who has done this and why?' I wondered aloud.

" 'I should not like to rush to judgment, Captain, but—' Dabir hesitated and glanced at Mahmoud. 'Your nephew is rightly suspicious of the Greeks. There are three of them; there are three sets of tracks here. Or at least there were, before your men moved over the area." He pointed to an undisturbed corner to the right. "One of the them had a small, slippered foot, like the daughter of Corineus.'

" 'So they did this?' I asked.

" 'It would seem likely.'

" 'Very well. I will wring the truth from them,' I said.

"Dabir shook his head at this. 'Be cautious, Captain,' he said. 'The Greek and especially his daughter Lydia wax high in our master's esteem. If you confront them when he is nearby, he will likely excuse the matter and they will be alerted.'

"I saw the sense in this, so I said, 'Let us call upon Jaffar and see if we can pry him from Lydia. Then we shall tell him what we think.'

"Near the midday hour I thought to find Jaffar dining in his tent, but he too was admiring the art of Kalhu. The two guards I'd assigned that morning were with him. Naturally so too was Lydia and her guard, a large-thewed Greek. His girth made my soldiers nervous even though he carried no sword, and they prudently flanked the master.

"The daughter of Corineus turned at our approach, brushing a lock of dark hair from her high forehead. She and Jaffar were looking over a carved relief of bearded figures rowing a warship amid wondrous fish. Now Mahmoud has said that Lydia was lovely, and it was so. She was in the flower of her beauty, and the wind against which she struggled blew her long dark hair across her face, shaping soft curves with her green dress. Lest you think the master charmed merely by eye, I should make it clear that she was very clever, as well. Too clever for her own good, as it turned out. She was witty and laughed pleasingly at the master's jokes. She understood his talk of history and literature, and seemed to share his thoughts on many subjects but added observations that impressed even Jaffar. Her Arabic was pure, but she spoke it with the faintest trace of an accent that was somehow"—I labored for the right word. In truth her voice was alluring, but I did not wish to say that—"endearing. I know not why. In any case, Jaffar's eyes sparkled whenever he looked upon her."

Mahmoud laughed at this. "It is true!"

"We told Jaffar that we wished to speak with him alone on a matter of import," I said. "It was clear to both Dabir and myself that Lydia was concerned over what we might say, for she eyed us with suspicion. Jaffar reluctantly bade her to excuse us and cast a long look her way as we moved off. I immediately suggested that he should not trust her.

"Jaffar's eyebrows rose, and I sought quickly to explain the matter of the goat. Somehow my telling failed to sway Jaffar, for I saw a smile play about the corners of his mouth. It grew even larger as he glanced at Dabir, as if he thought the scholar behind some game.

"'You jest, surely,' Jaffar said. 'You think she has slain animals and drawn strange pictures upon their horns?'

"With his wording, it did sound somewhat preposterous. Dabir bowed and tried to explain that we had found tracks at the site that looked very much like those of Lydia, but Jaffar only chuckled and said that we must be mistaken."

Sabirah interrupted then. "I have heard this story many times, and I have never heard my uncle say the Greek woman had so captivated him. Is this true?"

"Oh, yes," Mahmoud agreed.

"I'm sure you did not hear it this way because Jaffar was in the room," Hamil said, laughing, and too late I wondered if I should be so honest in front of the little man. But the poet seemed truly to be enjoying himself. "Speak on, Asim! What happened next?"

I glanced over at Dabir, wondering if he, too, were concerned with the way I told the tale, but he gave me an encouraging nod, so I took a breath and continued. "In the end we managed to convince Jaffar that at least we were concerned, and so, mostly to humor us, he allowed us to accompany him through the rest of the day. To protect him from the girl or any goats, he said. I cannot speak for Dabir, but I was somewhat embarrassed by then.

"It was later, during evening prayers, that the slaves broke through the rubble Corineus was having them excavate and found a hidden passage beneath the ruins. Corineus sent word to Jaffar, and Dabir and I hastened with him to see what was found.

"The whole of this section of ruins was built into a hillside, and Corineus earlier told us he thought it Kalhu's citadel. The slaves had been digging into it for three days, and this day Corineus had pushed them hard, commanding they dig into the evening. The rubble that they'd cleared was piled in a great mound. They stood, leaning heavily against their spades, some quaking with exhaustion. Corineus, though, grinned at sight of us and urged us to follow him into a dark archway.

"Jaffar asked him what he'd found.

"Corineus answered eagerly. 'I have discovered a huge repository of vibrant frescoes, and a great library of tablets with fascinating ancient markings.'

"Jaffar said that they must get Lydia, then, and insisted Mahmoud be sent to find her. We could not know that Mahmoud's search was a waste of time, for the daughter of Corineus was already deep underground. The Greek knew this, but said nothing, keeping her doings secret. Dabir and I and two of my soldiers walked with Jaffar into the tunnel, Corineus preceding. Dabir shot me a look which I took as a warning to be on guard—as though I were not already. Jaffar was altogether too comfortable with the Greek.

"I took a torch thrust at me by a dirty slave and followed Corineus and Jaffar into the tunnel. It widened until three men might walk abreast, but it was not so tall. I had to bend forward or the top of my turban brushed against it.

"The stone was covered in fading paint, depicting blue water and a great walled city. I would gladly have examined it more closely, but was more concerned with those about me, and my senses stretched taut against sign of betrayal—swift footsteps, a sword pulled from its sheath, whispered words. I heard none of those things, and there were only three turns of the tunnel before we came upon an opening in the right-hand wall. A great stone door had been swung aside. Four sweat-streaked Greek retainers labored at a mound of slabs five paces farther down the corridor.

" 'The wonders await, honored one.' Corineus halted and wiped sweat from his brow. Foreboding filled me.

" 'Let me look first, master,' I urged, 'lest there be some hazard the infidels have missed.' I drew my sword, and its curving length shone with a red tongue of reflected flame. I stepped lightly into the room, advising vigilance with a glance to the two rear guards I left by Jaffar.

" 'I, too, will go,' I heard Dabir say. I think he wanted a first look at the tablets."

"I also wanted to make sure it was safe!" Dabir objected good-naturedly.

"Almost I lost my balance, for I stood at the edge of a narrow stairway. There were but four steps descending into a wide chamber supported by a forest of square columns around its perimeter. Between the columns were stacked thousands of clay tablets, some tumbled and cracked upon the floor. I saw nothing else.

"I climbed down, and Dabir's feet scuffed the stone on the stairs behind me. And then I heard Jaffar cry out. I whirled in time to see my men sinking under Greek knives and Corineus wrestling Jaffar from the threshold. The great stone door swung in toward me, faster than I thought possible. It shut with a thud as I took the stairs in a single bound. Dabir and I pushed against it as one, but it did not yield.

"I sheathed my sword and threw my full weight against the door. It budged not an inch. Outside I heard the dull ring of hammer on iron and guessed they spiked the door.

"I cursed them, as you might expect, and my voice echoed from the stone. The torch flame shuddered as I thrust again against the door. Only my shoulder felt my efforts.

"Dabir remained infuriatingly calm, and told me that there was no getting out through the door. I scowled, shoved the torch at him, and charged the door a final time. It still did not move. We were trapped, there in that dusty room that had not been opened in a thousand years. And it might not be opened for a thousand more."

I let the thought of that sink in as I looked over the faces of my listeners. All of them waited expectantly, even Dabir. I judged my telling to be a success so far.

"Anger gripped me like a mighty flame. I could not help thinking of the worm-eaten goat and its severed head, and wondered if that is what the Greeks intended for my master. How could I protect him, trapped as I was behind the stone?

"Dabir stepped away from the door and followed the wall, torch in hand.

"'We can hope there is another exit,' he said, adding more softly, 'or Kalhu's future visitors will find our bones in this room amongst the tablets.'

"I eyed the darkness and then joined him in stalking around the room. The torchlight spilled over the plain stone columns and the stacks of clay tablets. They were decorated only with triangles and bird scratches, for the people of Ashur did not know the proper method of writing. I wondered if Dabir could make sense of it. He could, as I learned later, but I did not ask him then.

"It took less time than I had feared to make a complete circuit of the walls. Everywhere were the piled tablets and the stone pillars. There was no other way out, so I started back to the door. Dabir put a hand on my arm to stay me, and I was so tense that I spun on him and demanded what he wanted. He only pointed into the darkness.

"'What?' I asked him.

"'There.' Dabir carried the torch closer to one of the walls.

"'What?' I growled.

"And exasperation rang in his voice. 'You look, but you do not see! There! An arch!'

"I scowled at him, but followed his pointing finger. Once more I saw only the piled tablets and the rough square columns upholding the level ceiling, and yet . . . one mound of the tablets was different from the others. A black, crescent-shaped sliver showed at their height, instead of the flat, broken bar of dark above the others.

"We advanced together. Dabir began to carefully remove the tablets and set them aside in similar order, but I knocked them clear. They shattered into pieces as they struck the ground. Dabir looked horrified for a moment, but did not protest, and within a short time a dark gap below the curving door frame was revealed.

"'Now do you see?' Dabir asked me.

"The torch sputtered in his hand. The tablets had been stacked to my height and three quarters my sword reach but I'd soon scattered enough of them to widen the entry before my eyes and stare down the throat of a tunnel. After a little more effort I had cleared the opening to my waist. That was enough, and with sword in hand, I clambered into the passage, urging Dabir to hurry.

"But Dabir told me to hold, saying that the torch needed more fuel, and thus we took off our turban cloths. We had little else at hand with which to feed it. He wrapped the cloth about the flame, singeing his fingers more than once, and then we resumed our exploration. The dark tunnel curved to left and right, then branched in two, widening slightly. Along the left wall the ancients had stacked some stones and broken bits of columns, blanketed now by dust. Dabir thought the left tunnel would be the better choice; I know not why."

"I thought it would veer toward the central passage," Dabir explained.

"The torch gave out fifty paces farther. A light is great comfort in a strange warren of enemies and who-knows-what ancient evil, and I was

85

not pleased to lose this one. Dabir lay the cursed thing quietly along the wall, saying we might find some use for it later, then I moved forward by feeling along the dusty, uneven surfaces. My imagination populated the dark with crawling things and black efreet and vengeful spirits.

"And then I saw something that set my heart to racing, for there, in the thick black ahead, were six dim red points of light. They were grouped in twos, at the height of a man, and I thought that, not one, but three efreet with flames set in their skulls awaited us. I clenched my sword and bared my teeth.

"'They speak,' Dabir whispered in astonishment.

My audience there on the boat looked almost as surprised as Dabir and I had been. I let them savor the moment before plunging on. I was thoroughly enjoying myself, which assuredly had not been the case when I was experiencing the events I was then relating. "I heard the voices as well, despairing. How might I fight invisible demons with glowing eyes? But then I recognized the voice of Lydia, and Corineus in answer, though I could not make out their words.

"'Ah,' Dabir said in realization, and he urged me forward with a tap on the back.

"I drew close enough to see that the glowing eyes were but six small holes cut in the wall. Light from another room showed through them. I shook my head in relief, and put my face to one set as Dabir stepped to another. No doubt ancient spies had used the holes in the exact manner we did.

"Two low fires burned in a square chamber. I saw Jaffar, standing as yet unharmed, though Lydia's muscular guard held his collar with one hand and a sword to his neck with the other. He swayed slightly, as though stricken with fear, or drunken, but he looked whole. I breathed a prayer of thanks to Allah. Corineus and slender Lydia stood nearby, their faces turned to a square column into which a bearded face was carved. The Greek's servants were nowhere to be seen. So intent was I on Jaffar's welfare that I had to look twice before I saw the horror they ad-dressed. The wet, red thing hanging from the lips of the carved stone face was a tongue—the shining orbs in its sockets were goat's eyes. I made the sign against the evil eye.

"'The wealth of your kingdom, majesty?' Corineus was saying.

"And then the stone lips moved. I do not lie. There came a hoarse rumble from the stone: 'It shall be yours.'"

My listeners gasped audibly.

"'Have I not kept my promises?' the deep voice asked. 'But first you must keep yours. Is this the ruler?' The eyes moved. Somehow this was more awful even than the voice, or the tongue. They were prominent and staring, and their stone lids did not blink. 'He is not arrayed like a king.'

"Corineus bowed his head. 'As I feared, majesty, I could not bring the caliph himself. But this man is his trusted friend—'

"The stone face cursed him. But then Corineus told of Jaffar's power, and how he had the ear of the caliph, and that he was one of the most powerful men in all the caliphate, and the voice grudgingly said it would take him. While this went on I sought vainly for a release in the stone—a catch, a latch, something that might be a sort of opening. There was nothing. And then I heard Lydia speak.

"'Wait—' she said, 'you have not yet passed on your secrets. You have not fulfilled your bargain.'

"The stone lips curled. 'You accuse Tiglath-Pileser of deception?'

"'No, no, majesty,' Corineus said quickly in a tone even more ingratiating than he'd used with Jaffar. 'She wishes merely to hear a sampling of your promised wisdom. As do I. It was no easy matter recontacting you once we came here, or readying this man for you. We have proved our faith. Now show us yours.'

"'Very well,' the eerie voice continued."

I lowered my voice and straightened my back, doing my best to imitate that ancient, regal manner of speech. "'Gather the strongest about you, and arm them well. Send them to take from the weak, take a part for yourself, and reward them with what remains. Give them riches, and women, but do not let them rest. Most will die, but more will come, eager for the treasures. In this way you build your power.'

"Lydia did not sound pleased with this advice. 'This is no secret,' she said. 'There has to be something else!' She calmed herself and asked if there were more, and that old stone face spoke on.

"'Leave no enemy alive. As your forces grow, you ride forth, and take more. So long as you gather the strong to your side and reward them, there will always be more!'

"'This spirit has no secrets,' Dabir whispered to me. 'He taught those tactics to the world all too well, alas.'

"I asked Dabir what we could do, and he wondered if the two of us might lift one of the broken pillars we saw earlier, saying further that the wall seemed thin. Eagerly I grasped his idea, and we hurried off, for Lydia had begun to chant as she walked about a circle drawn on the flagstones before the face. Dabir said this was a spell. As we moved off into the darkness, I told Dabir I wished we still had a torch.

"'I wish I were in a warm bath,' he said sourly, then urged me to haste."

Dabir cut in quickly. "You leave out part of their doings, Asim. Corineus and Lydia argued at greater length."

I shrugged.

"It is Asim's story," Hamil said.

"I think it important to note," Dabir continued stubbornly, "that Corineus said the king had doubtless learned many things other than Arabic in his millennia in hell, and he looked forward to knowing those secrets. A king from his time, you see, would not have spoken Arabic, though I have often wondered that they did not converse in Greek. Perhaps he was practicing for his new role." Dabir said the last as if speaking to himself.

I waved this off. "That doesn't matter."

"A good storyteller must tailor his story for his listeners," Hamil agreed. "Go on, Asim. If someone cuts in again, the rest of us shall stare him down." Everyone seemed to agree, and nodded, then looked at me to continue.

I cleared my throat. "Well. We moved into the darkness, feeling our way. And before long I struck the pillar's end with the toe of my boot and cursed mightily—under my breath, but mightily. I do not think that sort of thing ever happened to Rostam. Then Dabir and I lifted a part of one of those broken pillars. Even quartered as it was, the thing was quite heavy, and I staggered to bear it.

"With it in my arms I jogged back into the darkness, my sheathed sword slapping my thigh. I hurried both to build speed for ramming and because I feared if I did not move fast I would have to drop the thing. Dabir followed, breathing heavily and supporting the pillar's back end.

"This time when I saw the burning eyeholes it was with relief, and I increased my pace. I grunted against the burden in my arms. My back ached, my biceps began to numb. And my toe still hurt. Still I ran, building speed, and we smashed the pillar into the wall. Chunks of masonry flew away and a jagged opening was torn from the spot where the eyes had peered, almost to the floor. Something sharp struck my head and then I was through the gap. We pushed the pillar away from us, and it crashed into three long pieces. I drew my sword.

"Our entrance had in no way been quiet. Every eye in the chamber stared at me, even the horrible ones shoved into the stone face, even Lydia's. She paused in her magics. I called to God and ran forward, whirling my blade over my head.

"Corineus yelled something in Greek and the burly Greek guard shoved Jaffar away to come at me. Our swords met, throwing sparks.

"The Greek was strong and no stranger to the blade. We struck and parried, trading blows again and again. Each time I swung, his weapon was there to block mine, as mine was for his. It grew clear to me swiftly that we were matched in both speed and strength. I could spare little attention to anything else in the room. I did know that Dabir had run forward to confront Corineus, who had grasped a wobbly Jaffar and held a knife to his throat. I could hear him call out for the two of us to stop, but there was no stopping the Greek, and I had no mind to be killed by him, so the two of us kept fighting. Lydia, meanwhile, resumed her chant. And that awful old voice from before Muhammad roared for her to hurry.

"I had a plan then, and I increased my onslaught. The Greek warrior blocked expertly as I came on, not realizing my objective as he retreated. I swung from my left, locked his blade, and in a flash stepped in to clout his face. He leapt backward. Lydia cried out.

"The warrior landed in the midst of the circle. Instantly he threw back his head, staggering. His mouth shook, straining against a scream that did not come. The blade fell from twitching fingers and rang against the floor. Backing him into the sorcery had worked even better than I'd supposed. Whatever dark magics the circle contained were now afflicting him. He crumpled to the floor. It was no warrior's death, but I dared not cross the circle to finish him with steel. Lydia swore at me, but I paid her no heed. Jaffar, shaking his head as though dizzy, wrestled awkwardly with Corineus, whose knife was gone. Dabir watched, sword poised. He dared not strike for fear of hitting Jaffar.

"I had more faith in my arm. My blade cut through Corineus's clothes, and his spine, before he knew I was there. He collapsed upon Jaffar, flopping and bleeding. The girl screamed rage behind me. I bent to help up Jaffar, who expressed gratitude to us both, though he seemed to have trouble focusing. I learned later that he had been drugged, so that he was ever after unsure about what he had really witnessed.

"At a noise from behind, Dabir and I whirled as one.

"The Greek guard was back up. This time he growled wickedly. His eyes were lit with vicious intelligence. Behind him the tongue hung slackly from the stone lips and the eyes that should never have moved were dull and glazed.

"The warrior laughed and came for me once more! I thrust, but he deflected it with an effortless twist of his hand. The old dead king had taken the warrior's body, and the old kings, you see, were not the sort who waxed fat on their thrones watching dancing girls. This one knew swordcraft. As he swung high and low against me, now feinting, now thrusting, it was all I could do to defend. Mayhap he had learned a trick or two in the nether realms, for I was panting hard in only moments.

"Again he laughed and his deep voice bore that strange ancient accent. 'You will die first!' There was pleasure and hunger in those words.

"I pressed my attack, but that was just what he wanted. He parried and thrust, slicing through my jubbah and drawing blood along my side. If I had not slid back he would have struck me dead. Pained, startled, I leapt away, watching his eyes. He grinned wickedly. Beyond me, Dabir busied himself with the circle about the stone; Lydia knelt over her father's body.

"The dead king whispered in a dark, low tone and the shape of my sword blurred! It took the form of a hissing snake and snapped at my wrist." I paused in my narration to find the audience's attention anchored surely to my every word, then resumed in a confidential tone. "Now here is where the old dead king made his mistake, and you soldiers should heed well. He *had* me, understand. He had more skill than I, and more power. I was fighting purely on the defense. All he had to do was keep pressing me, and he would have won out. Instead, feeling cocky, he sought a more complicated victory. When my sword transformed into a snake he probably meant for me to fling it aside—but I flung it at him.

"A curious thing transpired. The snake struck him and stuck out of his chest. Then its form blurred once more and I saw that my blade had pierced his side. He looked down in bewilderment as blood gushed from him. He staggered slightly to one side, my hilt wobbling in him. The blood flowed down his tunic and his thighs.

"'No matter," he said, sneering. "I will simply take another . . .' And he stepped toward the circle, only to utter a strangled cry, for Dabir had stepped into the circle and stood beside that hideous stone. You might think that was a foolish thing, but he had broken the protective magic and written the name of Allah across the top part of the stone. When I snatched the blade from the Greek's body and struck him again, he fell and died, emitting a wail of terror as the dead king's soul fell back to the court of Iblis."

I was quiet for a long moment, letting them picture the scene, and finally little Abdul could take it no longer. "What happened then?" he asked.

"Well, Jaffar was grateful, as you might imagine, and showered us with praise. He might have doubted his senses, but he was certain we had saved him. Lydia rose stiffly from the body of her father, her head high. No matter that she was a short woman; she looked tall with dignity. 'What will you do with me?' she asked.

"'I do not know,' Jaffar admitted. That he said this was remarkable given the usual duties of his office. He pressed a hand to his head, visibly forcing himself to concentrate. 'You have been party to murder and lies.' He looked away briefly then added, 'I don't suppose you were made to participate unwillingly?'

"'No,' she said fiercely. A silence grew before she ended it. 'Your man killed my father.'

"'That is regrettable,' Jaffar said, 'but all these events are of your making. Were you so desperate for power that you would let no propriety interfere?'

"Her lovely face screwed up in anger. 'Desperate?' she snapped. 'Yes. Now, I suppose, you will take me before other men and pronounce a man's justice upon me. Do so. My only crime is wanting some share in a world ruled by bearded fools.'

"Jaffar's eyes widened a little, then he frowned sadly. His voice, when at last he spoke, was soft. 'Ride, Lydia. Take one slave and ride, as swift as you dare, and do not darken this land again. I wish never to look upon you.'

"She stared at Jaffar as though she had not heard him properly. Finally she said, 'But my father's body—'

"'Go!' Jaffar barked.

"And thus she left, though she gave me a final dark look. She hurried from the room and was gone. There is not much more left to tell. My wounds were bandaged. We never found any gold or jewels, though we dug for a little longer because we'd heard the spirit saying such things were hidden there."

"There were the tablets," Dabir countered. "We took wagonloads back to the House of Wisdom."

"There was that," I said. "Most of them spoke of the deeds of that dead king, though, and made for gruesome retelling. Dabir and I prospered and stand high now in the master's favor because of that day. And . . . there is nothing more to tell."

Everyone praised me then, saying that I had done a fine job. I concealed my pleasure with a long stretch and yawn and rose, saying that it was time for all but those on watch to settle in for the night. A few of them lingered.

Mahmoud drew close. "Last time you told the tale, the dead king called forth a demon with a man's face and you fought it while Dabir struggled through the magic circle."

"Well," I said, "a good storyteller tailors his story for his audience."

Hamil, waiting beside him, laughed. He actually slapped me on the back. "That was nicely done, Captain. Nicely done. The ending could have had a little more punch, but I have heard worse from folk who make their living with such things."

"Thank you, Hamil," I said.

"We should talk more, you and I," he said. "About storytelling."

I nodded my consent, feeling odd at this change in his usual manner with me. I'd hoped for a quick word with Dabir, but I saw him withdrawing with Esfandiar. I started to follow, but Sabirah was there, and clearly wanted to speak. She looked up at me and I was struck by the way her eyes silvered in the moonlight.

"I have heard Uncle tell that tale," she said, "but never in that way. He said nothing about any magics."

"Aye. The bhang made him witness many odd things. He only thought himself the victim in a strange murder ritual." The master had never directly accused either Dabir or me of fabrication, but subtle remarks he'd made discouraged us from arguing against his version of events. He'd once told us, smiling, that no extra details were required to earn his favor, for he was already grateful to us.

"He never spoke so about the Greek woman. Was she truly so captivating, or was that just for the benefit of your listeners?"

"She was a striking woman," I said. "Though short. I expect she will age less gracefully than you."

Sabirah blinked at me, seeming not to know how to absorb this information. I guessed that I misjudged the purpose of her query. "I have another question, Asim."

"Aye?"

"Have you had any storyteller's training?"

"Nay."

"So your skill is all learned by listening to others?"

"I suppose it is."

"And natural instinct, I expect. Do you still think that those bowls were confused?"

I said nothing for a time, for all good feeling left over from my success as a storyteller fled on the instant. I had momentarily forgotten such things. "Good night, Sabirah," I managed finally. She studied me for a moment, then walked off for her cramped quarters. I stepped away to where Dabir and the Magian sat quietly together. The spars rattled gently against the mast, and the insects chirruped among the grasses.

Esfandiar paused in midsentence to glance up at me, then continued. "—disclosing any more."

"Pardon my saying this, Dastur," Dabir went on without looking to me. "You are no young man. A desert trip will tax your energy."

"I know this."

"The trip might kill. What harm, then, will come from sharing the route with me? Tell me the way, so that you can return home with Sabirah when we arrive at Basra."

Did Dabir, then, mean to learn Ubar's location? Could this be what Jaffar had warned me of? Was Dabir trying to take more power for himself?

"You words hold wisdom," the old man said slowly. "And I will consider them carefully. It may be that it will do good to have more than one of us knowing the way . . . but I mean to go with you."

"Why?" Dabir prodded.

"I am at least partly to blame for Firouz," Esfandiar said, then sighed deeply. "He is my son."

"By the nine and ninety names," I said softly, then crouched down beside them. "Why did you not say something sooner?"

"I think Dabir has guessed for a while. Have you not?"

Dabir turned up an empty palm, but said nothing.

"If he is your son," I said, "then you can tell us his nature—his weaknesses, and what other sorceries he might know."

The priest breathed in deep. "He is my son, Captain," he said in his soft, low voice. "It is a sad thing to contemplate the downfall of one's own child; it is a worse thing to aid in its planning."

I studied the old man anew. His eyebrows were coarse and thick; he smelled of sweat and old paper. Almost I told him that I was sorry, but I did not know how.

"He was a good son," he continued in his slow, sad way, "quick to learn, slow to anger. I thought surely that the breath of God moved through him, and it may be that I spoke too pridefully of him, both to my friends and to him. He mastered the hymns and the teachings and much more, but I think now that he learned too fast to gain wisdom at the same moment."

"You said he was angered," Dabir prompted.

"The poll tax and land tax weighed heavily upon the community in Mosul. There was a matter of property being confiscated when monies could not be paid, and"—he glanced hard at me—"some of the folk yelled too loudly. Soldiers were called in. My son's wife and many of his friends were killed when the uprising was put down."

Dabir nodded with a knowing frown.

"Firouz turned inward, then, and hate took root and flowered darkly. At first he tried to sway others to heed him, but we warned him it was not the way of Ahura Mazda to seek vengeance, and that he walked a dangerous road. He grew silent; we found, though, that Firouz had sought out hidden texts and lost knowledge." Esfandiar finished after a long pause: "He refused to explain himself, and showed no remorse. And thus we revoked his title."

"What has he studied?" Dabir asked.

Esfandiar looked up at him. "I did not know this until later, understand. He unearthed secrets of old Ashur, and wizardry of the Hebrews and Babylonians. He read dark texts that have no business upon this earth. He sought to master the pure flame of God." The old man shook his head. "Would that I could have recognized the path that he was on, so that I might have turned him from it. I think the best I can hope for him now is an end that falls swift and painless."

What can you say to a man such as this, a wise man, a good man, who has raised a venomous son and who suffers in the coils of that knowledge? I had not the words to soothe him.

"Do you know a way to stop his sorcery?" Dabir asked.

"There are certain ancient cadences and signs that I have studied. They might protect us."

"Will you share them with me?"

Esfandiar eyed him sharply. "Your thirst for knowledge reminds me of his."

"I seek merely to shield us."

"Be certain you mean what you say," the old priest said, rising. He moved aft.

Dabir and I remained where we were.

"I think," Dabir said to me after a time, "that this voyage will not end as happily as it has begun."

"Perhaps. We may yet triumph, though, God willing." I did not add my chief worry: that our mission would not end well for him regardless of outcome. Jaffar could not be pleased that his niece chased after her tutor, and Dabir was likely to be blamed whether she came to harm or not. And what if the priest was right, and Dabir sought knowledge for the wrong reasons? Jaffar had warned me of just such a thing. Dabir might have guessed my thoughts, for he studied me closely before rising and following the Magian.

The next day Mahmoud spotted the bird.

6

My nephew brought Dabir and myself to the prow after midday prayers and pointed at the creature; Dabir immediately pulled his arm down.

"Do not draw attention," he whispered.

A small bird sat atop the forward mast. I could not tell if it was the same sort as the first, not with the sun high and blinding careful view.

"It sits there and does not flit about, nor make outcry," Mahmoud said. "I saw it land before prayers and watched it for a time. Still it sits."

Dabir walked away; I followed. "Should we let it be?"

"Nay," he said quietly. "We must kill it. Or stop it," he finished, and I felt a chill, knowing that he had changed his wording because he suspected, as did I, that it was already dead.

"Last time you said it would—"

"This time is different. I do not want him to know our position. Firouz cannot have an endless supply of these things, and they must cost him something. He is a man fleeing on a boat—his resources are not unlimited. Have your best archer shoot the thing. We shall arrange a disturbance—"

"Dabir!" Mahmoud called his name as he jogged to join us. "The bird has flown."

Dabir cursed lightly. "I wasted time in talking. When next it returns, shoot it."

But it did not return that day, or the next. At least, with Mahmoud now as earnest about the matter as myself, the other men took their orders seriously and also watched the skies. It availed not. After another two days I almost convinced myself that it had been a living bird and not a sorcerer's undead scout.

The character of the river had slowly changed. The Tigris broadened, and the plants along its banks multiplied. So too did the insects. I had never journeyed this far south before, and the captain informed us that we had reached the marshes. Basra and the ocean lay only a few days off. Between then and now, though, we would have to navigate through a swarm of little islands and lagoons. The already heavy traffic thickened with local boats on their way to and from nearby settlements. The little brown Marsh Arabs poled hither and yon on their rafts from their villages, which were made up of reed houses floating on great reed mats tethered to the palms and poplars. Dogs they kept, which barked at us, and water buffalo, which would graze among the lilies in the shallow channels. Birds of many kinds were thick here, duck, geese—thousands upon thousands of both—as well as teal, pelican, and many other waterbirds. Dabir told me that the bugs would be worse if the birds were not so numerous, and I praised God for sending them to this place, for it had altogether too many insects as it was.

The sunsets were worth praise, too, for they fell glorious and colorful both days we sailed the marshes. The frogs came out and sang, a sound loud enough to waken all the djinn said to slumber along the old banks. It was a disturbing, foreign sound at first, but after the first night it grew to be almost a comfort to hear that cacophony, such an omnipresent noise that one ceased to pay it notice. I think those beasts were pleased the heat of the day at last was over and celebrated in the only way they know, although Dabir said they called for mates.

By day the river was often lost in the chains of lagoons and winding lakes fed by a profusion of channels. Sometimes I knew the bank for a long straight line of palms bordering open water, but we could not have found our way without experienced hands. The captain told me the watercourses changed from year to year, season to season and that only the Marsh Arabs knew their true paths. I doubt any man could have known the whole of it. A maze of alternating water and reeds stretched in every direction, as though the whole of the world was made up of such features. Only the occasional bank of willows or floating village provided variety.

I told the men to make frequent display of their arms and helms. River pirates were well known to prowl this stretch of water. My men sat in shifts along the deck, absently polishing their armor or swords so that they could be seen by the shore, or pretending to do so while playing shatranj or backgammon.

That second evening we heard a muezzin calling, though we could not see him or the settlement. I set Mahmoud and two soldiers to watching while most of the rest of us knelt to pray.

In the midst of our prayers the captain's son shouted and flung up an arm. I looked up and beheld a flame arcing over the water toward us from a bank of reeds. Then I recognized the hiss of arrows as more spots of flame arched over the marsh grass toward our ship.

"Seek cover," I cried, pushing Sabirah bodily aft. I snatched up my sword belt and buckled it as I shouted at my men to ready their bows.

The first of the arrows bit into the deck. Two extinguished immediately; a third bloomed along the rail.

More soared after them.

"Fetch water!" Dabir cried. Sabirah called out something at me, but I dashed forward as Captain Ibrahim shouted his men into place. They rushed to obey and bring up the buckets. I spotted the reed bank from where the arrows came some thirty feet out, and cursed my men to hurry, for they were still stringing their bows. Even if our arrows did not tell, their coming would give the enemy pause.

One enemy arrow had apparently struck canvas, for fire raced along the sail. The ship's captain screamed for a sailor with the first bucket to hurry. He jogged up, water slapping the deck from over the bucket brim. Then fate dealt us a bitter blow. If the sailor had been a moment slower the next arrow would have missed him utterly; but as he raised his arm it struck him in the side. He dropped with a little gasp, the bucket falling with him. The water drenched the deck, not the fire.

The captain himself snatched up the bucket, firelight painting him in flickering reds and oranges. Dabir had organized the sailors into a chain that waged battle with three water buckets. The fire had spread fast.

Finally my men reached the rail with their bows.

Mahmoud, being the strongest, had strung his bow first. His arrow streaked off; on came another ragged volley from the shore. The arrows were striking aft, now, for we had drifted on.

The ship's captain ordered men aloft to cut the burning sail free.

My men fired together under my command, and there came no answering volley. Instead there was a roar from behind me.

I whirled, only to find flame spread across the desk. It reared up like a living thing and took on the shape of a monstrous human hand.

At first I thought it a fleeting image, a trick of perception, but while its outline wavered, as with any flame, the shape remained well defined. The two bucket men halted before it, gaping. For a moment all was still save for the shifting, crackling fire.

And then the palm slapped down upon the deck and across the captain and the two men with water. They screamed as fire wrapped them, pressing them down, and the deck erupted in lines of flame. The hand rose from the three black and smoking corpses, and then it clasped the main mast. Fire raced up its length even as a second hand of flame rose from the deck fires.

All had transpired in the time it takes to draw two quick breaths. One of the bucket men, wrapped in flame, staggered to the rail and threw himself over. Other sailors leapt after. All about us were cries of consternation and shouted prayers.

And then Esfandiar stood before the second hand, head high. His silvery hair glowed red in the light. He raised one arm and the fire hand paused. What the priest said I know not, but he pronounced it in a sonorous, authoritative voice.

The flames licked on across the planks until nearly the whole of the deck crawled with them, and the first hand rose once more to stand on its wrist beside the second. Esfandiar lifted his hands and repeated the words forcefully.

"Uncle," Mahmoud urged me, "we must swim for it!"

I glanced about. Dabir stood with Sabirah near the aft portion of the vessel. He called for the priest to run, even as flames ate their way toward him.

The hands backed away and, for a moment, I thought Esfandiar had won. And then his own hands began to shake, as if with palsy. At that moment the fiery hands leapt up and caught him between themselves, as though they clapped. He did not cry out, but was consumed in a blazing blue pillar.

Sabirah screamed in horror.

My men looked at me, their eyes wide as childrens'.

"Jump, dogs!" I shouted to them. I could no longer see Dabir through the rising curtain of flame.

My men leapt over the side. I cast my eyes about once more, saw the poet leaping after the captain's son. The boat was an inferno. How swiftly do fortunes fly! Moments before we had been masters of our fates, and in the space of a hundred heartbeats our craft was kindling and half of us were dead.

I hit the water and sank beneath the surface.

Now I wished I had looped my sword about my shoulder, for I immediately felt it drag me down. As a matter of fact, everything seemed to drag me down, jubbah, boots, sword belt, knife . . . but I have always been a strong swimmer. I kicked to the surface. The flaming ship crackled behind me, easily showing the bank's outline only a bow shot away. I stroked toward it, kicking with my booted feet, which might as well have been leaden weights. Would the archers be waiting on the shore? Possibly. But there was nothing to be done for it save hold on to my father's sword, even though it pulled me down like an inflexible metal tether hooked through my belt. I managed to keep my head above water and thrash forward.

I saw three of my men's heads bobbing in the water ahead of me as they too advanced on the shore, all but one of them turbanless like myself. Where were the others? Was Mahmoud among them? Where was everyone else?

It occurred to me then that the sailors had all been dropping off the far side. Dabir and Sabirah, if they'd survived, would have gone that way as well, separated as they were by the line of fire down the ship.

Mostly, though, I concentrated on reaching the shore. Qudamah, the first soldier there, reached down to help me up, his beard and mustache dripping water. More clearly now I heard calls for help over the splashing. The boat still burned upon the water, the timber popping as the fire roared in glee.

Qudamah's sword was gone, so I thrust mine into his hands. "Watch for the archers," I said, then pulled off boots and jubbah. Muti was staggering up into the reeds, but Tahir struggled mightily. I dived out and swam for him.

If you ever seek to aid a drowning man, be warned that they are maddened in fear. Tahir grasped desperately at me, as though he thought I stood upon some rock and could pull him to safety.

"Calm yourself!" I cried. Yet he clasped at my arms and I went under, gulping water. His grip shifted to my left arm and I kicked up to the surface. Tahir's eyes rolled madly, then relaxed after I clouted him in the face. I clasped his collar, keeping his nose above water, and swam one-handed, kicking with my legs. I staggered up with him onto the muddy bank and struggled up through the reeds, wondering where Qudamah and Muti had gotten to, wondering if Mahmoud and Dabir and Sabirah and the rest were already dead somewhere in the water.

I bent down, rolled Tahir over on his stomach, and pushed his back until he coughed and water rolled out.

I did not hear the bandits until they stood in a half-moon behind me. I whirled, and there they were. Two had arrows knocked in bows. Three others had swords drawn, one of which was my own. They were short men with evil smiles and tattered clothes.

Two of the swordsmen moved aside at a word from behind, and out stepped the smaller man I'd encountered in the Baghdad market, the snake who'd commanded the attackers. His gaze was cool, appraising. His face was round, almost boyish, his eyes bright.

Behind him came a tall, turbanless man in fine boots, robed in red. The others moved aside for him, but even without this signal I knew by his commanding presence that he was the one in charge. Was this Firouz? I searched him for obvious signs of Magian heritage, and saw none. His beard was full but well trimmed and he would have been handsome if not for his cold and haughty manner.

"Where is Qudamah?" I demanded.

But the red man did not answer. I rose, and the bowmen tensed.

"No further, foreskin," said the knife man.

I bristled at the insult; the men about him laughed.

Tahir, meanwhile, had finished coughing, and sat up weakly.

"Diomedes," the red man said commandingly, and then the thick grasses parted once more and the pop-eyed Greek arrived. He took in the whole scene with distaste.

The fellow in red spoke again, his tone clear and precise. It was an orator's voice, certain of response. "This is the guard captain?"

"Yes, Firouz," Diomedes answered.

"Kill the other," the red one said.

"No," I cried, but the arrows flew and Tahir died. I bent by him as light faded from his eyes, and anger filled me. I bared my teeth and rose, my hand reaching for my knife.

"Don't," said the little snake man, and his own short sword was in his left hand, while a knife glinted in his right.

"Where is Dabir?" Firouz demanded.

Rage and disbelief had stolen my tongue; I made no reply and did not, in that moment, even wonder that he asked for the scholar.

"Kill him and be done with it," Diomedes instructed.

"Nay," said Firouz. "There are questions that must be answered."

"Where are the rest of my men?" I demanded at last.

"Burning in hell with that one," Diomedes replied.

104

"You murdered them, too?" I knew the answer, but the words were torn from my lips in disgust.

"As you and your masters have murdered so many," Firouz said.

"You're the fire sorcerer? Do you realize you slew your own father?"

Firouz shook his head slowly. "If you practice magic, you must be ready to pay the ultimate price. Besides, it was my father's blindness that led him to death. It was his choice, not mine. Now, come, tell me where the others are. Have they drowned, or swum to the far shore?"

I only spat.

"Talk!" the snake snarled at me.

"He will not talk," Diomedes said. "He knows what you plan for him."

"But you do not," Firouz answered Diomedes with disdain. He stepped briefly aside with the Greek and they held a swift, whispered conversation. I saw the Greek nodding and looking back at me.

When Firouz returned to me his tone was more agreeable. "We have many things to discuss, you and I, and if you cooperate I shall let you live to deliver a message to the caliph. Who better to testify to my powers than someone who has witnessed them, and who better to be trusted by the listener than a guard captain?"

"I shall tell you nothing."

"Of that we shall see. Bring him." He turned his back and stepped away, his boots rustling the marsh grass as he parted the reeds and vanished behind them.

7

Now after my mother and my father and my eldest brother, there was no relative I treasured more than my eldest brother's son, my nephew Mahmoud. It may seem that he was at the bottom of a long list, but he was at its height in a way, for he was the only one of these still living. I knew him for a strong swimmer, better even than I, yet I had not seen him surface, nor had I seen him lying among the bodies my captors forced me past. I was in agony to ask if others had surfaced, but if Mahmoud had survived, I did not wish to give away his existence. Worries that he had not, however, tormented me: perhaps Mahmoud had struck his head upon the wood, or inhaled when he should have exhaled, or tried to help another swimmer as I had done and not been so lucky when the fellow panicked. If he *had* survived I wondered if he'd held on to his weapons, and prayed quietly that he did as they dragged me through the swamps, for Firouz had told a half dozen of the men to stand guard and look for other survivors, with specific instructions to kill all but Dabir.

I revealed none of this; did not, in fact, speak another word. Neither did my captors to me, save to curse when they thought I took too long pulling on my boots. My feet and socks were wet and filthy. I produced squishing sounds as I walked.

Before long we descended another bank into a marsh channel where we climbed into a boat of sewn skins. The marsh tribe was named Al-Bu Chilaib. Why anyone should intentionally name themselves after dogs I

106

do not know, but it was the way of these people. There was a lean, hungry aspect to them. I have heard some say that all Marsh Arabs are thus, and that may be true, for they live in a wild place where living is hard. Not all, though, are so hostile to outsiders, which I later learned.

As we rode through the maze of channels I contemplated throwing myself over the edge of the craft and swimming for freedom, but I did not know where I would go. It might be that some better chance of escape would be granted me, but I confess that I thought my fate was writ. In the scheme of things I knew that my death would be no great event, and that the frogs would continue their singing and the stars their wheeling whether I lived or died. This might have provided comfort to some philosopher, but none to me.

Eventually dark structures loomed up out of the night. I knew them for the houses of these people; they were long and narrow with rounded roofs. We did not stop at the first, or even the second, but drifted toward the largest structure of all, standing on its own little island. My captors tied the boat off on a pier, beside the more sturdy craft that bore Firouz and the others. Diomedes and most of the bandits traveled on; I could not see their destination for I was hauled out of the boat and shoved roughly along. Nearby two water buffalos were roped under a fragile looking lean-to: one snorted at us as we walked by. Somewhere farther off a dog barked until shouted into silence.

This building was the mudhif, a sort of a tribal gathering spot and guesthouse. It was an arched chamber of reeds that stretched twice the height of a man and extended more than three times that width from side to side. Once the door was thrown open for Firouz, who preceded us, I saw the mudhif's floor too was built of reeds partly concealed by dirty old carpets just visible by virtue of the hearth fire built up in the building's center. A hunched servant tossed willow branches into the fire's midst and set it crackling.

Firouz paced for a moment on the other side of the hearth, then collected himself and called out orders. Most of the men he sent away. Two stood with me, as did the snake man, whom I now knew to be named Ali.

"Sit," said Firouz. He swept a hand down toward some dark lumpy cushions near the hearth. "Take your ease. We need not be enemies."

He must have thought me an imbecile to trust his changed tone. I did not move. "You have stolen from my master," I said, "and slain my men."

He laughed almost warmly, then moved closer to me. His tone was fatherly. "By what right is Jaffar your master? He has no power over you than what you give him. You might slay him in an instant."

What madness was this? I knew no proper answer.

"And your men—again you say that I slew them, but would they not have done the same, to me, given the chance?"

"They would not have slain you when you were helpless."

He made a rude noise, and his voice grew mocking. "We were not fair, were we? Should battle be fair, Captain? Should we measure out our swords to make sure that they are all the same length and sharpness?" He drew even nearer and crossed his arms. I am by no means small, but he had a little height over me, and so looked down. "Should we ensure that only warriors of precisely the same skill cross blades? Should we roundly measure their muscles?"

I frowned at him. "There is such a thing as decency."

"You are merely annoyed that I killed a man that you had troubled to pull from the water."

I was, it was true, but there was more to it than that. I had liked those men. I had trained them, praised them, cursed them into action; I knew their wives, and their families. And it was I who chose them for this mission. I could imagine them laughing or striving on the practice field, or boasting to one another over their games of chance. Now that memory was marred by sight of their twisted, arrow-ridden bodies, left for carrion.

"War is not fair, Captain. You know that. Certainly Jaffar knows that. It only seems fair to the victor. And somewhere"—he pointed vaguely at my heart—"you know that as well. Now, come." He turned and barked to the guard who had stolen my sword. His name was Pig—the Marsh Arabs had strange names for one another. "Bring us wine."

"I do not drink the wine," I said.

"Then you shall be in a sorry state, for the water here has an unpleasant tang, and you are likely thirsty."

"I do not mean to share salt with you in any case. Nor to drink any liquid of your stinking Marsh Arabs."

One near me growled and his hand whipped to his sword blade.

Firouz raised a palm and gently motioned the man at ease.

"Take care, Captain, lest you offend someone."

"What is it you want, Magian?"

"A simple thing. A trifling thing. Sit."

"I prefer to stand."

"As you will." Firouz approximated a royal wave and lowered himself into cushions, his back to the fire. "You make my job as host challenging. I know your boat is only the spear point of a larger force from Jaffar. How many more men follow, and how far behind are they?"

It was only then I realized that I had some leverage. Whether it was merely because of a grand sense of self-worth or because he was up to far more than mere thievery, Firouz assumed we'd thought him a greater threat and had set more men after him. Might I spin a thread out of this web that led to a longer life?

While I considered this unasked for opportunity, Pig arrived and presented Firouz with a chipped brown cup. The Magian took it from him and drank. Ali, the knife man, waited on Firouz's right side, seemingly idle.

"I thought your birds would tell you all you needed," I said at last.

"Through them I see, but do not hear," Firouz replied. "And I know Dabir's cleverness. He made show of the armed men on your boat. Those that follow are hidden, are they not?"

He had overthought the problem as well as overestimated his own importance. Still I knew not how to use his weakness to my advantage. And so I stalled.

"You ask me to lead more men to their deaths," I said.

"Deaths? No one need die. If I know how many there are, and how far behind, then I might avoid them altogether."

I grunted and said nothing. He took this as something other than what it was; perhaps he thought I considered his words.

"I really wish none of you, personally, harm. I know you are merely instruments. I actually hold some affection for Dabir."

It occurred to me then that he had mentioned Dabir by name several times, and I eyed him.

"Did he not tell you?" Firouz's eyebrows arched.

"Tell me what?"

Firouz laughed. "He and I are old friends. We were comrades in younger years. We both studied at the House of Wisdom, learning secrets."

The House of Wisdom was one of the most famous buildings within the whole of the caliphate—a great library and storehouse full to the brim with books and writings and the scholars who pored over them. I did not know that Dabir had been a part of the institution, although it did not surprise me. His relationship with Firouz did.

"You lie," I said.

Firouz chuckled. "Dabir and I were the only two in a generation who mastered Akkadian, and we worked for a time as translators. I'm surprised he didn't mention this?"

"It didn't come up." Was he telling the truth? Why would he seek to fool me with such information?

Firouz's head craned forward and he studied me. "No matter." His manner grew more brusque; it was as though he then addressed one beneath him rather than an equal. "Tell me the disposition of the men."

There were, of course, no men to tell him about. I decided to buy time by whatever means I could. "What will I earn if I betray them?"

"I will let you live, to send word to the caliph of my power."

"I don't believe you."

"I am merciful and compassionate. As a ruler should be. As your caliph is not."

Did he mean to compare himself to Allah the compassionate and merciful? "I would be a fool to return to my master and the caliph having failed at a mission and betrayed my soldiers."

"Then stay here, and live as an officer in my own guard."

I considered the dirt-speckled man at his side. "Your officers do not seem as prosperous as those of my master."

Firouz's voice grew sharp, his pronunciation precise and forceful. "I am tiring of this, Captain. There are less pleasant measures that I can take. With ease. Flame proves a fine persuader."

The door opened and in slid another figure. The sudden influx of wind in the cylindrical building set the fire wavering in the central hearth, as if to emphasize Firouz's threat.

Firouz glanced over, then back at me, then turned once more and stared at the newcomer. Ali drew his blade, and the two men to my side muttered in frank curiosity.

It was Dabir.

One of the Marsh Arabs came behind him, but it seemed not so much that Dabir was his prisoner as that the Marsh Arab was his attendant, so self-possessed was Dabir. True, his boots squished at every step, but his head was high, and his eyes bright. Also, his weapon was still at his side.

"Dabir ibn Khalil." Firouz pronounced the name with wonder and motioned his men to rest.

"Firouz Caspari. Peace be upon you."

"And upon you, the peace."

Dabir walked forward; the man behind him followed, hesitant.

"I wish that you had contacted me," Dabir said. "So much of this might have been avoided."

"I did not think you would pursue me so far," Firouz said, rising as Dabir drew closer. I looked back and forth between them.

"He is a murderer, Dabir!" I said warningly.

"I think I can tell whom to trust," the scholar replied without looking at me. "So you knew that I was looking over the door pulls?" he asked Firouz.

"I did."

"Then why did you not seek me out? All this"—Dabir encompassed the men about us with a sweep of his arm—"and your magical exertion, was unnecessary."

Firouz smiled almost sadly. "It is easy for you to say this now; you have no options now that my man captured you."

"Your man did not 'capture' me, Firouz. I walked to him"—he indicated the Arab behind him—"and demanded audience."

Firouz looked to the big-shouldered man behind Dabir, who assented with a nod: "It is true, Sheikh."

"Well, you had few options in any case other than throwing yourself upon my mercy."

"Nay, I have many options. The simplest would be to find my way to another village and thence to Baghdad. But I would not have volunteered for this mission had I not thought that I could catch and join you."

I could not hold back a gasp. So Jaffar was right, and Dabir was a betrayer.

Firouz continued to stare at him, saying nothing for a long moment. "Why would you join me when you do not know my aim? Or have you guessed it?"

"It is easy to see you seek knowledge from the Keeper of Secrets."

Firouz smiled, saying nothing.

"There are grievances I myself nurse," Dabir continued, "not unlike yours. And questions I would like answered."

"You have done nothing about your grievances."

"I lack your ambition. But I am not shamed by that. You know well how much use I might be to you."

Traitor! If I could do nothing more before I died, I would slay the pair. The attention of my guards was clearly held by the drama before them; I slid my hand toward the knife pommel jutting from the belt of the man on my left.

Firouz stroked his beard thoughtfully, still considering Dabir.

My hand closed on the hilt and I pulled it clear. I heard a cry of surprise from my right, and whirled in time to see the pommel that struck my forehead. My own sword had been used against me!

Bright motes danced before my eyes and I staggered, but I lashed out at the man and heard an outcry. I meant to leap toward Dabir, but my legs were uncertain.

Ali appeared before me. His leg slammed mine and suddenly I was kissing the rug and his foot was pressed down against my hand.

"Should I kill this clown?" Ali asked.

Firouz's voice was almost a purr. "What do you think, Dabir?"

The traitor did not answer immediately. "He is a buffoon," he said slowly. "But I cannot condone his death outright, Firouz. He once saved my life."

"He has refused my service," Firouz said.

"Perhaps you can send him back to the caliph with your demands."

"This, too, I have offered him," Firouz said. "He has been rude."

I glared up at them both.

"Jaffar's niece is my prisoner," Dabir said. "He values her greatly and will pay well for her return. I'm sure this one will agree to convey a ransom demand."

Firouz laughed. "I thought you lacked ambition."

"I do not lack the eye to see opportunity."

"Where is she?"

"Bound; safe until you and I strike a compact."

"Very well. Pig, take your men and escort this lout"—he pointed at me—"somewhere safe. We will save him for Dabir."

"He sliced my arm!" someone above me wailed.

"You heard me," Firouz said sternly. And so I was hauled to my feet with an encouraging kick or two, and then marched outside.

"He didn't say you had to be left whole," Pig whispered to me as we moved through the doorway. His greasy fingers wriggled on the hilt of my sword.

The traitor and the murderer remained by the fire, gabbing like the old school friends they were, and the only thing that pleased me was that it took three armed men to guard my steps. My gait was still unsteady, but I pretended my balance was worse than it was in truth. At that moment I had no desire beyond killing Dabir and Firouz. The door closed behind us. All my senses were alert to seize any opportunity, and all my thoughts bent to that one end. I would die in the process, aye, and Sabirah would likely perish, but the greater evil would be eliminated. To think that I had considered Dabir a friend!

Outside the air was still, though the croaking of frogs was more pronounced. Two guards sat near the boats, dark shapes against a darker shore.

Pig ordered one of his men in the boat while the brute I'd wounded shoved me after. And then, at the dock's edge, I heard him gurgle. I turned in time to see the fellow go down. Behind him was a broad, dark shape with glinting steel in his hand.

"Mahmoud!" My voice was a glad whisper.

"His sword, Uncle!" Mahmoud hissed.

The man I'd thought a guard had already risen and stabbed Pig from behind. The Marsh Arab grunted, clutched at me, and fell lifeless into my arms. I took my father's sword from him, praised God, and dropped the dead man into the boat.

The last of my guards was sinking into the reeds. I grinned, for with their faces turned toward me I recognized one of those I'd thought a waiting guard to be Lufti, my soldier. And the man who'd stabbed Pig was the poet, Hamil.

I grabbed Mahmoud and kissed him on both of his hairy cheeks. Also I slapped his shoulder. The other men, too, I clasped, even Hamil, who grinned at me. Water dripped from his little beard.

"I feared you were dead!" I told Mahmoud.

His easy, lopsided grin reminded me suddenly of his father.

"Now we strike," I said. "There are three of them, and four of us."

"Dabir said we should wait for his signal," the poet whispered.

"Dabir betrayed us," I said. The moment I spoke this aloud I realized that his entire appearance must have been a ruse. I groaned at my own foolishness. "What is he doing?"

"He aimed first to free you," Mahmoud relayed, "then to learn more from the leader."

"Where is Sabirah? How many others survived?"

"Sabirah waits in the boats with Ghalib."

I smiled again; so another of my men was left.

Mahmoud waved generally toward a dark patch on our right; the reeds were tall enough that I saw nothing. "Five sailors live." Mahmoud continued softly. "We slew a score of the river men. But there are many more in the homes about us."

I nodded, considering. Dabir was braver even than I thought, to walk boldly into the camp of his enemies with a lie framed upon his lips.

"There are but three other men within," I said. "One is a knife fighter, another the mage who wielded fire against us. The third wears a sword, but I do not know his skill. We four—we five—can take them quickly, and flee."

"Should we not do as Dabir commanded," the poet asked, "and wait for his signal?"

"We are exposed, here," I said, "in the midst of our enemies. We must strike fast, while we have the advantage. Dabir is no military man—though I praise his courage. I can playact as well, and make a fine diversion. Once I have their attention, you and Lufti will charge in after. Hamil will wait by the door and move in if needed."

The poet sounded skeptical. "Can't that sorceror just set us all on fire?"

"I will trust Dabir to slay him, as he is standing close."

Mahmoud looked doubtful, but I clapped him on the shoulder. "Do as I bid. We shall strike the head from this snake, retrieve the treasure, and be on our way."

8

I flung wide the door and brandished my sword, striking left, then right. I meant to play my role even more finely than Dabir had played his, so I spoke in a booming voice.

"Dabir! There shall be a reckoning! Stand you forth, betrayer!" Again I slung my blade, and its passage through the air set it humming with menace. "You will pay! Serpent! Prepare thee for a smiting that shall rend your flesh, smash your bones, and send you to the courts of Iblis!"

It was a darkened room save for the fire that burned in its center hearth, yet there was light enough to gauge the reactions of the men within. Firouz and Ali whirled in surprise, while the swordsman fumbled for his weapon. Dabir managed a look of dismay that was utterly convincing.

"Ali," Firouz shouted, "silence that cock's crowing!"

The little knife fighter leapt to his feet, a blade in his hand before I'd crossed half the distance to him.

Dabir and Firouz stood as well, and the swordsman looked to his master for instruction.

"Lay down your weapon, fool!" Dabir demanded.

"He is too much of a nuisance," Firouz remarked. "We shall find you another messenger."

Reflected fire shone on a short length of metal in Ali's hand that a moment later twirled through the air toward me. I sidestepped and swung and somehow deflected the knife, which slashed into the reed wall on my left.

I closed on Ali, laughing, but the little fellow had no end of tricks. He flung powder before me, and there was no help but to blink at the stuff—sand, I think. In that moment he leapt and thrust with his short, fat sword. I had to parry in close, deflecting the strike near the very hilt of my own blade. Dabir and Firouz argued over some point that I could not hear.

The little man spun with more acumen than many dancing girls. There were no wasted movements or flourishes—he was economy and grace and I would have admired him had I not been fighting for my life. I am used to the offensive, but between his skill and the grit that I still blinked away I found myself on defense. Worse, the swordsman was closing in on my left.

A rush of feet came from behind, at the same moment that Mahmoud's voice called, "Right with you, Captain!"

I laughed deep in my throat then, glad to see Ali retreating. Lufti dashed in to engage the swordsman. Dabir and Firouz struggled over a satchel while Firouz hurled imprecations. Dabir snatched it clear but overbalanced, God be praised, for as he dropped Firouz swept out a hand. Flame from the hearth followed at the gesture, missing Dabir's head by only finger spans. The fire struck the reeds on the right and licked greedily up and over the walls in a moment, spreading faster than hungry ants. Dabir scrambled off the floor and dashed toward me, teeth set in determination, a satchel hugged to his chest.

Firouz was illuminated behind him, backlit by fire like a demon, his hand uplifted. I thought then that he and Dabir and Mahmoud and I would all be suffused in flame. Yet for some reason he did not grip us with fire.

"Stop them, Ali!" Firouz's voice cracked in desperation.

Mahmoud leapt ahead of me with a glad cry and struck at Ali. Dabir reached me, glared darkly, and moved past. I stood guard as Lufti backed from the opponent he'd slain, then called for Mahmoud to follow.

And then we were through and out the door; Mahmoud at rear guard while the height of the reed house flared blinding red.

Outside the poet waved us into a captured watercraft. Our sailors, manning the paddles, struck out furiously before any of us were settled into place. Sabirah huddled in front, watching with wide eyes. Mahmoud, the last one in, landed heavily behind us even as our vessel shot away. Ali shouted fury from the pier, already three spear lengths behind us.

"Faster, dogs!" I barked. "It is too soon for paradise!"

Other men were venturing from their own reed huts and staring as we poled past, and behind was the sound of Firouz, shouting, "Slay them! But bring me that pack!"

I grabbed up a paddle and set to work, yelling over my shoulder for Mahmoud to set his lazy arms to motion, for there was another paddle at my feet. Instead, Dabir took it up and stroked on the other side.

We sped on past two reed huts and out into the maze of lanes. "Left!" Dabir called from behind me, and I heard the poet, who sat aft, calling for the steersman to swing wide.

"How do you know the way?" I asked Dabir.

"I paid heed," Dabir said. His voice was tight, controlled.

Mahmoud was hunched against him.

"Dabir, give Mahmoud the paddle; he is stronger."

Dabir hissed through gritted teeth, as if he were keeping in a curse. "Left again!" he called, then, "This was your plan? To blunder through the night with no clear exit?"

"I rescued you!" I reminded him.

"I rescued *you!* Didn't Mahmoud tell you to await my signal?"

"We outnumbered them and had the element of surprise. It was time to strike." Why was he complaining? We were away and we had what we'd come for.

Dabir called for us to turn right. I risked a glance behind and by the light of the flaming reed house saw the outline of at least one boat under way behind us.

"Mahmoud, how many are back there?"

I thought at first that he was silent because he was assessing their numbers. The quiet, though, stretched on.

"Your nephew is dead, Asim." Dabir paused between gasps for breath, for he worked the paddle furiously.

I was not sure I'd heard him properly. "Dead?" I repeated stupidly. "How?" After all, he'd thrown himself into the boat like Dabir and myself.

"A knife cast from Ali struck him between the shoulder blades as he leapt."

The breath caught in my chest as if I myself had been struck.

"I am sorry," Dabir said.

"Why did you say nothing?" I had a mind to turn back and seek Ali.

"I am sorry," Dabir repeated.

And then there was nothing to do but row. It was fortunate indeed that Dabir knew the way, for I could not have seen through the tears that blinded me.

9

For all of Firouz's power, he could not inspire those men to follow us into the dark for very long. Men given over to vengeance or greed might have pursued us more vigorously; these men, though, were weary, and it must be remembered that bandits by inclination are lazy, else they would have chosen a profession that required more sustained effort and less hazard of life.

We too were weary; but we were desperate men in fear for our lives, and so we rowed. Even when we struck the main channel of the Tigris, we rowed.

A quarter hour downriver we came upon a vessel at anchor. It was a one-masted flat-bottomed affair. The Marsh Arabs who manned it at first obeyed us out of fear, but by morning, when they better knew our circumstances, they proved generous, sharing bread and drink and telling us of the depredations of the Al-Bu Chilaib tribe. I shall be forever grateful to the ugly little monkey of a man who gave over a shroud to me, and clean dry linens. These things he did, unasked, and without mention of payment.

By midmorning it rained. The skies were gray as tombstones and there was no seeing beyond a half mile. The poet kept a lookout anyway; I sat by my nephew, and if I do not dwell upon my thoughts at that time it is because I do not recall them. I swam in grief. Each moment of that day passed like a hundred hours.

We transferred to a larger vessel come evening, Dabir and the poet convincing all that we were official representatives, despite our condition, and then came to Basra by nightfall. I would that we might have buried Mahmoud as soon as we reached dry ground, but a grave could not be readied until the morning. When at last the prayers were said and we placed him facing Mecca I knew a deeper sadness even than before, for he had no family to mourn him in that place aside from myself. His bones lay in a city strange to him and all who loved him; only I and a few comrades set him to rest.

Dabir put me in charge of Sabirah in rooms he had obtained from the city governor. For the next two days he and Hamil and the soldiers went out again and again to arrange for our return trip and certain other matters to which I did not pay heed. I had been entrusted with the contents of the satchel. The door pulls remained within, but Dabir took a folio of documents with him. He reasoned those documents alone had kept Firouz from blasting us with flame as we fled. It was all one to me.

Even now I shake my head and become silent when I recall Mahmoud. He had grown sharply, that one, and came to the sword like a fish to water—which might also describe the way in which he swam, for he was a natural with that skill as well. He was not rash, nor did he display temper; he obeyed his elders and commanders and abstained from wine drinking. In the months before his final days perhaps he had had an eye toward women overmuch, but that was as God willed, and he did not shame himself in that way either.

I had found him his post, and I was ever proud to say so. He was not one of those relatives you shamefacedly found minor positions for while hoping no one would later recall your blood tie; he was the sort you boldly pointed out as sign that God had smiled upon your family.

It saddens me even now to think of him.

I sought comfort somewhat in a Koran Dabir had obtained for me; mostly, though, I took solace from silence. And that is the one thing, that afternoon, that I could not have. Hamil and Dabir were gone, so Sabirah took it into her head that I must be lonely. First Sabirah asked if I preferred to be alone; she walked away for a time then asked if I really wished to be alone or if I were simply being polite, before again departing for the back room. Then, some minutes after that, she announced that she thought it a poor thing not to keep a man company when he had lost a close relative as I had done, and said she would sit in the same room with me.

"Perhaps we might recite a sura together."

"No."

The apartments had come with servants, who busied themselves in the kitchen area. Judging by the smells they had but lately come to the study of culinary arts. I thought they were about a fish meal, for which I do not especially care.

Sabirah got up to look through the tiny petal-shaped openings in the window screen, then returned. She sat down at my right elbow, looked long at me, and sighed.

"You mustn't blame yourself, you know," she said.

"Blame myself?"

"For your nephew's death. It wasn't really your fault."

"It was not my fault at all," I said. "It was the fault of the wretch who threw the knife."

"Oh."

She fell silent. Something in her manner was clearly amiss. I do not think I normally would have pried; I was, however, not in the best of moods.

"Why do you think I blame myself?"

"Well . . . you just seem struck especially hard. I thought perhaps you blamed yourself for not listening to Dabir's plan."

"Dabir did not tell me his plan."

"Ah." She paused briefly. "Hamil said Mahmoud told you to wait for Dabir's signal."

A great rage roiled within me then, and it was all I could do to keep from shouting. "Now I have it, by God. You think if I had waited, Mahmoud would still live?"

122

"Oh, no," she said, backing away. "I wasn't trying to say—"

"Are you one who can divine the different roads of fate?" I demanded.

"No . . ."

"Is that what the stupid poet thinks? Or is this the word of Dabir?"

"I'm only trying to help!"

"You are *not* helping! When do you ever help?! You have no care but for your own desires."

"How dare you!"

"Oh, I'm *sorry*, mistress; a thousand pardons—"

"You mock me?"

"I call you to account! Someone should! You've been nothing but trouble since you joined the household! You're selfish, and willful, and heedless. You've damaged your reputation, embarrassed your family, and probably doomed your teacher by mooning after him instead of doing as you're told."

The dark eyes over her veil blazed angrily. "I do *not* moon after Dabir!"

"He's liable to be sacked or executed now because you stowed away! Is that what you wanted for your love?"

"I don't love him!"

"Do you think we are blind, Sabirah, not to see the way your eyes light when you look upon him?"

Her eyes lit now, but it was not with pleasure. "Ai-a! At least he has a brain, which is more than I can say for you!"

She sprang to her feet and fled through the curtains into the back room. I heard a sob choked from her.

Now she may truly have meant to aid me, but for her efforts I was more angry even than before, and I took to pacing, my teeth gritted. Would that I could have faced Ali then at that moment! It was all I could do not to follow her and give her more of my mind. I had just enough sense to let her be. Arguing with a woman is always problematic. Even when you win, victory can scarcely be endured, for women are poor losers.

After a long while my mood calmed somewhat, and hunger settled upon me. It was a great hunger that gnawed at me, for I had consumed little in the last three days.

I stomped into the kitchen area to see what the servants were fixing. It was a fish stew. The two old women were all smiles, which made me regret the harsh words I uttered about the stench when I walked in. Thus I took a large bowl and pretended that, being closer, the smell had grown upon me and that I looked forward to eating.

"Where is the young lady?" the leaner of them asked.

I explained that she was in her room, and they conferred, saying that they would be sure she ate. They then asked whether they should keep the food warm for the other gentlemen, and I said they were not likely to return for some hours.

I hadn't been in the mood for company to start with and wished it even less now. I drank the stew quickly, chewed the fish down—which did, indeed, taste as unpleasant as fish does normally—and retreated to the main room. Bad as that meal was, I debated returning for more, for I was still hungry. I sat down to stare at the stew bowl, weighing my choices, when a weariness stole over me. I had never slept on guard duty, and knew the old trick of reciting suras to stay awake. This I did . . . and yet somehow I fell to slumber anyway.

My dreams were languid. I swam upon great currents of air, pressing a cloud to my belly. All about me were red monkeys, who pounded drums while lovely women danced. My spirit must have been lascivious that day, for those dream women were curvaceous, wide-hipped beauties bedecked with carbuncles and diamond necklaces. Even the slippers on their tiny feet sparkled with jewels. They leapt in unison as clouds transformed to floor tiles. Great too was the skill of the monkeys, and I asked the man on my left where they were from. When he told me that they had been trained upon the north sea, my dream self-recalled that I had heard of the red monkeys of the north before.

The drumming was interrupted by a weeping Sabirah. I pointed out to her that she should be silent to hear the monkeys, and she left. Then there came a sharp pulling on my beard; a crab with the knife man Ali's face was there, smiling at me.

The crab tugged a little more and then scuttled away. I chased him with a broom handle, then tried to rediscover the room of the monkeys and dancing maidens. When I could not find them, I lay down and slept in my dream. I dreamt that I dreamt, which is an odd memory indeed.

"Asim!"

The voice was insistent, and my body shook. I opened my eyes only reluctantly, ordering the man to leave me at peace.

"Asim!"

"Dabir." Even I was amazed at how groggy I sounded. "Leave off. I am looking for monkeys."

"It looks like he's been drugged," I heard the poet say.

Dabir's voice was heavy with sarcasm as his head turned away. "Really." Then he was staring earnestly down at me, concern in his eyes. "We thought you were dead at first. Sabirah has been taken!"

I struggled to rise. Each of my movements came only with great labor. I felt just as I had earlier in the week after I'd leapt from the boat. Reaching the surface this time was an even greater challenge. Even though I heard what Dabir was saying, his words lacked a connective sense. "What? What's happened?"

"I say Sabirah's been taken," Dabir said with greater emphasis, "and the pulls as well. How did they get in?"

I felt my head as I sat up. "I know not. Who got in? The monkeys?"

"I do not think it was monkeys," Dabir said quietly. "Asim, focus. Do you remember anything?"

"I remember the fish," I said slowly.

"Listen to him," the poet said. "Fish, monkeys—it is the bhang talking—"

"No, no . . ." Things were starting to make more sense. I knew a great irritation at the poet, and a growing sense of worry. Had I heard Dabir right? "The fish stew. It must have been drugged. Did you say Sabirah's gone?"

"I did," Dabir said shortly. "So it was the servants. They drugged Asim and let in Firouz's men."

"Allah!" I struggled to sit up and put my hand to my head. My senses were becoming my own at last, although the room spun. My left eyebrow felt stubbly under my fingers, and I knew a sudden sickness of heart. "Firouz came, and I lay sleeping?"

"You were drugged," Dabir said simply. He crumpled a paper in his hand.

I winced, horrified. I had never failed to keep a watch; I had rarely failed at all. "The pulls? Did they take the pulls as well?"

"They took the girl and the pulls," Hamil said. He stood just to the left of Dabir, who knelt dejectedly beside me. He added. "And they took your hair."

"What?" I put my hand to the left side of my face. My beard was fine there, but my mustache had been trimmed.

"The left side of your beard," Hamil said, "the right side of your mustache, and your left eyebrow. You look like you were cut by a drunken barber." I knew by his tone that he was amused, but trying not to show it.

I groaned. My fingers proved his description accurate.

"Why did they not just kill me?" I half wished they had. Shame coursed through my veins, burning more surely than the sorcerer's fire.

Dabir glanced absently at the note crumpled in his hand. "Firouz wrote that he would not stoop to slaying my sleeping dog, though he had him shaved."

I scowled.

"He meant to humiliate me, I think, more than you."

"Your hair is intact." I sat forlorn, feeling the stubble of my mustache. I desired a mirror, but there were more pressing matters than my appearance. Light through a high screen window had a wan, afternoon cast to it. I wondered how long I had been asleep—several hours, by the look of it. There would be no hope of pursuing them.

"I have failed completely."

"This was not your fault, Asim." Dabir's voice was strained, but not unkind. "The servants must have been paid by Firouz. Why should you have suspected them?"

Miserable, I shook my head. "What do we do now?"

Dabir lifted the clenched fist holding Firouz's letter. "Firouz writes that no harm will befall her if we meet him in Ah' Sila and turn over the documents I took from him. That is on the coast across the gulf."

"Do you believe Firouz will keep his word?"

"He has no interest in hurting Sabirah," Dabir said, though he sounded troubled.

"The master is going to be furious," the poet said.

Dabir's eyes suddenly blazed and he snapped his finger. "That for the wrath of Jaffar. That girl is a treasure worth more than the sum of the caliph's rubies. I would not see her harmed!"

"I like her, too," offered a chastened Hamil. "She is a special young woman."

Dabir turned back to me. "Come, Asim, find your strength! We must be off!"

While Dabir conferred with Basra's governor, Lufti and Ghalib and I waited in the palace gardens. I'd had a look by then at my true appearance, and understood why children pointed at me and adults stared, for Ali's shaving had left me looking like a clown. At least my men did not laugh. Ah, but I was a wretched sight. Even the governor's slaves covered their mouths, trying not to chuckle as they hurried on their rounds.

Dabir emerged from the meeting looking grim, though I did not see why, for when we headed straight to the docks Dabir procured a ship by waving a paper and looking in the know. She was not the tallest of the ocean rigs, but small and sleek, and the taciturn captain had her under way after evening prayers.

Our ship took its head like a mare eager for the field. Out we sped through the vast flock of ships from distant lands—junks and high-prowed craft from far ports, boasting three or even more masts, tiny rivercraft nosing after them. I kept watch for ill-omened birds and saw none. In truth, though, birds were thick in the sky.

As the sun sank, the rest of the river widened and the ship began to rock in a way that sickened my stomach again. Dabir said the ocean's waves were hitting us. Lufti and Ghalib were already retching over the side, to the amusement of the sailors. I retreated to a narrow cabin off the main deck.

For three or four days I could hold little solid food and lived chiefly on broth and water that possessed an odd, metallic taint; the fare matched my mood. The only good thing to come of my seclusion was that my mustache had partly regrown. My eyebrow still appeared stubbly and my beard mismatched despite my efforts. Perhaps if the ship did not rock so much I would have done better, but I resolved to find a barber upon landfall.

When I finally emerged on the worn planks of the main deck, who should I first spot but the poet. The sun was high and bright in a clear blue sky, the ocean calm. The wind came from my left. It was a beautiful day, and for whatever reason the ship's rocking had ceased to trouble me. This was by necessity a larger ship than the river vessel, with greater canvas and higher decks. There were more sailors, too, though they did not look very different from the rivermen. The weight in my heart had lightened but a little.

The poet looked up from where he sat by the rail. I had not considered him closely in a while. He seemed thinner, and his long face with its high forehead struck me now as more tragic and weather-beaten than arrogant. "Peace be upon you, Captain."

"And upon you, Hamil," I answered warily. Truly, I expected a jibe at my expense at any moment.

"Your complexion looks almost normal."

I hazarded a guess. "Are you writing a poem about that?"

"Nay." He scribbled down another word or two as I started past him. "I am working on a memorial."

I stopped then. "For whom?"

"I mean to write one for your nephew, but . . . do you recall the captain's son? Little Abdul?"

I told him that I did.

"He leapt with me into the water," the poet said quietly. And he had me; I stepped closer as he paused to choose words, for I wished to hear what he would say.

"He could not swim that well. I am no strong swimmer myself," the poet conceded, "but I strove to aid him. We were almost to the shore when he slipped away from me. He just . . . went under. I reached for him. I touched only feathers of his hair as he went down. It was as if he ceased to try."

I had not expected to be in sympathy with the poet, in any way, this day or ever.

"I could have saved him had I been a better swimmer," he said mournfully.

"Nay, his fate was writ."

"Was it? If I learn nothing else from this trip I have learned that I must become a better swimmer."

That gave me pause, and I looked away, wondering what lesson I would be taking home, and what my reception would be. Even if we were to succeed now, Jaffar could not be pleased. We had lost his niece, after all, and she had been in my care. I considered the horizon, which seemed to bob as the ship nodded up and down upon the waves. The solitary figure near the point of the ship, I realized, was Dabir, standing with his back to us. I would have to speak with him. Soon. I delayed, though, and addressed the poet once more, for I feared the coming talk would not be easy.

"Are you still writing a daily account of our voyage?"

"I was at first. It all went down with poor Ibrahim and his ship."

"Can you not rewrite it? It would be nice if Jaffar were pleased with one of us."

The poet laughed. "Surely, I can rewrite it, but what glories are there to report so far? Wonders, surely, but battle is a different thing than we are told, isn't it? Perhaps I should tell of that."

"You should lie," I said, "like other poets, so that you will be showered with gold rather than with kicks."

"Perhaps you're right."

"Do you really think the master will use your account to write one of his own?"

"Eh, who can say? He has a fine hand. He writes well of the law. But storytelling is a different art, is it not?"

I said I supposed he was right, though I did not quite understand his meaning. In these later years I have thought upon it more deeply and found truth in his simple observation.

I bade Hamil farewell and walked on across the deck. Ghalib and Lufti loitered disinterestedly playing dice, and rose to pay respects as I approached. I asked if they had seen any black birds, and they had not, so I bade them to look over their gear when their game was done, and passed by. They made no mention of my appearance, for which I was grateful.

The deck creaked beneath me, the ship swayed; I rolled to meet it. It was something of a game and it pleased me that I could keep my step so well on a platform that constantly heaved.

Sails shone like white wings here and there on the horizon, and I wondered if any of them might belong to the thieves, and if so, whether we might face a great flaming hand aboard this vessel. There would be no swimming ashore from here.

Sailors on this rig for the most part worked bare-chested. For all that they were small men, they were broad, their arms knotted with ropy muscles, their skin darkened black as a Nubian's. The ship's captain, an Indian by the look of him, with large mustaches, spoke with the cadaverous helmsman, whose lean arms clasped the wheel almost negligently.

I stepped up to the rail beside Dabir and we greeted each other. From where we stood I could see the back of the ship's figurehead, but had no idea what it truly was. A woman, likely, or mermaid.

"So," I asked softly, "you plan to hand over those papers to Firouz?"

"Asim," Dabir said slowly, "if we do not, now, work with the same aim, we will fail once more."

"We do have the same aim," I said reflexively. Was he suggesting that we did not, or was he dwelling still upon my failure? "What are you talking about? We were sent to recover the door pulls."

"We have to work together," he persisted. "You must hold off second-guessing me in the midst of action."

"You mean among the Marsh Arabs? How was I to know your plan, or whether it had any merit?"

"I must be able to depend upon you," Dabir concluded with a wary look.

Heat spread across my face. "Do you suggest that I am not dependable?"

Dabir shook his head, frowning. "I cannot fully focus on solving the problems before us if I must look over my shoulder when you are behind me," he said. "You were ready to believe the worst of me the moment I pretended before Firouz."

"Why should I have not? You did not tell me that you knew Firouz!" He opened his mouth as if to respond, but I did not let up. "And you certainly *acted* like you were in league with him! Why didn't you tell someone sooner that you'd been friends?"

"I did not want you to be suspicious."

"How well did that work out?"

The corner of Dabir's mouth turned up in a wry smile.

"What else do you keep from me?" I asked him.

Instead of answering, he countered, "What special orders did Jaffar give you on the dock before we departed?"

I scratched my head; suddenly many things were clear. "So that is it. You saw us talking."

"Asim, let us not dissemble. Jaffar no longer trusts me, and you are his eyes and ears. I am watching every word, every action, lest it be taken the wrong way by you and reported to him."

"I am no spy; I do not record your words and listen in to your talks."

"But you do watch me."

"Yes, I do. And I have seen nothing but honorable conduct and sound judgment. If Jaffar were to ask me, I could only report praise."

"Oh." He sounded surprised, and, it may be, a little pleased.

"Aye! If Jaffar wants black words from me about you, he will not hear them unless you perform black deeds. And I do not think you will."

"Well." Dabir was at a rare loss for words, and hesitated before speaking further. "That . . . that is good to hear."

"The next time you act, make sure that I am in on your plan. You were quite convincing."

Dabir smiled. "We could not have conferred in that instance, but . . . perhaps I should have told you I knew Firouz."

I shrugged. "That day is behind us. Besides, if I had known, I might not have been so convincing."

Dabir's smile widened.

"Put these worries aside," I said, waving them away. "We are both committed to recovering the pulls and stopping Firouz; also the rescue of Sabirah. We will see that these things are done, or die in the trying. Now tell me. What is in these documents that Firouz wants so badly?"

"The most important of them are calculations about the heights of the doors of Ubar. If the doors that he builds don't match the originals exactly the pulls will not open them in any magical way."

This was all new information to me; now I understood how Firouz meant to open doors that had surely collapsed long ago. "So he will make new doors?"

"That is his plan."

"Why didn't he just build the doors wherever he was, and open them there?"

"He has to erect them on the site that leads to the djinn, or it will not work."

"Very well. So you're going to meet with him and give him his papers back?"

"I have subtly altered the numbers upon them."

"Heh."

"If my plan fails he at least will not be able to use the pulls for the purpose he intends. We may have to sacrifice the pulls to save Sabirah."

"Do you not mean to recover them?"

"Stopping Firouz and rescuing Sabirah are far, far more important than getting the pulls back. We shall try to recover them, but we may simply have to trick Firouz so that he cannot use them."

"I see that." I pointed at him. "You see that. What will Jaffar see?

Only that we did not recover what he sent us to find. Only that we did not protect his silly niece. As to the rest, it will be nothing but stories to him." I shook my head.

"Sabirah is not silly," Dabir said, staring hard at me.

His fascination with the girl beggared my understanding. "Other than her birthright, what special quality does she have that a hundred other women do not? There are many who are more pleasing to the eyes and less irritating."

"Her mind is amazing. Surely you've seen that? She is so swift to grasp understanding. Did you not know that she had learned the suras by the age of seven?"

"I have heard tell."

"Did you know that she has nearly mastered Greek in less than four months?"

"No."

"What other girl could do that, Asim?" Dabir demanded emphatically. "What man? She has but to read something once to know it forever. And not in the way that you and I remember it—she can recall more than the meaning—she knows a piece word by word."

Although I wondered as to the worth of any of these skills, I understood now that there would be no changing of Dabir's mind. "I see why you are drawn to each other."

"She is not drawn to *me*, Asim."

How could he deny the obvious? "Hah. She hangs upon your every word, Dabir."

Dabir sighed. "That is because she is interested in what I am saying. Especially when I talk about *you*."

I heard these words, but it took me a moment to swallow them, like a man who momentarily has a grape lodged in his throat. "Me?" I finally managed.

"You," Dabir confirmed softly.

"Why me? I've never thought of her as anything more than Jaffar's niece." A dalliance with a woman in the master's family was tantamount to a death sentence, and I had no interest in Sabirah in any case. Why would I? She was too thin for my tastes, and young. Only seven years separated us, a gulf many men were willing to cross for a comely face. I, though, had long ago supped my fill of drama prepared by the hands of women her age. "Why is she not in love with you?" I asked Dabir. "I have no gift with books, or math, or science."

"No," Dabir began hesitantly, "but she has told me that you are kind, even if you are gruff. She said that you were brave and honest."

I groaned.

"You should have heard her fish for information from me about our battle in the marketplace. She was thoroughly impressed by your bravery."

I put my hand to my face. "I never noticed." I knew my measure as a man, that I was broad-shouldered and tall, and clear-eyed. I was no stranger to women who had praised my appearance and made sheep's eyes at me—and knew they would do so again when my hair had regrown. How could I be faulted if Sabirah found me attractive? It had not been my doing. "I am through with wives for a while," I said.

"You have been married?"

"Aye. Once, to my sorrow, and once more, to my regret. And I can tell you that Sabirah is not at all the woman I would wish for a wife."

"She is not yours to be had in any case," Dabir said, as if I needed reminding. "Her family is grooming her for an alliance that will cement their power. She'll probably end up bored and lonely in some rich man's harem," he added, "all her talents wasted."

I could not help thinking that we would all be better off if she'd already *been* married. "I pray that Jaffar does not find out about this. You do not think the prophecy referred to me losing my life over her, do you?" I could not imagine that I might fall for the slip of a girl, but are we not all slaves to fate?

Dabir snapped his fingers again. "That for the prophecy."

"The bowls were switched, weren't they?" I asked. "You have lost your heart to the master's niece."

His sigh told me all I needed to know. "The bowls were not switched," he said, "I watched the woman the whole of the time. As for Sabirah . . . Sabirah is young, and impulsive. And she is beyond my station."

I felt for him then and knew not what to say. Even if he had watched the fortune-teller closely it was clear to me now that there had been a mistake. I decided to change the course of the conversation. "This whole rescue would be easier had we more soldiers."

"The governor would not give us more—he is miserly, or suspicious, or does not wish to aid an enterprise he thinks will fail. It was all I could do to procure a ship." Dabir frowned. "He was more hindrance than aid, though when he told me I could take only one of his smallest ships, he did not forbid me from taking his swiftest."

"How do we oppose Firouz with but me and you and Lufti and Ghalib?"

"I have thought long upon that."

"Ah' Sila must be a secure place for Firouz, else he would have arranged for this exchange in Basra."

"Yes," Dabir answered.

"He is sure to have more men there."

"This I know."

"And how will we stop Firouz's sorcery?"

"I have a few ideas. Where do you think I was when Firouz took the pulls?"

"Finding supplies?"

"In a way. I thought it likely Firouz would strike again, and I sought tools to aid us."

"Where? What tools?"

"All will become clear. Now, let us discuss strategy."

After only a few moments I understood that while I had been wrestling with grief and the sickness of the sea Dabir had assembled the components of a plan. Dabir's cleverness was not in the creation of an overly complex scheme—for those tend to unravel—but in certain preparations that Firouz would be unlikely to anticipate. After a quarter hour I understood Dabir's aim well enough to carry out his orders, though it was not time to do so for another day and a half.

God blessed us with calm waters, clear skies, and a fair wind, and thus we reached the coast in good time. Ghalib, Lufti, and myself left the ship three hours north of Ah' Sila and made our way down on foot. If we were questioned we were to say that we had been set adrift after a pirate attack—but we were to avoid conversation if possible.

Our seaside trek was warm, the terrain scrubby and ill-favored, even if it was not true desert. The water in our skins was somewhat stale from long days in the ship's casks, but it was good against our lips.

Before very long we saw the flat outline of a village on the horizon. Only a minaret and a handful of buildings rose higher than a single story. Lufti relayed that the sailors had discussed the place with scant praise, and in a little over an hour it was clear to us all that Ah' Sila was no garden spot. The buildings along the village's winding streets were crumbling, poorly tended, and held together more by encrusting dirt than any mortar that happened to linger between their bricks. Most of the folk seemed unfamiliar with the habit of cleanliness, or it may be that they did not chance entering the bathhouse, against which slouching, shift-eyed ruffians leaned and watched passersby like vultures. Almost no plants were to be seen, and no public gardens were anywhere in evidence, only weeds, which grew up along the sides of some buildings where men lay, dead or drunk. We were not inclined to look close enough to learn the difference.

Ah' Sila was a village developed by trade, and thus there were a half-dozen caravanserais on its outskirts. It was not a matter of choosing the best of the caravanserais so much as avoiding the worst. I settled on one in short order, then retired to a room above an empty stall and sent off my soldiers. Any or all of Firouz's men might know me on sight, but were unlikely to recognize Lufti and Ghalib.

I spent an anxious hour there after evening prayers—for I did not go to the mosque to answer the muezzin's call—sharpening my sword and awaiting their return. They came back with provisions and, better, report of a meeting with Hamil, who had been playing for coins down by the wharf and managed to pass on a message from Dabir. The scholar had drafted a succinct note: he was to meet Firouz in the marketplace at the tenth hour of the night. No other communication was required, for I already knew that the men and I would have to scout out the exchange point as soon as it was revealed. Lufti and Ghalib knew this as well, and sketched out the area for me. Lufti had paid especially close attention and from his observations I made our plans. I would have preferred to venture to the souk myself, but even those who were not familiar with me might have been told to look for a big man with a patchy beard and a missing eyebrow.

The town was laid out along three roads, coming together at a central well squared by shabby market stalls and dilapidated dwellings. My men had found all the best places for concealment and cataloged them for me, enumerating their strengths and weaknesses. I soon made my choice.

We ate well, then readied our gear. By the ninth hour we were walking the market. The street vendors were gone, but the place was not completely empty, for men passed hither and yon, walking for taverns, which outnumbered all other institutions in that place. A dirty fountain spattered water into a cracked pool in the center of the market.

Ghalib and Lufti and I bided our time in the shadow of an alley.

Dabir had soaked a set of our robes and turban cloths in a barrel for the duration of our sea voyage, and we wore them now. They smelled strongly of soaps. Also we had gloves basted in the same stuff, and veils about our necks. We waited in the darkness beside a roped pyramid of barrels, and Ghalib could not leave off fiddling with the neck cloth; he feared it would look unmanly were he to pull it up.

"I feel ridiculous in this," Ghalib said in his slow drawl.

"You will feel worse if your face is burned off," Lufti countered.

Ghalib turned to me—I saw his hook-nosed profile against the greater darkness. "This cloth will really shield us from the sorcerer's fire?"

"So says Dabir the scholar," Lufti cut in.

"Dabir is a wise man," I reminded them. "The burak is a special salt that makes clothes resistant to flame. Remember that it will not protect you completely, and you will still feel a good bit of heat."

"Then what is the point?" Lufti asked, a little grumpily.

"We will not catch fire and die from a burst of flame. It is like wearing armor. It may protect you, but you still want to avoid getting hit."

Ghalib laughed in his quiet way.

I stepped closer, emphasizing the point to assure myself they understood. "If the mage throws fire," I said seriously, "do not stand still. If you move, the flame cannot settle upon you."

"God will it to be so," said Ghalib.

We were mostly silent after that, but Ghalib did not leave off adjusting the veil every few moments, and I was hard put to keep from snapping at him not to fidget.

As time went on a number of people entered the souk and milled about in little groups. They were young men, mostly, although I saw a few bent backs amongst them. Clearly they were expecting someone. Surely they could not all be in service to Firouz. They had come to hear him speak, just as Dabir had predicted.

A little before the tenth hour of the night, more folk shuffled in to the market, many bearing lanterns.

"Hsst," Lufti called quietly; "here they are."

There was no missing Firouz, for two swaggering bravos bore torches before him. He strode boldly into the souk as though he owned the place, turbanless head held high, his robes, dark red with deep black folds, trailing behind him. Ali, my nephew's murderer, walked at his side, and I bit back a curse at sight of the little man. Behind them came a veiled woman, walking with downcast eyes. Usually Sabirah moved with the pride of her station; I thought the figure to be her by size and shape, but I worried that they had either a counterfeit in her place, or that they had harmed her in some way to break her spirit. She was guarded by three cautious men in dark robes, one of whom I recognized for Diomedes after I saw him in profile. Six ruffians strolled after, their hands on their hilts. Firouz said something and waved them out toward the crowd. They spread out as Firouz advanced on the fountain.

"There are more than I thought to see," Lufti told me.

"Aye," I whispered back to him. "But look. They are puffed up with importance. I wager but three or four have any real backbone or skill."

"Where is Dabir?" Ghalib asked me.

"He will be here. Mark where the sentries take their posts. We will slay them first. Remember to stay to the shadows."

"We smell too clean for this place," Lufti remarked.

I signed for us to move apart, then strolled along the edge of the crowd toward a grim fellow who'd walked to the east. The crowd had grown quiet in anticipation, and I reflected again upon Dabir's shipboard predictions. He'd foretold that, as Firouz loved an audience, he would likely seek one out in making the exchange.

I feigned only casual interest in the goings-on, and made no direct way toward the sentry. In the darkness my gloves might go unnoticed, but not the scent of the burak soap, as Lufti had pointed out.

A deeper hush settled over the crowd, and I paused in my movements to see why they had fallen so silent.

Dabir advanced alone into the clear space before the fountain. I knew then that the woman had to be Sabirah, for she pressed her hands to her breast in worry.

Dabir wore a treated robe like us, but had forgone the wearing of gloves because he did not want to draw attention from Firouz. He carried a stoppered leather tube in one hand. His sword hung at his side.

Firouz beamed at the sight of him and stepped up to the rim of the fountain. He called out to the folk and his words reached me easily even at the edge of the crowd.

"People of Ah' Sila—pay heed! Look who has come to call upon me! It is Dabir ibn Khalil, emissary of the caliph! Tell them, Dabir! Is it not true that you have come at the behest of Jaffar the Barmacide, son of the caliph's vizier?"

"It is true," Dabir said in an even voice that carried only because the crowd waited in silence.

Firouz swept one hand high, dramatically. More and more folk were gathering along the outskirts of the marketplace, talking quietly among themselves and pointing.

"He has come to me because I commanded him to follow me from Basra!"

"I came," Dabir answered swiftly, "because you abducted a girl under my protection!"

"It is no fault of mine, Dabir, that you cannot keep track of your things."

Men laughed at this. All eyes now were upon the drama at the fountain. I slid closer to the sentry. He was no professional, for he watched just as intently, craning his neck for a better look at the goings-on.

"Dabir was once a promising student," Firouz continued. "But he labors now under the iron heel of the caliph and his ministers." Firouz raised an empty palm. "The caliph brings you nothing, but takes all! His vizier would sell the marrow from your bones if he could, to bring dinars to the treasury. Your home, your wives, and your children are nothing to the vizier, who would slay them if they stepped in an inconvenient place."

Almost I was upon the sentry. I stepped back into the darkness and slid along the wall of the building behind him.

"What good is the caliphate to you? It is a blight upon the face of creation, a yoke around your necks! Are you slaves?"

"No!" the men cried.

It was then that I struck, grabbing the sentry about the throat and pulling him backwards onto my knife. He struggled only briefly, and then I dragged him into the darkness. No one noticed. I hoped Ghalib and Lufti were equally as successful. So far, no alarm had been raised.

"The caliph lives in splendor while you live in poverty. Yet they call him Harun the Upright! Is that just?"

The crowd answered in one voice. "No!"

"It is time for true justice," Firouz cried, "and I am the man who will give it to you! This I vow—in three weeks' time, by my hand, Baghdad itself will fall, perishing not by conquering armies, or illness, or famine, or flame, but by the power of Almighty God! These shall be the hands of justice!" He raised clenched fists and the people cheered.

I wished that the miserable place had a governor and a garrison. But like many frontier towns, taxes were levied but once yearly, and it was only then that the caliph's soldiers were to be seen in the streets. None would be found this day.

"Are you a man of your word, Firouz?" Dabir called out. He brandished the leather tube. "I have brought what you demanded. I will give it to you if you will release Sabirah."

Firouz smiled. Diomedes leaned over to whisper something to him and the Magian nodded, still smiling.

"You may advance," Firouz said with royal benevolence, "so that I may see the papers."

"First you release Sabirah."

"Dabir," Firouz said with an amiable laugh, "you are surrounded and in no way able to make demands of me."

Ghalib and Lufti and I reconvened midway along the west side of the square, then pushed forward through the crowd so that we were but ten paces from the guards around Sabirah. One old fellow sniffed at our approach and shot us an odd look. All the others were too busy watching to be truly suspicious.

A seemingly resigned Dabir walked forward. Ali watched him warily, but all Dabir did was hand up the tube.

"There is nothing in here other than what I have asked for, is there?" Firouz asked. "The girl's life hangs upon your honesty."

As if to emphasize this, a Greek guard held a knife near her throat. The point winked in the flickering light. Sabirah did not flinch.

"I've given you only the papers," Dabir said.

Firouz uncorked the tube, tapped out the papers, and unrolled them with a flourish. For a long, quiet moment, he glanced over them, and the crowd was altogether silent. You would have thought those young men were awaiting advice from a famed mullah.

The Greek lowered his blade from Sabirah's flesh, waiting for orders.

Firouz studied the papers intently, and Diomedes stepped close to peer over his shoulder. The Magian frowned, considered one page with great care, then smiled. He lowered the documents. "What charming additions you've made, Dabir." He handed the papers off to Diomedes. "He's altered some of the numbers," Firouz said, almost purring. "What do you think that does to our agreement?"

It is well that we watched so closely, or we would have missed Dabir's movement. Suddenly his arm was up, and as a round object shot from his hand I urged the men forward: "Go!"

The crowd parted for us in alarm when they saw our blades. We ran for the fountain. The fragile glass shattered against Firouz's shoulder, spraying him with a colorless liquid. He flinched and cried out.

"Sabirah!" I called. She and her guard and Diomedes looked to us, and their surprise was a pleasing sight. She ducked low as her guardian fumbled to replace his knife. A more experienced man would have dropped it and grabbed his sword, and thus he perished as I brought my blade crashing through his skull.

A roar of surprise swept up from the crowd. I yelled for Sabirah to run to Ghalib, and locked blades with another beardless fellow I knew must be Greek—a minion of Diomedes, most like. I saw a gout of flame from the corner of my eye but could not spare a glance. Following the flare came a cry of agony, close at hand. I later learned that Firouz had used his fire sorcery against Dabir, projecting a burning stream from one of the torches. He'd struck Dabir but the flames had failed to catch the scholar's treated robe. Lashing out in anger, the Magian had failed to realize the obvious—working with flame while splattered with distilled spirits is in no ways wise. The cry had risen from Firouz.

I beat down the Greek's blade and slashed through his chest, then kicked him aside. I glanced up in time to see Firouz's right shoulder wreathed in flames. Ali beat at the fire with his hands. Aye, Firouz had seen through Dabir's ruse with the documents, but had otherwise played his pieces as predicted.

"Fall back!" Dabir commanded.

It seemed likely that if we advanced the rest of Firouz's warriors would scatter, but I had promised to obey, and thus I retreated.

Firouz's men, untrained as they were, seemed hesitant. Some looked to Firouz, still smacking at the flames in his clothes with Ali, others to us. Lufti let out a war cry and plunged ahead.

"Fall back, Lufti!" I called.

Diomedes himself stepped up to Lufti, parrying the swing with his long straight blade. He barked a command and a furred shape leapt up from the darkness about Diomedes's feet, clawing at Lufti's chest. It was one of those cursed monkeys.

Lufti cried out and beat at the thing's skull with his pommel.

I advanced too late; in the moment of distraction, Diomedes, teeth bared in a grimace, chopped halfway through Lufti's spine. I shall never forget the way he crumpled or the way that hideous monkey gnawed on his face as he screamed, still trying to pull it free.

I took an automatic step toward my dying soldier, and then Diomedes's eyes fastened on mine. The monkey looked up at the same moment, the black stones in its face glittering redly in the torchlight.

God forgive me, but I had my orders, and no wish to cross Diomedes while that thing chewed upon me. Lufti was done for, and there was no way I might recover his body without losing my own.

I backed away. Diomedes followed. "Come!" he shouted, and the men about him found their spirits and raised blades.

I risked a glance behind me and saw the final part in our plan—Hamil had arrived with horses. Rangy nags they were, but each had a saddle, and while Ghalib's sword kept the hesitant crowd back, Dabir and Sabirah mounted.

"Asim!" Dabir called.

I turned tail and hurried toward them. Footfalls pursued me across the square. The faces of the crowd were blurs to my left and right. It had not seemed so far to run as we'd attacked.

At that moment we all heard from Firouz, who screamed so loud it must have carried all the way to the harbor. "Get back! They are *mine!*"

Ghalib and I reached the horses. One of Firouz's bravos crossed swords with Ghalib before he could mount, but the path between us and the fountain was otherwise clear. Firouz stood beside the fountain, left hand held up to the right side of his face. Smoke curled up from the shoulder of his smoldering robe. Ali was positioned beside him with a torch.

I pulled up my veil and leapt to the saddle. "Ghalib!"

His opponent was not so much skilled as enthusiastic. Fighting one such as him was a matter of time, and we had none. Hamil and Sabirah were already galloping down a side street. Dabir lingered, his horse dancing impatiently. "Hurry!"

As I leaned down from my saddle and lay open the bravo's scalp, Firouz cast more fire. It left the torch in an arc and struck me in my sword arm. The fire might as well have been thrust at water, for it blew out, swirling off in tiny sparks. I was unharmed, though startled, but this was all too much for my horse, which was no war mount. It whinnied in terror and sprang forward after its mates. I twisted the bit to the right, forcing the beast into a tight circle; Dabir had less luck and his galloped away, with him barely holding his seat.

I glanced back to check on Ghalib and saw him sinking to his knees, pawing at a dagger haft protruding from his throat. Ali had advanced, grinning wickedly, and even now reached at his belt for another blade.

I cursed Ali and kicked my mount into a gallop after the others. I thought to feel his blade between my shoulders at any moment, but I think my speed and the dense shadows beyond the square made me too poor a target.

My heart was heavy as I galloped down a side street eating the dust of the three before me. I had lost two more good men, the last of my command. Six of my finest soldiers were dead now, five unshrouded, their families all unknowing. I imagined facing the anguished eyes of Ghalib's sister and Lufti's young wife as I relayed that not only had I failed to bury them, I had left their bodies among enemies in the street.

Dabir awaited me at our rendezvous point at a caravanserai along the wharf. Our ship was silhouetted against the lesser darkness of the star-speckled sky, a block away.

At this late hour the caravanserai might as well have been a tomb, so quiet was it within. Dabir peered behind me as I swung off the saddle. No one looked down from the balcony; on the ground level with us were only sleeping camels and a few horses, who whinnied back and forth with ours.

We led our rented mounts into a wide stall to join Hamil and Sabirah. I let go the horse and it wandered over by one of its fellows and munched on its fodder.

"What of Ghalib?" Dabir asked.

"Slain," I said. I was almost speechless with fury. I forced myself to calm so that Sabirah would not hear language to scorch her ears. "The little knife man," I managed. I smacked fist to palm. "Some day there will be a reckoning."

"God will it to be so," Dabir said, sighing. "But now we must get you two and Sabirah onto the ship."

Sabirah startled me with a tight hug before I could respond to that. "I'm so glad that you're all right," she told me. "I wasn't sure what they'd really done to you."

I patted her head, pleased to see her happy, then remembered she loved me and swiftly broke away. "What do you mean, 'you two and Sabirah'?" I asked Dabir.

But now Dabir ignored me. "Did they harm you?" he demanded of Sabirah.

"No. Dabir, did you really give over the papers?"

"You're sure you're all right?" Dabir pressed her.

"I am fine," she said, and in the moonlight, smiling up at him, she was suddenly beautiful. "Ali frightened me a little, but Firouz let no man touch me."

"He is not completely bereft of honor, then," Dabir said darkly. "I am glad for that. Now it is time to get you to safety."

"Dabir," I began, but he cut me off sharply.

"You promised to obey. There is no hope for it. You two must escort Sabirah home."

"What?" Sabirah asked. "What of you?"

"I must remain here. The pulls must be recovered now, or Firouz will take them to the desert."

"You cannot move against them alone," Hamil countered.

"There is no time for discussion!"

"What talk is this?" I asked Dabir. "I will go with you. The poet can return with Sabirah."

"That is enough!" Dabir said through gritted teeth. "Do as I say, all of you! We've little time!"

Outside then we heard the shouts of men and the pounding of feet, and we fell silent. The volume faded with distance, but the number of voices raised in outcry grew more numerous. Dabir and I crept to the mouth of the caravanserai and peered out.

I had assumed that the whole city had risen against us and was hunting us down with torches and swords. What we saw was worse.

Our ship was wrapped in flame.

10

We had no friends in that place, and no allies other than the Bedouins from whom Dabir had rented the horses. They loaned us robes that night and rode with us out to a small camp a mile from the city, where they invited us to rest in an old tent. I thought Dabir was entirely too trusting of them, but when I pointed this out he said only: "What would you have me do, Asim?"

Thus while we talked I sat at the tent flap, listening, expecting at any moment to be surrounded by Bedouin foes who had sold our location to Firouz and meant us to remain until he could come for us and pay them more.

"This is better anyway," Hamil said once he had taken his place on the rug across from Dabir. "You would have been killed trying to stop Firouz on your own."

"Better?" Dabir repeated bitterly. The hot coals from the cooking brazier we'd borrowed threw shadows across him, emphasizing the lines in his face. He looked years older. "With thirty more men dead at Firouz's hands?" He referred to the sailors, killed aboard the governor's vessel. "Better, that we chase him into the desert with Sabirah? We cannot leave her in the village, either alone or with the two of you. Firouz has too many allies and spies there. This is hardly 'better.'"

Hamil smiled glumly and looked down.

"I know the way he is going," Sabirah said with great seriousness.

"You do?" Dabir asked tensely. I might even have detected a note of hope in his voice.

She nodded. "I overheard them speak of the course to take via the stars. Though I did not understand all, I can remember clearly the constellations and numbers."

"Dastur Esfandiar never shared the location with me," Dabir said. "What precisely did they say?"

Sabirah proceeded to rattle off a series of numbers and degrees, interspersed with commentary. It made little sense to me but I gathered the information would help determine the positions of stars at certain times. "You know the use of an astrolabe," she finished. "We can find the way!"

"You see," Hamil said, "all is not lost." He fought a smile, then could contain himself no longer. His hands rose with his voice excitedly. "You must not be sad! You achieved the impossible! You rescued Sabirah! And your trick worked, by Allah! Firouz set himself on fire! And your clothing protected you from the flame!"

"Sabirah is free." Dabir frowned. "But I was not so clever as I thought. I wish I'd thrown the spirits a moment sooner, while Firouz still held the papers. I'd brushed them with oil."

"It wouldn't have mattered," Sabirah interjected. "Firouz insisted he had already memorized the calculations, but Diomedes would not trust him. You saw that he recognized your changes."

"Why would the villain bargain for papers he'd already committed to memory?" Hamil asked.

"On our journey here," Sabirah answered, "Firouz and Diomedes often argued. Firouz assured the Greek that it did not matter if you appeared with the documents or not, because he could reproduce them at will. But Diomedes was not convinced and insisted that the original papers be found before they moved forward. It seemed to me that Firouz agreed because he wanted rid of me and because he relished the opportunity to demonstrate superiority. But then, too, Diomedes is the chief source of the monies used to outfit their expedition. They seem to respect each other, but maintain some suspiciousness."

"I wondered at their resources. So Diomedes is an agent of Empress Irene?" Dabir prompted.

"I am positive. Diomedes was angry, and said this to Firouz: 'Perhaps you think that my mistress will only be angry with me, should I fail. Her reach is long, my friend. Her coffers are not so deep as the Muhammadens, but she will spare no expense in hunting down those who have failed her.' Firouz then said: 'The empress will be fully pleased with the both of us, you may be sure.' Following that their voices grew more indistinct as they stepped farther away from the wall I listened at, and I could not hear more."

For the first time I truly understood Dabir's appreciation for the girl's mind.

"He is more than an agent, though," Sabirah said. "Diomedes has mastery over dead things, Dabir. I saw him at work on a seabird one evening, sewing its belly closed."

"Aye," I agreed, "the monkey protected him this night."

"He told Firouz how he would soon have need of more black stones if he was to keep losing servants. They guessed that either you or predator birds had finished some of his spies."

"It was not us, alas," I said.

"So we face two wizards, not one," Hamil said thoughtfully. I wondered what he would make of that in his poem.

Dabir's attention remained fixed upon Sabirah. "Did you learn exactly what they intend with the pulls?"

"They mean to return from the desert with a stone," Sabirah replied.

"A stone?" Dabir repeated. "What sort?"

"I wish they had said more, but Diomedes was cautious, even though I pretended meek stupidity. Firouz is confident that what he recovers from Ubar will doom Baghdad. He said, 'When we switch out the stones, the caliph will well remember the day his people destroyed mine.' He worried most about the timing of his expedition, and any delays, for it was important to him that he return to Baghdad on the anniversary of some massacre."

"That helps," Dabir said. "Now at least we have a timetable, and a final destination. Did they mention the Keeper of Secrets? If they sought some kind of magical stone, he might bestow it."

Sabirah shook her head, frowning. "I never heard the djinn mentioned. But then they often spoke in lowered voices, and I was kept in a tiny cabin separate from theirs, so that there is doubtless much that I missed."

We spoke on for a longer while, Dabir probing for more information with his questions, but soon I suggested that we gain what rest we could.

I remained awake through the night, alert for the betrayal that did not come, thus, when I lay down for a brief sleep that morning I was not awake to stop Dabir's reconnaissance of the village in disguise. He returned shortly to announce that Firouz had departed for the desert before dawn.

We had enough money to hire guides for the desert, or to hire passage on a ship, not both, and Dabir had decided that we would chase after Firouz. When Hamil asked how we would return to Bahgdad after the desert, with no money left, Dabir said that there were many troubles before us and that one came later than others. I myself wondered if any one of us would be returning alive, but did not voice my worry.

The chief Bedouin was Hadban, a lean fellow on the steep side of forty. Dabir and I sat down with him inside his tent before midday prayers and bargained with him to purchase passage and the aid of desert guides. After much talk, Hadban agreed for a princely sum—most of the rest of our money, as well as those rings Jaffar had purchased for us in the marketplace—to lead us into the empty quarter with his son and nephew, though they assured us that there was nothing much to be seen there. Hadban advised against the woman joining us, suggesting even that she could stay with his women. I did not know enough about Bedouins at that time to take him at his word. They are shrewd negotiators, the Bedouin, but unfailingly polite and garbed in honor. Which would have seemed worse to Jaffar? To leave her under the care of strangers, or to take her into a deadly desert in pursuit of enemies? We were so far gone at that point there was little worrying what Jaffar might say; I doubted anything short of a miracle would see us into his good graces again.

So it was that we climbed into saddle and rode south into the wilderness. The deserts I had known were flat, barren, and rocky, and so was this one for the first day. Come evening its character changed, for we entered the empty quarter. If the empty quarter has rocks, they are not to be seen, for they are buried beneath vast drifts of sand.

It is hard to portray the lonely immensity of the place with any justice. The brown dunes roll to the horizon, rising sometimes for hundreds of feet, gentle on one side and precipitous upon the other. From the height of the greatest of them one can see far, and the monotony of the view both disheartens and inspires awe. There is nothing to be seen but the dunes, identical in their composition but infinitely variable in their shape, height, and sweep.

My recollection now of that journey has blurred the events of the days and nights so that it is impossible to separate them aside from a few key moments, rising above the tide of memory as small peaks. During the days I looked always for one of the birds, but saw none. As a matter of fact, I thought at first that nothing lived out there but occasional scrub brush until Hadban one evening reached into the sand and pulled forth a small scaly lizard. Hadban grinned at me. "They are everywhere, below the surface, if one knows how to look."

I tried mastering the how of looking and must confess that I never did learn, although once I spied a tiny spider.

I hope I need hardly emphasize the heat. We would pause in the hottest hours of the day, and sought ever to move from shadow to shadow. I had thought we would move at night, remembering that Dabir had told me our way would be pointed to by the stars. Night travel, though, was too hazardous, for one could not see the footing as well. Besides, it was very cold in the night. Thus we readied for travel every day before first light, then traveled from shade to shade—when we could find such luxury—until midday, then again through the afternoon and evening. Dabir and I were more accustomed to the sun, but Hamil and especially Sabirah had to contend with its burning rays. The Bedouins, noting their difficulties, provided them with traditional desert garments. They apologized that they had no clothing suitable for a woman. Sabirah did not mind, and donned a loose white robe and head cloth along with Hamil.

During the first three evenings the wind gusted out of the emptiness and blew energetically into the night, coating everything with a fine layer of sand. The grit lodged everywhere. In my boots. In my underclothes. In my food. In my nose. Yet these were not sandstorms; Hadban assured me that I did not want to experience a sandstorm in the empty quarter. No, the evening winds were merely another dependable feature of that place.

There was no sign of Firouz. The sand shifts so much one should not expect to find tracks. I had thought, seeing as how Firouz had left only a half day before us, that we might sight them.

"Are we headed the proper direction?" I asked Dabir the second night. There amongst the endless expanses it was easy to imagine losing one's way.

"Sabirah said that they meant to follow the position Merak held on the eighth hour of the night of the twenty-first. That is the direction we follow—her memory is flawless."

He sounded as if something still troubled him. "And yet?" I prompted.

He lowered his voice. "Suppose that there was some detail they did not discuss? She would not know if they did not speak of it that night."

"Will you know if we have gone too far?" I asked.

"At the end of six days. And we will not be able to search much longer than that with the supplies we have."

"God give that the girl overheard all that there was to learn," I said.

Sabirah was no longer the girl holding court, as she had been upon our river travel. She was more subdued. But though the heat and the thirst encouraged silence upon our travel, it did not altogether still her tongue. Of the Bedouins she asked many questions concerning the desert and camels. Always the Bedouins were courteous and polite. From time to time she would look over at me with a curious, questing look, but I in no way encouraged her attentions.

Except during a few short evening hours, all of us spoke less than was our habit, even Hamil. Perhaps it was the place imposing its spirit upon us. The dunes crouched like hungry cats, a force both patient and irresistible. Only the camels seemed unaffected by the environs. They snorted, they snuffed, they bayed. They made noxious noises and smells.

At least my she-camel, Ghadah, was a cooperative creature. Dabir's was stubborn in the mornings; mine never gave me a moment of trouble. Indeed, if God had fashioned more camels in her likeness it might be that everyone in the world would have desired the beasts. It took me a few days to accustom myself to her gait, for camels run differently from horses. Both legs on one side move, then both legs on the other, imparting a swaying motion. It is not unpleasant. One always hears about the trouble mounting the animals; the trick is to twist their head to one side as you climb into the saddle. You must lean back as they push up with their rear legs and lean forward as they push up with their front, or you will surely spill, as happened three days in a row with our poet. The second day was especially amusing. As the camel pushed up on its hind legs Hamil soared over its head not so much like an arrow, but a drunken bird, and continued to flutter his arms in the sand upon landing. The Bedouins thought this fine entertainment, and it was the first time I'd heard Sabirah laugh since we'd crossed into the dunes.

I am sure they thought her manner unconventional, but it was clear that the Bedouins had judged that she was not shameful; indeed, they were almost as solicitous of her welfare as Dabir, who was on hand whenever she climbed on or off her mount lest she suffer from the same troubles as Hamil.

On the fifth evening, Dabir told the Bedouins that we must talk of things to come.

The seven of us sat about a tamarisk fire, the Bedouin each resting one arm on a knee while the other leg was thrust out before them, as is their habit. The wind for once did not assault us. Venus shone high over Sabirah's shoulder.

"The winds are low tonight," Dabir said. "It is time to push on. The stars will guide us from here."

Hadban shook his head. "You know that the sands are treacherous at night."

"I have no choice," Dabir said. "We should be nearing the place Firouz seeks. If Asim and I travel on through the night, I hope to catch them unaware before further trouble may be unleashed."

Hadban pulled at his beard. His nephew and his son looked back and forth at each other and at their patriarch, waiting for him to speak. He said nothing.

Hamil, though, had grown agitated. "I'm coming with you."

Dabir shook his head. "You must stay here with Sabirah."

"You two are pledged to recover the treasure," Hamil said, and I groaned, for the Bedouins knew nothing of a treasure. "I am ordered to write all that transpires for Jaffar."

"Jaffar!" exclaimed Hadban's son.

Hadban looked at the youth, then back to us, and smiled thinly. "We knew that you were in service to some great lord. We were not sure which one."

"We serve Jaffar the Barmacide," Dabir said. "This is Sabirah, his niece. If we fail he will reward you handsomely for her return."

"You speak like men who expect to die," Hadban said.

"I must plan for contingencies."

"There should be none of this talk," Sabirah said. The Bedouins looked at her curiously. "We should strike at Firouz together. With the swords of these brave men beside yours, you will not fail, and then honor will come to all of you."

Hadban's nephew and son heard this with keen interest and watched Hadban for response.

"We need numbers," Hamil said. A plaintive note entered his speech as he thrust up his chin. He looked over at the Bedouins. "Will you and your family join us? Think of the reward of a grateful caliph."

"Hamil, Sabirah," Dabir said quickly, "I did not hire these men to fight for us. They must see you safely from the desert—and perhaps to another port."

"But we need more numbers," Sabirah said, sounding agitated.

Hamil started to object once more, but Hadban gave off tugging at his beard and spoke. His voice was thin, but certain. "It is true that we did not agree to fight. We pledged to safeguard the four of you in and out of the desert, and that we shall do." He gestured to Dabir. "You need not worry for the girl if you do not return; we will see that she is sent safely back to her uncle. Take Hamil, for you will surely need another sword against these enemies. Sabirah will come to no harm while under my protection."

"Father," said Naji, Hadban's son, "do you not think—"

"I have already said what I think," Hadban said smoothly, and his gaze brooked no argument.

"Should we not bargain?" Naji persisted quietly.

Hadban turned a kindly eye toward us. "Do they look like men of great resource, Naji?"

Naji said nothing.

"They are servants come to the end of their rope," Hadban continued, "sworn to reach the bottom of the chasm."

"We are honorable men," the poet declared, "and if we succeed, we will see that you are rewarded."

Hadban seemed faintly amused. "I thank you. Now you should rest before making your way."

"I thank you, Hadban," Dabir said formally.

We stood then, and moved for our separate tents. I heard Hamil telling Dabir that he'd thought that had gone well, and then I felt a hand upon my shoulder. It was Sabirah. She beckoned me to follow.

I steeled myself for the awkward duty of breaking her heart. I would strive not to wound her too severely. She turned and regarded me after we walked around the side of the tent. Her dark eyes mirrored starlight.

"Asim," she said tensely, "you are a soldier. You know that we should stick together."

These did not sound like the words of a lover to me. She raised a finger to tick off a point in the air, just as her uncle Jaffar often did.

"If you three go alone," she continued, "you shall be outnumbered, but if we stay together, we are likely to be an even match." She raised a second finger.

"That cannot be," I said.

"Listen!" Though her voice was low, she was still emphatic. "I can stay back while the six of you sneak up on their position at night. I will be perfectly safe. But for your sake—"

"Sabirah, we cannot ask the Bedouins into a fight not of their making."

"Then pay them to fight!"

"We have no money, Sabirah, and someone must protect you."

"But I don't need protection!"

"Clearly you do. You should never have left home," I added.

"But you'll be killed!"

I sighed. Now came the challenging moment. "I know you think you can't live without me," I said, "but you will live on, and bear strong sons to another man, and have a comfortable life."

Her brows lowered and she started as though she'd suddenly spotted a dog's leavings upon a valuable rug. I recalled that my eyebrow still resembled an old man's knuckle.

"You're . . . very nice," she managed in a quiet, embarrassed tone, "and I don't want you to die . . . but I do not think of you in a . . . a marrying way."

I myself was surprised by the defensive sound of my voice as I responded. "Dabir said that you did not hold off talking about me."

"Oh," she said, and cleared her throat. "I did not mean to suggest . . ."

Suddenly I understood that she was trying to be polite about not breaking my own heart, and I sighed. Dabir, for all his intellect, had completely misread the girl.

"Sabirah," I said, "be at ease, for I have no interest in you either."

She let out a great breath but did not relax: still she held herself tensely, hunched slightly forward.

I stepped closer. "Sabirah, it is bad enough if you fancy me, but Dabir? By the Ka'ba, Jaffar is angry enough with him already. You see that, do you not?"

She was wide-eyed but mute.

I wanted to make sure that she understood. "Assuming we survive and succeed, do you think Jaffar's going to like Dabir enough to marry you to him?"

I knew my arrow had found its mark, for she looked away and down.

"It can never be. Jaffar will send one or the both of you away. Allah help me, but the lives of both of you may be at risk for all that we have undergone. You must forget Dabir, and do what is best for *you.*"

She spoke quietly now to herself, much as Dabir sometimes did, but in an utterly different spirit. "I do not wish to live without—"

"Now that is folly. If you truly love Dabir, you must honor his sacrifice this night."

Her eyes burned into mine then and I saw that they glistened with tears.

"If you love him you must turn away from him," I told her. "All else is fantasy." Her lips moved as though she wrestled over an objection, and I cut her off sharply. "You know this is true. Always Dabir praises your wit. Use it. When you persist in loving him, you doom him. If, God willing, we survive these next days there is still your uncle's wrath to be faced. These dreams you have will be the end of you both."

She did not answer for a time. She wiped at the edge of one eye and looked up finally, though she did not meet my eyes. "I wish you had never gone to the marketplace," she confessed slowly, softly. "Then the day would dawn tomorrow and I would go down the hall after prayers and have a simple lesson of Greek, or history, or medicine."

Those lessons did not seem simple to me. "That cannot be. And you cannot love him."

She lowered her head then and tried to hide the tears that she wiped away. Before I could reach forward she turned and hurried away. I followed only far enough to see her enter her own tent. I watched for a time to see that she did not exit, and then left her.

Dabir and the poet both waited for me in ours, and asked what Sabirah had desired.

"She fears for us," I said simply.

"Ho!" cried the poet. "She fears for the handsome guard captain."

"Not so much as you might suppose," I said.

Dabir's response was curt. "We should rest a short time. There is a long night before us."

11

The new moon was a slim, shining sickle when we rose later. We bade farewell to Hadban and his family, and Sabirah, who bade us go with God. She embraced us all, then looked fiercely upon Dabir, as though it angered her to pull her eyes from him. He smiled sadly at her and turned away and my heart ached a little for both of them.

The camels objected no more than usual as we mounted. We were up over the first dune in only a few moments. I saw Dabir half turn to look over his shoulder for the campsite at the apex of the next dune. Already the tents were hidden and might almost have been figments of our imaginings.

The stars shone coldly down, and the Milky Way gleamed like a twisting silver ribbon. The wind was light, the night cold. I had not realized the comfort of my threadbare roll until I could not lie within it.

Dabir carefully picked our way forward, slowing at the height of the dunes to trust to his own judgment, or perhaps his camel's. Next came the poet. I brought up the rear.

The moon sank low as we traveled deeper into that wasteland, and I fell to thinking upon Mahmoud, and my father and brothers, aye, even my wives. I wished that I might only ever consider my first wife, but alas, when I thought of her I naturally thought of the second who had proved so wanting in comparison.

After a time the poet fell back beside me. We exchanged greetings, and then he said: "I think that in the darkness beneath the stars the desert evokes even more loneliness than the sea."

"That may be so," I conceded.

Hamil must have been musing on this for a while, for he continued: "Both stretch in every way around you, dwarfing your existence to insignificance. Upon the sea is constant motion and the sense that you are in a place you were not meant to go and do not belong."

"That is true." Fish belonged in the sea, not men.

"The desert is entirely different—it moans like a ghost; everywhere about you is the sensation of ineffable antiquity. Beneath the dunes at every hand might lie some ancient palace, vanished from the knowledge of man."

As if he had bid me to do so, I considered a long dune on our right, wondering if it might conceal the tomb of some storied king, or the treasures of djinn, or other things. The poet was not the only one who fancied wild things; I was simply not as used to giving tongue to them.

Up ahead Dabir was dismounting to examine something along the base of the next dune.

"What do you think that's about?" Hamil asked.

"Let's find out," I said.

We dismounted behind Dabir's camel so as not to tread across whatever he examined, and I led the way to his side. Even by starlight I saw that Dabir's expression was grave.

The sand was marred by a set of lion prints.

"It came down here from the west," Dabir said, "and stood." He rose from his crouch and stepped sideways. The wind pushed at his robe. He knelt once more. "Then it turned, here"—he touched the sand—"and started back up."

"I did not know lions could live in the desert," Hamil said.

"They do not," Dabir answered.

"There is no food for them here." I myself had hunted lions near Baghdad, but there was game there. In truth, the big cats were so numerous in some places that they dared to stalk men on horses.

Dabir was correct, though; these were lion tracks. I could not mistake the shape of the paw. "There must be scrubland close by."

"I don't think so," Dabir said. "The closest scrub is that we left. We brought our own water with us; the lion would have none."

"Then the lion has wandered from its hunting ground," the poet said, "and is dying."

"That may be," Dabir said. "It would be very hungry, if so."

"What do you think it is?" I asked, fearing his answer.

He did not come right out and say what I suspected. Not directly.

"It is hard to gauge," Dabir said, "as I am unused to these sands. But . . . the prints do not sink to the proper depth for a creature of a lion's weight."

"It is likely starved almost to nothing," the poet offered. "That would make it light."

"Yes," I agreed. "And the sand may have shifted, so that the tracks are not as deep as they once were."

"Perhaps." Dabir stood.

"There is something else?" the poet prompted.

"We have seen our enemies command a bird and monkeys. Why not a lion?"

I blinked once, slowly, knowing that it must be so.

Hamil let out a low whistle. "Surely not!" he said.

"It would explain what the lion is doing here," Dabir said. "And also warns me that we must be close to Diomedes."

"But how could such a thing be concealed?" Hamil asked. "Surely we would have heard of a lion's corpse walking the streets of the village."

"The thing would be dead, and easily stuffed into a sack. It would not be heavy with life." Dabir glanced back at the prints. "That would explain why the tracks are so light."

"But how do we kill something already dead?" the poet asked.

Dabir nodded slowly. "A fine question. Had I known the extent of the power of these sorcerers before we departed Baghdad, there are ancient . . . tools within the caliph's palace we might have asked to take with us. One at least would surely have come in handy now. But we must stop Firouz without magic. When I inspected the bird Asim killed—should I say killed again?—I found a shriveled black stone in its chest. I think Asim dislodged the stone when he struck the bird. That is what we must do if Firouz sends any other creatures against us."

"How will we know where the stone is kept?" Hamil asked.

"We can surmise," Dabir said. "The black bird's stone was sewn into place beneath the breastbone. I expect stones in the other creatures would be stored similarly. I presume the magics are disrupted by dislodging the stone, as Asim did, but probably not by merely striking it."

"I hope you are right," I said. "I need to know where to swipe should I face the thing."

"You're both so easy with all this," Hamil said. "So the matter's that simple? A dead lion may attack, and if it does, you will knock its heart free. A simple thing!"

"I lack other options," I responded.

"We aim to stave off dying," Dabir finished dryly, which pleased me.

Hamil shook his head again. "You needn't worry about Jaffar," he said. "After he reads my account, he'll know how brave you truly are."

"You're still working on that?" Dabir asked.

"Why do you think I'm coming with you?"

Dabir clapped the man on the shoulder and gave him a knowing look. "I'm glad you're along to help."

Hamil looked down at his feet. Beyond us the wind picked up, and the poet shivered in the cold.

"Let us go," Dabir said.

It was good to hear Hamil's words. Yet his was a lone voice crying in the desert against the wind. I wondered if that were the case for the words of all poets.

Hamil looked thoughtful as he climbed into the saddle of his camel and bid it rise. I was pleased to see he retained his seat this time.

We were off once more. I guessed it to be somewhere around the seventh hour of the night. In another quarter hour we came upon more lion tracks, and from that point saw them regularly. We pressed on with-out consulting. The poet, as usual, spoke the obvious.

"Dabir must be right," he said to me as he rode at my side in one of the vales between the dunes. "We are on Firouz's trail, and the lion re-treats before us, watching." He stared up at the outline of the next dune, a curving line of darkness against the stars. "It might even be watching us now."

"It might be."

"I can't believe you're not troubled by this, Captain."

"I'm more worried about the number of Firouz's men," I answered.

An hour or two later we came upon the track of camels. Dabir be-lieved that they had been made late in the day.

"What are their numbers?" I asked. I climbed down and consid-ered the prints with him. After a time we thought it likely that there were less than a dozen and more than three. Some of these were surely pack camels.

There was no sign of lion tracks amongst those of the camels.

"Maybe we're jumping at shadows," I said. "Maybe it really was some half-dead lion lost in the desert."

"That would be nice." Dabir's voice was weary. "More likely Diomedes is using the thing as a scout."

While that was possible, even likely, I held out hope for the more conventional explanation. At least we had a better sense of the numbers and the direction of our quarry.

By and by there came a change in light quality all along the horizon, a predawn glow that was little more than a promise. The camels sensed it and picked up their pace. We grew more alert; soon the sun itself would throw off the dark cloak that had concealed and protected us.

A few moments later, as Dabir started diagonally up the face of an-other dune, a strange sound echoed over the desert stillness. It sounded like a nail being struck into wood. In the countryside or city such a noise would have gone without remark or notice. Here, where it was utterly out of place, there was but one explanation. Firouz's men were at work building their doors. They, and the sorcerers, and the dead lion, and even dead Ubar itself, might lie just over the next rise.

Dabir left his camel and crept forward to the next dune, a tall one, to see what might be. I went with him. At the sound of rustling sand behind us we looked back to discover that the poet followed.

The light along the horizon revealed all. There, in the sand beyond, sat Firouz's camp. The tents were arranged in a rough circle, and two men sat at its center by a campfire, readying the morning meal. Their camels were tethered to the right. Off on the left, out in the sand, two carpenters worked with a pile of lumber consisting of small straight pieces of cedar.

Dabir and I watched them hammering for a minute or more then dropped back out of sight, for nothing else was to be learned at that juncture.

"What's going on?" The poet's whisper seemed overly loud.

Dabir glanced sourly at him. His answering voice was much softer. "They're building doors. Perhaps frames as well."

"There are no ruins there," I said.

"Some stone thrust up here and there through the sand," Dabir said. I was not sure how he had seen it and I had not—likely he had not been paying as much attention to the position of the sentries and the camp layout.

"What do we do?" the poet asked.

Dabir did not immediately answer. He considered me for a moment. "You two will quietly approach the camp from the right and make loud noises. Better even if you can creep close enough to chase off the camels, but that may not be possible."

"What will you do?" Hamil asked.

"When the carpenters leave to investigate, I'll crawl forward and set fire to their wood. With no frames and no doors to this other realm, Firouz can achieve nothing more."

It was a reasonable plan, and one to act swiftly upon, while there was still darkness to shield us. "Good. I will go with you, though. The carpenters may not depart, and someone will have to shield you."

Dabir shook his head. "Nay. You must live on, to get Sabirah back to Baghdad."

"The Bedouins are seeing to her," I reminded him.

He frowned and seemed to purposefully conjure some inner strength. "She . . . cares for you, Asim. She would be happier, I think, if you lived."

"It is you she loves, Dabir," I said.

"It is?" Hamil asked.

Both Dabir and I shot him a look.

"Then Asim should go forward so that Dabir might live," the poet said.

I sighed. "You're both idiots if you think *any* of us are coming out of this alive."

"I tell you, Asim," Dabir said, "she talks of nothing but you—"

"Because she loves the sound of your chattering and you will not speak of yourself. She said as much to me! Now forget Sabirah and focus on what lies ahead, while there is still some darkness."

Dabir chuckled quietly to himself. His voice was very soft. "All is clear to me." A joke for his own ears, I think. "Very well, Hamil, you perform the distraction. Asim and I will set fire to the wood. Perhaps working together we might yet escape alive. Remember that the burak in our robes will still shield us, since the clothes have not been washed."

"How could I not forget?" he asked. "When we finally get out of this desert, you will have to pry me out of the bathhouse."

We'd donned the robes this morning. We had kept them packed away to better preserve them. They still smelled of soaps, but were fragrant with other odors as well.

We divided then, the poet and the two of us, knowing it would likely be the last time we drew breath together, and then went our ways. Perhaps this should have been the time for long heartfelt words of sonorous power, but we three, with time pressing, only locked eyes briefly before we hurried on.

Dabir and I strove quickly, running along the sides of surrounding dunes, our boots dislodging sand as we ran. It is a fatiguing way to move. The sun brightened the sky to a greater and greater degree so that the mission seemed all that much more impossible. The light must have

165

worried Dabir as well, for he managed to whisper, between breaths, "I hope that your sword is sharp."

I smiled. For some reason the comment struck me as absurdly humorous, much more so than the situation warranted.

Soon we were looking down again on the carpenters. Both were bent over their wood, hammering, completely absorbed. From this angle we could not see much of the camp save for the backs of some tents. We dropped flat below the ridge of the last dune.

The horizon was changing to light sapphire, with rose trailings where it touched the earth.

Still the poet's promised distraction did not come.

"Where is Hamil?" I hissed.

Dabir, lying beside me, grabbed my arm. "Asim!"

I whirled to follow his gaze.

A beast was in motion across the face of our dune. It was a lion, naturally, scattering sand as it bounded down.

I scarcely had time to stand and draw.

Its flesh was withered so that bones showed through. Light glittered from the dark recesses of the lion's sunken eyes.

It leapt without a growl or tail-lashed warning—one moment it ran, the next moment it propelled off back legs and came for me. Knocking a stone from its chest seemed well and good, but there was the matter of the claws. I leapt, slicing as I did so. I struck flesh and cleaved through bone then fell to the sand as the creature passed by me.

I hit the sand and rolled to my side, frantic to keep the lion in my sight. It landed with a stumble, as it was now missing half of one of its forelegs. If it had been alive, it would have been stunned or enraged. This thing merely turned as swiftly as it could, fangs bared. It sprang at me again as I scrambled to my feet.

My blade swept down and glanced off the skull, merely crumbling the paper dry ear. The lion's glittering stone eyes stared into mine and it showed its teeth.

Dabir landed a handsome blow on the thing's neck. It hopped toward him, whereupon I slashed out and struck off the other foreleg.

The front of the beast fell forward, the jaw raising a spray of sand. It struggled to push itself up on half-severed limbs.

"Slice the back legs," I said, dashing as I did for the right side. Dabir raced for the left. We struck almost simultaneously. I do not think his sword was as fine as mine; certainly he was not as strong or as practiced, for he had to hack twice whereas I had little trouble cutting through the brittle flesh and bone in a single blow.

Then the dead lion lay in the sand, rolling a bit from side to side as it sought purchase.

"That worked nicely," Dabir said.

"In the light of day the idea of the thing is not nearly as unsettling."

"We dealt with it easily enough," Dabir conceded.

It seemed so harmless that I did not trouble to pierce it repeatedly in search of its chest stone. I slipped one of the mummified paws into my pouch as a memento of our victory and rose to take stock of the situation.

What I discovered was far from pleasing. Two men stood on the dune's apex with arrows knocked to bows. A few paces off I recognized a small figure ready with an arm cocked back for a knife throw. To his right stood Firouz himself, standing insolently with hands on his belt. One side of his face was blackened; the eyelid on that side drooped.

"I'm glad you've found us," Firouz said. "I have use for you."

12

After we surrendered our swords Firouz's rogues marched us over to a high spot west of his camp, where we were reunited with Hamil, guarded by Diomedes.

The Greek gnashed his teeth at us. "Do you know how many hours it took to prepare that lion?"

"It is not my fault if you chose a clumsy beast for your spell," I said. Dabir smiled at that.

Firouz turned his back to us and took in the view. I gave off considering where best to place a knife should I obtain one—for men with swords still guarded us—and studied the view myself, seeing now a few hunks of stone protruding from the sand both to right and left and, indeed, for some several hundred feet in every direction. To our left, in fact, a square stone platform poked from the dune.

Ali rejoined us to report to Firouz. "There were no others with them," he said.

"They probably had guides," Firouz said. "They've likely fled and are of no consequence." He trudged up the dune toward the platform and spoke without looking back. "Bring these three."

The light on the horizon had pulled forth the sun itself, a wedge of brilliant orange.

The guardsmen and Ali urged us before them. Firouz turned to regard us, smiling, and mounted the stone square ten paces off. In the sunlight his once handsome face was even more ghastly, black and red and wrinkled. I wondered if he had any sight from that drooping eye at all. To Firouz's right, on the lee side of the dune, a sunken series of stone merlons thrust up from the sand. I realized then that he stood atop the remnant of a tower, or perhaps even a city gate.

"Imagine my surprise," Firouz called down to Dabir. "After all my preparations, I had thought simply to wander into the city and find my portal." Firouz's scarlet sleeve billowed as he took in the sand with a sweep of his arm. "There's nothing to be seen but the capitals of some pillars."

"I hope you brought shovels," I murmured. Dabir caught my eye but remained serious.

"I have something better," Firouz replied in good humor. I hadn't thought he would hear me. "And that's where you can help me."

At my side, Dabir tensed when Firouz produced a small stoppered bottle from a pouch at his waist.

The Magian held it up to the sky in the palm of his hand, and it shone crimson in dawning light, as though it were coated with blood. "I anticipated a surprise or two along the way," Firouz continued, lowering the bottle, "and took precautions."

"Firouz, do not," Dabir urged. "You're dealing with more than—"

"Do not provoke me further, Dabir!" Firouz snapped. "I have much to thank you for already!"

Dabir said nothing, and Firouz continued in an imperious tone. "Stand clear of the prisoners."

Our guards, looking confused, moved away. Ali hesitated, glared at me, then stood aside.

Diomedes joined Firouz on the stone.

Firouz popped free the cork. He held it out from his hand and blood-colored smoke boiled forth into a churning cloud.

"What's he doing?" the poet demanded of Dabir.

As if in answer, a whirlwind rose suddenly along the crest of a dune some distance to our left and skipped over the sand toward us. Its form shifted between a dense cone, roughly man-sized, and a wider shape the height of a ship's mast, spread thinly enough that the horizon could be observed, as if through the slightest of fabrics.

Hamil whispered a prayer and I made the sign warding off the evil eye.

"He's summoned a djinn," Dabir said grimly.

The whirlwind slowed beside Firouz, and the crimson smoke swirled into its form, coloring it in bands and striations that spun until the whole of the thing was red as a battlefield. The smoke then diminished, and the djinn cloud ceased its whirling. A powerfully built man was revealed at its center. He was all of varied shades of red—a light red shirt, pants and hair so dark a shade that it approached black, skin a modicum lighter. He wore no turban or other head covering, and the wind raked his hair. The turbulent air buffeted his clothes unceasingly.

I recalled then that the old dastur believed Firouz sought a djinn. Could this djinn be the one? If so, how had he been called without the doors and their pulls?

"Again you summon me," the djinn said. His voice was deep and resonant, like a distant storm roaring in the depths of the night.

Firouz gestured to us. "Again I offer a gift."

The djinn frowned. "You bring an audience that I may amuse?"

"Nay, one of them is your gift."

The djinn's gaze turned over us. I saw to my surprise that he had no eyes, only bright orange holes where such organs are normally found.

Firouz pointed stiffly to Dabir. "The one on the right there is wise with lore. You might collect it and derive endless fascination."

The djinn made a scoffing noise. "Your lore is darker and more interesting. But here, the one on the left is fresh, not weighed down by responsibility and remorse. It sparkles a bit with purple images and dances with the rhythm of words." He turned back to Firouz. "Very well. What do you want of me?"

"The sands obstruct my view of the ruined city. I wish you to cast the sand away to the north so that I might enter it."

"You would trade a soul for such a paltry thing? Four thousand years

170

I have dealt with mortals and I am ever amazed. I thought sure you would ask for more sorcerous power."

"Nay, only the removal of sand."

"Done." The djinn's head turned and his hand outstretched. The fingers beckoned minutely, and then a spinning bubble passed ghostlike from Hamil's chest, gleaming like gold-flecked marble, and shot into the hand of the djinn. The poor poet collapsed upon the instant and moved no more.

I shall never forget the last stricken look upon Hamil's face. I had seen the end come for men before, and there is often an anguished display of surprise as though they did not expect death to ever reach them. Normally, though, death seeks those who actively put themselves at risk, or who lie in sickbeds. To have it lunge forward with such unexpected ferocity would have been a shock to any man. In that moment the petty hatreds and little annoyances that we had handed back and forth over the years paled to insignificance against the callous evil that dispatched Hamil. He had gone bravely forward with us, lacking polished martial skills, because he thought to help. If he and I had not quite been friends, we were comrades of the road, striving as brothers toward our goal. Somewhere along the course of our travels I had come to like the little man and raged that he had been slain with no more regard than a bug is squashed by an idle youth.

The djinn slid the poet's shining soul into a pocket of his robe. Out swept his hands; they struck thrice and then the whirlwind consumed him. The red-hued cyclone soared out and beyond and settled on the ground two bow shots distant. At once there rose a column of sand that tunneled through the djinn and drifted to the north. In the time of ten heartbeats, flagstones, columns, and fallen stone stood naked beneath the rising sun. More followed as the djinn roared on, and the city's structure shone clean; fallen walls, causeways, wells. Temples. Streets. Here and there an ancient roof slanted green slate across a shorter structure, and in the distance square watchtowers stretched toward the heavens. In the space of a hundred heartbeats ruins stood revealed that had not known the sky for a thousand years.

The djinn did not remain to admire his miracle; he spun faster and wider until all was visible through the substance of his whirlwind. And then he was faded to nothing, though the wind still whistled. Despite all, I could not help muttering my surprise and turned to Dabir to gauge his reaction.

Dabir was kneeling at the side of the poet, watched by the guardsmen and the Greek. Diomedes's look was grim.

Dabir closed the poet's eyes. Slowly, methodically, he straightened the man's limbs.

Firouz was laughing as he rejoined us.

"There will be an accounting with God for you," Dabir said, his voice, though quiet, shaking with passion.

Firouz laughed the harder. "You can say that? You who serve a tyrant? I am striking the tyrant down, Dabir!"

"If you had a djinn," Diomedes interrupted, "why didn't you send him after the cornerstone?"

"You know nothing of the way djinn think. Once he felt its true power he would not give it up. We are fortunate he did not sense it in clearing the city."

Ali grunted. "Why didn't you send him to kill the caliph?"

Firouz laughed with disdain. "You think so small! I mean not just to destroy the ruler, but the machineries of his government! The caliph, his ministers, and his generals will be swept away. Nothing shall remain!" The madman started down toward the city, calling to his men without looking back. "Have Dabir and the captain cart the wood!"

"We should bury this man!" Dabir stood stiffly beside the poet's body.

Firouz halted and looked over his shoulder. "Why? His soul cannot rise, can it?" He turned then half toward us, his drooping eye twitching slightly as a smile flashed across his face. "It might have been you, Dabir. You should give thanks. Now instead this other will decorate the djinn's mantle, or provide him a snack, or whatever it is that pleases him. Assuredly the soul will not be journeying to paradise."

Dabir stared hard at him, then bent to the poet and started to remove his satchel. Our guards had already confiscated our weapons and thoroughly searched us, but they leapt quickly to lay hands on it as though it concealed riches.

"Leave off, jackals!" Dabir cried. "I mean to keep his writing!"

"It will end up in the dust with you," Ali said.

"Let him have it," Firouz said, managing to sound almost magnanimous.

The thugs released the satchel. Dabir rose with it over his shoulder and turned away as the men looted the body of coins and tore a ring from his finger. Firouz and Diomedes continued into the city.

The men with us were Muslim in name only and did not pray that morning, though I suggested it would be good for them. We were not permitted to pray either. When I moved to unroll my prayer rug, Ali only laughed and charged us with shouldering the timber. "You might as well be of use in your last moments," he said. "A shame—your eyebrow's almost normal looking again."

"Give me a sword, and I shall trim your hair by a head," I said. But Ali only smiled. Little could be gained by refusal except a swifter death, so we did as we were commanded and lifted the wood.

Aside from Firouz and Diomedes and Ali there were four, two rogues and two lackeys who proved to have knowledge of carpentry. It was they who had been nailing door frames together, and they who led the pack camels.

Ubar had not been so large as Baghdad—I guessed the city walls encompassed no more than a few miles. Probably there had been farmland and estates without the walls, but the djinn had not troubled to unveil them.

Even though I knew death was close at hand I could not restrain my curiosity. How often does one have an opportunity to walk a city destroyed by the hand of God? The street was flagged with great slabs of stones cut with the images of fantastic beasts set in malachite and lapis and other stones, each creature paired with a mate. Every hundred paces was an iron ingot with a scrawled symbol; numbers or a street name, I supposed.

173

Ubar's avenues were long and straight. Those who had dwelt here would never have had to wind their way down twisting concourses of different sizes.

Most buildings had collapsed inward upon themselves, leaving only broken walls to suggest their general shape. Here and there a structure stood complete enough to support portions of roofs, slanted always with interlocking green tile made from—as God is my witness—jade. Ubar had been destroyed, after all, in part because its builders thought to rival the splendor of heaven.

The men about us muttered to themselves. One called to Firouz, "Where are all the jewels?"

"Be patient," Firouz said. "Do you expect to find gems glittering in every opening?"

They did not respond, but grumbled quietly.

Dabir hissed to gain my attention. He swayed his head to the left to point me toward something.

A shining white skull rested in a nearby doorway, vacant eye sockets aimed toward the street. With my right hand I briefly relinquished my hold upon the wood to make the sign against evil.

After Dabir pointed out the first I began to notice the skeletal remains every few steps: curving ribs lying just inside another doorway. Finger bones thrust out from beneath a collapsed pillar wrought with thousands of tiny splendid dancing figures. Here and there dried and withered flesh still clung to the bodies, which lay brown and unmoving upon the pavement stones, their mouths gaping in horror below empty eye sockets.

Great indeed must God's wrath have been.

The men guarding us were untroubled by the dead; indeed, they found the bones appealing, and if it had not been for Ali sternly warning them to keep watch of us they would have rooted amongst them for valuables. Such is the way of insects and greedy men who are untouched by the plight of their brethren.

Firouz walked the central road for more than half the length of the city, then stopped at the edge of an immense rectangle of pavement framed by larger ruins. The area was littered with columns, stones, and the broken limbs of dozens of bronze statues. A few metal legs still stood noble and proud upon square plinths at the edge of the rectangle, otherwise all had tumbled as though this had been their battlefield.

I thought for a moment Firouz was struck by the tragic grandeur of the place. He paused to look to both right and left. He chose right, cutting across the courtyard at a diagonal and around a fallen column. I marveled as I passed, for this column was fashioned with figures even more amazing than the first. Tiny warriors and heroes marched in relief all across its surface, presenting arms, smiting foes, riding in chariots pulled by marvelous steeds, bowing to long-tressed, high-breasted women who pressed garlands to their heads. The women were shameless in their attire, but, as I am not fashioned from stone myself, I could not help admiring their charming forms.

A jumble of dried brown bodies littered the wide marble stairs of the building Firouz had chosen. On either side of the entrance were long walls, mostly intact, from which two stories of empty windows stared down. Huge figures were carved under the arch of the roof; robed men working at various tasks, for the most part, although their doings were mysterious. One bent to look into a tube pointed at glittering gold stars above; another measured building stones. Others were poised over jars, scrolls, and tools I did not recognize. Dabir studied the figures with great interest.

The stones of this building were fashioned strangely. I had never seen their like. Instead of ordinary bricks stacked in alternating rows they were interlocking hexagons. Those above the doorways were incised with the scribbles that served for writing among the ancients, filled in with gold. One of our keepers cried out and pointed to the high arches framing the doorways, where emeralds gleamed in a long row, and much talk followed of building a ladder to pry them free.

"Let's look inside," Ali suggested smoothly.

Firouz led the way up the stairs. Through the gaps that had once held doors we looked into a cavernous room open to the sky, for the roof lay in pieces at our feet.

"Quickly." Firouz's voice betrayed excitement, and he waved us all forward before disappearing within.

Once we passed into the interior I wondered if Ali had been counseled on what to expect by Firouz, for gemstones were worked into the colorful wall mosaics. I passed close by one fashioned as a seascape. Its ultimate border was a thick line of what appeared to be gold. Sapphires shown amongst the glorious blue tiles in the deep, and after a long look I saw that they were the eyes of beasts hidden in fronds of seaweed. The early morning light set the jewels glittering brilliantly, shining with such beauty that even the no-accounts with us commented upon their loveliness before setting to work prying with daggers. Ali called them back, cursing them, reminding them that they were contracted to build Firouz's frames before they did anything else. Ah, there was grumbling then. Dabir shot me a sidelong glance. He supposed, like I, that their distraction would be to our benefit.

I am no student of art, yet I would gladly have spent time staring at the craft there. Time was not my own, however. Dabir and I were ordered to follow, and thus we went with the rest down a long straight corridor. Firouz walked with purposeful stride, here and there stopping to consider writing highlighted in the walls with gold.

"This is a place of study," Dabir whispered to me. "Like the library of Iskander was said to—"

"Quiet," Ali ordered.

We passed intersections with other halls, and everywhere were openings into other rooms. Finally, though, the hallway came to a halt below a grand arch. Above was a mosaic of a large white serpent with whom a group of sages seemed to speak. Below was a gap where a tall double door must once have stood. Through it we looked into a sunlit courtyard.

Diomedes commanded us to set down the wood, and carefully. We did as we were bade.

Diomedes looked pointedly at us and then addressed Firouz. "What do you intend with these two now?"

"I might not need them at all."

"Kill them, then. They are trouble."

"Should there be difficulty I may need to bargain with the djinn once more," Firouz said. "Whose souls would you rather I trade?"

Diomedes frowned.

I did not wish to spend eternity on the curio shelf of a djinn beside the poor poet, and I resigned that if nothing else I would see that I was knifed, although I still meant to slay as many as I could reach, and most especially Ali. I pretended indifference.

"Ali." Firouz pointed at us. "You and your men watch those two. You carpenters—this doorway—these are the ones. Set to work."

Neither Dabir nor myself said anything at all. Ali's eyes never left us, but for his men the riches upon the walls were clearly of far greater interest. Their eyes roved longingly from place to place, for the walls that led to the opening were more richly decorated than anything else we had seen.

I think the carpenters would have behaved in similar fashion had they not been so busy. Perhaps thoughts of wealth inspired them, for the frame rose quickly. Firouz walked back and forth almost the whole of the time they worked, trying to interest himself in the murals but more often observing the construction. For his part, Diomedes stood to one side and fingered his cross, watching Firouz. I wondered what lay between them, and the limits of trust they held for one another.

In less than a quarter hour the lintel was up and work moved on to the doors themselves. Their construction was even swifter, for the majority of the craftsmanship had been completed that morning. I do not mean to suggest that these were well-made doors, for they were plain cedar and roughly assembled. They were solid, though, and arranged in panels that were nailed easily together. In half an hour the frame filled an interior archway and the two doors had been fitted into it. As the carpenters hammered the hinges into place Firouz studied the door pulls a final time.

"Firouz," Dabir called. We sat against the wall near a pile of roof shingles that had slid through a hole above. Behind our heads was a mosaic of galloping horses with ruby eyes and gold hooves that might have ransomed a small kingdom.

"You are no different from those you say you despise," Dabir continued. "You trade and bargain with lives that are not your own."

"I am past caring what you say or think, Dabir." He stepped over to him and looked down. "You have never been willing to pay the price of your convictions. You have achieved nothing, and you will die forgotten." Firouz leaned over Dabir, a mad glint in his eye. "When I die, men shall speak of my fall for a thousand years!"

With that he turned away and lifted up the first of the plaques bearing a pull and carried it to the door on the left while one of the workmen waited to the side. The central panel of the door had been prepared with a slatted frame to hold the device. Firouz slid it carefully into place and then held it there while the workman nailed a board across the upper portion of the plaque, so it rested snugly.

The process was repeated for the second door. Expectancy grew thick in the air. Diomedes stepped up to the side of Firouz, then withdrew. The workmen set down their tools to watch. The promise of the unknown even captured the imagination of the criminals guarding us, who gave off staring at jewels to watch the Magian.

Firouz bowed his head in thought, then traced his hands almost lovingly over the stones and figures upon the door pulls, his right hand brushing over one, his left across the other. I glanced to Dabir and saw his eyes narrowed in concentration.

The Magian clasped the rings upon the door pulls, and his fingers tightened upon them. Yet he did not move further.

The simpletons guarding us could not hold off asking, "Is it going to work?"

"Silence," Ali hissed.

A longer interval of quiet followed. Firouz was so still he might have been a statue. I grew conscious of a low, tuneless humming originating from him. I think he was muttering foreign words under his breath as he made the noise. The men stirred uneasily as the sound rose in volume. I realized suddenly that it did not all arise from Firouz—it seemed also to be coming from beyond the sealed doorway.

There is a tension in the air during a lightning storm—a clarity and crispness as if the skies are pregnant with danger. I felt that same tenseness then, within that ancient room of riches with its holes where sunlight streamed down. One of the carpenters stepped back and the scuff of his boot upon the old stonework was like a thunderclap.

Firouz lifted the rings in the door pulls higher, then stepped back. The rings grew taut against the ancient metal, which clunked against the frames holding them in place, and then the doors swung outward.

There was no longer an empty ruin beyond, but another room—its walls shining with dull blue flame. The true chamber could be seen dimly through the stones, as one can look through poor quality glass and observe the distorted suggestions of shapes.

Firouz laughed with pleasure. He pulled the doors the rest of the way open and let them stand there. The two workmen watched with wide eyes; Firouz ignored them and grinned first at Diomedes. He stared at Dabir in triumph, despite his earlier claim of indifference, though he said nothing.

"Watch well, Ali," Firouz warned. Then, to the others, "Come!"

Diomedes came forward; the workmen seemed less inclined.

"There is nothing to fear," Firouz said.

"It glows like the gates of hell," one of the workmen managed.

"This is not hell," Firouz said. "It is the gateway to more riches than you can comprehend! Come with us, and see them!"

They looked back and forth at one another, then shouldered their tool packs. I think they might have hesitated longer if Diomedes had not put his hand to his sword.

Firouz strode through first. The angle of my view was poor, and I could not be certain, but I felt something changed in his stance as he entered. His very form swayed and shifted. Before I could focus fully upon him he had stepped out of my line of sight.

The workmen followed, and their forms, too, blurred and changed. I heard Diomedes let out an oath even as he stepped after; before the open door blocked him from my line of sight his clothes transformed to dark purple robes, his form blurred, then he passed from view.

179

"Look at that!" one of our guards said.

"Firouz became a demon!"

Ali's clever face screwed up in puzzlement, but he did not step away to investigate. "That's none of your concern," he said. "Come back here, though."

"What kind of treasure do you think they'll find over there?" the skinnier of the two men asked.

"None I want to see," Ali answered quietly.

His henchmen seemed willing to settle for the treasures nearby. Their attention turned to us.

"We could be seeing to our pockets if we didn't have to watch these two," the thin one said. His eyes were deep-set, his beard patchy.

"We can take turns," the other said. He was more thickly built, his beard ungroomed and tangled.

"Silence," Ali hissed. "Firouz said to watch. We watch. Unless one of these gives us an excuse."

They turned as one and I could sense them considering the possibilities. I think that if Dabir or I had moved too swiftly at that moment it would have been the end of us.

"We could assist you," Dabir said reasonably.

Ali snorted.

"We can help you pry out the treasure," Dabir continued. "You can watch us while we work."

"Pry them out?" Ali asked. "With weapons? Do you take me for a fool?"

"Nay," Dabir said. "I thought you might put in a good word with Firouz for me. I mean the two of us," he added quickly.

Ali's mouth turned down skeptically. His men, though, embraced the idea.

"Why not?" the thickset one asked. "Firouz just said to watch them. What harm if they do the work?"

"Aye, Ali. If we hold swords on them, what can they do with a hammer? Gamali left one, see?"

Ali thought for a long moment. "Keep an eye on him and it might be all right. This one, though"—Ali indicated me with a casual wave of the long knife he seemed always to keep ready—"you can have him root through that pile there in the corner. But watch him closely."

The thickset guard grumbled but assented to watch me sort a pile of rubble while Dabir pried rubies free. "We share everything they find," he called over his shoulder to his comrade.

I expected no treasures amongst the roof debris. After a moment or two of checking through the cracked stone and shattered tile I discovered a wedge of jade with a jagged point, half again as long as my hand. Normally a cracked roof tile would hold little interest for me. Today, though, it seemed a find of fantastic wealth, and I hesitated with my hand upon it.

"What is it?" The thickset man crowded close. His sword was out, but pointed away from me as he bent forward.

It was almost too easy.

"I think I saw an emerald in here," I said, pretending to root further.

The fool drew near, making his end absurdly simple. Still crouched, I spun on one leg and drove the jagged point of the tile into his thigh. He tottered and screamed; I dragged him up by the wrist of his sword hand and snatched the hilt from his nerveless fingers. His mouth was still open in agony when I drove the sword edge into his neck.

I heard Ali's curse and swung the dying man's body as a shield in time to catch the little man's knife. Blood fountained all over my shoulders and face, but I was grinning as I dropped the twitching corpse and tore across the floor toward Ali.

"Now comes your reckoning!" I shouted.

Ali grabbed at another weapon. Dabir's guard watched stupidly, raising his sword but not daring to intervene as I charged in and slashed at Ali.

My reach was longer; he was swifter. He ducked under my blade and lunged. His thrust passed so close it sliced through the cloth of my robe and cut my flesh. I leapt back, smarting, and he pulled a short knife free for his other hand.

I pretended not to notice Dabir's warden creeping up on my left.

"This looks like an excuse," Ali said. He flourished his sword and dashed in. His aim was to drive me toward the other man and I played along, even as Dabir cried warning. I jumped back, as they wanted, then spun to my left, which they surely did not expect. The lean one's sword was raised for an overhead blow. His mouth shaped a ring of surprise as I slashed half through his chest. Blood spurted and his lips worked in a silent scream.

My blade, though, had caught in his rib cage and I knew Ali was closing behind me, so I let go the sword and stepped behind my dying foe to take his instead. I grabbed for it, but he had a literal death grip on his weapon, and I was forced to kick him in the spine toward Ali as I wrestled it free. That won me the sword; Ali jumped clear of his henchman, who collapsed into an expanding pool of his own blood.

Ali's knife hand went back and I knew there was little hope of dodging. But Dabir hurled a chunk of masonry into Ali's shoulder a moment before the release, and the knife clattered into a wall behind me.

I rushed in before more knives could be readied.

Ali did not smile now. His teeth were gritted, his eyes narrow. My sword arm was sure, yet I knew better than to be reckless with this man, for I had seen his speed. My strength was the greater, though, and when he caught my blade with his own I forced it down, down. He strained with every fiber of his being, with both hands upon his sword, but he could not withstand my power.

I am not one to talk in a battle, but this man had slain my friends. My nephew. My Mahmoud. "Down to hell with you!"

Ali pressed once more against my own sword, as if with all his strength, then suddenly stepped to the side and let the weapon go. I could not help stumbling. From the corner of my eye I saw his hand dart for another knife. Desperate to reach him before he struck, I pushed off one foot and twisted, swinging wildly. I was off balance and I knew I would hit the ground hard.

I fell heavily onto my shoulder but fortunately my blade had raked him under the lip. Ali reflexively clutched at his face; it was then that Dabir stepped in to slam his hammer into Ali's temple. The knife man went down. He was struggling to rise by the time I got to him and drove my sword through his throat. I snarled down at him as he died.

"To hell with you!" I said again.

I watched him move his last, then took in the room, and the bodies. Dabir joined me.

"Are you all right?"

"Aye!" I patted my side. "Nothing deep." I chuckled, still breathing hard.

Dabir looked concerned. "Why do you laugh?"

"Because we live!" I raised my hands to the heavens. "Praise be to God! It defies belief."

After a moment, a smile spread slowly over Dabir's lips. "Our survival smacks of absurdity, now that you mention it."

"Quickly, let us slam shut those doors. We can take down the pulls and then Firouz and the Greek will be trapped within."

Dabir started forward, then halted. "A fine idea, but what if Firouz calls another djinn?"

"How could he get out if he couldn't get in?"

"It cannot be left to chance," Dabir said. "Firouz seeks a mighty weapon—we can't just lock him in there with it and hope for the best. We have to make sure he's stopped."

I sighed. "You're saying we have to go in there after him."

"Indeed."

"Fate and random chance—and more than a little bit of skill," I said, thinking of my swordplay, "have so far acted in our favor. I'm not sure we should press our luck."

Dabir hefted his dead guard's sword in his hand as though testing its weight. "We must, Asim. Besides, aren't you curious to see what's on the other side?"

"Somewhat," I answered after a moment. I scratched my head. "It is always better to fight on the ground of your own choosing," I said. "But you may be right. Let us at least gather our own weapons. This blade is notched and poorly balanced."

"They are stowed in the pack on the left side of the second camel," Dabir said. "Let us wrap your wound, then fetch them."

13

So it was that I, Asim el Abbas, and Dabir ibn Khalil donned our swords and advanced through the doors into another world. Or, as Dabir explained to me, a different aspect of our own.

Dabir, eager to be off, started through ahead of me, but I caught up and we passed through the portal side by side.

Before us was a wide courtyard with a small central portion open to the sky, and against the walls to either hand were workrooms where glowing spirits were in talk. Transparent images of men wandered up and down along the paved walkways, lost in speech that we could not hear. Two burly spirit men dragged a two-wheeled cart piled with thick wooden boxes.

There was no sign of Firouz or Diomedes; presumably they had passed through the open doors on the far side of the courtyard, a hundred paces on.

All this I noted in the space it takes to draw a breath; though I did not release it, for I was too surprised to finish. The powers of the place had worked upon Dabir. His shape had broadened; his clothes were of a finer cut, and his blue eyes shone as though manifest with the wisdom of the ages.

"Dabir," I said, "the place is changing you!"

Dabir looked down at his hands and his sleeves, then over at me. "You are a bit different as well."

I looked down at myself. Perhaps the cut of my sleeves lacked unraveled strands; I saw nothing else, however. It was then I noticed that I felt no pain, and that the wound in my side and the stain upon my clothes had vanished utterly.

"What's going on?" I asked.

"This place is a passage to another side of our world, Asim. It is like walking beneath the floors of a bathhouse, where you can see all the piping. We are seeing the energies around us. The life force. The magic. I think we see ourselves as we truly are within." He smiled. "You are little changed, which speaks well of you."

"I do not follow."

"You are the same person within as you are without," Dabir said.

"And what are these?" I encompassed the ghosts, who had taken no notice of us, with a wave.

It was quiet as the desert at midday, though all that the ghosts did should have produced a great clamor. I saw now that their images were overlaid across the city's ruins, so that workmen laboring with hammers behind ghostly stones were truly working behind the jagged, shattered wall that existed in reality and that I perceived as through a fog. The fish statue that sprayed water was not truly present, but it was superimposed over the faded structure that had toppled into the broken tiles of the fountain's pool.

"Are these spirits?" I asked Dabir.

"I'm not completely sure," he said, a thoughtful note in his voice. "But I believe this is the city's ideal self, or its memory."

I did not understand him right away. That day I was to be confronted with a staggering number of new ideas. Or should I say I was to be confronted with a small number of new ideas that staggered me. Now was not the time for philosophical considerations. "How do we find Firouz?"

"If he is after the city's cornerstone, we must find the city's center."

I am not ashamed to admit that my hair stood on end as one of the walking scholar ghosts brushed past us.

"What is this talk of a cornerstone?"

"Diomedes mentioned it after Hamil's death—they are after a cornerstone."

"And not the djinn? The Keeper of Secrets?"

Dabir shook his head. "Nay. Even though this complex was clearly constructed to gather knowledge from that djinn. These rooms on either hand are set up as laboratories. Look, those two men labor at metallurgy; those three over there are mixing chemicals—maybe medicines—from those shelves with jars." He shook his head. "Much could be learned here, if we had the time."

"The cornerstone," I prompted.

"I do not know why they seek it. Perhaps it hides a spell or an artifact. You heard Firouz—he said that it was very powerful. I wonder which building here was first erected?"

"We shall have to look," I said.

"Let's circle around this complex and return to the square before it. If they're chiseling a stone free anywhere nearby we should hear them at work. Be on your guard," he added, a remark I found altogether unnecessary.

Even though we hurried for the open doors on the far side of the courtyard, Dabir did not leave off looking into the rooms where the ghosts or memories or whatever they were toiled with strange apparatus and made notes on clay tablets.

When we reached the exit, I looked through the doorway first and beheld a stream of ghosts moving about the streets of a city long vanished. Transparent women strode with spirit children in tow to vendors and merchants. On my right a throng of men gathered to consider a pair of stallions of noble bearing. All, though, were more translucent even than the stones of our building, and I made the sign warding against the evil eye. The sun burned high above, but gave off only a soothing warmth no matter that it seemed brighter and larger. The sky, too, was a more brilliant blue than it was in reality.

A child chased a dog toward us. I stepped to the left to avoid the animal, and then the boy, hot on his heels, passed directly through me. I felt nothing, though I gasped.

Dabir led us down the outside of one long wing of the temple, or whatever it was, and did his best to weave around, rather than through, the people.

I marveled at the ancient place brought to life before my eyes. Who would not have stared at the glowing stones and the ghosts, or the city's memory of folk, or just the city's dream of people who might have lived within its walls. I do not mean to suggest that I was lost in idle speculation, for I was primarily on the watch for men I meant to kill and who would be only too happy to slay me. Still, a part of my mind ruminated on these strange matters.

Shortly thereafter we looked out upon the square. Now the columns stood straight and tall, and each was topped by the statue of a powerful-looking man or noblewoman, long-haired and large-eyed. Were they gods, or rulers? I remembered that the folk of Ubar were said to have worshipped stone idols. Were these them?

The real world's columns and statues still littered the pavement—but they were not quite there. By this I mean that they were wavy and distorted, as a distant man is when riding across the desert in the heat of day. I reached down to touch the obscured leg of a fallen statue, and I could feel it, just barely. There, where our camels should have been tethered to more antique stone, I saw only a group of shadows. When I tried touching them, my hand passed through the space they occupied.

"I do not wish to be trapped in this place," I said quietly to Dabir.

"A sound sentiment," Dabir replied. He stood for a long time and studied the buildings. Which one would hold the city's cornerstone? It could be any one of the great, marble-faced buildings that sat at the height of long stairs. What were all of them for? I could not guess, for I could not read the symbols inscribed upon their porticos, but I was witness to the beauty of the place. Gold gleamed on the leaf of the roof eaves. Everywhere the colors had grown brighter. Vibrant tones from the whole of the spectrum met my eyes, and I could hear the sounds of the city now, though only faintly, as if they reached me from a long distance away, or if I were at the bottom of a well.

The ground shuddered beneath us. My hand went instantly for my sword and I searched to right and left, thinking that Firouz worked sorcerous mischief.

If he did, then he was greater than I had feared him, for the city's ghosts reacted to the shaking with me. They cried out in alarm and called to one another. Mothers hugged infants close. Some of them pointed to the heavens.

How to describe then what next I saw? You who have never seen doomsday cannot properly imagine it.

From out of the sky fell flaming hunks of stone. The people screamed; some ran while others huddled together. The statues atop the columns swayed even as the rumbling grew to a growl. The sky darkened and the wind roared as one of the massive rocks smashed down through the roof of a nearby building. The eaves splintered and shingles flew as though they were light as feathers; huge chunks of rock erupted from the impact site.

"Let's go, Dabir!"

He hesitated a moment, then his eyes met mine, full of horror. "I know what he plans, Asim!"

A column came down just behind us, the statue tumbling from its height to shatter into pieces, one of which fell right where its transparent suggestion had lain when I sensed it moments ago.

"Hurry!" he cried.

We ran back the way we'd come. I instinctively dodged the falling masonry and running folk, even though I knew that they would not touch me.

Just when it seemed things could not be worse for those doomed ghosts, the wind rose and sand swept in across the city. A young woman running just ahead of me covered her head and ducked low, only to be knocked off her feet. She passed through the hand I threw out to catch her and smashed into the side of a building to my left, where she lay crumpled and still. I gritted my teeth as the sand that was not there blasted through me. All about me the ground still shook and the wind howled and the heavens flew with flaming stones that smashed in the roofs of buildings.

I had to shout to be heard above the din. "What's happening?"

I made out only part of Dabir's answer. "Its final moments . . ." he answered. "Memory . . . Firouz triggered it . . ."

I did not ask him how; now was not the time for extended talk.

The ghostly doors to the back of the temple complex were closed now, but we passed through them, for their real-world counterparts were long since rotted away. I thought Dabir meant to make a stand to either side of the door, to ambush Firouz and his men when they came through, but he darted instead for one of the workrooms, racing right through a trio of ghosts. Had fear gripped him so surely?

"Hurry, Asim!" he cried.

For a moment I thought he meant me to take shelter with him, but I soon saw that he was straining to lift a rounded, waist-high jar with a strange metal pole thrust up from its center. A moment later I saw that it was mostly gold, or at least wrapped in it. Did he mean to carry the thing out with him? I had never known him to be covetous.

"We can even the numbers if we hurry," he called over the wind. "Carry this to the gap in the wall!"

I did as ordered, though this activity defied my understanding. Still, when he raced out from one of the other workshops with golden chains and then set to rubbing a chunk of glass touched to the top of the great jar's pole with cloth torn from his robe, I had to ask.

"What is it you do?"

"I am readying a surprise! Keep watch, Asim!"

I left him on the left side of the entryway and steeled myself, for huddled there beside me were three robed men, cowering and pointing at the sky. I did my best to ignore them, occasionally thrusting my head into the transparent door so that I might better observe the street beyond. Sand lay calf-deep now and still the ghost winds did not cease. People took shelter in buildings. This, I understood, was Ubar's end, or its recollection of its end, somehow playing out before us.

Dabir swept long, swift strokes at the glass, pressing it all the while to the metal pole as though our lives depended upon it. I assumed they did, though I knew not how. I stepped back to his side.

"There is no sign of them yet," I said. We had to raise our voices still, to be heard above the sandstorm.

"Good!" Still he continued to strike. He glanced up at me, his eyes betraying concern. "Firouz's magic may be stronger here."

I started to ask why, but the matter seemed clear. "Naturally," I said. Why would sorcery not be stronger in a place that was rich with it? "What magic are you working?"

"It is not magic, but science. Secure that chain around the gold cup I brought and leave it near the threshold. Then take that second chain and secure it around the vase—on *no* account are you to touch the chains at the same time. Understand?"

I nodded.

Both of the gold chains were so finely crafted that they might even inspire comment from an emperor. One was looped about the metal pole that thrust up from the lidded vase. Having carried the thing I now knew that the vase could not have been fashioned wholly of gold or I could not have carried it. Instead it was sheathed in the metal. The cup about which I wrapped one of the chains was broken in the real world, though its ghostly image clung to it so that when I lifted the piece it seemed whole. Both the half I held and the half that was imagined were studded with diamonds.

I set the cup in the portal, and peered out.

My view was obscured by the mistlike sand that wasn't really there. One cannot open one's eyes in a real sandstorm, of course, or one's nose. I could see through this one, as through a thick morning fog upon the river, and observed forms moving around the other corner of the building. My eyes widened in shock, no matter my instinct to keep them narrowed. One of the figures stood taller than a human, and glowed a blazing red. I knew instantly that this was the shape I'd glimpsed as Firouz's form upon entry into this nightmare.

"They're close!" I said.

"Get the other chain out there," Dabir urged, continuing his rubbing. "Just beside the cup."

I followed the mysterious command, then looked carefully out a last time.

Firouz was a red spot burning through the sand. By him walked a man swathed in purple. Two other figures went before them. These were the laborers, also transformed. One, squat and powerful, carried a burden in his arms. The other, absurdly thin, walked before him, clenching and unclenching his oversized hands.

I motioned to Dabir and then took my place, sword at the ready. I reflected now that I felt none of the knocks and bruises and fatigue that most surely should have been mine. Instead I knew a great power within me, like a young man awakening to his strength. I almost laughed with the joy of it.

Dabir tossed down the glass and the cloth and drew his own blade, waiting to the other side. We exchanged a glance. He too looked eager for the fight.

An unfamiliar voice whined over the wind. "I can hardly wait to get out of this place."

"All you do is complain," said another.

Then came the unmistakable voice of Diomedes, strangely altered; it was richer, darker, heavy with menace. "Silence!"

The admonition must not have sunk in very far, for when the lean figure with the large hands stepped through the ghostly doors—with a noticeable shiver—he let out a cry of excitement.

"Look at that!" he said, and both of those oversized hands reached down for the treasures shining through the ghost sand. His grasping hands closed about the gold chain and the cup.

Never before had I witnessed a thing like that which followed. I knew Dabir had crafted a trap, but when it went off, I myself jumped in surprise. The moment that man touched the treasures, a blinding blue spark lit up his hands and blew him back through the ghost doors with a loud pop.

I blinked in amazement, then gathered myself. "God is great!" I shouted, and charged into battle.

The greedy laborer lay twitching just beyond the threshold. The other, bearing a large rectangular stone flowing with variant rainbow energies, hurried to step from my path. Beyond him stood whatever Diomedes had become in that place, which was not so much a man as a dried-out husk of skin draped in tattered purple robes. A bejeweled crown rested upon his head, which was as withered and dead as those of the corpses that littered Ubar's streets, and a great black bird with shining black eyes sat upon his shoulder. A sickly green color burned within the Greek's eye sockets, and his mouth moved into a scowl. As I brought up my blade he spread his fingers and shouted words unknown to me.

Before Diomedes could finish his phrase, I'd sliced his hand half off. Desiccated fingers fell away, following the arc of my sword. He howled in agony.

And then his cursed bird came at my face. I jumped back. I did not mean to leap so far, but there, in that otherworldly place, my own abilities were enhanced as well. The bird flapped its wings to follow.

Dabir sidestepped an attack from Firouz, who swept out his palm. Flame shot forth in a massive stream—Dabir did not chance its touch and leapt behind a mound of debris that existed now in both the real and imagined Ubar, for part of the wall had tumbled in.

Firouz turned toward me, a shining blue flame flaring in the black of his eyes. He snarled and extended his hands. I dropped.

I missed heaven only by inches that moment, for a great sheet of flame passed over me. The heat of that attack burned the cloth of my turban and shoulders. In that place Firouz's fire was of such intensity that the burak was almost no help. I scrambled out of the way just as a second blast licked the ground at my side.

"Stop cringing and move!" Firouz shouted, and kicked at the man with the cornerstone. "I will—"

Whatever he meant to say was cut short because Dabir leapt up from behind his cover and flung a small wheel at Firouz. Both the rusty metal of the real wheel and its ghostly wooden frame with shining bolts slammed into the Magian's side. He groaned and stumbled, lashing out with his hands. Flame sprouted from his fingertips, roasting the stones behind which Dabir had ducked again.

I got to my feet just as the burly man with the cornerstone approached my position. "Drop that!" I shouted at him. I had not the heart to cut him down, though I knew I should. The fellow grimaced and tucked his head low, probably fearing his masters more than me.

Just as I raised my sword, the bird dived at me once more. I swung at it but the damned thing was fast, and I did not connect. Again I leapt back, striking this time against the edge of the fountain. The bird cawed and came after. In that respite I saw Firouz blasting Dabir's hiding place with flame that streamed from both hands. The stones themselves glowed cherry red. I could not see Dabir, obscured now by ghostly sand, real and imagined brick, and swirling masses of fire.

I struck at the bird diving for my face, clipped away a stream of feathers. Diomedes dashed past me, holding his injured hand, the servant lumbering after.

"Dabir!" I called. "They're getting away!"

Firouz, not Dabir, turned at my call and extended a hand to me. I dropped.

A smaller stream of flame struck the diving bird, and fire raced over its dry feathers.

Firouz laughed as the flaming bird dived yet again at my face.

I leapt to my feet and slashed out; firey plumage rained down. The thing came at my neck, claws extended. I dashed to my left and cut again. This time I hit the burning center of the creature; it fell apart in two halves, still afire.

I looked up. Dabir was rushing from his hiding place. His turban smoldered, but he otherwise looked unharmed.

I turned then to our foes. Diomedes and the laborer had already passed through the portal; Firouz was but a few feet away.

I sprinted after them.

In that place Firouz's sorcery was great, but so, too, was my own prowess. My legs struck the earth with such power that I closed the distance in six bounds. I felt near panic. If I did not stop them, they would pass back through the portal and strand us.

Firouz threw himself through the doorway even as the doors were swinging closed. I reached them just as they shut and slammed into the one on the right with all my weight. It creaked against me.

"Stand up and put your back into it!" Firouz screamed from the other side.

Dabir reached my side as we heard hammering.

"One, two, three!" Dabir cried, and then we pushed together.

The door gave and we raced into the corridor beyond, ready to smite Firouz or Diomedes or a thousand ghosts; whomever had been present would have felt our wrath.

But there was nobody there. Firouz or Diomedes must already have removed one or both of the door pulls, for we had emerged into a ghostly rendering of the corridor, not the real world. There was no sign of them here, not even a suggestion of their shadows.

We were trapped.

14

Meteors screamed from the sky and cratered the earth. The ground trembled; buildings wobbled and pillars toppled. We retreated into the learning complex, for we knew it would survive intact. Though we were fairly certain we could not be harmed by the memory of the city's end playing out before us, it was too disturbing to stand in the midst of God's wrath.

We were not alone in that place: A handful of spirits had taken refuge moments before us and huddled in a far corner, oblivious to our presence.

"I wish," Dabir said softly, "that I had thought to block off the exit doors."

The ground rumbled ominously.

"I wish we had stayed on the other side of the door," I said. "Although," I added, "I, too, wished to see what lay beyond."

Dabir grunted acknowledgment. His eyes strayed to the group huddled there—three men, a pregnant woman, three little girls. "What do you think happened to them?"

"They perished," I said. "Swallowed by the sand, most like."

"Their bones were not in the corner."

"Who can say what happened?" His idle speculation had begun to frustrate me. "More importantly, what is to happen to us?"

"I'm thinking."

I sighed. "It is too bad your trap killed their man. He could have told us much."

"I was not sure it would work at all," Dabir said. He rubbed his forehead and looked out the doorway as another column tumbled. The statue upon its capital was flung to the flagstones, breaking at the waist and head. The sand, rising fast, drifted over its limbs in a few short moments. "I have no idea how to get us back, Asim. None. I barely even understand where we are."

"Well, you understand it better than me," I reminded him.

"It seems we are neither here nor there, in reality," Dabir said, almost to himself.

The spirits in the corner vanished as utterly as a snuffed candle flame, though they left not even smoke coiling in their wake. Dabir stared at the spot they had vacated, then rose and hurried to the outer door. I followed.

The ghostly storm was vanished. Yet we were not returned to the normal world. The ruins stood stark and forbidding with just the suggestion of their ghostly overlay. The colors were too intense, and occasionally misplaced, like the vermillion halo around the risen sun.

"What's happening?" I asked.

"I think," Dabir said slowly, "Firouz must have taken the cornerstone completely from the city."

"What difference would that make?"

"Firouz has stolen the founding stone of the city, Asim," Dabir said slowly. "Its heart and soul, if you will."

"Its soul?" I asked. No matter the wonders I had witnessed of late, the concept of a city with a soul strained my credulity.

"Yes. The doomed and haunted soul of Ubar. That is why all this"—he waved a hand dismissively skyward—"faded when Firouz passed beyond a certain range. He took the soul with him."

"Cities cannot have souls," I said.

"Does not a city take on the character of its people, and the people the character of the city? Do not different cities have different personalities? Is Basra not different from Baghdad?"

"Well, yes," I said, "but that is merely because—"

His eyes flicked up to mine, glowing intently. "Because?"

"Even if true," I conceded, "what use would Firouz have for such a thing?"

"He means to replace the soul of Baghdad with the soul of Ubar."

"Can he do that?" I asked. "What would happen?"

Dabir seemed frustrated with me. His voice was sharp. "Take the soul of a mighty city blessed by God, thronging with art and music, and home to scholars, then trade it for one doomed by God, haunted by spirits, and blasted by sand for a thousand years? What do you *think* will happen?"

I swore. Aye, I could imagine it now, having seen the ghosts of Ubar living through their final days.

"With Baghdad destroyed," Dabir continued, for he had pondered the ramifications for a longer time than I, "the Greeks will sweep across the borders. Our lands and treasures shall be theirs. Firouz will have his revenge. And Diomedes will have the blessings of his empress."

"The caliphate is not Baghdad alone," I said. "We would not bow to the Greeks."

"The caliphate will writhe, and some may die in its coils, but the end will still come." He frowned. "We are but a few weeks off from the anniversary of the massacre that killed his family, Asim. I know it well, for I saw Firouz mourn when I knew him as a younger man. The sixth of Dhu'l Qa'dah. That explains the timing. He means to take his vengeance on that day, three weeks hence. And from here there is nothing we can do about it!"

"It seems not."

Dabir turned to face the eastern horizon and then he looked hard at the sun. He looked in each of the directions, his brow creased. "Asim," Dabir said after a moment, "do you feel anything? Heat, cold, wind?"

"Nay," I said after a moment's reflection.

"Well, then at the least we can leave Ubar."

"But where will we go? We have no food or water to speak of."

"Do you hunger or thirst?"

Now that he had brought the matter to my attention, I realized I did not. "No." And I should have been thirsty after my exertions. A thought struck me. "Are we spirits, Dabir?"

"No," he said, "I don't think so. We are something in between, here. But think—since neither heat nor thirst nor hunger troubles us, we can cross this desert. Other conditions may affect us, but not those."

I wondered what conditions he might possibly refer to, but held off asking, for there were more practical worries. "All well and good, but how are we going to find a way back to our world?"

Dabir seemed to be thinking of something else as he answered. "Surely we are not the only people in the whole of creation who've come through to this realm. There may be another access point."

"So we'll wander the world until we find another open door?"

"I don't have the answer," he snapped. "Do you want to stay here? No? Then let's go."

We headed down the avenue toward the remains of the city's towers and wall.

The desert lurked in great mounds without the walls. In this other place even the sand was different. On close examination it proved not to be hardy grit, rough edges all of slightly different shapes, but dark brown spheres all of the same size.

Dabir and I walked, and the strange sun climbed higher, glowing but not burning. We strode up the ridges and down to the valleys and our pace was almost tireless. I say almost, for by the time the sun, now a solid pink disk, hung directly overhead and we stopped for prayers, Dabir declared that he wished to rest for a moment longer. He lowered himself against a dune. I lifted the water sac to my lips. When the cool liquid hit my tongue my eyes widened in shock, for it was sweeter than honeyed nectar. That single draught was like an elixir of youth, sating and restoring me.

Dabir, meanwhile, had nibbled on a dried date.

"You must try this, Asim! The taste is exquisite! I do not think I can finish it!"

"I am full on the water," I said.

Dabir nodded. "Of course—the food, too, is in its perfect form." He nibbled the date, smiling, then replaced it before contemplating the sky and the distance before us. "This crossing is apt to be more pleasant than the first," Dabir said.

I think he had lost sight of our greater predicament because of the seeming ease of our movements. I was sharper with him than I had intended. "You're really trying to sell this ass as a stallion, aren't you? What will we do when we reach the coast? Even presuming we can find our way out of the desert and don't spend the rest of our lives wandering around the empty quarter, we can't talk to anyone."

"A magician might be able to see us," Dabir said. "And there might be one at the village."

"That's all you have?"

Dabir sighed. "That's all I have, Asim." He stood, dusted sand from himself, and stalked off into the dunes.

I followed him. What else was there to do? We did not speak, though, for long hours. I held my tongue, for it seemed pointless to revisit the difficulties before us. Even I, annoyed as I was, knew that there was no benefit to remaining within the ruins. It wasn't as though Firouz would have a change of heart and return with the door pulls to set us free. Weighed against that possibility, circling the world in search of another exit looked far more likely to yield success.

After evening prayers we took a second break, again at the base of a dune.

"The sun is magnificent here," Dabir declared.

Surely it was, for as night came on the sun swelled as it sank, no longer pink but red gold. I discovered that I could look upon it without fear of blindness. "There is flame upon it," I said.

"Yes."

Our silence then was more companionable.

"If nothing else," Dabir said, "we have been granted the blessing of seeing marvels few others have looked upon."

I grunted agreement, but added, "I wonder if men are meant to see such things?"

"I do not know. God gave men intellect and a mighty puzzle to unravel. How many thousands of years were required for men to invent mathematics by which to measure a glimmer of God's creation? How much more is there yet to learn? There are surely greater mysteries out there of which we remain ignorant because we lack the tools to find them."

I had then the first inkling of the reason behind his fascination with knowledge and it set me to wondering. I asked, not unkindly, "How did you come to have so many questions?"

He finished chewing the date, then wrapped up the pit. "I do not think it belongs here," he explained before answering. "My mother was very thoughtful and curious. I suppose I learned it from her. Her father had been an astrologer."

Dabir stood, brushed sand from his clothes, and indicated the horizon. We fell in step.

"What of your father?"

"I did not know him; I was not so fortunate as you, Asim. I have no extended family."

"I am sorry to hear that."

"When I was very young there was an uprising in Mosul. The folk of the city thought the taxes being levied by the caliph were . . . somewhat harsh. And the caliph feared that the Greeks were fomenting the trouble, for Mosul is close to the border. I think that may be why he struck so forcefully."

"Your folk were rebels?"

"I cannot say. My mother would not speak of it. Thousands were killed in a fire begun during the confrontation, and my father and other relatives were among them. Half the city burned to the ground. My mother was forever scarred, on her face and arms, so she did not remarry."

I would not have guessed any of this; to look at him I would have thought him the son of some minor bureaucrat, raised through the ranks on favors first and then his own ability.

"I did not know."

"I was an infant when it happened," Dabir said. "And my childhood was not unhappy, though we were very poor."

His words struck a familiar chord. "This is what Firouz alluded to in the hut."

"Yes. We both lost family to the caliph's soldiers. When I knew him, Firouz was understandably angry, but charming. He was driven to learn. He could be generous and amusing. And he was brilliant. He was very kind to me actually, Asim, when he learned my own history. But I think it is ever simpler to be kind to individuals than to groups."

"You may be right. Dabir, you studied with Firouz. Did you not learn magic?"

"Nay," Dabir said sharply. "Our paths diverged. I read of sorcery, but I do not practice it. The cost is altogether too high, in both worldly goods and souls. You heard Firouz. I think it likely he has traded more than one soul with the djinn, and he will have an accounting with Allah come judgment day."

"I did not think you knew a hidden way home," I admitted, "but I had hoped."

"Nay, I have none. Unless the practitioner be very careful, using magic is like slowly slicing away layers of your own spirit. And lest you forget, its practice is forbidden."

"So is the drinking of wine."

He shot me a sidelong glance. "I might drink wine, my friend, and ask forgiveness. Enough. You have not told me what you were like as a young man."

"Me? I was impatient. Always I strove to be as my father, then my eldest brother, wished me to be."

"Are they soldiers?"

"They were. Both are dead."

"I am sorry."

I nodded slowly in acknowledgment. "I have many nephews and cousins, some of whom came to Baghdad after me. Mahmoud was my favorite. My eldest brother's son. Should I ever remarry, I shall name my boy after him."

"That would be a fine thing," Dabir said gently. We walked in silence as memories came unbidden to me: young Mahmoud racing after a young horse that had thrown him; the stern tone he first adopted when speaking to the troops as an officer; his consummate skill with the bow almost from the moment he picked one up.

"I did not know," Dabir said finally, "that you had been married until you spoke of it on the ship."

"Twice," I said. "And I had no sense either time."

Dabir laughed. "Why do you say that?"

"Well, my first wife talked too much—ever and on with whatever thought entered her head—but she was kindhearted, always trying to help. I did not appreciate that enough until she was gone from me and I came to her cousin, my second wife. They were much alike in figure—I like women round, soft—and in their talking, but with her . . ." I shook my head. "Her tongue always wagged about the faults of others or the things she lacked. We divorced, and I am far happier. I heard she married a paper merchant."

"How did your first wife die?"

"An illness that killed many in Karbala that winter. She was dead a month before I knew. That is a soldier's lot. I was on campaign when she sickened, and could not have come to her even if I'd gotten word sooner."

Dabir nodded in sympathy.

"What of you?" I asked. "Have you had a wife?"

"Ah . . . yes. She is dead these two years." His voice grew very soft. "She did not live the night, birthing my son. And he did not live the day."

It seemed that we had both known sorrow. I knew not what to say, so fell back to the wisdom of the Koran. "She will dwell hereafter in a garden watered by running streams, my friend."

"Inshallah. She was a jewel, Asim. I thought I had treasured her enough, but I think back sometimes to ill words I shared. Should I remarry, I will do better."

"It is difficult to imagine you not handling a woman in a wise way. Although how you escaped noticing Sabirah's interest confounds me."

Dabir winced. "You thought she was interested in you."

"Only after *you* convinced me."

He sighed. "I concede. Well, my friend, like many men, I'm afraid my mind is sometimes clouded when it comes to women. I dared not act on my attraction for her sake and mine, so perhaps I deliberately misled myself. And it may be she worked to conceal her interest from me. I was a fool."

"Women make fools of us all," I agreed.

It was not too much longer before the sun gathered up the last of its colors and sank in a glorious bed of gold below the horizon. Then the stars came out and if there is one thing I could pluck from my mind's eye so that all might see, it is the sight of the stars glimmering there above the Desert of Souls. Although heavens are usually beautiful and clear in a desert, here they were impossibly glorious, flaming balls of different hues set in velvet folds of deepest indigo. No gold nor silver nor precious gems can equal the beauty of that vision and the words to describe that magnificent, splendid web of light do not exist, or at least cannot be commanded by this feeble hand.

Dabir and I agreed that the stars were an awesome sight. We admired them as they rose, and stared long at them as we walked, for they marked our route. Almost I was glad that we might be trapped there, to have seen such a thing.

The moon gleamed, too, like a silver ball unmarred by the mottled circles which usually decorate its surface. I fancied that I detected waves sweeping its face. Might there be a glistening sea there onto which brave souls could venture out in ships?

"What is that?"

Dabir's question interrupted my imaginings. He pointed off to our right. A vast glow rose up from the sand somewhere to our northeast.

"Is it a city?"

"I have no idea," Dabir admitted. "It might be something useful. We should go see."

"What if it's something dangerous?"

"It might well be," Dabir acknowledged, but did not leave off trotting down the side of the dune toward the glow.

I sighed inwardly and followed him. The light source did not prove to be as close as it first had seemed. Down we went, and up, and down and up again, and still the light remained mysterious and distant.

"Is it a mirage?"

"Mirages do not occur at night," Dabir said.

"Maybe they do here," I replied. He grunted, which might have been a yield to my point.

A half hour or more we walked before finally reaching the crest of a high, rippled dune and looking down upon a shining mystery.

All the sand had been cleared from a vast swath of the desert that stretched on for miles, exposing black bedrock. Set into that bedrock were countless thousands of twinkling lights.

"They look like the stars," I said.

"It is a map," Dabir said softly. "Someone has made a map of the stars. But it is backwards. See, there is the Coffin, and the Mourners. But Alioth is to the *left* of Mizar."

While I do not know the names of all the stars, I know many of the constellations, and I saw that Dabir was right.

"Who would go to all this trouble," I asked, "and set it up the wrong way?"

"And to what purpose?" Dabir asked. Doubtless he did not expect an answer from me. "Notice that some of the flickers burn more brightly than others, just as real stars."

"Magic," I said.

Dabir crouched. "I would like a closer look."

"I do not recommend it. We cannot delay—we must find a way to stop Firouz."

"I thought you were the one who doubted there was a way out. If we are trapped, where lies the harm in looking?"

"I thought you were the one who said we could escape from here."

"Well, here is a marvel on our journey. We should stop to investigate, or we shall ever regret it."

"You said something like that before we walked through those doors."

"Asim, you told me not an hour ago that you were glad for the sight of these heavens."

"That does not negate my point! It *is* possible for things to get worse."

"Man"—an immense voice rang out of the stillness behind us—"what do you here?"

I whirled, hand to my sword, an oath on my lips.

A great serpent scaled in iridescent feathers rose from behind us, sand grains sliding silently from its long length. Wide around as a buffalo, it curled on down the dune for the length of a dozen horses. The head swayed for a moment a few feet above our own, then it drew higher and glared down with poisonous, radiant green eyes.

I have seen snakes widen their mouths to engulf large prey, and did not doubt that this one could manage me in a gulp should it choose to open. The wonder was that it had not done so when it stole up behind us.

"Do not meet its eyes!" Dabir commanded, and I looked away with reluctance, for truly there was something compelling in the malignant depths.

"You are men, and not djinn," the thing said, opening its jaw but a tiny fraction as it addressed us. Its voice was rolling and powerful; it echoed like a winter wind against the trees, or the roar of waters in flood. "It has been long and long again since men came freely to my haunts. Who are you, and what do you here?"

My hand still on my hilt, I stood tall and made to answer. "I am As—"

I fell silent, for Dabir had fixed my arm in a viselike grip between his fingers.

"We are travelers," Dabir said quickly, "and are known by many names in many places."

The head swayed—I resolved to stare at the snout so that I could see where the eyes tracked without being lost in their depths.

"I am known sometimes as the Seeker of Truths," Dabir continued, "and my friend as the Lion of Battles."

"Those are very grand titles for such little creatures."

"It is a pleasure to meet you," Dabir said. "You must be the Keeper of Secrets I have read so much about."

The serpent's tongue licked the air, and then its head reared back. I tensed, thinking it meant to strike. Instead the snake writhed up the sand to our left, then raised its head to regard us, once more from a few feet away and a spear's length above.

"You show no courtesy," it said. "You do not announce yourself, nor bring me gifts. If you wish to know a secret you present yourselves poorly." The head tilted so that one eye shone brightly, reflecting the brilliant arrangement behind us. Did it mean to trick us into staring at one or the other?

"In truth," Dabir said evenly, "we did not expect to see you here. I was led to believe that your dwelling place was closer to Ubar."

"So might a thief say, come to steal my treasures." Again it tasted the air.

"I have no interest in your treasure," Dabir said.

"Now you lie. Else you and your battle lion would not have stood marveling upon it."

"I have no interest in taking your treasure," Dabir corrected.

"Why do you have a backward star map?" I asked.

The head rose and I felt the power of its eyes upon my own. "That is a secret! Are you prepared to make a formal request?"

"He is merely curious," Dabir said quickly.

A scheme had presented itself to me. I cared little about the serpent's backward star map. It might, though, tell us how to return to our own place. We had a handful of precious gems Dabir had pried from the wall while I gathered our gear. Perhaps the creature would find them of interest? "What is your asking price?"

"There are two acceptable offerings," it said reasonably. "The first is a simple matter; a soul, freely given."

It paused as though it felt the chill spreading down my back and savored it.

"The second," the beast continued, "is novel information of import to me." The neck bowed out as the head sunk to the level of our own and it confessed: "I almost never hear information I do not already know."

"How are we to know whether you already have the information we offer?" I asked.

"You do not. I will tell you."

I glanced to my side, realizing that the serpent might sling coils about us while we were distracted by the head. Its sinuous length, though draped about the mound, was no closer.

"That seems to leave you at an advantage some might call unfair," Dabir said.

"I am honest to a fault; however, most do prefer to approach me with souls rather than news. You have but two." It hissed. "Are you sure that you are not thieves? I do not think you came to offer your souls to me in trade."

"We have no need of these souls," Dabir flung out his hand to indicate the sparkling sight below. "I find my own sufficient."

The thing hissed. "I had forgotten," it said slowly, "how interesting mortal folk could be. How did you know that my star map was made up of souls?"

"That," Dabir said with dignity, "is a secret."

The creature stared at him, hard, then broke into a long, hissing chuckle. When humans laugh it is usually infectious. This sound was as warming as the rattle of bones.

"Oh, you are amusing, Seeker of Truths. I have not bantered with anyone but djinn since the fall of Ubar. Yours is a little secret. Do you have something better?"

"It might be that I want only to hear a little secret from yourself. It might be that I have more. Perhaps a mound of little secrets could equal a large one in trade."

The snake turned from considering him to considering me. Staring at the snout and not at its shifting emerald orbs was a challenge.

"Do you have secrets?" it asked.

"That is a secret."

The serpent was unimpressed with my wit. "You are not as clever as your companion." The head lowered toward Dabir. "If you convince your comrade to give up his soul, I shall share a great secret with you."

I was pleased that Dabir's answer came swiftly. "I do not want my friend to spend eternity anchored upon a star map."

"It would not be for eternity." The serpent sounded offended. "I am not cruel. Once the map is finished, I shall release them. I apologize for not making that more clear. I am out of practice speaking with mortals." It looked once more to me. "Why, a soul, once removed, scarcely feels the passage of time." Its tongue snaked out as if it sought for answers in the air before me.

Its words had stirred my thoughts until understanding rose up from the depths and floated high upon the surface of my mind. Somewhere on that black bedrock Hamil's soul was pinned. The serpent had said it spoke only with djinn, and below us were the flickering lights of souls, in all ways resembling the radiant sphere wrenched from the poet. Firouz's djinn had brought it here, for payment, and received a secret in return.

Great must be the creature's store of secrets, and great must those secrets be, if enough souls had been traded to it for the star map to nearly mirror the sky.

It watched me still.

"I am not interested," I said.

"Perhaps you will reconsider. I think it would be a comradely thing to do—a noble gift—to loan me your soul so that your friend could prosper."

"I must decline."

"A pity." It returned to its consideration of Dabir. "What are we to do then, Seeker of Truths? Surely there is some secret you would know, else you would not have troubled to find your way here. For I am inclined now to believe that you are not a thief. Perhaps you want to learn a magic spell, or the location of a whole book of them. Many mortals desire riches? Or mastery over the opposite sex? No? You must have grander ambitions."

It was maddening. This thing could tell us how to escape the ghost desert, but what could we trade it? If we could not escape, then Firouz would triumph, and Firouz had much to answer for. I had been ready to die in service to Jaffar before; what was so different about this circumstance? I steeled myself for the grim duty I knew lay before me.

"Oh Wise and Beautiful One," I said, "there is a secret I would know."

"Ah!"

"Would you allow me to confer with my friend?" Dabir said quickly.

It tested the air with its tongue. "Of course," it said after a moment. "I shall go down among the star field. Call to me when you are prepared to speak."

It turned away, then undulated down the slope with surprising swiftness for a creature so immense.

"Dabir," I said softly, watching as the thing retreated onto the glowing field of souls, "if I trade with the serpent, you can get out, and stop Firouz."

Dabir's eyebrows shot up in horror. "I was afraid you'd take that notion. No. I will not agree to that."

"Firouz must be stopped," I said. "I will trade it my soul, so that you can escape and finish him."

"*No*," Dabir repeated forcefully. "Do not trust the creature, nor believe its promises."

"It says it will set the souls free."

"It said it would release them from the star map, which is not the same thing. It might just as likely eat them when it did so."

That was no comforting thought. What solution might there be, then? Were we no better off than before we'd found the thing? I stared at the serpent as it writhed among the constellations, and I was struck by the thought that it seemed an even more immense beast crossing through an ocean of stars.

"Why is it making the star map?" I asked.

"I cannot be sure what it seeks."

There was a questioning note in his voice. "You think you know."

"I have an inkling. Who alone could look down upon the earth and all the stars in the firmament?"

I hesitated only a moment. "Allah."

Dabir nodded shortly. "Perhaps it wants God's perspective on the matter, though I know not why. There are secrets amongst the stars, of this I am sure; it must know more of the matter than I can guess, else why would it strive for so long?"

All that was interesting, but we still had the same problem—the creature was likely our only way back to our own world. "What can we trade it?"

"If we knew why this map was constructed we would be closer to answering that question," Dabir said. "Let us see if there is more we can learn." He struck off across the sand. I fell in step with him and we walked about the rim of the map. The serpent's head snapped up. Though I could not see its eyes, I felt them upon us.

"The serpent watches," I reported.

Dabir glanced over at it. "I wonder how much time we have before it follows."

"What is it we look for?"

"I'll know when I see it."

Someone less polite would have commented that Dabir obviously didn't know himself. I said nothing on that score. "It is a large beast," I said, "and swift."

Dabir guessed my thoughts. "Fighting it should only be a last resort. It has held off attacking because of some manner of conduct code, but seeing how it so easily obtains souls that are not willingly given up, it might find its way to break that code and take ours. I think that wandering onto its map without permission would be taken as intrusion, which would be an excuse to attack."

"Also it might try to provoke us."

"Possible," Dabir conceded. "We must seek to hold its interest. I do not think much happens here, in this place. It seems to crave some kind of diversion, even if it does not realize it."

We had walked many hundreds of feet, and still covered little territory. The map was even larger than I had first imagined. Artificial starlight glimmered on the dark stone as far as the eye could see.

"It must have been constructing this for thousands of years," Dabir mused. "Depending on how swiftly the souls were brought to him, of course. We have no way to know how often they are delivered."

I was more interested in watching the serpent, which slid along below, sometimes closer, sometimes farther, occasionally pausing to look about. Whether its examination of the soul stars was genuine or merely a ruse to disguise his monitoring of us, I could not tell.

"It might have been here for tens of thousands of years," Dabir said.

"Why does it need souls, though? If it wants a star map, mightn't it simply paint one in the sand?"

Dabir looked at me sidelong and raised a finger. "That is an excellent question . . ." I had the sense he started to use my name, for his voice trailed off. He confirmed my suspicion a moment later. "We should not use our names here. The proper name of a thing gives sorcerous creatures power. It is possible it heard me call you by name earlier, as it snuck upon us."

"Is that bad?"

"The less it knows about either of us, the better. Reveal nothing. Say nothing about your desires."

It was not too much longer before the creature came soundlessly up the slope and undulated along beside us, its head at the level of our own. "Have you come to a decision?"

"I am overcome with curiosity about your map," Dabir answered. "Do the djinn come to admire it?"

"Not any longer, no. Not for a very long time."

"It is quite lovely. It is more than that, though." Dabir looked sidelong at the thing. "I sense a powerful intellect here. Yet what is intellect without purpose?"

The serpent said nothing; I knew almost nothing of what it thought from its face. But it seemed to me the beast hungered and that its eyes burned only for Dabir.

"You wish to know my purpose, do you now, Seeker of Truths?"

"I believe I have some inkling of your purpose, wise serpent."

"Do you?"

"Somewhere below, in a gap between stars, or somewhere along the ridgeline I will find your instruments."

"My instruments?"

"Instruments—calculations—some might even call them incantations."

The serpent sidled around me and swung up beside Dabir. Starlight gleamed on its scales. "You are an interesting man, Truth Seeker. I cannot fathom your aim yet for seeking me out."

Dabir did not see fit to correct its misinterpretation of our presence, so I kept quiet as well.

After a brief pause, the serpent continued. "There is such a place, and I would show it to you to see what more you can guess. You and the lesser one may follow."

It slithered effortlessly ahead of us. I could not help staring at its long, long length, all covered in shimmering rainbow feathers that shifted as it moved, as though kissed by starlight.

We followed along the ridgeline for what felt like an hour. At last the serpent stopped in a low spot adjacent to the star field but apart from it—if the star map was an oval picture frame, then this low spot was a notch in the frame directly below the picture. Easily two hundred feet across, the hollow resembled nothing so much as a quirkat board engineered by a madman. Long deep lines were etched into the bedrock, crossing one an-other in a pattern of triangles set also with round indentations studded sometimes with jewels the size of ostrich eggs. Here and there mathemati-cal scribblings in a fine, elegant hand were etched in stone, though the numbers made no sense.

"What can you guess from this?" the serpent asked.

"Do we have your permission to walk out for a closer look?" Dabir asked.

It hissed. "I give you permission. Move nothing."

I felt the thing's eyes upon our necks as we walked past and out. Dabir bent to consider one of the strands of numbers and symbols, then walked on to one that was much longer, a maddening string being subtracted and added and connected by signs I did not recognize.

"What is all this?" I asked out of the side of my mouth.

Dabir glanced over at me, saying quietly, "Think of the star map as a ship."

"A ship?" How could I think that? The analogy eluded me.

"If you think of the star map as a ship, this is the wheel that controls it in the wind."

"I see," I answered, though I didn't really. "How does this help us?"

"It is keeping us alive," Dabir replied very quietly, "for we have the creature's curiosity."

"What is this control wheel for, though?"

"Now," said the creature as it slid up from behind us, "you have even more questions, don't you? Tell me, Seeker of Truths, if you understand any of this."

"Some of these calculations are for measurements," Dabir said.

"Good, good. What is measured?"

"In part, the spaces between the stars. There is more, though."

"Oh, very good."

When monsters confront heroes in the old tales there is usually a predictable pattern; either the creatures attack instantly, or hero and monster trade clever riddles until one is outwitted. Never before had I heard of a monster taking on the part of a mentor, but that seemed to be what transpired before me. The serpent no longer challenged Dabir as a cat with a mouse, but as a tutor sounding out a talented pupil; one seeking to lead the student to greater wisdom. Its malevolent eyes followed Dabir as the scholar walked from equation to equation, prodding him to consider the meaning of what he saw. Sometimes it told him the meaning of this or that symbol—enough for Dabir to gain some small measure of comprehension. I cannot recall most of what they said for the simple fact that I could not understand it. They might as well have been two philosophers debating, or lawyers, for all that the words meant to me. What became apparent, though, was that the relationship had changed.

Almost an hour passed with Dabir and the serpent in dialogue, I following after. They spent the greatest length of time considering a complex equation at the root of an intersection of many of the lines. After the prodding of the serpent, Dabir's face suddenly cleared and lit in amazement.

"What is all this?" I asked.

"He will not understand," the serpent said.

"All this . . ." Dabir's voice trailed off as he mused. "This vast field is like the furnace where heat is stored prior to forging."

I struggled for meaning. "Does he mean to make a weapon?"

"No . . ."

"He will not understand," the creature repeated.

"If an attentive student does not understand, it is the teacher's fault," Dabir told the thing, though not unkindly.

"If the student has not the wit," the serpent countered, "what can be done?"

Dabir ignored the question and addressed me. "This map is like a net that has gathered fishes—but the fishes are heat. Do you see? If enough fishes are gathered, then a large fire will blaze up."

That really didn't help me either. "What will he do with a fire?"

"It is not a fire," Dabir said, confusing me further, "but it is *like* a fire. A power. He has gathered power. He has harnessed these souls, like horses, to carry him."

"That is interestingly put," the serpent said. "Long ago—long beyond your human understanding of time, when you and your friend were not even a dream of the things that slept in the primordial slime, my folk"—it paused, hissed—"came here."

So much was missing from this pronouncement. From where had they come? Why? Had they come of their own volition?

"We immediately set to building a power field. It did not have to

215

have the power of the one above us, just the semblance of it. One by one the others drifted away or died. I alone remain. And someday, soon, I shall have enough power to return to my homeland."

"Where is your homeland?" Dabir asked.

The thing's head lowered closer to his. When it spoke, it was a conspirational whisper. "Get this one to give up his soul, and I shall tell you."

"I will not ask him," Dabir said.

"I will do better. Give up his soul, and you may stay with me, and labor, and learn secrets no man living has ever dreamt of. You barely perceive three dimensions of this tiny spinning rock—I can show you the universe, Seeker of Truths. You can travel with me to the depths of the cosmos!" It paused briefly, then lowered its voice. "I had not thought," it confessed, "that I was lonely until I fell into conversation with you."

It may be that I saw longing flare in Dabir's eyes at that moment. Certainly there was an electric tension in his posture. Recall that here, in this other realm, his eyes blazed. Well, at that moment they burned hotter, like the blue flame that is strongest at the hearth's center.

"There are things that I must do," Dabir said. "Here, upon the earth."

"Earth is nothing," the creature said. "We are prisoners here. I offer you the key to the door that closes us in. Be not so quick to disregard my offer. The creatures about you are insects crawling over dung! Why care you for their troubles? You and I can swim amongst the suns!"

"I cannot agree to what you ask," Dabir said resolutely.

The serpent hissed at him. "I thought you understood what I do here." The scales set some five feet below its head fluttered. Two spindly limbs, ghastly white, unfolded themselves from the body at a man's length below its jaw. I mouthed a blessing, for at the end of those limbs were scrawny skeletal hands ending in fragile, four jointed fingers. They had a semblance to human hands, save that a thumb offered itself on either side of the palm. "I shall show you something," it announced.

The serpent's body slid forward to the intersection of multiple lines below the equation and there those ghastly fingers manipulated jewels I had not noticed set into hollows. One it set skidding away on its track. Another it rotated. "Come, Seeker of Truths," it said as it worked. "Tell me what you see."

Dabir was either fearless or trusting, for he stepped closer to that thing than ever and bent down beside it. I tightened my hand upon my hilt, knowing that I could not smite it before it struck Dabir.

"Clear your head and look just above the juncture of the lines."

I contemplated the point it indicated, seeing there a kind of haze one might observe rising from the sand at midday.

Dabir looked, and gasped. "Subhan'Allah. It is the face of the moon!"

"It is nothing. We can gaze upon the surface of the stars. We can look upon the planets of stars throughout the heavens. We can journey there. We can journey to whichever place we desire. We can know all there is to be known."

"You said that we might travel there?"

"Oh, yes. That we shall do."

"Why have you not traveled yet?" Dabir asked.

"I have far to go," the thing answered. "I am close. Very close. But I have not yet gathered all the power to project me the full distance."

"Can we look upon the earth?" Dabir said.

"Why would you wish to do so?"

"Show me something that I already know. This desert, say."

"I thought you more imaginative." Still, the thing shifted gemstones, going so far as to bring some back that it had sent spinning off in their tracks.

Dabir's attention was so centered upon its doings that I do not believe he blinked.

"Look there, now."

Dabir's gaze settled upon the hazy place the monster had already shown him. This time I inspected it more carefully. The longer I stared, the clearer it struck me that there was more there than I first had seen. Through that haze, beyond it, fluttering like a moth at the edge of my vision, lay a proper landscape. I narrowed my eyes, like a dazed man intent on keeping the world from spinning. I swear that I stared so hard my head ached.

And a desert of earth, lying below a blanket of stars, appeared before me.

"You see?" the serpent asked of Dabir. "You may look upon as dull a setting as you desire."

"Thus do you gain your knowledge," Dabir said.

"In part. Mundane doings interest me little."

"Is it possible to focus upon a single being, or group of them?"

My head throbbed and my vision wavered; staring with such concentration was more than I could endure, and, indeed, there seemed no call for it. I let my attention go and once more the stark unreality of this new world shone vividly on every hand—the gleaming black earth, the dark humpbacked dunes, the impossible, haunting beauty of the night sky, the immense serpent with its lambent green eyes.

"It is," the serpent answered. "Though rarely is there a single mortal being worth the observation."

"How do you find them?"

"If I seek a djinn with which I have had contact, I hold their image in my mind as I search the map. You are inquisitive, Seeker of Truths."

"And you could use the same process to join them, if you wish."

"Somewhat," the serpent answered. "It is not that simple. It requires little energy to view a place, more to step through once the place appears before you." It stared at him, unblinking, then seemed to come to a decision. It turned and lowered into position once more. "You could be taught to do it, I think. Once you have seen the marvels beyond, you will have the scope to appreciate the limitations of this plane." It raised up, facing Dabir, and folded those awful arms back into its body. It slid back.

"Now you have seen what you might learn."

"I begin to understand." Dabir bowed his head in respect. "But I must know, wise one. My people believe that it is forbidden to take an innocent life. I infer that these souls are your power source. Are they not

218

like logs tossed upon the fire, which are consumed as they furnish heat? Will these souls not perish as you work your scheme?"

"Your thinking is too pedestrian, Seeker of Truths, for a mind so able. You are rooted to your time and place. You no longer need to be so. Now, though, you must decide."

"I must consult with my friend."

The monster stared at Dabir, saying nothing for a long moment.

"I will wait only a little while, Seeker of Truths, before I lose interest in your decision and regret the time I have spent upon you. You may speak with the lesser one over there, away from the grid."

Dabir bowed his head once more. The thing watched us as we retreated, my hand on my sword.

We walked up the dune for some hundred feet. Dabir turned its back on the thing while he spoke to me; I turned to the side so that I might watch them both. It did not leave off staring.

"I think that I can get us home," Dabir said.

"The creature will not permit it."

"Indeed not. We must return, later, and hope to manipulate the instruments before it senses our presence." Dabir's glowing eyes sought mine. "We may have to fight it."

I didn't relish that prospect, but I nodded once. "This is our way back."

"Most likely." Dabir massaged his forehead. "So long as I can recall the creature's motions."

"Do you?"

"It is a dangerous thing, my friend. I understand only the movements it made, not the reasons. The result, not the meaning."

The creature's head lowered—its tongue flickered toward us, and then the serpent slid effortlessly through the gem board where it controlled its sorcery and onto the sand. For a creature so large I was struck again by its speed.

"It's coming," I said.

"I shall make apologies and say we will depart."

"What if it does not permit that?"

Dabir watched the serpent's inexorable approach. "Do you think you can hold it?"

He must have read my doubt in the look I gave him, for he answered swiftly, "Do not forget your heightened speed and strength here. I need only a moment."

"God gives," I said, though I had no faith I could hinder it for very long, or survive the trial.

The thing stopped before us, its head leaning over from a height of two men. Gone was any pretense of civility, any intimation of comfort, or the suggestion of a meeting between equals. I widened my stance.

"Your time is at hand, Seeker of Truths. To you I have gifted my time, infinitely more valuable than you simple beings can perceive. You have given me nothing. Now I am owed."

Dabir bowed. "I am grateful to you for the consideration you have shown me. I will happily impart information to you."

"I am no longer interested in information."

I sidled to the left. Why should we make it simple for the beast to keep both of us in its sights?

"You do not know the information I hold."

"I can know all, once I have your soul."

"I do not freely give it," Dabir said.

I took another step left. The serpent's long length rotated in the sand toward me, a long wall of scaled muscle, for the feathers did not conceal its belly.

"I shall either have one soul, or two, depending upon your choice, man, and you must decide now." The head rose up above Dabir.

If I was to distract it, now was the time. I made a rude noise.

The thing's head turned toward me, and the tongue licked out. I grasped my sheath and unslung my curved blade. "This is what the wisdom of ages has made of you? How many human lifetimes have you skulked in the desert, serpent? To achieve what?" I continued to step to the left, hoping Dabir would take the hint and move. So far he only watched.

"You prattle on about your mighty intellect," I continued, "but you bargain like an innkeeper. Nay, like a moneylender."

"Do you mean to insult me, man? Do you think your opinion carries any value? I am as far above you as you are above the worm."

"And yet you would spend the whole of creation digging in the sand and robbing wayfarers! What mighty work!"

It reared up, and for the first time I saw a frill of feathers rising along the back of its head. These shook back and forth.

I saw Dabir poised to spring, watching me. Did I truly have the beast's attention? "You are nothing more than a thief," I said, "stealing the gifts of Allah, shielding your honor with grand words! You hoard souls like stinking beetles hoard dung! Who is closer to the worm, wyrm? Is it me, or you, who slith—"

Feathered lightning streamed toward me. The serpent's maw spread in a death grin crammed with hundreds upon hundreds of pointed triangular teeth.

I should have ended my days there. Yet mine was a gazelle's leap, twice higher than I could have managed in the real world, and three times as far. I laughed, for it is a joyous thing to command such speed. Then the snake's tail whipped toward me and my laugh died. In that half breath I saw my fate writ; the strike would cave in my chest and send me flying the length of an arrow's flight, then the monster would devour my twitching body.

Sometimes it is well not to overthink a problem. I twisted in the air so that I flew with outstretched arms, my back arched above the earth. The tail swept so close below me that the feathered scales brushed my clothing. For the briefest moment I thought I was free and clear. Then a mighty blow crashed across the heels of my boots. Aye, it stung, and moreover I was sent spinning and my sword tumbled away as I closed on a dune that looked solid as a wall.

I called out to God to preserve me and wheeled off balance into the sand, landing awkwardly on my off side. The impact stole my breath. I thought it likely one or more of the toes on my left foot were broken. Yet it was no time for counting injuries. I rolled to my feet and dived for my sword even as the serpent reared. Sand still rattled down the slope from where my sword had landed. I did not see where my weapon lay so much as feel it, so fine were my senses honed in that strange land. Relief swept through me as my fingers closed around the pommel, and I climbed to my throbbing feet, sword raised fanglike. When the serpent struck it would feel my sting.

Its head reared back, and my neck hairs stiffened in alarm. Its mouth widened farther and it must be that angels whispered a warning, for I knew to jump. Pain lanced through my foot as I sprang away, and instantly I heard a popping and spattering behind me. I took the brunt of the landing on my right heel, spun in time to see the great snake vomit steaming green venom. Sulphurous smoke completely obscured the sand where I'd stood only a moment before and I swear the sound that rose from the place was like that of lamb flesh tossed across a hot brazier.

The serpent shut its mouth and spun toward me, its green eyes burning hate. I fixed upon its snout.

Suddenly, though, its attention wavered and it lifted its head higher still, looking away and to the right. It hissed volubly and rocketed away. Almost I looked after, knowing that it had caught sight of Dabir. Instead, I struck down with all my strength at the tail sliding past.

The impact rode up my arms and strained the muscles of my chest. My wrists were all but numbed. Yet I laughed, for dark blood fountained out as my blade raked through the feathers and deep into the flesh below.

So hard did I pull to free my weapon that I stumbled as I came clear.

The beast swung back toward me.

Though I had feared that it would ignore me to go for Dabir I did not now rejoice at success.

A long black tongue licked out over those deadly teeth, which once more faced me from on high. It was the eyes, though, which concerned me. They throbbed, the glow about their edges now brighter, now dimmer, like they answered to a steady drum. There was power there, and as the thing began a singsong chant in an unknown tongue I understood that it worked sorcery.

Instinct screamed to run at top speed as fast and as far as I was able. Instead I charged.

I was but a pace or two from its feathered scales when the world twisted. A haze passed before my eyes and then all was different. Instead of strangely beautiful iridescent feathers, the serpent's body was slick with ebon scales marred by welts, scars, and yellow pustules. I too had changed—the lightness in my step was gone; my foot ached to the point of distraction. My breath was labored.

It was too late to question; I slashed and stinking blood erupted from the furrow I carved through the ancient scales.

From above came a birdlike caw of anguish.

Gone were my fantastic reflexes and superhuman strength. It took a moment too long to pull free my sword. The scabrous tail struck me full in the side and I soared some twenty feet, my sword trailing away in a glittering arc. So busy was I marking its progress that my impact into a dune came as a shock. My breath roared out of me in a gasp.

I lay stunned, expecting death to come, in pain from calf to shoulder. I rolled onto my back so that I might see my end.

The thing was retreating, its length arched above the sand in the places where I had struck it. No longer did it seem a creature of alien beauty, but a decrepit ancient monster, its scaly flesh mottled and worn and failing. Everything about me had altered. The stars, which I tried to blink into focus, were cold and remote and hopeless. They stared down unblinking, uncaring, and I was reminded of looking into the sockets of a skull.

I forced myself to rise, knowing that the serpent closed on Dabir. The moon loomed huge on the horizon, the craters and scars on its surface livid with dark shadows that rendered it a landscape more barren even than this. By its light I found myself on a chalky gray white powder. Here and there amongst this sand was a larger hunk of similarly colored substance and in a chill moment I realized it was bone—ground-up bone—as if every man, woman, and child who ever lived had been rendered fleshless and pounded by time into tiny fragments.

I climbed to my feet. I could not shake off my weariness, but I would not delay, and so I staggered off in the track of the worm. There was no time to seek my sword, so I pulled free my long knife and forced myself to a run.

The serpent had worked a spell, somehow stripping me of my ideal condition and rendering me a normal man. Was this landscape, then, in its true state? I did not know. More important, had I delayed the thing long enough for Dabir to work the sorceries? I could only hope.

I reached the height of the dune and looked down. No longer was there a star map, but hundreds of thousands of transparent figures lying supine and writhing silently in viscous black fluid that restrained their struggling limbs. Only the lines over which Dabir was hunched were unchanged. It was not gems he manipulated, but skulls. He himself was the same fellow I knew on earth, oblivious to his death sliding up from behind. Closer and closer it drew, and he all unaware.

"Dabir!" I screamed.

He whirled, caught sight of the beast.

"I have your name!" the serpent wheezed.

I forced iron-stiff legs down the slope. "God give me strength!" I cried, and plunged into a run. The moment I reached the slope's bottom I pushed harder and sprinted, my legs and foot and side protesting earnestly.

The serpent reared up over Dabir, chanting in its language. Now and then I heard Dabir's name worked into whatever dark sorcery it practiced. My friend staggered as if struck and raised trembling fingers to his face.

I tore forward as pain lanced my side like sword thrusts. My only hope was to cause the serpent such agony that it could not complete its spell.

Then Dabir sought my eyes. He still clutched his face with one hand, but with the other he jabbed out at a skull fifteen paces to his left. It was huge, misshapen, blackened and yellowed with age. I could not guess to what manner of earthly beast it had belonged, or if it were some creature only of nightmare.

I changed direction, panting so loud that I wasn't sure I heard Dabir clearly, for his voice was weak and strained. Had he commanded me to smash it?

I looked to him for confirmation, but Dabir had sunk to his knees. The very substance of his body wavered and smoky wisps of color broke away from him as though he were being consumed from within by fire.

There was nothing for it. I leapt as high as I might and landed with both feet full upon the skull. It must have lain there for eons, for it was almost as fragile as glass and it splintered as I crunched down. One sharp edge sliced straight through my clothing and into my calf. My own grunt of pain was drowned out by a hoarse, deafening scream.

"*No!*" The serpent's upper length reared high, shaking in fury. It whipped toward me as I jumped up and shattered the remaining fragments into powdered shards.

The snake's shriveled mouth opened. Its sunken eyes and pointed snout looked entirely different from that which had sprayed me earlier, but I sensed its intent and sprang away. This time I was no superman, though, only a battered Asim el Abbas, and I did not completely clear the spray. I heard it sizzling on my boot as I came down on my bruised ribs.

Dabir was up and shifting another skull to the right, yelling for me to hurry. Out beyond the panel the souls were rising, drifting up and farther up, into freedom, toward the moon and the stars. They shimmered in gold and red and blue—aye, they were lovelier even than the stars of which I already wrote—and there were thousands upon thousands of them. How to describe what I saw in only that brief moment as I ran toward Dabir? Behind came a horrified bellow from the snake thing. Ahead I saw a coruscating multitude. It may be that all souls are beautiful, for I saw none that day that were old, diseased, or ugly. No, what I beheld were the smiling faces of men and women and children. Here was a grinning ancient black in strange red robes, rising heavenward. Nearby was a young child with pudgy cheeks and slanted eyes, all in green. There was a woman with long red hair who met my eyes. At that moment I felt her relief, and her gratitude poured into me, granting me strength. Beyond them were countless more, whose faces come sometimes in dreams. Farther out were stranger shapes and forms bending and shifting in ways human forms could not, too obscured by the press of bodies for me to closely watch. Whether they were fellow serpents or some other race unknown to scholars that had lived and fought and died on earth in ages past I shall never know.

Dabir was yelling for me to hurry. In the air beside him was a ripple of energy. His teeth were gritted, and one shaking hand was pushed to his temple as a man will do with a head wound, or a noble will do if complaining of a headache. The other hand, likewise shaking, was stretched to me.

A shifting ghost shot from the star field and straight at me. I recognized Hamil, his face beaming, triumphant but determined. I cried out in wonder, cursing him, for he did not veer. He crashed straight through me. I felt only a cold tingle; I heard a laugh, as if from far off, and then I reached Dabir's hand and clasped it. Somehow then the wavering image beside him clarified into a dunescape beneath the stars.

"Jump!" he shouted, as though I needed urging.

We dived through as one and landed in the dunes of earth. I turned my head in time to see a wavering image behind us of the serpent's head rearing away as the poet's soul flew at his face and rose up. Then the wyrm's head was down on level with our own, maw open wide.

The shimmering around the rim of the portal grew more pronounced as the serpent neared, then rim, portal, and snake all wobbled and faded from view as a final tormented shriek of fury echoed through the night.

15

The deathless still of the desert night rendered the sound of sizzling all that more ominous.

"Your boot's smoldering!" Dabir shouted.

My muscles strained in protest as I fumbled with the top of my right boot. After all that I had just experienced, it was the thought of having my foot cooked away by serpent venom that nearly unmanned me. I clasped the leather about the ankle tightly and jerked my foot clear, then hurled the boot into the darkness.

"Are you all right?" Dabir asked.

"Yes." I did not mention that I'd likely broken a toe or three.

Dabir loped off down the side of the dune—I knew not why—while I inspected the bottom of my sock. It did not seem as though the venom had eaten into it, Allah be praised.

"Keep your hands from your weapons!" a stern voice cried out behind me.

I groaned. In all the vastness of the desert, how is it we had come upon some place where there were men?

"Raise up your hands," said a second man, his voice less certain.

I lifted my hands and turned, holding in a grunt of pain as my side protested.

There on the ridge above two men were silhouetted faintly by the starlight and the moon. Bedouins holding bows. Of course. Who else would be out here in the desert?

"Asim?" one of them asked, and it was then that I recognized his voice.

"Hadban?" I asked.

At the same moment I realized I faced our guide and his nephew I also heard the sound of footsteps brushing through the sand behind me. Dabir trotted up, my boot dangling from one hand.

Hadban's nephew fired.

Dabir dropped like a stone.

"Idiot!" The pain was nothing to me then. I sprinted downslope in a lopsided gait, scattering sand with my booted foot and sliding with the other. Hadban cursed at his nephew.

I reached the scholar and sank down on one knee. "Dabir!"

He lay on his side.

"Dabir, where are you hit?"

"It is my arm," he said.

I rolled him over gingerly. He cradled his left arm in his right. Search though I might, I saw no arrow shaft. "Did you already pull it clear?" I said, grasping his arm and straightening it to better see the wound.

Dabir yanked his arm back. "Leave off," he said through gritted teeth. "He shot your boot, not me."

"My boot? Then why are you holding your arm?"

"Because it hurts! I landed on it when we jumped the first time, and again just now, when I dropped as yon idiot tried to skewer me. I'm trying to feel if it's broken."

"Let me see."

"Thank you, no." He looked up, then added more gently, "I'll be fine."

The Bedouins joined us then. The nephew bent down and raised high the boot. The arrow shaft had punched through both sides.

"Congratulations," I said to him, then asked Dabir why he'd gone after my footgear.

"I thought it likely you would need it for the return journey," Dabir said dryly, "and that we could repair its sole. It may be mortally wounded now."

"Come," Hadban said, smiling. "We will stir up the fire, look at your arm, and have some food."

Dabir and I struggled to our feet like crippled old men and followed the two Bedouins back to the campsite on the other side of the ridge. The camels were tethered there, and shifted their ungainly bodies around to stare at us. Three narrow tents had been raised up. Hadban's son stepped forth at his command to stir the fire.

"Is Sabirah safe?" Dabir asked.

"She is," Hadban answered. "She sleeps deeply, for she has grieved for hours, thinking you perished. Naji saw the wizard and two of his followers returning from the way you had gone. We stayed well clear of them." He peered closely at us. "We thought you dead. How did you come to be here?"

"That is a long story," Dabir said. "Let us talk over a meal."

At my insistence Dabir allowed me to look over his arm while Kafiq, Hadban's nephew, produced some dried fruit. I am no hakim, but have some experience with injuries. He fretted at my touch, for his flesh was tender, but I could find no break. "We should probably prepare a sling."

"I will help with that," Hadban said, for which I was thankful. Weariness had settled heavily upon me, my foot was throbbing, and Dabir was testy.

Hadban rigged up a cloth to support Dabir's arm, then sat down with us around the fire while we nibbled on dried meat and fruits.

The son, Naji, presented us with two battered mugs of tea. It is a pleasure, on a cool night, to sit among friends and clasp a warm cup between your hands. And on this night, with the miraculous improbability of our survival and return sinking in, I felt truly blessed despite the new aches I discovered with every movement.

"We have seen wonders," I said. "There was a vast city of ghosts, and an ancient feathered serpent longer than a camel train." Dabir looked up companionably.

"Dabir? Asim?"

My sluggish brain identified the quavering voice as Sabirah's only a moment before the slim figure dashed into our midst and flung her arms about us both. She sat with us then, demanding answers faster than they could be supplied. Dabir calmed her, and then he and I relayed all that had transpired.

At first Sabirah and the Bedouins interrupted us with questions. We patiently demurred, as would polished storytellers, saying all would be revealed in time. They listened to our words. Dabir and I traded off our narratives smoothly enough that it might have been rehearsed, and judging by the rapt attention of our listeners, we told to good effect. It may be that Dabir was too detailed and that I had more natural flair, but in all honesty it would be unfair of me to pass judgment.

Dabir even answered some of my own questions as he talked, providing greater detail of how he had found the location of our current company through the serpent's sorcery, and opened a way to them. Also I heard specifics concerning the numbing pain he felt while manipulating the serpent's magic, and the soul-wrenching agony of the serpent's assault upon his mind and spirit.

Even then our listeners asked questions of us.

"So which was it?" Kafiq asked. "An ancient diseased worm, or a beautiful snake?"

"A worm," I said.

"Something of both, I think," Dabir said.

I drained my cup. "Whatever it was, I regret I did not slay it. The thing was evil."

"I feel sorry for it, in a way," Sabirah said after a short moment. She sat between us, huddled under a blanket.

"Sorry?" I said. "You did not see the souls trapped for eternity like so many bugs. One of them was our friend! How can you feel sorry for it?"

"I didn't mean . . ." she demurred, embarrassed.

"No," Dabir said. "Ignore Asim's manner. Speak on."

"It's just . . . it spent how many years do you think? Thousands, tens of thousands, trying to build a way back home. And you said it was close to completion. What will it do now?"

"Die, I hope," I said.

"It will probably start anew," Dabir said quietly. "I, too, pitied the creature. I wonder—was it always evil, or did it become that way out of desperation and loneliness? Is that how all turn to evil?"

I sighed so that no one might mistake my feelings in the matter. "We freed tens of thousands of souls, Dabir, and found our way home. I am only sad that our friend died; at least, though, we should rejoice that he moved on to God. There is nothing to lament. Unless"—I pointed my finger at him—"you consider our current circumstance." I shifted, testing the pain in my foot—which predictably reflared with movement. "Hadban, how far is Firouz ahead of us?"

"At least half a day, I think," Hadban said. "We kept watch upon them from concealment until they passed. Then we waited longer before moving ourselves so that we would not accidently come upon them."

"So," I continued, "our enemy lies before us, and they have their artifact, as well as great sorcerous power. I've lost my father's sword and"—I glanced to Dabir—"we're in no condition to fight."

"And Kafiq shot your boot," Sabirah interjected.

"Yes," I agreed, although at the same moment the others chuckled at my misfortune. Sabirah, too, smiled.

"Asim," she replied, "you and Dabir have returned to us against all odds, and done deeds the caliph himself would praise. The gems you showed us from Ubar . . . won't they be enough to buy passage back to Basra? If there is money left over perhaps we can even find you new footgear."

The Bedouins laughed again at this.

"Allah has smiled upon us, Asim," Dabir said. "We must press forward."

I had never suggested abandoning our mission; I had just meant to point out difficulties.

I pitched a tent with no further word to the rest of them, though I was quite sore and would not have objected to the offer of aid. Once bedded down my mind retraced our many steps and I thought back to all that we had lost, soldiers and sailors, Mahmoud, Hamil, the sword of my father. And what had we gained?

These thoughts were poor company. Fortunately, sleep came fast. It was dreamless, and I was so tired still when I was roused that it felt as though I'd just closed my eyes.

Neither Dabir nor myself were in high humor for the next few days, for a camel is a poor seat when one is already in pain. Aye, between the aching and the baking beneath the sun it was easy to forget how glad I was not to be trapped in that land of ghosts and serpents.

I wore both boots. The venom had burned a great oval in the bottom beside the heel, but it was still better than nothing. The holes, Sabirah had pointed out, would aid in cooling. Of all of us, she was in the finest mood. If she was concerned about our final fate or how her family might receive her after so long an absence, it did not show in her manner. She did search the horizon like the rest of us, but I began to wonder whether she was apprehensive about finding Firouz, or about reaching the ocean and beginning the return trip.

Alas, though we pushed hard, we did not catch up to Firouz. It may be that we lost too much time when we overslept that first morning, for the Bedouins thought to aid us by letting us rest. Or it may be that Firouz and his men had too great a start and, in Firouz's eagerness to carry out his plan, pushed just as hard as we did.

Whatever the case, we'd had no sight of them when we reached the scrubland, and we yet lacked sight of them when we saw the outskirts of the village. As a final thanks for their services, Dabir gifted the Bedouins with two fine stones we'd pried from Ubar's ruins, asking only that they return the coins with which we had first paid them. This they did gladly, for the sapphires more than doubled that amount. The treasure set their eyes to popping.

Hadban weighed the sapphires in his palm, then considered us.

"I am not one to offer advice that has not been asked for," he said.

"Especially not to men who have hired me. But you have paid us, and I no longer am in your employ."

"That is true," Dabir agreed.

"Then I speak as someone who thinks of you now as a friend, and not as an employer. And as a friend, I have words for you."

"Speak on," Dabir urged.

"You go to your death," he said. "You face a wizard with dark powers; moreover, you face the caliph's friend, do you not? And he would not look well on your love for his niece."

Dabir started at that, but Hadban went on, ignoring the scholar's reaction. "If you even survive the wizard, the caliph's friend will be a graver threat."

"There are challenges before us," Dabir admitted.

Hadban's smile enlivened his face with wrinkles. "More challenges than even brave men like you can overcome."

"What can be done?" Dabir said. I do not think he expected an answer.

"You are good men," Hadban said. "Given time, you could be desert men. I have nieces and granddaughters who bloom like flowers when they smile. Asim, they would look fondly upon you and bring you strong sons. Dabir, you and the girl could marry here and remain with us."

"But what of the caliph?" I asked.

Hadban snorted. "The caliph would assume all three of you perished."

"All of Baghdad may fall if we do not stop the sorcerer," Dabir said.

"That may be so, but what is that to you?"

"Thousands will die; the Greeks will likely overrun our lands."

"They will not come here," Kafiq pointed out.

"Silence, nephew. So might many die if the sea floods the land. Who knows what Allah will bring? Have you not striven enough? I would not think you cowards. Stay, my friends, and live."

Dabir smiled sadly. "You are kind, and I shall not forget you. But I cannot accept your offer."

"Nor can I," I heard myself say, though in truth a part of me had come to appreciate the wide spaces. I knew I could accustom myself to the heat, and I was not altogether incurious about the beauty of Hadban's nieces. Yet I was sworn to serve Jaffar.

"Go with God then, my friends. Allah is merciful." He added this last resignedly, as one will who sometimes sees God's mercy delayed, or delivered in a different way than hoped for.

I bowed my head to him and made to return the sword I had borrowed to wield should we encounter Firouz. He held up his hand. "Nay, it is a gift."

And so we left the Bedouins and slunk into the village, like rats into the grain house. We could not know if Firouz had truly leagued with the city leaders. Surely he could never have anticipated that we would return from the desert. Still, there might be those who had been told to seek us out before, and would recognize us now. Thus Dabir lingered in the shadows with Sabirah while I did the bargaining, for my face was less well known. We bought boots and simple food supplies, then booked passage on an Egyptian rig and all of us embarked for Basra early the next morning.

We had only one cabin between the three of us, which proved somewhat awkward. There was nothing to be done for it, though.

Sabirah's mood changed when we boarded the ship. Once more she was reflective and subdued. I thought at first that her stomach was troubled by the waters like mine. After the first day I grew more accustomed to the churning again. I lay on an upper bunk, she on the lower across from me. She sat with arms wrapped about her knees, and stared out the open portal, high in the wall. Dabir had vanished to the deck. Although the scholar was slighter than I, in all the years I knew him I never once saw him suffer from seasickness.

Afternoon light flowed through that port, lighting the sad eyes of the girl. The air was touched somewhat with the taint of bilgewater, but freshened by the salty tang from outside.

"Does your stomach pain you, Sabirah?"

"Nay," she said without looking up. She had put her veil aside.

"You are sick of heart."

She did not answer.

"It is no good life," I said, "to be married to a scholar. His life will never be his own, and on a whim livelihood might end. Nay, you will have a wealthy husband, secure in his place, and command many servants."

Sabirah sighed, drew her legs even closer, and rested her chin on her kneecaps. It was as if she sought to fold up so compactly that she would shrink away to nothing.

"I hear again and again of your brilliance," I said. "Surely you have deduced by now that life with Dabir is an impossibility."

"Dabir's *life* may be an impossibility," Sabirah said softly. "It's not fair. His bravery, and your own, are likely to mean nothing to my uncle. I have been thinking that we would have been better off remaining among the Bedouin."

"If we were to think only of ourselves, aye."

Her eyes lit upon mine, a rebellious fire burning in their depths. "I know my duty," she said sharply.

Someone less wise than myself might have pointed out that someone who knew her duty would not have stowed away on the ship to start with.

She looked back at the port. "Do you think we can catch them, Asim?"

"God gives," I said.

"Do you think we can stop them if we catch them?"

"Dabir and I shall stop them or die in the trying."

"You always end up talking of death, Asim."

I grunted. "Would you rather I talk of ponies and sweets and perfumes?"

She scowled, saying nothing.

"You must make clear to Dabir that you two cannot be together."

She sighed in disgust. "Do you think we are both idiots, Captain? Do you think that he does not know?"

"He needs to know that you know. You have acted as if all was well."

"Could I not snatch a few moments of happiness before it all comes tumbling down? Would you have preferred me to sit weeping upon the camel the whole of the ride back? What would you have said then, Asim?"

"I would have said you were being too dramatic," I said.

"Ai-a, you have studied at the foot of brilliant teachers!"

Staring as she was once more at the port, she could not see the dark look I gave her. I said nothing more. After a short time, she spoke again. "I would rather be alone, Asim. Leave me, or roll back and fasten your eyes upon the wall, so that I can pretend you are not here."

"On a ship," I said, lowering myself to the deck, "it is not called a wall." I would have corrected her more completely, except that for the life of me I could not remember a wall's proper shipboard name. I staggered slightly with the roll of the waves, reached the door, and departed.

On the deck, sailors worked the masts while officers barked. A course correction was asked for, I think, because the wind had changed. Water rolled on every hand, as far as the eye might see, thrusting like curving fangs and then dropping from sight.

Dabir sat in a low-slung rail-side chair, staring out at the sun. The wind buffeted my sleeves as I stepped to his side. He glanced up, nodding his greeting.

"Are you feeling better?" he asked.

"I am well enough. Do you think it is the food I ate before we sailed?"

"Who can say? Some are born with sea legs, some are not. You should count yourself lucky, for you at least adjust after some days. The ship's captain was telling me of a passenger who was green for almost two weeks. All he could eat was broth, and he was almost a skeleton by the time he left the ship."

I gripped the rail and set my mind upon the sway of the ship, as one sets their mind upon a camel's movement to adjust to its ride. After a time you cease to pay it heed, and your stomach settles.

"It was difficult enough getting the governor to give us a ship," Dabir said.

"Aye, and he will be wondering what happened to it. He will not like the tale."

Dabir nodded. "I must find the words to convince him to turn out the whole of his guard to search the harbor and seal every gate. And Firouz is ahead of us. We must have speed. Can we catch up to him before he leaves Basra? I am . . . at somewhat of a loss. I can think of no other steps."

"You have thought us out of all our troubles so far," I said. "Yours are the eyes that see and mine is the hand that strikes. Together we will succeed."

He smiled thinly then, as if he had been distracted by something unexpectedly pleasing. "I hope you are right, my friend. By the nine and ninety . . ." His hand clenched, then he let it fall to the arm of the chair. "If we had but known the extent of their power, we could have borne tools to stop them. Do you remember the boy bragging of the treasures in the caliph's stores? I helped catalog some of them, Asim. I *know* some of what is down there."

"I doubt Jaffar would have given us leave to remove any of it," I reminded him, "seeing as how he'd already lost one thing he'd borrowed from the caliph's storehouse."

Dabir nodded slowly. "Aye. But if . . . when we face him again, I shall ask for such things, and I pray that Jaffar will have the sense to give them."

"I hope that it will be so," I said, and then we both watched the sea and said naught of what we thought would truly happen.

After a time I said, "Sabirah is moping below."

"And I mope above."

We listened to the wind lash the rigging, and the steady swish of the water against the wood. I wondered for the first time that day if there was something palatable aboard.

"I will have to talk with her," Dabir said.

But if they discussed anything substantive that day, or that evening, I did not hear it; little was said the next day, or the following, when the sailors feared the dark clouds all along the horizon. Sabirah was young and her mood was black; it occurred to me that young women in love were inclined to foolishness. If, in her despair, she were to throw herself overside, or stab herself, it would be the end of not only an innocent life, but of Dabir and myself as well, in all likelihood. Thus I kept careful watch of her. When I was not in her presence I contrived to venture close enough to monitor her by ear. By nature I am not one of those who delight in the private affairs of other folk, so it troubled me to spy upon someone in so pitiful a state. I discovered that by standing along the rail by the port side I was close to the window in the deckhouse that was our tiny cabin; from there I could overhear what passed within.

That evening the sun burned like a great red eye that bled down upon the waters; it was as though a grisly end were come to the world, and judgment were at hand. The evening star gleamed low and proud, like a tiny candle held aloft by a soul drowning in a sea of blood and darkness. Dabir told me it was time to have a word with Sabirah and left the rail. A few moments later I took my listening post under the eyes of the sailors. They knew what I was about, and their amused smirks shamed me; they thought I listened in so as to take pleasure from carnal doings.

There was nothing carnal in the subdued greeting shared between Dabir and Sabirah. A long silence followed before I heard Dabir speak.

"Tomorrow we will reach Basra. Things will be different from there on out."

"I know," Sabirah answered.

"Your uncle will not be pleased."

"What if we catch up to Firouz in the city, and stop him?"

"That is my hope."

"Then," she continued, excitement creeping with a stammer into her delivery, "you would be a hero."

"Sabirah—"

"Heroes might ask for *any* boon."

Silence followed. Thinking that they whispered, I leaned closer. Still I heard nothing. Might they be kissing?

At last, Dabir's voice rose weakly, as if weighted down with great chains. "Here is the boon I would ask of you, Sabirah. Live long, live well. You are young—"

"That is not my fault!"

"No. It is a blessing."

She choked back a sob. So strained was her voice that I barely made out her words. "I do not wish to live without you."

Ai-a, what would Jaffar say to that?

"Sabirah . . ." Dabir's voice faltered. "Sabirah, you are a gift from Allah to the world. Do not throw that gift away. You are stronger than that. You have so much more you can learn. So much more of God's tapestry remains to be unfurled, and I know that your hands will be upon that cloth."

She said nothing, and a long pause followed.

"Think of the wisdom you can share with your children."

Her voice was very soft. "I wish no children but yours."

"That cannot be."

There came soft weeping, then a quiet confession from her. "I know all this, Dabir. Yet my heart still hopes. Sometimes . . . sometimes I imagine that after all this . . . maybe you could tutor my own children. We would not be husband and wife, but you would still be there, near me. It is foolish, I know."

His voice was tender then. "I would that I might wake to find you lying at my side each morning, your hair across the pillow. That I might take your hand as you woke."

Allah, it was heart-wrenching. Silence fell again, and then I heard her voice, strained and quiet.

"I wish you to have this," she said.

Whatever it was, he demurred, saying, "Time with you has been treasure enough, and one I would cross an ocean to win."

"Nay, I wish you to wear it, always, and think of me."

"I shall never leave off thinking of you," he said.

That was the end of it; when Dabir returned to deck I was far from the railing near the cabin. He took up station near the bow, far from me. I could guess that he needed no company, and so let him be. It was not until the following morning that I saw her emerald upon his finger for the first time. On one of those desert nights she'd told me how it was her favorite ring, and that her father had gifted it to her before his trip to Syria. Now she had presented it to Dabir, and save for short intervals, when he removed it to engage in tasks that might have soiled or damaged it, and twice when it was taken from him by force, the ring never left his possession for all the span of years I knew him.

There are some who have said, when I tell them this part of the tale, that Dabir and Sabirah must surely have kissed there in the cabin. I do not think either would have done that, but it may be true. If they sinned, I have it in my heart to forgive them, as Allah the compassionate most certainly has done, for they had been unfairly burdened with troubles not of their own making.

16

Basra lies not upon the coast, but a day's travel inland up the Tigris. From far Hindu lands and tropic isles come dark-waisted boats with high prows and short brown men; slant-eyed Chinamen with singsong voices cast their lines near the Arab voyagers, who are as at home upon the waves as I am upon the horse. Small boats moved amongst all, laden with melons and breads and wine. Urchins shouted up the worth of their wares while their fathers and uncles rowed. I thought it surely the busiest river in the world until I saw the Nile's mouth some years later.

Repeated contact with Dabir had convinced the ship's captain that the scholar was no charlatan: Dabir had promised him compensation from the state if he made good time, and so he did, navigating through the mass of ships and on up the river. God was with us, for he sent a wind at the right angle for the sails. We reached a berth that evening and Dabir paid him with the last of our gemstones.

Basra began its life as a garrison town, although I think there must have been some village in its place beforehand. It grew fat on the grains and produce brought through its winding lanes and waterways. And because merchants are drawn to money as unerringly as flies to rotting meat, the population swelled. With more markets there came more traders from farther afield.

Scholars came too, in greater number than are found even in Baghdad. It can grow warm in Basra, but rarely does it grow as hot as a rooftop on a Baghdad noon, though I know not why. I think the scholars came because it was cooler, though they may also have come to sit at the feet of wise men who settled there.

I shall say one other thing for Basra—it was well watered. In some parts of the city the streets themselves are stretches of river. Some Marsh Arabs make their living there, poling folk about or making boats. Dabir thought it most likely that Firouz and Diomedes would be found in their district of the city. The three of us certainly had no chance of finding them in that warren, though, and so we moved as swiftly as we could for the governor's palace.

It was our bad timing to have arrived at the moment just before evening prayers, when the folk are out dining or hurrying to their homes to eat. The beggars know always to be out in force at such times. I lost count of those who plucked at us. The throngs reeked of sweat and fish; for the first time in my life I longed for the open sea breeze. It amazes me to this day how much a little travel changes one's perspective.

To avoid a second marketplace, we turned down a side street in an older section of Basra. In such places the building heights lean out over the streets themselves, leaving all below in shadow save for at noontimes. I was alert for ambush in such a place, and it may be that is why I saw the figure pass a block ahead, on an intersecting street. Something about the man's gait caused me to stare; though clothed in desert robes, his head wrapped in a turban, there was no mistaking the long straight nose or the protuberant eyes. Aye, he was far away, and might have been anyone. I knew he was not.

"Diomedes!" I said to Dabir, and, pressing hand to sword belt, bolted off after him, never mind the fresh ache in my toes.

I imagined success ran with me—that if I caught the man our problems were near to over. I was certain I could convince the Greek to lead me to Firouz, and it might even be that Firouz walked in front of him and I had not seen. Thus I cornered the building with a grin. Before me lay a wider avenue sloping up from the river; on it more of the city folk hurried. Twelve paces on, passing by a fruit vendor who was rolling up his awning, walked Diomedes.

I steadied my sheath, whipped my blade free, and hurried after.

The vendor gasped as I dashed past; a man with a thick white beard coming out of a leather shop stared openmouthed.

I was almost to Diomedes when he turned. First I think he saw the blade in my hand as my left reached for his shoulder. Then his eyes met mine and the startled look transformed into recognition and horror.

I clamped down on his shoulder, and brought up my sword. And then something dropped onto my back, digging with sharp talons through my cloth and deep into my flesh. I'd meant to press the sword to the Greek's neck and demand answers; now I gasped in pain, groped to find a furry body shifting for position. I recoiled; my hand had brushed across a moving skeleton wrapped in dry hair and flesh; one of the Greek's monkeys. It sank teeth into my neck.

I grunted in pain. From behind came the sound of running feet. Dabir called my name as he neared.

I grabbed at the thing, clasped fur, closed around the monkey's neck even as it bit down again on me. Pain lanced through my shoulder; blood ran down my clothes.

A cry went up from one of the vendors, who rushed off, calling out for aid: "Help! Murderers! Robbers!"

In my distraction I'd failed to pay heed to Diomedes; he bore a blade in his off hand—his right was swathed in bandages—and his lips were pulled back in a grimace. The monkey clasped my chin with both hands and jerked it to the left.

It was not enough to break my neck, but it was a distraction at the worst possible time. Diomedes darted in and swung. I threw up my sword and caught his blade on the tip of my own.

The monkey bit my neck again, and as I shouted, Diomedes drew back for another strike.

I sliced out at him, meaning to disarm, but Diomedes was leaning in and the monkey was digging into my back, and I misjudged. Instead of striking his sword clear, I sliced deep into his belly. Instantly he dropped his sword and fell, howling, trying to stay the flow of blood.

The damned monkey renewed its efforts.

I tossed down my blade and reached back with both hands.

"I've got it," I heard Dabir saying, and surely there were two other hands on the beast, trying to wrestle it clear.

"Watch its teeth!" I heard Sabirah urge.

"Forget me!" I cried. "Question Diomedes!"

But Dabir did not leave off. Sabirah stepped over to the Greek, still thrashing in the dirt in a growing pool of blood.

I squeezed the monkey's neck until I felt bones break, yet it did not release its hold. Finally I wrapped both hands around its skull, my thumbs shoved deep onto the stones that were its eyes, and pulled.

In a living being, muscles, tendons, and skin connect one portion of a creature to another. One must have a sharp instrument to separate them. This thing was bound only by papery skin and dried-up sinew. The head popped free in my hands and I threw it onto the dust of the street. Dabir, panting, stood with me, faintly ridiculous with a severed, red-furred monkey arm in one bloody hand. The torso of the beast writhed on the ground, two limbs still scrambling for balance. I had never seen something as revolting, and without thinking I snatched up my blade and hacked the thing through the torso again and again until it had ceased movement.

The monkey was dead, and Diomedes lay in the mud, his legs churning feebly, moaning and clutching his belly with both hands, the bandaged and the whole. A copious amount of blood colored his tunic and the earth he lay in, and he was all but drained of color. A satchel at his waist had come open and spilled dozens of shining black stones. The eyes of the dead, I realized, and shuddered.

It was then that I paid closer heed to the onlookers. There was the old man with the thick white beard, and a handful of stout women with urchins, farther back. There too, advancing down the street whence the fruit vendor had disappeared, were four men in cuirasses and turban-wrapped helms. Their grim, competent demeanor did not bode well.

"We must see to your neck," Dabir said softly, then tossed down the monkey arm and stepped forward, hand held forth. I noticed again that it streamed blood and realized the unclean beast must have bitten him as well.

Then the guards were there about us.

"Peace be upon you," Dabir said.

The guards wanted none of that. "Put down your sword," one of them shouted to me. Knowing myself how swiftly violence erupts and how important it was to have these men upon our side, I set down the blade.

Their manner did not relax.

"These two attacked the man and his monkey," the white beard said.

The fruit vendor shouted in a high piping voice, "This one"—he pointed at me—"raced up behind the man and killed him when he sought to defend himself, then slew the monkey."

"The brave little fellow," one woman muttered, and others mouthed similar comments about the horror.

"It was an undead beast," I said.

By then the guards had closed on us more tightly, staring hard. Dabir was working his tongue. "We are servants of Quadi Jaffar, the vizier's son," Dabir said. "That man there is a Greek spy. We must keep him alive for questioning."

"It's too late for that," the old white beard scoffed.

"He is passed out or dead," Sabirah said. The guards had given her and Diomedes wide berth, though they watched her curiously.

"I think you are robbers," the stoutest of the guards told us.

"Please listen," Dabir insisted. "We work for Jaffar the Barmacide. This man is a thief."

The stout guard shook his head. "You and your friend here need bandaging. He's getting paler by the moment."

"Why would you attack a monkey?" asked a second guard, a tall young man with only a stubble.

"The monkey was already dead," I said, "and controlled by the Greek. Look at its body—"

The guard officer looked at his fellows, then back to me. "Either he's lost more blood than I thought, or he's the worst liar I've ever seen."

"It's full of sawdust!" I countered. "Look, shouldn't there be more blood?"

The officer considered the monkey corpse. There was, indeed, sawdust mixed amongst the fur and mud, and there were only little flecks of blood—probably mine—but I had so mangled the thing with slashing and stomping that such clues were not obvious, and simple to disbelieve.

"Look to the Greek," Dabir urged, "or thousands could die."

The guard shook his head. "He is already dead."

"By all that's holy, man, do not be a fool—"

One of the guards struck Dabir then, across the mouth. He stumbled backward. I grabbed for him, but my balance was off. I lurched when I meant to leap, and we held on to each other's arms, leaning against each other almost drunkenly. My head felt light.

Sabirah shouted that everything was true, and that she was the vizier's granddaughter, but the guards only laughed and told her to begone. They took our weapons, ripped my clothes to bandage us, and marched us off.

"I will petition the governor," Sabirah said, and dashed away even as Dabir called for her to wait.

"Your doxy has better sense," the youngest guard said. "You should have run from justice when you had the chance." His comrades laughed.

Dabir's mouth twitched; his arms actually shook as he balled hands into fists.

"Watch where your tongue flies," I said. "The woman is the vizier's granddaughter."

"So *you* say, slayer of monkeys."

The laughter rang around us again; the officer then bid all of us to silence. Not so much for our benefit, I think, but because he realized his men were distracted and undisciplined.

Dabir tried twice more to speak as we were guided to the palace.

Each time he was urged to silence, and the second time a fist was raised threateningly. He had wiped blood from the side of his mouth; already his upper lip was swelling.

We were marched onto the grounds of the governor's palace as the muezzin called for evening prayers, but we did not receive the reception we had counted on. Nay, we were hastily locked in a cell with a dozen foul-smelling gutter rats and drunks. Dabir was still shouting to them that they needed to alert the governor.

"If the girl dies because you failed to act—"

"Silence!" the officer snapped.

"You will live to regret it!"

"Tell your captain that I am Captain Asim in Jaffar's household," I said.

The officer hesitated, meeting my eye.

"You know I am a military man, like you. You see it."

The muezzin's call was fading. The officer lingered at the cell door, considering me by the dim light that came, like everything else in that place, only through bars.

"Think us liars about everything else if you will," I said, "but bring your captain. He will wish to hear my words."

The officer made a scoffing sound, but there was something in his look that gave me hope. I had set him to wondering. What I said to him was true; men who have served long enough bear themselves distinctly. I had recognized in him someone who well knew the early morning drills and the late-night rounds, the dusty rides, the meager food, the madness of battle. And he had recognized something of that manner in me, or he would not have lingered.

I had no rug, nor water, nor sand, so my wiping of hands and feet was only a formality as I knelt to pray. Dabir sank against the dark stone of the old dank wall and put his head in his hands.

"You should have prayed," I told him when I was done. I sank down beside him, nearly toppling. Fatigue swept over me in waves; my neck throbbed in multiple places; my back pained me to a lesser extent.

"Are you my mother?" Dabir snapped.

"What did you two do?" A greasy, light-skinned man asked us.

"We killed a man," I said, staring sternly at the fellow.

"He was asking us questions," Dabir continued.

The little man looked back and forth between us, then scuttled back to his corner of the cell.

"I am sorry, Asim," Dabir said softly. "It is just—we were so desperate for aid. When you spotted Diomedes, I thought the hand of God must surely be upon your shoulder. He could have led us straightaway to Firouz." A sweep of his arm encompassed the cell, darkening about us as the sun fell. "Instead we are here. And you have lost half your blood."

"I have had worse," I said.

"We need to wash those wounds with fresh water," he said, "and cover them with fresh bandages. I would not mind them for my arm, either."

"At least Diomedes did not poison the thing's teeth," I said. "We'd surely be dead by now if he had."

Dabir chuckled, then was instantly serious. "I am afraid for Sabirah."

"She will be fine," I said.

"I hope so. What if Firouz was close, though?"

"If he were close, I think he would have intervened."

He nodded, hearing the truth of my words, but fretting for the girl anyway, as will a man in love.

We sat there as the light dimmed and the cell grew more foul-smelling, for one of the drunks retched and another relieved himself, managing to miss the foul hole intended for waste by a considerable distance. Ah, the glory of the grape.

We'd fallen far, Dabir and I. Only a few short weeks before we had lived and worked in one of the most luxurious homes ever conceived by the mind of man, where our basic wants and needs were cared for with so little effort upon our part that I had taken those luxuries for granted. Now I had no kind of food or drink, nor even a carpet to sit upon. For all that, I did not despair. Foolish or no, I held hope, and I had a friend at my side. In such times that may be the greatest comfort of all.

Despite my aches and pains and a growing hunger, I nodded off, but I did not dream. I realized I slept when Dabir nudged me. I found that I was resting with my head held up by the corner of the room. Someone was calling to me, and Dabir was standing, offering his hand.

"Dabir ibn Khalil?"

I took Dabir's hand and he helped me to my feet. If anything, my balance was worse than before.

Two guardsmen stood at the barred door, playing shuttered lantern light into our resting place.

"By Allah, it is them," one of them said. "You two are the monkey slayers?"

"It is a long story," Dabir said.

"You said you killed a man," a ragged voice said faintly from our left. No one acknowledged him.

"My friend needs medical care," Dabir said, "and we must speak with the governor. The vizier's granddaughter may be in danger."

"Be at ease," an officer told him. "She is here, in the palace, and the governor wishes to speak with you both."

17

The governor was in no hurry. The officer, Captain Ratib, led us into the palace itself, where a grizzled hakim cleaned our wounds and set bandages around them. I had never seen a hakim more scarred and burly, but though his look was odd, his skill was beyond reproach. I have scars to this day from the monkey's assault, yet they do not ache when the weather changes, like many of my others.

We were offered clean clothes then. Dabir commented to me that they were rather simple garb.

"Is it not said that one should not examine a horse's mouth too closely when it is a gift?" I asked.

"I am grateful," Dabir replied more softly, "but wary. These are servant's garments. The governor knows we are agents of Jaffar. Would he not seek our favor?"

Dabir spoke aright. "What do you think it bodes?"

"A harder road," Dabir said.

I would have pried for a better answer, but there were platters of flatbread and fruits. There was other fare as well. Fish, naturally. Those who have lost blood know the hunger that comes upon a man, and would understand that I consumed the fish as eagerly as though they were sweet pastries—of which there were none. The governor apparently could spare no desserts.

Once I was sated, weariness fought to master me. I could not let it win; our fates were still uncertain. We had been pulled from the one cell, yet I understood that our freedom was still an illusion, for a guard stood watch outside our chamber. Dabir asked him if Sabirah were coming, or the governor, and the fellow said only that he did not know, and to take satisfaction from what we had, a simple yet reasoned enough response.

Dabir sat down with a foul look. I sat down apart from him and soon my chin was nodding against my breast. Now was not the time to sleep, so I climbed to my feet and paced back and forth along the wall.

Dabir followed my movements, his brow furrowed. At last he could not leave off demanding to know why I paced.

"So that I will not doze off," I said.

He muttered something under his breath and retrieved a bunch of grapes from the food platter, slowly turning each in his fingers before consuming it. I thought he inspected them for poison until I realized he was merely lost in thought and was not really examining the food at all.

Finally our room curtain was parted once more and Captain Ratib entered, holding the fabric back for Governor Bashar.

Dabir stood to receive him.

The fellow was stout, his clothes richly embroidered, his turban glittering with jewels. The stark difference between his attire and ours would have been apparent at any time, and by lantern light it was emphasized all the more, for those gems set into the turban gleamed like a halo of stars above his brow.

"Peace be upon you," Dabir said. He was attempting calm, but strain showed in his voice.

"And also upon you," the governor said airily. He glanced over at me.

I bowed from the waist and stepped over beside Dabir.

"You will be happy to know that your charge found her way to my palace," the governor said.

"Is she well?" Dabir asked.

"She is fine, though she seems half-starved, and has wild fancies."

"Her words may seem fantastic, Excellency," Dabir said, "but I assure you that they are true. The men we were sent to seek are here, in the city."

"So she said." The governor nodded with no great interest.

"Did you dispatch soldiers to find them?" Dabir asked. "They are likely to be hiding close to where we found the Greek."

"That matter's no longer of any real concern," the governor replied.

"What?"

The man's eyes narrowed at Dabir's breach of etiquette. "I have orders from His Excellency Jaffar that supersede other considerations," he said. "He is no longer interested in the thieves or their theft, and wishes you two and his niece returned at the earliest opportunity to Baghdad. He was more than a little vexed to learn that you had allowed the girl to be kidnapped, and that the three of you had all but disappeared."

"Surely Sabirah told you what those men intended," Dabir said.

"She said many things," the governor admitted. "She was quite agitated. But, as I said, His Excellency's orders were quite clear."

"Fine, then." Dabir sounded close to exploding. "I will not oppose them. But those villains must be stopped. Believe me, Governor, Jaffar does not know their aim. If he did, he would urge you as I do. Arrest them. At least detain and question them."

The governor turned up his empty palms, smiling a little. "Unlike you, I do not presume to guess His Excellency's wishes."

"It is no risk to you," Dabir insisted.

"Well. I have been instructed to send you back; His Excellency is clearly unhappy with you. I think I would be a fool to take any of your suggestions after you lost my ship. So. You will be made comfortable, and at first light, you will be sent—"

"Whatever they paid you," Dabir cut in, "Jaffar will triple. You have no idea the threat these men form."

As he spoke, Dabir paid no heed to the expressions shifting swiftly across the governor's face—wide-eyed astonishment, openmouthed wonder, finally, lip-tightening anger. As the governor physically drew back without moving a foot: he squared his shoulders and lifted his head.

It was I who interrupted. "Dabir," I cautioned.

"You will leave at dawn," the governor said, and with that he stepped through the curtain. The captain hesitated a moment, and Dabir took this as an opening.

"Heed me, Captain—Baghdad and the caliph himself are in danger. It would take so little—a squad of men . . ." Dabir broke off as the captain, wordless, stepped after the governor. I watched the curtain fall shut and sway after their passage while Dabir vented his anger with curses.

"Sabirah is safe," I pointed out.

"Either the man is a lazy fool, or the Greek has paid him," Dabir said.

"It was folly to mention money," I said.

"What else would you have me do? If money is salve to his wants, I thought to offer more."

"You sound desperate."

"I *am* desperate. Asim, we must get out of here, and stop Firouz."

I groaned. "I ache throughout my body. I am weak and tired. And I have no weapons."

"All this is true." Dabir nodded. "But what are our troubles compared to those of Moses, who had to free an entire people?"

"Moses," I said, "heard the voice of God, who worked miracles through him."

"Mayhap it is time to work some miracles of our own," Dabir said.

His eyes burned with a feverish intensity. I met them, then looked away, choosing my next words with care. "Dabir, I lack a sword. Likely I could sneak up on a soldier, slay him with my knife, and take his blade, but I will be slaying none of these men, who have committed no crime; they are just following the governor's orders. Even were we mad enough to steal past them, how long do you think it would take for them to find us, two strangers, in the bowels of their palace, and, weak as we are, capture or kill us?"

"But we may have no better opportunity than this!"

"This is not a good opportunity. Firouz means to attack Baghdad—we can wait for him there."

Dabir's teeth flashed as he gritted them, then he dropped onto the cushions and placed his head once more in his hands.

It was a long time before he spoke again. "I know you are right, Asim. I clutch at straws."

"Let us rest, and see what tomorrow brings."

"I think it shall bring us nothing good," Dabir said softly.

The morning brought nothing good for me, to be sure, for I awoke with a fever. I have had fevers before after wounding, but never such a one as that. My energy ebbed low, and my body was so cold that it felt as though I had just dragged myself from an ice bath. Dabir and the governor's servants saw that I was bundled up as best they could. My friend insisted even that I be carried in a litter, which embarrassed me at first. I was embarrassed further to realize that I had fallen asleep while they bore me through the halls, for when next I was conscious I was lying upon a pallet on the deck. An awning shaded me. Dabir sat by my side.

"Asim?" Dabir asked. "How are you feeling?"

"I am not seasick," I answered, astonished by how weak I sounded.

"The monkey's bite must have been poisoned after all," Dabir said.

"I think so." My thinking was hazy enough that it took a moment for me to remember that Dabir, too, had been attacked. "What of you?"

"My wound aches, but I have no fever. But then I was only scratched. Who knows where else that foul thing had its teeth?"

I felt the spot above my collar where the evil little beast had seized hold of me; the skin there was numb to my touch and I did not recognize it as my own.

"Your neck is swollen," Dabir relayed.

The governor had sent a young hakim to tend to me—a student of the palace doctor, I found out. He was a quiet fellow, clearly unhappy with the trip away from the palace, but he did his job, which is all I would have asked of him. In truth, I did little asking, for I slept for much of the journey.

I felt fine enough by the afternoon of the fourth day to sit up and converse with Dabir. I was still beneath an awning near the ship's prow, propped against some tattered cloths. My clothes and blankets smelled of the sickness I had sweated out, and my neck, though sore still, felt like my own when I brushed my fingers over it.

Dabir was obssessed over the matter of Firouz and his arrival in Baghdad on the sixth of Dhu'l Qa'dah, and brooded silently about it when he was not running various scenarios aloud for me of how best the wizard could be stopped. I sat drinking broth from a cup, having little energy to speak.

"I knew that you were doing better when I saw you ask for a third helping," Dabir said.

At last I put the bowl aside, pushed the pillows and blankets off, and leaned back against the wooden rail.

"Where is Sabirah?" I asked.

"The women keep her sequestered in the cabin," Dabir answered. "I have seen her only at a distance."

"What women?"

"The governor sent some matrons and servants for her companions— and to watch her. She is allowed no contact with men."

I grunted noncommittally. That was probably a better arrangement.

"I wonder how much of that was the governor's doing, and how much was an order handed down from Jaffar?"

"There is no knowing."

"Sabirah has sent one of the matrons to ask of your health each day," Dabir said, adding, "From the matron's sour face, I think she'd prefer you dead so she would not have to be troubled with extra steps."

"I did not mean to inconvenience her."

Dabir chuckled briefly, then fell into a brooding silence.

We were on a quiet stretch of the Tigris at that moment; there was little to be heard but the creak of the ship and the wind breathing in the river reeds. Occasionally the sailors spoke to one another, but even they were quiet. The birds called to each other overhead, flying far and free.

"Asim," Dabir said finally, "Jaffar will be difficult to persuade."

"Sabirah and I will add our voices."

He nodded. "I know. If he will but place guards around the corner-stone of Baghdad's oldest building . . . then all will be well. At least for Baghdad."

"And us?"

"I think even a reasonable man might find reasons to be angry with us. All those under our charge have perished. His niece stowed away aboard our ship—"

"That was not our fault," I cut in.

"And she was kidnapped before she was returned. She then spent a month, unchaperoned, in the company of a man whom Jaffar suspects, rightly, is in love with her." He held up his hands as I started to object. "Then consider that we have failed to recover the golden plaques that were our goal, one of which was appropriated by Jaffar from the treasury of the caliph. Nor did we capture or kill the men behind the theft."

"The caliph does not lack for gold," I pointed out, knowing as I did so that the amount of gold was not the crucial part.

"That is not the point," Dabir said.

I sighed. "There were victories along the way."

"None that shall matter to him. We recovered the door pulls, only to have them stolen from us."

"What of the matter in the Desert of Souls?" I said. "Surely *that* was a victory."

"I doubt that it will have much bearing upon his assessment of us," Dabir said. Gloom fell thickly then about us.

I frowned, knowing he was right about all his worries. "No man could have done better."

"Do you think?"

"Aye. If not for you, we would not have survived in the swamps, nor would we have walked alive from the desert."

He pondered that for a moment. "It seems to me that we would not have survived if we had not stood together."

"Aye, that is the truth. Well, we have stood together, and we may well fall together, my friend."

My thoughts thereafter were mostly grim. Though my mind turned sometimes to Sabirah, I did not see her. Dabir, who must surely have been thinking of her even more frequently than myself, looked sometimes to the deckhouse windows. She was never there. He was lost in thought, and would pace the deck. Sometimes he studied the sky, mayhap searching for black birds with ebon stones for eyes.

As for me, I did not fear for Sabirah. She would be reprimanded, surely, but she was too valuable a commodity—a marriageable young woman in a powerful family—for Jaffar and the other elders to rebuke too sternly. Likely I would be called upon by Jaffar to testify to her continued chastity. Dabir's fate, now that I considered it, did not seem promising, and I wondered as to my own. Almost certainly I would be dismissed from service. If I were to face disgrace, what would happen to my cousins and nephews also in government service? Would they, too, face dismissal? I, who by my successes had opened the door for so many of them, might drag them down.

Suddenly I felt much older.

We reached Jaffar's palace in the middle morning of a warm spring day, the fifth of Dhu'l Qa'dah. One day before Dabir was sure Firouz would strike. The master was nowhere in evidence, but his orders reached us swiftly: we were to dress and wait in our rooms until summoned to speak with him. I need not remind you that Jaffar spent most of his working hours as a judge; we would not be facing casual questions.

Dabir glanced back at the deckhouse a final time, but the ladies were to be escorted last, so he had no sight of Sabirah. I thought that for the best, though I felt for him. Losing her company was one of many burdens he bore this day.

Jaffar's chamberlain, Boulos, walked with us for the brief moments that our journey saw us down the same corridor, warning us that he'd never seen the master so cross. "Things may not go well for you! Why didn't you send Sabirah back sooner?"

"We would have sent her from Basra," Dabir said, "but she was stolen from us."

Boulos shook his head. "You will have to be more convincing than that."

Dabir turned near a marble column, pausing only to nod at me. His quarters were in an entirely different portion of the palace from mine, for I bunked near the soldiers, he near the servants.

"Go with God, Dabir," I told him. I wished that Boulos were not there, so that I might say more.

"And you." He nodded and raised a hand in farewell. He looked very slight as he walked away from me, the light from high windows scattering shadowed rectangles into his path.

Boulos stayed with me as I walked to my quarters. "What happened to you? I swear that you look thinner."

"We were beset by troubles."

"And where's Hamil?"

"He is dead," I answered.

"Ho! Jaffar will be unhappy to hear that. Though I imagine you did not weep long!"

"He was a better man than I thought."

I felt the eunuch's small eyes keenly upon me. He did not speak for a long moment. "You mean that, don't you. But then you always say what you mean. Still. You seem a different man."

"Nay, just a sad and weary one. My nephew and my most promising soldiers were slain by treachery, and foul magic stole the life of Hamil. I saw Dabir strive every step of the way, and succeed against all odds. Yet I think it will end poorly for him."

"I am sorry for your losses, Asim," Boulos said, and I think that he was.

Boulos fell silent again, and our footsteps echoed together on the stone as we passed between carpets. "When you have rested, I would hear tell of your journey."

I was in no mood for that this day. "I might not have a room here much longer, Boulos."

"Oh, do not say that!"

He said nothing more, but walked with me almost to my door. Finally, he said, "It is good to have you back, Captain. I have other duties, though. I wish you well."

I thanked him. My chambers seemed smaller than I remembered. As guard captain I was given a balcony overlooking the front garden, and I stepped outside and placed my hands on its railing. Below me a fountain burbled water into a stone pool, and a little blue songbird perched upon the scrollwork. Whether it sang for a mate or for the sheer pleasure of being alive I could not guess, but I envied its joy. Still lying atop a chest just inside the door to the balcony was my shatranj board. Mahmoud never replaced the thing inside the chest after we played, always laying it there unless I scolded him. My first impulse was to take care of the matter myself, but I thought then of his hands upon the case for that last time and I stood staring at the old wood—for it had been his father's board before mine—and had to breathe deep lest sorrow drown me.

I left the board there when I headed to the north baths to clean up, then trimmed and changed. Though my back and neck were healing, I was still sore, and sudden movement pained me. Boulos sent one of the house slaves with a huge platter of food, and this I consumed eagerly. Ah, the things one can take for granted when exposed to them so frequently. I could not help wondering as I ate the finely seasoned duck and flatbread sprinkled with raisins if this were the last meal I would enjoy within the palace, or upon the earth.

We had been told we would meet with Jaffar in the early afternoon, and I did not anticipate a delay. Yet the afternoon wore on, and no one came to my door. It was not until the shadows lay stretched out across the floor like victims that I heard a dull knock. When I rose and bid the visitor to enter, it was not Boulos, but a houseboy I did not recognize.

If he was unfamiliar, the way he led me was not, for we passed into better traveled halls where servants even now hustled. Two passed me bearing platters of steaming slabs of mutton upon gold platters; shortly thereafter a trio of boys hurried with finely wrought goblets. Clearly a banquet was under way. As captain of the guard it was my responsibility

259

to be kept abreast of all scheduling so that I might ensure Jaffar's security, and it did not bode well that these servants were better informed than I.

At last we arrived at the polished walnut doors of Jaffar's main receiving room. The boy opened one of them and gestured; I heard him close it behind me.

Jaffar waited alone. I had thought to see Dabir and Sabirah and perhaps a contingent of guards, but there was only Jaffar, sitting upon the settee atop a raised dais at the room's far end. I bowed, and he waved me forward. Never had the walk down that brown carpet seemed so long.

I bowed once more when I reached the edge of the dais, keeping my eyes low and only glancing at Jaffar's expression. That day he wore finely tailored dark robes. Rings glittered on his fingers, and the sweet smell of his soaps was evident from many paces away. His expression was not angry so much as downcast.

"Peace be upon you, Asim," Jaffar said sadly.

"And also upon you, Master."

He raised his hands to belly level and tapped his fingers together distractedly. "I was sorry to hear of your loss, Asim. Mahmoud was a promising young officer."

"Thank you, Master." Was he merely marking time until the others might arrive? Where were they?

"You were my hope, you know," Jaffar continued. "Once I learned that Sabirah was missing, I sometimes feared that Dabir had leagued against me to gain the gold and my niece. But I always took solace in thought of you, for I knew well that you would never betray me."

I bowed. "Thank you, Master."

"I have heard from both my niece and Dabir how valiantly you labored over the course of your journey, and knowing you as I do, I am inclined to believe that portion of their tale. And here." He gestured to my neck, from which the bandages had been removed. My wounds still shown above my collar, scabbed and swollen. "Here I witness evidence of your struggles."

Where was he going with this? He was being extremely generous with compliments. His delivery, however, was slow, quiet. Sorrowful.

"I must put questions to you, Asim."

"I shall answer them, Master."

"You were the first to find Sabirah. Why did you not insist that the ship be immediately turned around?"

I bowed. "I spoke with Dabir about the matter. He thought it more important that we catch the thieves."

"Did he?"

"He was concerned about the appearance, Master," I added, "but he was trying to do what he thought best."

"Did you not think it likely that he wanted only to extend his time with my niece?"

"He seemed focused upon the mission, Master."

"Does that mean, then, that he took no joy in her presence?"

I saw then the road he meant to travel, and I hesitated before setting my foot there.

"Asim, answer me."

"I think that he did," I said. "But we all did, Master, for her company is a pleasure. And," I added, speaking quickly, for I'd seen him raise a finger as if he meant to make another point, "I guarded her well so that nothing unseemly took place."

"Did you?" His eyebrows lowered then, and he frowned. "Were you guarding her, then, when strangers broke into your Basra apartment and abducted her? Were you guarding her by leaving her with strange Bedouins? What about when she ran off after the Greek was slain?"

I bowed low.

"It seems that you did not guard her so finely as you would have me think."

"Master, the girl came to no harm—"

"Purely by chance, praise be to Allah."

"And I swear that I watched her closely when she was with Dabir."

Jaffar sighed. "You are a simple man, Asim, and I have always held that as one of your strengths. Surely I have few men so loyal. But Dabir and Sabirah, I think, are more clever than you. Do you insist, like these others, that you witnessed djinn and magical realms and giant snakes with feathers?"

"At first it was a giant snake, Master, but then it became a horrible worm."

"Dabir did not mention that."

"He did not see it."

Again Jaffar tapped his fingers. "Asim, Sabirah and Dabir both tell me that bhang was slipped into one of your meals."

"It is true," I said. "I did not expect the old women to be working for the enemy."

"That you were deceived is not my point. My point is that you have experience now with the consumption of bhang. Is it not possible that these other things you think you saw were hallucination?"

"I do not think so, Master."

"You did not consider your answer very long, Asim."

"I did not have to, Master. I know what I saw."

"So might a man say who took bhang." He cleared his throat. "I know, for I saw far stranger things even than you and Dabir reported when the Greek Corineus drugged me. Consider more carefully. You talk of djinn and giant snakes and strange landscapes—although Sabirah can only relay to me what she was told by the two of you. She did not see these things. I think that you were tricked into the consumption of drugs once more."

"I do not think so, Master."

Now Jaffar frowned.

"Is it not possible, Asim, that you are wrong?"

I dared not answer in the negative, and yet I did not wish to admit to something that was not true, so the moment stretched on and Jaffar's stare deepened. He cleared his throat.

"I suppose," I said, "that it is possible."

He nodded.

"Master, Dabir strove with everything at his disposal. We were out-matched by sorcery."

His brow darkened, his mouth opened, but I spoke on.

"You saw the monkeys—there were other dead things given life. Also the wizard Firouz controls flame, Master, and it slew your sailors. The enemy was leagued with a tribe of Marsh Arabs, and I daresay they may have bribed the governor of Basra."

He made a scoffing noise, but I persisted. "Yet against all of these odds, Dabir and I and Sabirah returned. If the governor had sided with us, we might have stopped the Magian there in Basra, and—"

"Captain!" Jaffar roared.

I stopped short. Jaffar clutched hard at the settee. "I no longer care about the theft—I have gifted the caliph with gold and ornaments ten times the worth of that stolen by the thieves and bungled by the two of you! What I care about is your failure, and the disappearance of my niece!"

I bowed low. "Master," I dared, "these men are dangerous."

"So too did the others say. And the city soldiers are alert for them. But that should not be your chief concern."

"But it is, Master." I looked gravely at him. "I have seen the Magian's power. He is evil, and he would bring that evil to Baghdad."

"You persist in this tale?"

"Aye, Master. It is no lie."

He sighed through gritted teeth, glared at me, then rapidly tapped his fingers together.

I bowed once more. "Do not be angry with Dabir," I said. "He—"

"You should be concerned with your own fate, not his!"

"My fate is as you will, Master. I stand ready to serve you, and the caliph, as always."

"Yes, yes." His scrutiny grew so great that I looked down at my feet. What was it he searched for?

After a lengthy silence, he sighed in defeat and addressed me softly.

"Poor, foolish, loyal Asim. Brave Asim. What could you do but follow orders?"

I looked up in time to see him spiraling one hand in the air as if conjuring thoughts with the motion. He sounded as though he meant to convince himself. "After all, I had told you to follow Dabir and seek the thieves, and this you did as best as you were able. You had no orders about the girl, thus it was simple for a more clever man to convince you that your mission—the mission I, after all, had given you—was more important."

"Master—"

"Do not interrupt, Captain! I hold you at fault, yes, but I cannot judge you too harshly." He nodded. "After all, you, more than any other, have paid more heavily, what with your own injuries, and the death of your beloved nephew."

I bowed my head.

"Here is what I judge. You, Asim, shall remain captain of my guard."

"Thank you, Master."

"I am more aware now than ever of your limitations, but knowing them, I yet value your strengths, which are many."

I bowed to the waist. "Thank you, Master."

"You may retire. Rest and recover for the next week, and then resume your regular duties."

I bowed low. "I am grateful, Master." As I rose, I dared the question that was on my lips. "But what of Dabir, and Sabirah?"

"That is not your concern," Jaffar snapped. "You are dismissed."

Once more I bowed. Usually Jaffar was not one to hold me to formalities of behavior, but given the tenor of the situation, I walked backwards, and made sure to bow once more before I opened the door from behind and slipped from the room.

The palace halls had never before seemed so empty. From far away, echoing and distorted by the stones and tiles, there came the drifting sound of music and singing. A celebration of some sort was under way, and for the life of me I could not imagine what it could be for. Not when Jaffar's mood was so foul.

I'm not sure when I have ever felt so small. Though we had suffered much, none of it had mattered. My friends seemed destined for a fate they did not deserve, and a grave threat loomed unheeded. Nothing I had said, likely nothing any of us had said, had convinced Jaffar. His reasoning was sound—so sound I almost doubted my own experience—yet the truth gnawed at the chain that bound it like a trapped wolf I was helpless to free.

I prayed alone on my rug at the call to evening prayers, then lit candles and set to an officer's most unpleasant task. With pen, parchment, and ink, it was time to write to the relatives of the slain soldiers and tell them that their men were perished. The worst of these letters would be for Mahmoud's mother. I could not quite imagine how to begin, so I left it off for last.

Who, I wondered, would write the letter for Dabir? And to whom would it be sent? Surely his fate now was sealed. And poor Sabirah, what was to be her fate? Truly her choice to follow had been foolish, aye, and disrespectful to her family, but I knew the girl well enough to know that she had not lain with Dabir.

Four times I began the letter to Mahmoud's mother—four times I crumpled the parchment and threw it aside. I had begun a fifth when I heard steps in the hallway at last. I set down the pen eagerly—an eagerness born of a desire for knowledge, I told myself, not of a desire to put off an unpleasant duty—and opened the door.

There were a trio of guardsmen in the hallway, one bearing a lantern. Omar and Saud were already unbuckling their sword belts, as a man will do when he is off duty and eager for the pallet. They started at sight of me in my doorway, then smiled.

"Captain!" Omar, the youngest of them, said with pleasure, "We'd heard you had returned."

"Is all well with you?" Latif, the lantern bearer, asked. I knew he meant to ask as to my fate and station in the palace. A homely fellow, his wit was sharp, and I had already decided he would be my new first lieutenant.

"Aye, I am your captain still."

They bowed their heads to me, and I think their pleasure was sincere.

Omar congratulated me, Latif praised God, and Saud simply smiled his gap-toothed smile.

"I have been busy with letters," I said. "What was the commotion about tonight?"

"Have you not heard?" Omar asked.

"If he had, would he be asking? Captain, the master's niece is to be married tomorrow, and tonight was the marriage banquet."

My first thought came to my lips. "That was swift. Who is the bride-groom?" Might Jaffar, suspecting the worst, simply have thrown up his hands and allied his house to Dabir's?

"Irfan bin Mubarak."

Ah, but I'd been foolish even to think that Jaffar would relent. Of course. The marriage to the son of a prominent Baghdad merchant would strengthen the family's ties in the south. Would Sabirah yet act properly for her family's honor? I hoped that she would do nothing rash.

"Have you heard anything about Dabir?" I asked.

Latif lowered his lantern and glanced over his shoulder. "The slaves were talking," he said quietly.

"The slaves always know," Omar added.

Latif continued. "Jaffar was going to behead him, but Sabirah wept and begged and pleaded and threatened to kill herself."

Oh, no.

"So Jaffar told her that he would send Dabir to the caliph if Sabirah pledged straightaway to wed Irfan without remorse."

"I wondered how it fell so quickly together."

"Who would not wish to marry into the master's family?" Latif said. "Even if there were some questions about the girl. Boulos says that you rescued her from kidnappers."

"Boulos exaggerates," I said.

"Nay, tell us the truth, Captain," Omar pleaded.

Their honest good fellowship warmed me, but in truth I did not feel like revisiting the expedition just then. Those memories hung like a lead weight around my neck. Also it seemed likely a different version of events was being shared through the palace, and I thought it wise to learn what it might be before I spoke.

And there was the letter still to write. Thus I bade them good evening and retired once more to my quarters. I tried to convince myself that Sabirah, at least, was no longer my worry. I took some comfort from knowing that Dabir was alive and safe. I left the letter to the morning, blew out my candle, and climbed into my pallet.

Long and dreamless was that sleep. On those rare instances when I fail to rise for prayers it is never sloth that keeps me to my bed. This time it was great fatigue. With no companions to rouse me I failed utterly to hear the muezzin's call. I did not wake until I heard my name. I blinked and sat up. Boulos stood at my shoulder, the little eyes in his fat face blinking rapidly.

"What are you doing here?" I asked.

The day was well on, judging from the light flooding my room. I regarded Boulos sleepily.

"You did not rise for prayers," Boulos said. "And you did not answer to my knock, nor when I called your name at entry. Forgive me."

I rubbed my head. "I did not hear you."

"Thrice I called. I had to shake your shoulder."

I sat up more fully and considered him. "Is there an emergency?"

"Nay." His head bobbed a bit. "I thought you might be dead," he admitted.

"Dead?"

He offered his palms.

"What time is it, Boulos?"

"Well into the noon hour, Asim. Or should I say, Captain?"

Noon. I had slept long. And today, I realized, was the day. The sixth of Dhu'l Qa'dah. I turned my head and looked out the window; all seemed well. There were no ghosts, nor fire streaming from the sky. "Does the master need me?"

"Nay, the master is not even here. I came to offer my congratulations."

"For what? Has Firouz been caught?"

"Firouz?" Boulos wrinkled his brow. "Nay, I meant for keeping your head. But then you did not show," he added quietly, "and I wondered if perhaps you might have been . . . dealt with in some less obvious way."

"The master would never do that," I said, and Boulos eyed me as though I were a fool. He stepped into the other chamber as I slipped out of bed and into my garments. I hurried to stand at my window and looked out at the clear sky. I heard a distant clamor of the city, nothing more. By Allah, if Dabir had been wrong . . . my one hope had been that Firouz would arrive to carry out his plan and my friend would be vindicated when the Magian was stopped. But there was no sign of Baghdad's doom. Normally I would have been happy of that.

"I've brought food," Boulos said behind me, and by way of verification I could hear the clink of plates and platters. I smelled sweet cakes.

More fully awake, I realized then that Boulos, gossip that he was, had come himself to learn the details of my meeting with Jaffar. It was not simply that he loved a good story, but that his position depended partly upon knowing all that took place within the palace. Thus he sought always to be near the center of understanding, like a spider crouched in a web of lines. When something interesting happened at one end of the palace, the line would shake and Boulos would scamper off to learn all that there was to know. I did not begrudge him this; we were not intimates, but I respected him. The warm food was such a welcome sight that I invited him to join me, which he did with obvious relish. Lest you think it strange that a free man ask a slave to join him at table, remember that he was Jaffar's chief steward and in many ways could be said to outrank me.

"I heard that Sabirah's being married off today," I said.

"True, true." Boulos passed over a plate with candied dates, and I took one. "The caliph himself will attend. Any hint of scandal has been brushed under the rug. But tell me—how many of Sabirah's kidnappers did you slay? Some say that you single-handedly fought off four of them, another that there were three, but that there were trained monkeys with poisoned claws."

I eyed him closely to see if he jested.

"There was one monkey that time," I said. "I do not think his claws were poisoned. His teeth did this, later." I tapped at my neck.

Boulos sipped at the fruit juice. "One of the most endearing things about you, Asim, is that you are such a poor liar."

"I do not lie about the monkey," I said.

"Oh, I know—I can tell."

If he could tell, why then was he amused?

"Is that why the master spared you?"

I grunted. "I told the master the truth. We all did—likely that is why he spared all three of us, though we failed his mission. Sabirah will be some other man's worry, praise Allah. Dabir may not like working for the caliph, but surely it will be better than lying in a shroud."

Boulos set down his cup. "My dear Captain. Do you really—are you really so blind?"

I had just selected a sweet bread and paused with it near my mouth. "What do you mean?"

He clucked his tongue. "Sabirah believed the master, but she is a girl, even if she is a clever one. She is young. What is your excuse?"

"What are you saying?"

"Do you really think that the master would spare Dabir?"

"Has he not promised Sabirah Dabir's safety? I was told he would work for the caliph."

"The caliph is the master's closest friend, Asim. What do you think he will do with Dabir, knowing that the honor of Jaffar's family name is threatened whenever Dabir's name is mentioned?"

A coldness spread through my skin; my face felt like ice. I set down the bread.

Boulos chuckled once. "You dear man. You really didn't know. Here I thought you had been shrewd."

"Is he still alive?"

"I expect they'll keep him that way until Sabirah is bundled away with her new husband."

"But . . . he is a good man," I said. "He never—nothing—" Words failed me.

"Here. Drink the wine." He tried to pass me a cup; my thoughts reeled and I pushed his hand back.

"There is no one here but us. Drink! The wine soothes the master when he is troubled."

"It is forbidden."

"God would forgive you this once, I think."

"Ai-a, what is it you want, Boulos? You tell me my friend will die, then press me to break the command of God?"

He sniffed, as though I had wounded his dignity, then leaned back against his cushion. "I sought merely to help."

"There is no help for me, Boulos. I am a fool. Praise be to God, who gave me a mighty arm and a keen eye for fighting. Who am I to question why he gave me so little wit! Maybe I miss so much because I look without seeing, as Dabir says."

"I did not mean to trouble you."

I nibbled distractedly on the bread. Hungry as I was, I had lost my appetite. And my need of company.

Boulos sensed this. "Eat, Captain. You have been wounded. You need your strength."

A thought flashed into my mind. Might Boulos be trying to poison me? Was that why he pushed food and drink upon me? But, then, if he was trying to poison me, why had he seemed concerned when I had been hard to wake? Surely the eunuch was not a poisoner . . . might it be that he had worried someone else had poisoned me instead of he, who wished the credit?

Tired of the second-guessing, I bit deeply into the bread and chewed with gusto. I would not be ruled by fear.

"Does not Dabir love Sabirah?" Boulos pressed.

"He is an honorable man."

"Even honorable men have temptations. And they were gone a very long time."

"It was not Dabir's doing!"

Boulos offered up empty palms. "It looks bad."

Anger roused from deep within me. "No one pays heed to the greater worry!"

"Which is?"

"The Magian and his plan! It is as if a clown dances and juggles on our left while an assassin stalks up behind with darkened blade."

"And what is his plan?"

"To destroy the caliphate! He is a master of sorcery and has the tools he needs to bring down Baghdad!"

The eunuch nodded. "Ah, yes. The master said that the Magian had used bhang upon you and tricked your senses."

Boulos seemed oblivious that I was clenching my fist so that the bread crumbled from between my fingers. He continued, "The master had bhang once, and wild sights. It may be that his experience saved you, for he understood how a man might be fooled."

"I was not fooled!"

"But weren't you tricked by Sabirah's kidnappers?"

"That is, that was—"

"Asim, let me offer you advice. The master is honestly fond of you. Now, his heart is easily moved, but I think you are one of those whom he truly favors. If you argue against him or his judgments . . ." Boulos's voice trailed off.

My thoughts churned and would not settle.

"So take it from me, one who has seen and heard much over the years, that you would be best served if you kept your tongue silent on this issue. Palace gossip has it that you are a hero—perhaps one that was tricked, but a hero who was stalwart and brave. All this is true. Why worry about the small details?"

A chill touched my flesh. "Small details like the truth?" I asked quietly.

Boulos shook his head. "Small details can make the difference between life and death. Your life and death."

Howard Andrew Jones

I said nothing.

"Think on it." He smiled and rose, bowed once. "God be with you, Asim," he said, and then let himself out.

I am a man of large appetite, but Boulos had set my thoughts tumbling at such a furious pace that it was long before I moved to consume the feast he had left.

I ate slowly and weighed my options. Outside, storm clouds gathered and the sky rumbled. I heeded the evening call to prayers, and asked God to help me in my steps, for I had chosen a path. And then I sat down to write a note to Mahmoud's mother. It was easier, then, for I had decided that there were things that I must do. I wrote my cousin in the caliph's guard. And I wrote a third letter, as well, the boldest, broadest lie I had ever composed, one that would surely condemn me to death and possibly damn me.

My most comfortable travel clothes had been worn threadbare upon my journey, and so I donned my finest jubbah, a dark, stiff-collared affair with intricate scrollwork, inlaid with pearl buttons. My turban wrap was threaded with gold. All this would better suit my purpose in any case. I had been gifted with a ceremonial sword, but this I left, preferring a sturdy blade I took from Mahmoud's quarters. Would that I might have taken up my own curved blade again, the only belonging of my father's I'd owned, but it was lost forever in the Desert of Souls. Almost everything I'd valued had been lost upon my journey, and now I was readying to abandon almost all I had left; my office, my oath of loyalty to Jaffar, and my pledge of fealty to the caliph. But not my honor. Nay, it was my honor that drove me to break those oaths and forswear all I had won by my service.

Well groomed, perfumed, resplendent from heel to helm, a sword at my side, I left my quarters and the wing of the palace. I did not expect to return.

I paid a servant boy to deliver the note to Mahmoud's mother, then turned toward Jaffar's office. You might think that I would feel fear at such a time; such was my state of mind, though, that I knew only a grim

272

sense of determination as I neared the door. I raised my hand to knock. An hour or more before, Boulos had relayed that the master was gone. Wherever he might be, he did not seem to be in his chambers. I stepped inside, closing the door gently behind me.

Jaffar had a number of receiving rooms and halls, but only one real office where inks and papers and a wide variety of books were stored. He worked here in the mornings sometimes, his chief secretary at a desk by his side. A wall of thick tomes stood upon shelves that stretched behind both desks. As you might expect, the office looked down upon one of the gardens, and the patter of rain upon leaves sounded outside the window screens. Always orderly, Jaffar had stacked a square of papers on the desk, and a pen was sharpened and ready for use beside them. I frowned then, for I saw no ink.

Jaffar's desk had but two drawers, one to left, which proved to hold only some unsharpened quills. The right drawer held his inkwell. This I sat atop the desk and unstoppered. I had not trusted to produce his signature from memory, so I lit a candle and stepped over to a neatly stacked sheaf of papers on his secretary's desk. Alas, the first of these were letters dictated to the secretary and awaiting Jaffar's signature.

A second, smaller stack on the right-hand side of the secretary's desk was a set of papers that had been signed and awaited only Jaffar's seal— thank-you notes to banquet attendees, by the look of them. Platitudes and pageantry, but they provided Jaffar's signature.

One of several flaws with my plan was that Jaffar had a fine hand—he was, in fact, well known as a talented calligrapher—whereas my writing was only passable. My thought was that I would copy the look of his signature, but write it swiftly, as though Jaffar had been in haste, or distracted.

I brought the paper back to Jaffar's desk and my note, stared hard at it, then dashed down my rendition of his name. I had not done it justice, but as I had but the one letter there was no chance to try again. My meager effort would have to suffice.

I replaced the letter, the ink, and wiped clean the quill. I folded the paper and was in the act of tipping the candle to provide the wax when I realized that Jaffar's seal did not stand on his desk in its accustomed place.

Thus did I face the first of my obstacles. It was my hope that, ranked as I was, I might bear a sealed note from Jaffar without question. Why, I might be able to declare what the note told me to do without ever having to present the signature for scrutiny. But waving it around with authority would only work if I had Jaffar's seal pressed into the wax. And it was nowhere in sight.

Once more I checked the drawers. They held only the styluses and ink I had noted before. As I stepped over to the secretary's desk I heard a noise at the door. I turned in time to face the man who thrust it open.

Boulos was framed in the doorway, a lantern in one hand.

"Asim?" he said.

"Yes."

"What are you doing here?"

I had no ready answer, and said nothing.

He glanced over his shoulder and stepped inside. "What are you doing?"

I dismissed the idea of slaying him, likewise the idea of taking him prisoner. Before I knew what I was about, I answered his question. "I am looking for the master's seal."

Boulos closed the door and stood staring at me. "Asim . . ."

"I need his seal, Boulos. I go to free Dabir."

He shook his head. "It will be your death, Asim. There will be no getting out of this."

"Dabir did not abandon me when enemies were leagued against us. I cannot abandon him."

"Do you think to use this seal and get back into the master's grace? It cannot be done!"

"The seal, Boulos. I do not care about the master. Just the seal. Do you know where it is?"

The eunuch sighed tiredly. "There. In the little box above your head on the shelf."

My hand closed upon a small casket of dark wood, enameled with green stones in the shape of an elephant. Inside lay the master's seal. "Thank you, Boulos."

He stood there, watching, as I dripped wax across the paper and pressed the seal in, leaving the master's official mark. I replaced it, then tucked the letter into my coat.

"Just because you have done this thing does not mean you have to go farther."

"The letter does not command me, Boulos, but loyalty to my friend."

The eunuch nodded, looking suddenly old and worn. He bowed. "I shall pray to God for you, Asim. And for me," he added, "that I might have a friend like you, someday, in my hour of need. But I shall pray in vain, I think."

I bowed my head in response. "Where is the master?"

"With the caliph, at the Golden Mosque. Asim, go with God. I *will* pray for you."

"Pray also for Dabir."

I clapped him on the shoulder, then bethought myself of something. "Oh, Latif is the brightest of all the guards. He is not much to look at, but he will serve the master best."

Boulos nodded. "I will urge his promotion." He smiled and shook his head.

"What?"

"You leave now on an errand that will be condemned as treachery, yet your last thought is for the safety of the master who will order your death."

I put my hand to the door latch. "I hadn't thought of it like that."

"I know. I will miss you, Asim. Try to get killed *before* you're captured. It will be much less painful."

18

Boulos's advice was sound, for if captured, I would almost surely die by slow torture.

I meant to bluff my way into the caliph's palace, pretend that Jaffar had ordered Dabir's company, then flee the city on our horses. It was a house of lies built over the bedrock of betrayal of my master, Jaffar. Fittingly, the muezzin made their last call to prayers as I rode through the city, and I did not stop. Certainly I had little time, but was I not making excuse after excuse for turning against my own beliefs and standards? How easily does man turn from God.

All these things were in my mind as I galloped, slowing only when traffic barred my way.

The storm had blown over by the time I reached the walls of the Round City. Even at prayer time there are those who must stand watch. I sat in my saddle under the long shadow of the frowning Iron Tower of the mad caliph as guards at the gate briefly scrutinized me. They recognized either me or my bearing, and waved me in.

The palace courtyard was mostly bare, and I rode through unobstructed, leading the extra horse I'd requisitioned from Jaffar's stables.

I left the reins of both animals in the hands of a stable slave with warning that they must be ready to ride, swiftly. I repeated the information twice, for the boy's glassy-eyed expression did not suggest a powerful intellect.

People were returning to duty stations from prayer as I stepped in through the service gate. I brandished my sealed paper to a turbaned guard with a waxed beard. "I've been sent to retrieve Dabir ibn Khalil, late of the household of my master, Jaffar. Do you know where he might be found?"

The fellow did not, and suggested I speak to one of the eunuchs. So it was in the caliph's palace as it was in Jaffar's—the eunuchs and slaves specialized in information. I asked the guardsman if he knew my cousin Rashad, and when he replied affirmatively I asked him to convey my letter.

I had meant to warn Rashad without being specific—lest someone else read the letter—apologizing that actions I felt honor-bound to take might jeopardize his own standing, and that Baghdad itself might soon come under attack by strange forces so that he should be ready to depart with his loved ones. I did not wish to detail information about the Magian any more than I meant to detail information about my own plans, nor did I wish to contact my cousin myself, lest he be seen as a conspirator. I thought it possible my letter, phrased as it was, could even serve as proof of my cousin's innocence in my planned actions.

The guard permitted me deeper into the household, in the company of a slave who asked another slave, and after a chain of exchanges I learned that Dabir was not in the servants' quarters, but already sitting in the caliph's dungeons. I strove not to reveal my concern. Did he still live? Had he been tortured? I faced an entirely new obstacle. Could I pass the level of scrutiny I would necessarily undergo when I presented myself to dungeon guards?

I was no stranger to the caliph's dungeons, for Jaffar, as a judge, heard many cases every week, and sometimes I oversaw the transfer of prisoners from holding cells in the palace to Jaffar's reception room. In other parts of the caliphate guards might lounge; never did they do so in the entry hall to those dungeons. As I turned the corner beneath the vaulted roof and descended the short flight of wide stairs, I immediately saw two large men at the hall's end seated at a table. They had ample time to stand and consider me during my approach, for the hall was thirty paces long. Both matched my height and girth. No matter that they had been playing quirkat—they were no sluggards. They wore armored cuirasses, highly polished, and jeweled scabbards hung from their belts.

I bowed my head to them. "Peace be upon you."

"And upon you, peace," said the taller of the two, a sharp-eyed fellow with a long nose.

"I am Captain Asim, of the household of his honor, Jaffar," I said. With these two, I did not wave the paper in my hand about. Why call attention to my lie?

"I know you," said the other fellow, and so I nodded once to him, though I did not recognize him. He returned my greeting politely enough.

"I've been sent to retrieve a prisoner in your holding, Dabir ibn Khalil, late of Jaffar's household."

"The scholar," the first man said.

"Aye."

"Have you an order?"

I lifted the paper.

The tall one took it from me, glanced at the seal, then back at me before breaking the wax and unfolding the paper. He leaned down toward the steady bronze light of the wall sconce.

I pretended calm as the fellow studied my scrawls. I tried to sound casual as I spoke to his companion. "I wish there was such a long hall opening to the cells my men guard."

"There can be no surprise here," the soldier agreed professionally.

I continued. "Though we expect no challenges in our dungeon, I tell my men that they must be careful. We have but a sharp turn, and then the desk."

"Everything seems in order," the taller one said as he folded the paper and set it down. His companion, anticipating the next order, moved to unbar the door in the wall behind them.

"I'd heard your master was furious with this Dabir." The tall guard chuckled. "It looks like his hand was shaking when he signed the order!"

I forced a laugh. "No one in his office dared even look at him at that moment," I said.

The guard gestured that the door was open, then said to his companion, "Take Captain Asim to the prisoner and bring him forth."

My guide lit a lantern, then bore it before him and advanced into the dark hall. On the whole, dungeons smell foully, for prisoners are not usually permitted access to water or soaps or other toiletry articles.

"Subhan'Allah," my companion muttered under his breath. "I never grow accustomed to it."

I prayed silently, *Allah, let him be well and whole! Let him survive his trials, and like Joseph rise to greater heights.*

Dark it was in that hall. We advanced almost to the point where it turned, and then the guard held the lantern up to the narrow aperture set in each of the iron doors along our left. He must not have liked what he saw in the first cell, for he wrinkled his nose and stepped to the next. A pitiful groan rose from one of the cells across from us.

"Nobody's in here." The fellow's voice betrayed concern as he stepped away. He meant to conceal his worry, but I knew his fear. Might Dabir have engineered his own escape?

The guard lifted his lantern in front of the final cell on the left, then let out a satisfied grunt.

"Is this him?" He passed me the lantern.

I lifted it and peered into the narrow space. Dabir, dressed still in his fine garments, blinked up at me from a sagging pallet.

"Asim, what are you doing here?"

It was a testament to my friend's character that I heard more concern than relief in his voice. For a moment only, I was puzzled. Then I understood that he was worried for me; he feared I, too, was being imprisoned, or that I was attempting something risky.

Thus it saddled my spirit with a great weight to speak harshly to him, so that I might maintain my ruse before the guard.

"Silence, dog! Who are you to ask why the master requests you?"

The caliph's man raised jangling keys to the lock. There was a click as worn tumblers turned, and then he threw open the door.

Dabir, still blinking, stepped into the circle of lantern light. I fixed him with a stern gaze. His return scrutiny was like a deep knife wound, for I saw that he feared I had betrayed him.

The guard slammed home the door. I motioned Dabir to precede me.

"The prisoner had a ring," I said, "valued by the master. Do you know its whereabouts?" I had not seen the emerald upon Dabir's finger.

"I know nothing about it." Likely he spoke the truth and some other enterprising fellow had appropriated the ring before Dabir was in his custody.

The senior guardsman waited alertly just outside the door.

He retained my letter, and brandished it on one hand. "I see you found him, Captain."

"I did."

"There was something I wanted to have made clear to me," he said.

Dabir, ahead of me, watched attentively. My companion guard seemed not to have noted the suspicion in his officer's voice, and stood to my left.

"What is it?"

"Where was it you rode from?"

"The master's palace."

The senior guard nodded, closing the letter. "There is a mystery then, Captain. This is an appalling signature. I have seen a number of your master's letters. Usually they are written by his secretary. Even when His Excellency Jaffar is in a hurry, he prides himself too much in his hand for it to look like this."

I sat the lantern down on the table with a thud. "He was not only in a hurry, but angry as well."

"Was his secretary also angry? I do not recognize this hand either." He slapped his own against the letter.

"The usual man could not be found."

He nodded once. "Can you also explain to me how it is that you rode from the palace to deliver the message your master sent when Jaffar has been with the caliph the whole of this day?"

Let the failure of my plan stand as an example for all men who think themselves clever.

"Impressive!" Dabir said.

The officer's gaze set warily upon him.

"I mean it," Dabir said. "It was truly a shrewd line of—"

I seized the lantern and swung it into the head of the poor fellow beside me. He groaned and collapsed drunkenly across the chair. As his fall began, I drew my sword.

The senior guard brought down his blade in a vicious overhead blow. It is always better to parry early in the strike, when it is weaker, but I had no choice but to block at the last moment. Catching his blade with such force numbed much of my forearm.

He snarled down and pressed with the blade.

Dabir dashed forward on the guard's left, and the fellow, being cautious, broke off so that he could see us both. I could not tell what Dabir was about, and did not trouble to look, for I sprang after my opponent with a swipe of my own.

He caught the blow on his armored chest; I ducked a savage head strike. It whistled keenly through the air. My opponent dropped back as I swung hard at his shoulder, then tripped against a chair that Dabir slid into his path. I was on him in a moment and was raising my blade even as Dabir shouted not to kill him.

The guard crashed to the ground and pulled a knife free as he struggled to his knees; my blade, though, was to his throat, and he froze.

"You have no chance of escape," the man told us. "Whatever you plan is folly."

"What is the plan?" Dabir asked me.

"We put these two in your cell," I answered.

This we did, leaving the one fellow rubbing his head still and the other glowering after us. "He was a very bright man," Dabir said as we righted the chairs outside the dungeon.

I offered that God might have bothered to leave such bright men off duty the day I chose to free Dabir from jail.

"What is the rest of the plan?" Dabir asked me then. "Why are you doing this, Asim?"

"Is it not obvious? I'm helping you get away."

"But what of you? You're throwing your career away. Your life—"

"I have horses for us; we will mount them and ride. It may be that we will escape and find our way to Spain, as you once joked; it may be that we will be hunted down and slain in our saddles. It shall be as God wills. Now gird that sword and come."

Dabir fell silent and did as I bade without argument. As we started up the stairs I noticed that the ring had appeared again upon his finger and I asked him from where it had come.

"I was not searched too carefully," he answered. "If I'd had a small weapon, they would have missed it."

As we turned the first corner a great hue and cry reached our ears. From somewhere far off came the screams of a multitude; the high, shrill sound of women mourning children or bereft of senses, the frenzied shouts of men calling out to God.

The wide-eyed guard at the stair height had no thought in his head to suspect us of mischief. He seemed scarcely to see us before blurting out his news and hurrying on down the hall. "Judgment! Judgment day is come!"

"What do you mean?" I demanded.

He looked back at us over his shoulder as he ran on. "God rains fire and destruction; the dead walk the earth!"

I cursed. "Well, my timing for your escape was poor, it seems."

"Nay, your timing was perfect, Asim. What better distraction could we have asked for? Firouz has gotten past Jaffar's guards and brought his vengeance home to us."

"If Jaffar even posted them." I shook my head.

"You and I are the only ones who understand what is happening—we are the only ones who can stop this."

It was a strange moment there at the head of those dark stairs, the screams of the populace echoing in the hall along with the pounding of hundreds of feet through the palace. I could not see my friend well on account of the dim light from the hall lanterns and the darkness without; still, I studied him.

"Dabir, Firouz has bested us at every turn. He has mastery of magic, and djinn, and God knows what else. I count it a success that we survived with our skins intact. Besides, we do not even know where he is."

"He will be close, so that he can gloat at his success in causing such chaos. And I did not say that we should confront him without taking proper steps."

"What steps? Are you to master magics?"

"Not exactly. But there is at least one tool here, in the palace treasury, that we can wield."

"What tool is that?"

But Dabir was already in motion.

I seized his arm. "Dabir, wait!"

He turned.

"Against great odds you have your life. Jaffar, the caliph—they will take it from you, even if Firouz does not. This is their city. Their responsibility. You owe them nothing at this point."

His face hardened. "I do not think of them, Asim. I think of the thousands endangered by Firouz's crimes. I think of the caliphate, weakened or fallen, and Byzantium crouched on the border ready to spring at the scraps. I think of our friend Hamil, and Mahmoud, and all the men slain by Firouz, and all those who might still meet their end because of him."

I nodded. "All this is true. But I will not think less of you if you depart."

"I could not stand to live if I were to abandon you to fight him alone. My honor would die beside you."

I grunted, for this answer pleased me. "This will likely be the end of us," I reminded him.

A grim smile turned up the corners of his mouth. "And that is different from anything we've done together in the last few weeks?"

"Together, then."

"Aye, together."

19

Screams erupted all around us and folk fled down the main corridors of the palace. Some had thrown down prayer rugs and bent knees in supplication. Others sobbed in corners. Still others had rifled through stores for wine and sat where they willed, sucking down the forbidden liquid. Here and there ghostly figures, glowing, ran through the halls, their mouths open as they screamed from long years before. A transparent pillar came crashing down and blocks of marble followed.

"The city of Ubar is superimposed over Baghdad's center," Dabir said, and as if to lend credence to his words, a chunk of burning matter hurtled through the roof and smashed into the wall near where a trio of servants huddled. The people were real and the aftereffects of Ubar were not, but it sent them screaming past us.

"Should we explain that none of this can harm them?" I asked.

"Do you think that would work?" Dabir asked.

I didn't answer.

"Do you think folk could live in such a place, even knowing that the images cannot harm them? Hundreds will die in the crush and chaos as they struggle to flee Baghdad and many hundreds more in the disarray to follow."

Eventually we arrived at the stairs to the treasury. Two wide-eyed guards stood sentry outside the door, watching a pair of ghostly figures limp through a wall, one supporting the other.

Dabir paid no heed to the phantoms, though he did walk around them. I gave them a wide berth myself.

"Halt," a guard said with quavering voice.

"We've come for an artifact to stop the magics," Dabir said.

"Jaffar sent us," I added. I had already lied so much that one more seemed a trifle.

"Have you a note?" the guard asked hesitantly.

Dabir threw up his hands in exasperation. "Do you think Jaffar took time to write a note? Throw open the door! If I seek to exit with treasure, slay me then!"

At some other time the guards would likely have bristled at this treatment, but both men bowed their heads and threw open the double doors.

Things were little better in the honeycombs beyond the portal. Even the stern veterans on duty within stood pale in the antechamber of the central hall, which burned thoroughly with ghostly fire. Only one of the three bureaucrats was with them. When Dabir told him we had been sent to find an artifact to put an end to these matters, he led us on without even asking who'd sent us.

Thus we wound through the dark, narrow corridors as the little man shone a lantern up to the numbers set upon the honeycombed vaults. At last we stopped before a small iron door, and the fellow passed off the lantern to me while he rustled in his dark robes for a ring of keys. A moment of jangling followed, and then he set key to lock and opened the door.

Only one item was within, lying lengthwise upon a shelf. Dabir set hand to it gently, then pulled the thing free, feeling the heft of it in his hand.

He held a wooden staff topped by a cat's head. It was fashioned of a rich black wood unknown to me and covered from head to pointed foot in curiously wrought symbols.

"It is an old staff," I said.

"It is a staff from the court of Solomon," the bureaucrat said, taking the lantern from me.

I showed him my palms. "What of it?"

"*King* Solomon, Asim," Dabir explained. "A magician in his court used it to slay enemies."

"It passed on to David, peace be upon him," the bureaucrat reported, "who wrought further wonders, through the will of Allah."

"God be praised," I said. "But do you know how to wield it?"

"I have never used it," Dabir conceded. "But I know through my reading that you must hold it high and trust to your faith."

He must have seen my skeptical look, for he continued, "We do not have time for burak treatment. If nothing else, the pointed end is still sharp. Come, Asim. It is time to act."

Dabir and I left the treasury and the guards and then the palace itself, he carrying the old, old wood before him less like a staff and more like the treasure it was . . . or might be. Men are credulous creatures, and it occurred to me that the thing might be any old stick preserved from ancient times and passed on somehow to the caliph with a grand note lying about its authenticity. I hoped that Dabir knew more about its history than me, but I did not question him. I felt then as though our boat had been swept out into the currents and there was nothing to do but ride the waves.

The night sky flamed with falling stars, trailing red and gold as they crashed into the ground on either hand. Transparent buildings dotted the open square and ghostly figures ran for cover within them even as pillars and cornices crumbled beneath the heavenly assault. Never before had I seen so many soldiers cowering, but there they were, outside the Golden Mosque, slack-jawed or weeping. Dabir and I dashed past them unchallenged. Some brave soul chose that moment to push open the door and stare from within at the madness without and called for all to enter and pray.

We kept on. Across from the square, looming above even the mosque's minarets, was the cold hard darkness of the Iron Tower. Only the falling stars themselves stood higher in the sky. From the windows in the tower's height shone a feeble yellow light. Wan and sickly though it was, it filled me with more dread than the glowing spirits crying all about us.

"You were right," I said to Dabir.

With all the shouting about us he must not have heard.

A half-dozen wild-eyed horses were tied to the posts near the tower. One poor mare was bucking madly as we came up, whinnying in fright. Her companions answered with calls of their own.

There was but a single entrance to the tower at its base, a thick metal door, its decorative leafing worn down by the years. I put first my hand and then my shoulder to it, and it opened.

"Why would he not lock it behind him?" Dabir speculated.

"Maybe your staff is already working." I peered through into the dark space. It seemed clear, so I unsheathed my sword, pushed open the door, and advanced.

Beyond the door was a small antechamber, and then a flight of steps that curved up around the tower. A figure was sprawled motionless across the bottom stair. Dabir bent briefly to him.

"Dead," he announced, although it was already clear. "Probably he questioned Firouz and they dragged in his body after slaying him."

Golden light fell briefly through a small tower window upon a run of stairs before disappearing as another ghost star plummeted outside.

I took a deep breath. "Should we go up?"

"Let us be on with it." He hefted the staff as if testing the weight of the old thing, then started forward.

Up we climbed, round and round the tower. We climbed in near darkness, the curving wall and steps before us but suggestions. We stepped quickly and for the most part silently, although we could not help sometimes scuffing our boot heels upon the stone.

Finally we arrived at a point where a dim but steady light shone ahead of us; we slowed to listen, for there was a man speaking. Firouz, I realized after a moment; he was exultant, commenting gleefully upon the confusion below. If he had companions, none of them answered.

I crept carefully up the final stairs, my back to the wall, and peered about the curve and up into the tower's only room. The mad caliph's tower was thick-walled, and this, its lookout, was wide and circular. Cobweb-strewn arches supported the domed roof, allowing access to a balcony that overhung the tower. The stairwell came up inside the tower; it was nothing more than an opening in the floor. I crept up the final curve of the wall until I had sight of our adversaries.

From my vantage point I saw the backs of only two men, standing stiffly near the stairs, looking away. I glanced back at Dabir and tightened the grip on my sword. Moving fast, I might be able to take them by surprise. Was one of them Firouz? I could not tell with certainty, but I did not think so.

I would trust to God, who had seen me through intact, and who knows the fate of all men. I looked to Dabir, and though I could not see him clearly, I saw him nod to me. I nodded back. It was no time for words, or hesitation.

I sprang up the stairs, and my blade swept deep through the first man's flesh. I spun and swung again as the second target turned to me. He fell back, silent, even as a pair of other men stepped out of the darkness toward me.

A single lantern burned upon the floor beside the railing. One figure raised it, casting light toward me as Dabir came up from behind.

"Dabir and Asim?" I knew the amazed voice for Firouz, though I saw him not, for it was he who blinded us with the lantern. "You live? Did the caliph send you?"

Then I understood that there was greater challenge here than I had expected. Aside from Firouz and ourselves, no one standing in that room was alive. Aye, there were four other men, but they were dead, with black stones for eyes, which now threw back lamplight coldly. The two I'd struck upon entrance drew their swords and readied themselves, not caring that I'd slashed them deep.

Sand slipped steadily from the slit in the belly of one, hissing gently to the floor. Their faces were dry and drawn. The stiff ends of thread stuck up from the corners of their mouths where they had been sewn shut. Only one of the four looked more fresh: even in death Ali held a throwing knife ready.

As if things were not already bad enough, the last of those damned monkeys sat hunched by Firouz's feet.

Dabir carried the staff before him in both hands, his face intent.

"A parting gift from Diomedes," Firouz said with a royal wave over his minions. "What does the caliph say to my summons?"

"It matters not," I cried, "for you shall be dead in moments." I raised my sword to charge him, but Dabir swept his hand to stay me. I did not long wonder why, for Firouz snarled a cryptic phrase and flame rolled from the lantern in a widening line. Dabir tapped down the staff, the cat head tilting toward the flame, and the point rang against the old stone. By Allah, the compassionate, I swear that the fire broke upon the wood like water striking a cliff, rolling to either side of us without so much as singeing our clothes.

Dabir raised an eyebrow at me and grinned and I realized, to my horror, he hadn't known what would happen.

The lantern flame sputtered and died, plunging us once more into black. Green afterimages of flame obscured my vision.

"Die!" Firouz roared. This time white-hot lightning coursed down from the sky, skipped into one of the wizard's palms and across his chest and out through his extended fingertips. It arced toward Dabir, but was drawn harmlessly downward into the staff. Its cat's head glowed with a brilliant blue white nimbus that threw the shadows of dead men on the floor.

Firouz, panting, snarled in frustration. "Slay them," he shouted. "Take the staff!"

I stepped in front of Dabir, swinging my sword in a figure-of-eight meant to keep them at bay until my vision cleared. A small blade clanged against my own, winged off to the right, and clattered down the stone stairs on our flank. I guessed it had been a knife cast by the corpse of Ali. Allah most surely was with us, for I had seen neither the weapon nor the throw; what's more, my vision began to clear.

Ghost meteors painted the floor in reds and oranges as they fell, keening. With the shifting light and my uncertain vision all I saw of the monkey was a dark, scrambling shape that somehow unnerved me more even than the dead men who stalked in front of it.

Ali's corpse came at me, blade in hand. I slashed down and caught my sword in his collarbone. This troubled him not at all, and he stabbed out at me, wedging the tip of my blade deep into his neck. It was only by holding my blade arm stiff that I kept from injury.

The monkey leapt at my right leg. I kicked at it, missed, and it bounded for the left. I gritted my teeth in loathing, bracing myself for it to latch on to my calf. At that moment Dabir slammed the point of his staff through the monkey's head. The blow delivered a satisfying crunch and dropped the beast flat, where it lay still at last.

"Praise Allah," I breathed.

Dabir turned back to his own battle; a glance showed me that one of his swordsmen was down. The other swung his weapon wildly back and forth before the scholar, advancing behind a barrier of swinging steel. "A moment," I told him.

My sword arm wearied from keeping Ali at bay. I did not feel the same fury for this shell of the man I'd slain, only a mounting sense of dread because the dead man did not trouble to struggle free, keeping me locked in position. "Dabir," I said, "fall back!"

He did not question. We two trusted each other now, and moved together in combat like the hands of one warrior. He stepped to the stair edge. I rotated, stiff-armed, directing my ghastly opponent into the track of his. The swordsman's blade lodged in Ali's spine with a mighty blow. The strike must have upset the corpse's equilibrium, for Ali's arms flailed uselessly. As he dropped, I wrenched my weapon free. Dabir leapt in and smashed the swordsman across the head with the staff. He, too, dropped. I understood then that a strike from the staff was enough to destroy the unholy things.

The final corpse, a pale Persian in armor, rushed forth even as Dabir raised the staff. The dead man grabbed the wood with both mailed hands.

The two wrestled as footsteps and the shouts of men rang up the length of the stairwell.

"Dabir, duck!"

When my friend let go the staff and dropped flat, I smote the corpse in the chest with all my strength. I meant to dislodge the magic stone, as had been done with Ali's body.

Instead, I knocked the thing off balance. It staggered backwards heel-toe, heel-toe, and it would have been comical if it hadn't struck the tower railing and fallen silently over the edge, staff still clutched tightly in his dead fingers.

"Oh," I said, my hopes dropping like the body. But at that moment I heard a new man's voice near at hand call breathlessly to Allah, and I looked up.

The black-garbed soldiers who had reached the landing ignored Dabir's call to douse the lights. They were the elite of the elite, the personal guard of the caliph himself, and boots, robes, turbans, and belts were all of them black. Three were as tall and broad as me, with short, pointed black beards, and two bore shining lanterns. The fourth, towering over the others by half a head, was the mighty Masrur, the caliph's chief body-guard and executioner. Beside him stood the caliph himself, a tall young man with large, sad eyes and round cheeks, garbed this night in a black robe decked in gold. It was he who'd seen the final moments of our battle, and cried out in surprise. Behind them, still on the stairs, was my master, Jaffar, also in black.

Dabir called again to blow out the lights. "That man is a wizard, and commands fire!"

"Oh, I will not kill the caliph," Firouz said calmly.

He sat now on the railing, one hand resting upon a large smooth stone balanced beside him. Spotlighted now by lanterns, it was clear he had dressed for effect. His robe was crimson, ornamented with little gold patterns of flame, cinched at the waist. He smiled as though greatly satisfied.

"What is the meaning of this?" the caliph demanded, his voice low-pitched and crisp.

"You received my summons then?" Firouz asked him. "Good."

"I received a message from a strange bird, telling me the power to stop this madness lay at the tower's height."

Firouz's smile broadened. "I sent that message. We have business." His fingers tapped the edge of the block, though the hand did not leave it. I guessed that if he lifted his hand it would overbalance and topple. "This is Baghdad's cornerstone, the first stone laid when your predecessor built over the tiny village that had stood along the riverbank. It is, for all intents and purposes, the soul of Baghdad. If I drop it, all this chaos you see around you will continue for eternity."

"Let me kill him, Master," Masrur said in his even, mild voice. There are those who think all eunuchs are fat and womanly; any who met Masrur encountered the finest contrary argument.

The caliph raised a single hand, and Masrur fell silent. "Who are you," he demanded of Firouz, "and what do you want?"

Firouz's mouth rose in a tight smile; his good eye gleamed. "I am Firouz, of the Magian. Our civilization was old when your folk were still wandering the desert chasing goats. You stole the wisdom of our sages, but ignored the most important of their teachings. But, fear not, I will instruct you."

The caliph frowned in irritation. "What is it you would have me know?"

"That all actions have consequences, that no one escapes the balance due. You tax us into poverty under a guise of protection. You confiscate our properties on any pretext, and slay all who dare to cry out against your injustice, killing any innocent in the way. You sit remote, amongst your luxuries, careless of the atrocities committed to secure your ease—"

"How many have you slain," Dabir interrupted quietly, "in your quest for vengeance?" All eyes turned to him.

"It is not the same thing!" Firouz answered angrily. It irked him, I think, to leave off the speech he had prepared.

"Is it not?" Dabir countered. "The caliph gave no orders for your family."

"Aye, they were slain out of hand. An accident; a happenstance by a government that cannot be bothered with such details."

Both the caliph and Jaffar watched Dabir with interest. I could not tell if they were affronted or startled by his involvement.

"And all the deaths at your hands were deliberate," Dabir said.

"That they were." Firouz almost purred.

"Do not do this thing, Firouz," Dabir said. "Set the stone upon the floor, and surrender yourself."

Firouz laughed. "Or what?"

"Think of your soul, Firouz."

Firouz chuckled once.

"Think of the souls of others below whose lives you disrupted. The loving wives and sons and daughters whom your actions are wounding and slaying even now. Do you wish to leave countless others with the misery you feel yourself?"

"I wish to destroy him," Firouz said, "by destroying his empire! Back!"

At mention of a personal threat to their master, two of the guardsmen had moved forward, hands upon hilts.

"Hold!" the caliph cried.

"I am surprised," Firouz said to him, almost regaining his composure. "I felt sure you would offer me money. Wives. A province."

"Is that what you wish?" the caliph asked.

"I want to know what you would offer me," Firouz said, "to spare the very heart of your kingdom. Would you promise me a kingdom of my own?"

"He is toying with you, Excellency," Dabir said.

"Silence!" Firouz shouted. "You should be silent before your betters, Dabir! I would have thought you had learned by now that you cannot stop me!"

"I can," Dabir said quietly. "This is why I ask you one more time to surrender, for the sake of your soul."

Firouz laughed. "You're bluffing."

Dabir raised his fist. In it I saw a small reddish vial. He flung it to the floor, where it shattered. Red-tinged smoke billowed up immediately. Masrur cursed and pulled the caliph back.

Dabir continued, "I took it from your pack in Ubar, after we had slain your guards the first time."

"Now I know that you lie, for if you could command a djinn, you would have used it before this moment."

"Unlike you, Firouz, I had no souls which I meant to sell."

Firouz's head rose minutely, calculating, and then his eyes widened in fear.

The djinn swirled in through a window arch, his appearance shifting so that he seemed at one moment a man and at another a dust devil and at another a blending of the two. The caliph and even his guards stepped back, muttering in amazement.

"But I never expected to live past this moment, Dabir," Firouz said, almost sadly. "Can it reach me before I strike the ground?" With a mocking laugh he pushed the stone over the edge and hurled himself after.

Dabir did not wait for the djinn to put question to him. "Restore the city's soul," he cried, "and Firouz's soul is yours!"

Without a word the djinn hurtled past. The wind of his passage staggered Masrur and the guards. I raced to the rail, the caliph himself at my left side, Dabir on my right. A ghostly ball of fire screamed down from the heavens at that very moment so that we saw Firouz's garments billowing about him as he plummeted to the courtyard. A red blur of smoke flew after.

The cornerstone shattered against the pavement. I remember thinking that Firouz had won, and then noticed his descent had stopped. He was suspended but a few feet above the stone. He must have realized it, too, for he cried out in dismay.

It was then that the djinn enveloped him.

A ghost meteor crashed through a spirit tower just outside the gate, lighting the whole of the courtyard. The djinn rose with this as his backdrop, Firouz's body struggling in one hand. The Magian screamed even as the djinn's other hand plunged through his chest. A moment later the djinn's fingers plucked forth an ebon ball shot through with jagged patterns of shining red and gold. He raised Firouz's soul to study and cast off the body, which struck the ground with a grisly crunch—it was as if the momentum of Firouz's fall, halted by the djinn, had suddenly been restored to him.

"But the stone," the caliph said. "He was not quick enough."

"Wait," Dabir told him.

The djinn tucked Firouz's soul within his robe and then hovered above the ground and extended both hands. Fragments and slivers of stone whirled up from the pavement beside Firouz's still and twisted corpse and hung before the djinn in midair. I swear to you that the djinn did nothing more than hover there, with hands extended—the stone rebuilt itself, chunks and specks and shards all blending one into another until the thing was whole and unflawed. Masrur let out an exclamation.

The cornerstone intact in his palm, the djinn rose up and sped off across the rooftop with the speed of a shooting star.

All about us the night still flared with ghost meteors and the screams and cries of men. The caliph looked after the djinn's course, then considered Dabir.

"Will the djinn do as you bade him?"

Before Dabir could answer, the flames upon the sky flickered and vanished. One of the soldiers shouted that the ghosts were gone; surely they were. No more did glowing figures run the streets of the city, no longer did transparent buildings intersect with and interpose themselves upon the real world. While all looked as it should, panicked voices and the frightened calls of animals rang out through the city. In the distance a trio of roofs was outlined in fire and smoke.

The caliph stared out at his city for a long moment. Jaffar waited at his side, looking almost nervous.

The caliph turned to Jaffar. "See that the city is put in order. One fire is under way—there may be others. Rouse the palace hakims and all others that you can find. Some of the people will have been injured and require tending. Send out the guard to look for looters. They are to instill calm, not add to the panic. Is that clear?"

"I hear and obey." Jaffar bowed very low, then hurried off down the stairs after a brief, unreadable glance toward us.

The caliph then turned his full attention to us. "You are Dabir the scholar," the caliph said, "and you are Captain Asim."

We bowed our heads.

"You," he said, pointing a finger at Dabir, "were last in my dungeons. How came you here?"

I bowed again. "I freed him, Your Excellency."

"On whose authority?"

"On none but my own."

"I see."

I did not know what he might say then. His look was grave.

"The two of you have saved the city," the caliph told us at last, "and the caliphate itself."

Again we bowed. He raised a ring-encrusted hand to stop us. "We are not at court this day. Ask any boon of me; it is yours."

I looked to Dabir to speak first, and so did the caliph. Dabir, though, said nothing, so the caliph turned to me.

I caught myself as I began to bow again, so that my head bobbed. "Your Excellency, my nephew died in the fight against the wizard, and his body now lies in Basra. I would have it brought here, and a tomb built to house it."

"Is there nothing else?"

I nodded my head once, feeling foolish. "Aye, the wizard also slew brave men under my command, soldiers and sailors, and a boat captain and his son. If monies could be given their families, I would be grateful."

The caliph shook his head, smiling wryly. "I shall do these things, Captain, and also I shall gift you with a robe of honor and a fine sword, and a horse of quality. Indeed, you shall lack for nothing."

I bowed to him; overcome, I had forgotten not to do so.

"And what of you, scholar?"

"I have grown homesick, Your Excellency. I wish only release from Jaffar's service, so that I may return to Mosul."

"Surely you jest! I mean to raise you to a station of honor, Dabir. You shall sit at my right hand, and I will value you among my counselors."

But Dabir only smiled sadly. "I cannot, Your Excellency, though it pains me to reject your offer."

The caliph studied him for a long moment, and I sensed that he understood some small part of what Dabir might be feeling, for he nodded slowly. "So be it. But when you return to Mosul, it will be to a home furnished with servants, with gold stores that will leave you wanting nothing. Captain, you are to go with him."

"Excellency," Dabir started, "that's not—"

"Nay, say nothing. You are a treasure to the caliphate. Asim, you are to guard him by day and by night, as you more swiftly understood his worth than all the rest of us."

"I will be honored," I said.

The caliph stepped away from the balcony then and contemplated the bodies that lay across the tower floor. My eyes fell again upon the twisted furry mass of the monkey. The flickering lantern light stretched and shortened its shadow, granting the thing an illusion of movement. I had trouble taking my eyes from it.

"There is much yet I wish to know," the caliph continued. "We will celebrate your victory at a banquet tomorrow evening, but I would first hear the details now, privately."

Dabir bowed. "It will be an honor, Your Excellency."

"Come with me then. Masrur, see that someone cleans out this tower. It is past time I had the thing torn down."

20

We near the end of this story, but I would be remiss if I did not recount the splendid banquet within the caliph's palace the night following. The Palace of the Gilded Gate was not some monolithic structure, as those looking from without might suppose, but a great warren of many rooms and wide gardens, some of which contained small palaces of their own. Harun al-Rashid favored us mightily, for we and his nadim—his closest friends and advisors—dined that evening at the Palace of Marvels, which sat in the Garden of Delights. The caliph brought only his most cherished companions to the Palace of Marvels, which was but one immense chamber lit by a hundred windows in the day, and a great glittering chandelier come evening. All about us as we ate were the voices of women raised in song—not cacophonous screeching, or the warbling of strings, but soothing sounds as might lull even the most troubled of hearts to rest.

Dabir and I were clothed in fine robes aglitter with jewels, and sat very near to the caliph himself, who was in fine high humor. After the first courses there were dancing girls and acrobats, and then some more energetic singers. I do not care overmuch for music, and by that time my stomach was more than ready for a full meal.

When the food at last was served, it was most fine: roast fowls and sheep, pastries of sweet cheese and honey, and marvelous fruits of all kinds. Delicate cakes dripping with syrup were brought forth such as they must serve to visiting governors and ambassadors from great lands.

The caliph asked again for our tale while we ate. Jaffar insisted upon starting out, and he passed lightly over the incident with the fortune-teller, saying only that she had predicted Dabir would be a slayer of monsters. Since Dabir did not see fit to add details to this account, I did not do so myself. Dabir and I told the rest of the story together, interrupted sometimes by questions from the caliph or one of the dozen nobles who thronged about the table.

There were certain moments Dabir left from the narrative, and I followed his lead—mention of romance between himself and Sabirah, or any conversation in this regard. When we came to the recounting of our arrest in Basra, Jaffar stepped in to explain that at the time he thought us failures and possible kidnappers, but the caliph waved him silent. Oh, there were skeptical looks from those who listened, but during the moments when we told of the dead city and the serpent worm and the final battle in the tower overlooking Baghdad, no ear turned from us, and even the servants and slaves delayed their departures from the room so that they might hear. The caliph himself attested to those gathered that he'd seen the bodies of the dead men we had fought, and witnessed the appearance and departure of the djinn.

Dabir added, "Asim and I saved the work of Hamil, the poet, who'd chronicled much of our journey before his death. We have not had time to have it recopied, obviously, but—"

The caliph brightened. "Oh, I would be quite interested in reading that. Abu, when these verses are recorded, I wish you to finish the tale, based upon the account you have heard this night."

The caliph's favorite poet smiled a little too broadly from down the table. "With pleasure, Excellency!" he piped up cheerfully.

"Ah," the caliph confided softly to us, "he is drunk. The details will escape him. I may have to have you write them down and send them to him."

"A fine poet will improve upon our story," Dabir said, "and it may sound better through a drunken haze in any case."

The caliph laughed. He was a merry fellow in those days, bright-eyed and handsome, the very image of a prince. Always he sat straight-backed, his head high, but such was his manner that he did not seem aloof or formal, but relaxed, for his commanding presence was natural to him. When he wished to be, formality mostly dropped from his manner and he seemed eminently approachable. Such was his attitude when he eyed us seriously then. "Are you sure I cannot convince you to stay?"

"No, Excellency," Dabir said. "Though I would ask that you do not make Asim's companionship a command."

"I will go gladly," I said, for in truth I did not know how I might return to my normal life in Jaffar's household after all that had transpired. I had broken into his office, forged his signature, and released a man he'd condemned to death. I had assumed, in other words, that I had known better than my own master.

"What of Baghdad, Excellency?" Dabir asked. "How much damage was done?"

The caliph nodded once. "The destruction was not extensive. Fires were quickly put out once order was restored. Saddest of all were the two dozen who died in a rush toward the river gate, where they were trampled underfoot."

"It is fortunate more did not perish," Dabir said.

"We're fortunate you and Asim fought so hard to stop the sorcerer," the caliph said. "A few poor souls were said to have dropped dead from fright at sight of the spirits. I cannot say that I blame them." The caliph's tone grew more reflective. "Dabir, you knew this wizard. Was he always an evil man?"

"Nay, Excellency. Misfortune twisted him."

"I have thought long upon his words. Is it true that his family was slain? Were they rebels?"

"Not as he told it, Excellency. They were killed when the conflict raged on."

"It is difficult to govern without the spill of blood," the caliph mused. His voice took on a sad, wistful quality. "Someone starts a fire smoldering and I must send men to stamp it out. Sometimes the fire rages too far; sometimes those sent to quell it know not how to stop, or lack the wisdom, or have aims of their own. God alone knows, and will judge them by their deeds." He looked long at Dabir. "You are wise, I think, to leave this, for a simpler place. I have no choice but to stay."

Now I had known many men who envied the caliph, but I had never guessed that the caliph might envy the station of someone beneath him, and I sometimes think upon that moment even today, for the young and thoughtful caliph was to age swiftly and die before his time.

We left him late in that evening, and as we made our way down the dark hall, we heard the rush of footsteps behind us. Jaffar called out to us. "Dabir, Asim, wait!"

We obliged him at the top of a stair, the little slave boy holding our lantern waiting discreetly to one side. Jaffar had been in such a hurry he'd come with no servant of his own.

He reached us, panting a bit, then stretched out a hand to support himself against a wall, none too steadily. Jaffar had been drinking. His shadow, thrown upon the wall from the lantern, shook as Jaffar himself panted.

"I wanted to . . . to give you my thanks," he said, "and personally congratulate you." He spoke slowly, and the struggle to find the proper words was writ large upon his face.

"Thank you, Master."

"You faced many obstacles." He stared at us, glassy-eyed as drunk men do, so it was hard to tell if he was intent upon a point, or ready to throw up. The grape makes fools of the wisest men. "I had my hand in setting some before you," he said finally, sounding almost sober as he did so, "and I deeply regret it."

"It is already forgotten," Dabir managed evenly.

Jaffar grinned. "You are a good man." He clutched suddenly at Dabir's arm. "Do you think it's true?"

It took Dabir a moment to decipher the meaning of the question. "The wise woman's prophecy? Is that what you're asking about?"

"Yes—do you think it was true? Do you think she mixed up the cups?"

"Oh, surely so," Dabir said compassionately.

Jaffar beamed like an imbecile.

"Clearly," Dabir added, "I was the one doomed by desiring someone beyond my station."

Jaffar's brow creased, and he waggled a finger. "But no man may avoid his fate."

"I did not avoid it—Asim altered it without my asking."

"Ah! That makes sense! I'm so glad he did." He put his hands together, beaming. "It has all worked out! There are no hard feelings, are there? You both have riches and honors. Sabirah is well, and married to a good man. And you, Dabir, can marry any woman you want!"

"Yes," Dabir said, though he did not laugh when Jaffar did so, nor did he respond as Jaffar wished us well and told us to go with God. He waved us away and turned into the darkness.

"He's still desperate," Dabir confided softly to me as we fell back in step.

"What do you mean?"

"He knows that the fortune-teller spoke truly, and that the cups were not confused, yet has twisted all his reasoning to convince himself they were."

"Who is above him?"

"Did you not mark the screen directly behind the caliph?"

In fact I had—a fine cedar panel had stood behind him, with latticework above head level—but I saw no connection to the subject at hand. "What has that to do with anything?"

"Above all others, perhaps even Jaffar, the caliph prizes his sister, Abbasah. She sometimes attends banquets thus, behind the screen, so that she can hear but not be seen. Did you harken how sometimes the caliph or Jaffar would lean close to the screen and smile or nod?"

"I did not."

"Doubtless she spoke to one or the other of them then."

"You think—"

"Shh," Dabir said quickly, adding softly, "I accuse him of nothing. I merely observe."

A fine observer he was, too, given what was to befall Jaffar in later days.

We passed that night in the sumptuous chambers given over to us in the caliph's halls, then rose after morning prayers to find a baggage train prepared for us, loaded down with gifts. No less than a dozen soldiers and as many servants and bearers were detailed to ride with us, so that such riches would arrive at our new lodgings unmolested. It was more than I had ever thought to see, and even Dabir, grim and tired-looking as he was, managed a smile.

As we wound our way through the city, riding for the northern gate, I bethought myself of all that had transpired, and how much my life had changed because of a parrot's death and my own injudicious laughter.

I considered many things, but one thing most especially, and thus I bade Dabir ride on, telling him there was a final stop that I must make; I would meet him on the road. Dabir looked curiously after me, but said nothing.

I found the little marketplace easily enough, then turned down the alley. The beggars and common folk stared at me as I dropped from the gleaming white mare that had been Jaffar's gift, doubtless wondering why someone attired in such fine raiment would venture here, for I wore my robe of honor and my boots were of new shagreen.

One of the fortune-teller's grandchildren answered the door, his eyes wide at my splendid garments, then called for the woman.

Old she was, but she smiled in recognition after she squinted for a moment. "You have come to know more?"

"Nay." I held up my hand. "I did not wish to know God's plan for me from the first."

"Then what is it you wish?"

"When you read our fates, is it possible that you confused them?"

She smiled crookedly.

"I am no writer," I said, "only a swordsman."

"Sometimes we choose our paths; sometimes we stumble upon them. Sometimes we must stride forward and seek them out, though the way is obscured by mist."

"That does not help me. Can a man change his fate, or another man change it for him?"

"I have seldom met a man who so feared taking up a pen."

I shook my head. "I do not ask any of this for myself, but worry for another of my companions."

She stepped closer to me. "All our lives are webs of choices, intersecting with other webs. But I think you know this."

I scratched my head, reasoning that I understood her, although I wished that she'd spoken more plainly. In any wise, I was not comforted, and I think she sensed this. To her I gave over the robe, which was altogether too fine a garment for a simple swordsman like myself.

She took it wonderingly as I stretched. Already the thing had made me overwarm, there in the street.

"Whatever is this for?" she asked.

"I think you shall put it to better use than I," I answered, and vaulted onto the horse.

"I shall tell you one thing more," she said, stepping after me and putting her hand to the bridle. "Cleave close to your friend. He will need you, and the world shall have need of you both."

I shook my head, knowing she was wrong. "I ride off to the hinterlands, where I shall grow fat and lazy guarding a man who will moon over books."

She only smiled, and bade me to go with God.

Once I rejoined him, Dabir said nothing to me until we stopped for a midday meal upon the road.

"Where were you?"

"Giving alms," I said, which was true in a way.

Dabir grunted. "Did she say anything more to you about our fates?"

"Bismallah!" How had he known? "Only that we were stronger together than apart."

"It takes no magic to see that," he said.

"Also she foretold that you would leave off book reading for basket weaving, and grow hugely fat."

304

"She did?" His eyes widened and I could not hold back my laughter.

Ah, I might say more, about our journey to Mosul, and the finding of our lodgings, indeed, of the many events which followed thereafter, but all of that must wait for another time, for this tale is done.

Afterword

Most of the characters in this novel are my own invention, with the exception of Haroun al-Rashid, Jaffar, much of Jaffar's extended family, and a few incidental characters like Masrur (Sabirah is purely fictional). It may be that I have been more generous with my depiction of Haroun al-Rashid than the historical record strictly bears out, but I have written him as the calm and wise ruler he was so often portrayed to be in story and verse. Surely there must be some truth behind tales that made him popular in his own day and for many generations thereafter.

In his lifetime Jaffar seems to have been just as popular as the beloved caliph, and was famed for his diligent work ethic and intelligence. He may well have been far more clever in real life than I have shown him.

I strove to portray the people, places, and customs of the eighth century Abbasid caliphate accurately, but the story's course and my own whim resulted in a variety of changes—referring to the Byzantine Romans (Roumi, to folk of the caliphate) as Greeks, moving the foundation of The House of Wisdom forward a generation or two simply because I knew how much Dabir would have loved to have studied there, and other matters besides. I tried always to make these changes in the spirit of the same unknown storytellers who spun tales for the *The Arabian Nights*, who seemed to know that while authenticity is important, it should never fetter the course of an adventure.

Readers interested in learning more about an ancient caliphate sadly

Afterword

bereft of djinn, sorcerers, and mighty wyrms have several excellent sources at their disposal. I have turned time and again to John Howe's translation of *Harun al-Rashid and the World of the Thousand and One Nights* by André Clot (New Amsterdam Books, 1989), *Daily Life in the Medieval Islamic World* by James E. Lindsay (Greenwood Press, 2005), and *Arab Seafaring in the Indian Ocean in Ancient and Early Medieval Times* by George F. Hourani and John Carswell (Princeton University Press, 1995). While the time period is centuries different, two volumes were of particular use in better understanding the outlook, mindset, and even tone of the people who lived in the region long ago: *The Travels of ibn Jubayr,* translated by Ronald Broadhurst (Goodword books, 2004) and Philip K. Hitti's translation of Usamah Ibn Munquidh's *An Arab-Syrian Gentleman and Warrior in the Period of the Crusades* (Columbia University Press, 2000). Though he wrote of an entirely different desert, William Langewiesche's excellent *Sahara Unveiled* (Vintage Departures, 1997) was a huge inspiration to me in bringing the desert quarter to life. Numerous other books and articles have been of use to me throughout the years, but I would be remiss if I did not mention two role-playing supplements, *GURPS Arabian Nights*, by Phil Masters (Steve Jackson Games 1993) and James L. Cambias' *Arabian Nights* (Iron Crown Enterprises, 1994) as good starting points for someone wishing to have a better sense of daily life in nineth century Baghdad as well as the caliphate's relation to nearby regions. The blog *Laputan Logic* introduced me to a number of books about the Marsh Arabs and showcased some fine photographs of the region, and an article by Brainerd S. Bates titled "Camping in the Empty Quarter" (Saudi Aramco World, Nov/Dec 1967) helped further my understanding of the desert environment.

In the realm of fantastic, there are of course many fine editions of *The Arabian Nights*, suited for many different tastes. I think a lot of preferences come down to what people are familiar with from their youth. I hope one day to read them in Arabic, but for now I have been enjoying the recent translations by Jack Zipes, collected in two thick Signet Classic paperbacks (Penguin Putnam 1991, 1999). Then, of course, there is the incomparable *Shanameh,* Ferdowsi's classic, which should really be read by any who love fable and myth. It belongs on the bookshelf next to your favorite volume of Greek mythology.

Neil Gaiman brought Haroun, Jaffar, and even Masrur to life in one of my favorite Sandman issues, "Ramadan," (DC Comics, *Sandman,* issue 50), illustrated with stunning clarity by P. Craig Russell, and that issue may well be the reason Dabir and Asim are adventuring when they are, as opposed to a generation or two or hundreds of years later. Or it may be that Gaiman's work served as a gateway drug for my interest, for once I began to read more deeply into the time period and realized Haroun himself figured in some of the Arabian Nights, the appeal of tales set at the same time was undeniable.

Probably my greatest inspiration came from Harold Lamb and Robert E. Howard. Lamb wrote with astonishing vigor whenever he drafted historical fiction, and his ancient Moslems were brought vividly to life, be they heroes or villains. It was my honor to collect most of those tales in *Swords from the West* and *Swords from the Desert* (Bison Books, 2009) so that more readers could treasure these undeservedly forgotten stories. Robert E. Howard is famous for creating the sword-and-sorcery genre with Kull and Conan, not to mention writing a whole host of amazing adventure yarns. Some of his best work, though, are his historicals, never as popular probably because there are so few recurring characters in them. One of my favorites of his, indeed, one of my all-time favorite short stories of any kind, is "The Road of Azrael" with its witty, flawed, and dangerous narrator, Kosru Malik. If you can take the same kind of delight in the exploits of Dabir and Asim as I have found in the tales of my own favorite writers, I will count myself successful.

Howard Andrew Jones